WHISPERING PINES

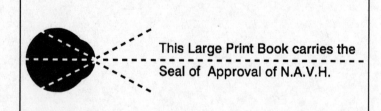

This Large Print Book carries the
Seal of Approval of N.A.V.H.

THE LANGTRY SISTERS

WITHDRAWN

WHISPERING PINES

SCARLETT DUNN

THORNDIKE PRESS
A part of Gale, a Cengage Company

GALE
A Cengage Company

Farmington Hills, Mich • San Francisco • New York • Waterville, Maine
Meriden, Conn • Mason, Ohio • Chicago

LIBRARY OF CONGRESS CIP DATA ON FILE.
CATALOGUING IN PUBLICATION FOR THIS BOOK
IS AVAILABLE FROM THE LIBRARY OF CONGRESS

ISBN-13: 978-1-4328-4288-8 (hardcover)
ISBN-10: 1-4328-4288-9 (hardcover)

Published in 2017 by arrangement with Zebra Books, an imprint of
Kensington Publishing Corp.

Printed in the United States of America
1 2 3 4 5 6 7 21 20 19 18 17

In loving memory of Jim Morgan —
We will see you again.

ACKNOWLEDGMENTS

I thank God for the many wonderful people He has placed in my path. I feel very blessed for the God-incidences every day.

Michael, I am inspired by your courage and tenacity, and I am thankful for your constant support. You have blessed my life beyond measure.

It has been a pleasure getting to know Shauna Johnson, and I thank you for your time and valuable feedback.

A big thank-you to Joey Judd for answering all of my questions. Always good to know a fireman.

PROLOGUE

Colorado Territory, 1865

"Look at the pinecones we found, Granny."
Pushing her plate aside, Rose emptied her
woven basket over the kitchen table, scatter-
ing her treasures for her grandmother to
see. She had been outside all morning with
her two older sisters, Adelaide and Emma,
searching for the perfect pinecones to add
to their Christmas decorations.

Granny placed the platter of sandwiches
she'd made for lunch on the table, and
picked up one of the larger pinecones. She
held it up and examined it closely. "Oh my,
these are beautiful. They will be very pretty
on our wreaths. Were you on Mr. LeMasters's ranch?"

"Yes, ma'am," Emma, the eldest granddaughter, answered. "But we were just in
the pines on the boundary, not near any of
his cattle."

Morgan LeMasters owned the large ranch

along the boundary of their small farm. Fortunately, she knew Morgan wouldn't mind the girls exploring on his land as long as they were careful around the longhorns. "That's fine as long as you don't get in the way of the men working the cattle. We will make Mr. LeMasters a pretty wreath for his door since the pinecones came from his land. You girls can take it to him tomorrow."

Rose's eyes widened at her grandmother's suggestion. "We'll make him a wreath, Granny, but you can take it to him. He scares us." Rose made it a point to steer clear of Mr. LeMasters whenever she saw him. Her oldest brother, Frankie, told her Morgan LeMasters was Satan himself, and she should stay away from him no matter what Granny said. Rose adored Frankie, and she believed everything he told her. But she didn't need Frankie to tell her that Mr. LeMasters was big and fierce looking. Every Sunday he sat directly behind her family in church, and she would always turn around and stare at the darkly ominous man. Her grandfather's sermons were often filled with stories about Satan, warning his parishioners to be aware of his presence, or they would face dire consequences. Rose could never understand why her grandfather allowed Satan in their church.

Granny smiled at her youngest grand-daughter. Rose reminded her of a fairy with her large eyes, delicate facial features, and small frame. While the other children had auburn hair and blue eyes, Rose had inherited her great-grandmother's light blond hair and unique green eyes. She was a remarkably striking child, destined to become a beautiful woman. But it wasn't only Rose's lovely face that drew everyone to her; she was also blessed with a warm, caring heart for one of such tender years.

It puzzled Granny why Rose was so afraid of Morgan LeMasters. The child never expressed fear; it was quite the opposite. She was such an inquisitive child that Granny often had to caution her to act with care. "Morgan is a very nice young man. You have nothing to fear from him."

Rose didn't respond; her thoughts had already skittered back to her treasures. She picked up the smallest pinecone, and thinking it was shaped like a tiny tree, she stood it on its base. She arranged the remaining pinecones around the first one, creating a small forest on the tabletop. As she concentrated on her task, she thought about what she'd heard in the forest that morning. "I heard songs in the pines today, Granny.

11

They sound as pretty as the songs Emma sings."

"I heard people laughing," Addie said, reaching for a sandwich.

"They were singing. I think angels were singing prayers," Rose insisted.

Granny sat beside Rose and ran her hand down her small back. "What do you mean, they were singing prayers?"

"Like the prayers we say in church, but the angels sing them. We tried to find the people, but we didn't see anyone. Why do they hide from us, Granny?" Rose asked.

Granny pushed the platter of sandwiches toward Emma. "Have a sandwich."

Emma grabbed a sandwich, and Granny slid the plate in front of Rose.

Under her grandmother's watchful gaze, Rose reluctantly picked up a sandwich and placed it on her plate. Out of habit, she began to pull off the crust. She wanted to remove the ham too, but she knew Granny would kick up a fuss. Granny was forever telling her she needed to eat more.

Granny fretted that Rose didn't eat enough to stay healthy, and no matter what schemes she employed, nothing could persuade her to eat more. "Honey, I told you the crust makes you pretty."

"Then she doesn't need to eat it," Emma

said as she snatched the tossed-aside crust from Rose's plate and shoved it in her mouth. "Everyone says Rose is the prettiest girl they have ever seen." Emma spoke without a hint of jealousy. The sisters were crazy about each other, and the older girls always looked out for their younger sister.

Rose giggled at her sister's antics, but she hadn't forgotten her question. "Why do the singing angels hide from us, Granny?"

"There isn't anyone singing in the pines, Rose," Granny replied.

"But I hear them," Rose said.

"Emma and I hear people laughing. Come with us so you can hear them, Granny," Addie suggested.

"I've been in there many times, and I think the wind blowing through the leaves sounds like wind chimes," Granny told them.

Emma expelled a loud sigh. "Granny, you are coming with us the next time. Then you will hear for yourself that someone is in there."

"Girls, you know Joseph Longbow, the man who works for Mr. LeMasters?"

"Yes, ma'am," the girls responded at the same time.

"Well, Joseph told me that the pines on Mr. LeMasters's ranch is a special place where the four winds converge. He says it is where his people hear the voices of their great spirits who have passed away." Joseph had explained the legend of the pines to her when she first moved to the farm.

Rose quickly swallowed the bite she'd just taken. "You mean his family in heaven talk to him?"

"You mean Joseph talks to dead people?" Emma asked.

Granny couldn't keep from smiling. Leave it to Emma to get right to the point. She was the most direct child with a no-nonsense attitude. "You know how you girls talk to your parents in heaven at night when you pray?"

The girls nodded.

"Well, that land is where Joseph Longbow talks to his loved ones. The Sioux have a special connection to the land. Joseph said the pines are where his ancestors offered praise to their creator. Church is our special place where we worship God."

"Granny, dead people can't talk or sing. There are people laughing," Addie said.

"Granny is just trying to scare us. I know people are in there," Emma said adamantly. She was too old to believe in ghost stories, and she was surprised Granny was trying to scare her younger sisters.

14

"I would never try to scare you girls. Joseph said that it's the heavenly sounds where the winds come together in the trees. He says different people hear different things, and only people pure of heart hear the pleasing sounds."

"What do bad people hear when they go in the pines?" Rose asked.

"I'm not sure what they hear, but Joseph said they get scared and leave. They never come back." Granny didn't dare tell the girls the many stories told of men who had disappeared or died in that spiritual place. Joseph Longbow told her the girls had nothing to fear if they wandered through the pines. The range of pine trees covered thousands of acres, and she didn't mind the girls exploring as long as they didn't go too far and get lost.

Rose and Addie exchanged a look. "I'm glad we are good girls," Addie said.

"What does Mr. LeMasters hear?" Rose asked. If he was Satan, like Frankie said, why wasn't he afraid to ride through the pines? Her grandfather said Satan was bad, so she imagined he heard terrible things in the pines.

Granny furrowed her brow, trying to recall if she'd ever asked Morgan about the pines.

15

"I don't think he's ever said. Why do you ask?"

Rose shrugged her small shoulders. "He's always riding through there. Do you think he's afraid?"

Granny smiled at her. "I don't think Morgan is afraid of much."

Rose looked out the window in the direction of the LeMasters ranch and the vast area of land covered with the massive pine trees. "Sometimes I hear whispers when I go in there with Frankie."

CHAPTER ONE

And I beheld, and lo a black horse; and he that sat on him had a pair of balances in his hand.

— Revelation 6:5

Kansas, 1876
"Throw your ropes over those trees." Morgan LeMasters pointed to the trees with limbs he deemed sturdy enough not to snap under dead weight. Morgan, and the four men riding with him, were somber, taking no delight in what was about to take place, but they were determined it had to be done. For the last month, they'd chased these men from Colorado, winding through New Mexico Territory, the Panhandle, and finally into Kansas. The band of thieves had splintered into two groups, and Morgan and his men had finally captured four members of the gang. Today was the reckoning.

Morgan's men pulled their ropes from

their saddle horns and fashioned the hangman's noose. After they threw the ropes over the limbs, they led the captives to their fate. One of the men ducked and weaved in his saddle, evading the noose Hank Murphy tried to place over his head.

"I keep telling you, LeMasters, we didn't do nothing wrong. We bought these horses fair and square," Frank Langtry yelled.

Hank didn't utter a word. He grasped the outlaw's neck in his large hand to prevent him from squirming about, looped the rope over his head, and tightened the noose.

"LeMasters, you can't do this! You know my granny. What are you gonna say to her? I didn't steal your horses, or rustle any cattle. You gonna tell her you hung me for no reason? You'll kill her for certain."

Directing his big black horse, Faithful, beside Frank, Morgan looked him in the eye. "Yeah, I know you, Frank, and you've been nothing but trouble most of your miserable life. Show me a bill of sale and I'll take you back to Denver. You can sit in jail until the territorial judge decides what to do with you." Morgan knew there was no way Frank could produce a bill of sale. One of his men had recognized Frank from a distance rustling his cattle, and Frank shot him. Fortunately, he hadn't killed him, and

Morgan had a trusted eyewitness this time.

Frank was right about one thing: Morgan knew he'd break Granny Langtry's heart when he'd have to tell her he'd hung her eldest grandson. She was a sweet old woman, with the kindest heart he'd ever seen. But he'd warned Granny about Frank's unlawful activities, and he hadn't minced words when he'd told her what he intended to do when he caught up with Frank. He should have killed Frank years ago and spared everyone a lot of years of heartache.

"They didn't give us a bill of sale. You know how it is," Frank said.

"No, I don't know how it is." Morgan recognized Frank for what he was, a no-account thief who had been lucky evading the law, until now. Even Granny Langtry admitted her grandson skirted the law. While they both agreed on Frank's short-comings, Granny preferred that the Good Lord handle Frank's comeuppance, but there was no way Morgan was going to wait for that day to come. He'd had enough. Today he was judge, jury, and executioner.

While Morgan waited for the rope to go around the fourth man's neck, he looked out over the landscape. It was just past dawn and the sun peeking over the horizon created glorious rays of color in the morning sky. *Too bad we have to hang men on such a beautiful morning.* He turned to face his men and was about to give the nod, but was distracted by the sound of horses coming down the trail. He held up his hand for his men to wait.

"Stagecoach," Hank said.

Morgan looked around and shook his head. He was so tired, he hadn't even realized they were only about thirty feet off the stagecoach trail. He muttered a string of colorful words in irritation. A hanging was not something he enjoyed, but he couldn't abide cattle rustling or horse thieves. He figured he needed to make a statement with Frank Langtry, or he would have more of his ilk trying him in the future. When Langtry and his men chose this profession they knew what would happen when they were caught. It was the cowboy code, and Morgan didn't want an audience of greenhorns who wouldn't understand.

"You best let them see you so they don't get the wrong idea," Hank suggested. Morgan's name was well-known in the territory, and if the stagecoach driver didn't recognize him by sight, he was certain to have heard his name.

"Yeah." Morgan turned Faithful and rode

back to the trail to face the oncoming stage-coach.

The driver slowed, and recognizing Morgan, he pulled the stagecoach to a halt. Once he set the brake, he jumped down and spared a quick glance to the gathering around the cottonwoods before he addressed Morgan. "You're some ways from home, Mr. LeMasters."

Morgan recognized the driver. "Hello, George." He hooked a thumb over his shoulder, and said, "We've been tracking these horse thieving sons-of-guns from Colorado for a month. Sheriff Roper is on the trail of their compadres. I think they were headed to Purgatory Canyon. Roper heard that's their hideout when they aren't rustling."

"I hear that's a dangerous place. The sheriff best have eyes in the back of his head." George glanced again at the men with ropes around their necks. He didn't give a second thought to hanging horse thieves. They were facing away from the road, and he was curious about their identities. "Glad you caught up with them. They rustle on Whispering Pines land?"

"Yep, several times. We're ready to get this over with and get back home." Morgan wanted to hurry George along. He didn't

21

want to get into a discussion over who he was hanging.

George had heard rumors about Frank Langtry rustling on Morgan's land, so he figured he was one of the men with a rope around his neck. "I think I have a problem with one of the wheels, something just don't seem quite right. When I saw you, I figured it'd be safe to stop. Can't be too careful out here with all the problems with the Indians, and I don't have a shotgun rider the rest of the way to Denver."

"Where is he?" Morgan asked.

"Had to leave him at the last stop. He caught a fever and was too sick to ride. I didn't have time to wait for backup." As he talked, he walked to the stagecoach door and spoke to the occupants. "You can stretch your legs if you want. I'll be a few minutes."

The door opened and a man jumped out. He turned to assist a young woman to the ground, and a second male passenger followed her from the coach.

The young woman glanced up at the imposing man on horseback. There was something familiar about the way he sat perfectly erect on that big black horse. She squinted against the glare of the rising sun in an effort to see his face under the wide brim of his Stetson. Unable to see him clearly, she looked past the big man and noticed the gathering of men on horseback. When she saw the ropes over the trees, her eyes snapped back to the man in front of her. "What is going on here?"

"Perfect," Morgan uttered to himself. Just as expected, the passengers from back East wouldn't understand cowboy justice. He took a long look at her. From the way she was dressed, in her fine blue traveling suit with a flowery hat to match, she was definitely an easterner. To make matters worse, she was holding a Bible, and he figured he was about to have a long sermon coming his way. "Ma'am, this is justice, don't concern yourself."

Morgan dismounted and walked to the front of the stagecoach, thinking to help George determine the problem with the wheel, and get him on his way a bit faster. He was worn out, and he knew his men were exhausted. They'd ridden hard, sleeping on the ground and eating mostly hardtack for days, and he wasn't in the mood to deal with meddlesome travelers. The only thing he wanted to do was get this hanging over with, get back to Colorado to have a decent meal and a long, hot bath, and sleep for twenty-four hours.

The woman thought she recognized Morgan's voice, but when he dismounted, she realized by the confident way he moved that he was the same man who had frightened her like the Devil himself when she was a young girl. "You're Mr. LeMasters."

Morgan turned around and walked back to her. He nudged the brim of his Stetson with two fingers as his eyes roved over her face. She was a real beauty, with eyes as green as fresh spring grass. There was something familiar about her, but he couldn't place her. "Yes, ma'am, but I'm sorry I can't say that I recognize you."

"You wouldn't remember me, I'm sure." But she remembered everything about him. From the first time she saw him in the small church in Whispering Pines when she was seven years old, she had been terrified of him. Her big brother told her he was Satan, and she'd believed him. Not only was Morgan's size imposing, tall and well-muscled, but his complexion, hair, and eyes were very dark, which confirmed her child's mental imagery of Satan's appearance. Morgan's deep, commanding voice didn't help matters. Then, there was the fact that she didn't think she'd ever seen him smile. Her grandmother always said he smiled with his eyes. She'd never understood what her grandmother was talking about. He scared the dickens out of her, and whenever he came to their farm she managed to stay out of sight until he was long gone. Taking a good look at him now, she judged he hadn't changed much over the years. Well, that wasn't quite true. He was even more intimidating than she remembered. He looked even taller, was much more muscular, and he wore his dark hair longer, which seemed to enhance his ominous appearance. First impressions said his demeanor had not softened either. Inexplicably, she almost felt like that small, frightened girl again. But she wasn't a child, she reminded herself. She was a grown woman, and there was no reason to be afraid of him, no matter the authoritative air that surrounded him like a mantle. "I'm Granny Langtry's granddaughter, Rose."

Of all the people to be on that stagecoach, why did it have to be a Langtry? When the Langtrys' son and daughter-in-law died of cholera, they'd taken in their grandchildren: two boys and three girls. The Langtry boys were well-known for their run-ins with the law, but the only time he saw the girls was at church on Sunday mornings. Tom Langtry had been the town preacher, and everyone called him Preacher. Preacher's grandchildren were always seated in perfect soldier formation next to Granny in the front pew every Sunday morning, listening intently to his sermons.

Morgan visited the Langtry farm on occasion to buy baked goods from Granny, or to take them a side of beef every winter, but the girls ran in the opposite direction when they saw him riding in. Of course, he'd never lingered overlong at their farm; ranch work didn't allow much time to socialize. When Preacher died several years ago, Granny sent the girls to live with her wealthy brother back East for their formal education. The two boys remained with Granny, and Morgan was about to hang one of them.

Unable to turn around with the taut rope biting into his skin, Frank yelled out, "Rose? Is that you?"

Hearing what she thought was her brother's voice, Rose stepped around Morgan and looked past the men blocking her view. She hurried to the men sitting on horses with ropes around their necks. Her gaze skipped from one face to the next, and when her eyes landed on her eldest brother, she gasped. She couldn't believe it was her brother at the end of that rope. "Frankie? What in heaven's name is going on here?"

"LeMasters said we stole his horses and

cattle, but he's got the wrong men. He won't listen to me and he's going to hang us."

Rose whirled around and rushed back to Morgan. "You can't hang my brother!"

Morgan remembered the youngest Langtry girl was the one with the pretty blond hair, but he'd forgotten her name was Rose. Surely, this couldn't be that same little slip of a girl who always shied away from him as though he carried the plague. He thought her name suited her; she was as pretty and delicate as a rose. "I'm sorry you arrived when you did, ma'am, but I'm afraid your brother and his friends rustled my cattle and stole my horses. You know what that means. I have every right to hang them."

"But he said he didn't do it!"

Morgan took a deep breath to try to keep himself calm. He didn't expect Frank's sister to freely admit her brother was a lying, thieving, miserable excuse of a man. "Did you really expect him to admit his wrongdoing?" He hoped she had more character than her brother.

"What do you mean?" She gaped at him in disbelief. "Of course I believe my brother when he says he didn't do it. Frankie wouldn't lie to me." Old memories surfaced in her mind. Frankie had always told her

Morgan LeMasters hated him. If Frank was right, Morgan wouldn't listen to the truth.

Morgan had a feeling this little gal didn't know what mischief her brother had wrought over the last few years. Maybe Granny didn't share what was happening in Whispering Pines with her granddaughters. "I haven't seen you at your grandparents' place for years. How long has it been since you've seen your brothers?"

"My grandmother sent me and my two sisters East to be educated. I haven't seen Frankie in almost five years. But I can't see what that has to do with this situation." Did he think she didn't know her own brother because she'd been away for a few years?

"Well, your brother hasn't exactly been a saint over the last five years. This time we just caught up with him."

She lifted her chin and stared him in the eye. "What is your proof you have the right men?"

She was a feisty little thing, he'd give her that. "Well, for one thing, you can look for yourself and see my brand on those horses that they've run nearly to death. I expect you remember my brand. I have an eyewitness this time, and your brother tried to kill him."

She had already taken note of the LeMasters brand on Frankie's horse. But Frankie said he didn't steal the horses, and she couldn't imagine her big brother trying to shoot someone. She had no reason to doubt him. She spread her arms wide and asked, "Where are these cattle you say they stole? I see no cattle."

People didn't generally question his word, and Morgan didn't feel the need to explain himself to anyone. He prided himself on his integrity, and it rankled him that she would doubt his word. He held his temper, thinking he should grant her some quarter since he was about to hang her brother. "They're probably scattered to Hades and back by now." He didn't need to be reminded how much money Frank Langtry had cost him over the years. But the way he saw it, you couldn't place a price on justice, and he was bound and determined justice would be served to Frank Langtry today.

"Why don't you take these men to jail so they can have a proper trial and defend themselves?"

"That's not the way it works out here. I'm sure you know a man can hang a horse thief when he catches him. We were riding with the law and we're deputized. The sheriff and his posse went after Frank's accomplices when they split up. Did you know your brother has his own outlaw gang now?"

One of the male passengers stepped forward. "Sir, it would seem that since this is the young woman's brother . . ." He stopped in midsentence when Morgan turned his ominous glare on him. The passenger immediately scurried back to the stagecoach and climbed inside.

Rose saw the determination in Morgan's eyes, and she didn't think anything she said would change his mind, but she had to do something. She couldn't stand idly by and see her brother hang. "Where is this eyewitness?"

Morgan noticed her lips trembling. She was putting on a brave face, and he admired her for not backing down. The woman had grit. Frank could learn a lot from his sister. "Joseph was shot by your brother. He never ventures far from Whispering Pines." Out of concern for Joseph's safety, Morgan told him not to leave the ranch. With the Sioux uprising over the dispute concerning the Black Hills, soldiers were combing the territories, forcing the Indians onto reservations, and Morgan tried to protect Joseph from that fate.

"Joseph?" Rose questioned, hoping he wasn't referring to the elderly Sioux who worked for him. He'd always been very kind to her, and taught her many of the native customs when she was young.

"Joseph Longbow," Morgan said.

"Was he seriously injured?" Rose asked.

"No. Thankfully, your brother is not a very good shot."

Rose was relieved to hear Joseph was not seriously harmed. She took a deep breath, determined to make her point. "These men still have a right to face their accusers."

Morgan glanced at his foreman. "Murph." If she wouldn't take his word about her brother's misdeeds, perhaps she would be persuaded by more than one account.

Hank Murphy tossed the rope he was holding to one of the men and pulled his horse forward. "Yessir?"

"Miss Langtry, this is my foreman, Hank Murphy. Maybe you remember him."

When she nodded her recognition, Morgan said, "Murph, would you tell Miss Langtry what Joseph saw? It seems she's not willing to accept my word about her thieving brother."

Hank cleared his throat. He didn't want this little lady to have to witness her brother swinging from a rope, but it wouldn't be fair to Morgan to avoid the question. "Miss, I'm sorry to tell you, but Joseph identified six of the eight men that rustled, and the man who shot him." He pointed to the men with the ropes around their necks. "There's four of the six men he recognized."

"He's lying, sis! We bought those horses fair and square from a man who told us he'd bought them off one of LeMasters's men," Frank yelled.

Rose also remembered Hank — he was almost as intimidating as his boss. "And you are Mr. LeMasters's foreman, correct?"

Murph smiled at her. "Yes, I am, and I remember you."

Rose ignored his smiling attempt to be friendly. "Being Mr. LeMasters's foreman, it seems reasonable that you would do his bidding."

Taking offense at her implication, Murph's smile faded. No man called him a liar and lived to talk about it. Seeing she was a female he'd make allowances, but not much. "Now wait a minute . . ."

Murph's words trailed off when Morgan took a step closer to Rose and laced her with his unrelenting dark gaze. "You've got no call to question Murph's word. He's not only my foreman, he's my friend and he's a man of character. Unlike your brother, he doesn't lie."

Rose felt guilty about her accusatory tone. "I'm sorry, Mr. Murphy, that was not my intent." Her eyes met Morgan's. "But don't you see these men have a right to face the actual person who is accusing them? I remember Joseph Longbow, and I'd say he is quite long in the tooth by now. Perhaps his eyesight is failing."

"They are facing the men who are accusing them." Morgan tapped his chest. "I'm accusing them. And Joseph's eyesight is just fine, and he doesn't lie either. He has no ax to grind against these men. As a matter of fact, Joseph has tried on more than one occasion to give your brother the benefit of the doubt."

"But . . ." She was losing control, and tears filled her eyes. "*You* didn't actually see them." She tried to collect herself as she searched for the words that would make him change his mind. "I know you are a God-fearing man."

When Morgan didn't comment one way or the other, he saw her glance down at the Bible she was clutching, as if she were drawing strength from the words through the cover.

"You were always in church listening to my grandfather's sermons. You know this is the wrong thing to do."

Morgan hadn't been in church since Preacher died. They didn't have a pastor now, and while some folks still gathered at church and sang songs, Morgan preferred to spend his time in his outdoor church. He figured he could talk to God under His big sky, and He'd hear him just as clearly as He did inside four walls. Like the Sioux, Morgan was a man who revered the beauty of the land. To him, riding on the range was the perfect place to have a conversation with his Maker. He pointed to the badge on his shirt, but he softened his tone when he said, "This badge says I have every right to hang them, and it's not wrong, it's justice."

"But . . ." Rose's lips started quivering and she could say no more.

Morgan wasn't a man to give in to emotion, but watching her trying to maintain control was tugging at his heart. He glanced at his men, and their sorrowful expressions said they pitied the young woman. At the same time, every man there knew Frank Langtry was a lying thief who deserved his fate. Morgan stared at his boots to keep from looking into Rose's tear-filled eyes. Once he'd steeled his courage to look at her again, a single tear rolled slowly over her cheek. That was his undoing. It broke his heart to see a woman cry, and he'd darn sure never been the cause of making one cry. At least, not to his knowledge.

He turned around and walked a few feet away and looked out over the countryside. He removed his Stetson and smacked it against his thigh in frustration. If he didn't hold these thieves accountable, he'd run the risk of his men not respecting him to do what was right. If he did go through with the hanging, then this woman would have a bad memory the rest of her life. By law he had every right to hang these men, but he couldn't say it was the right thing to do under the present circumstances. It was a difficult decision for him, and he was a decisive man.

He considered telling George to be on his way, and they could get the hanging over with once the coach was out of sight. Logic told him it'd be difficult to get Rose back on that stagecoach knowing her brother would be hanged once she was down the road. Even if he could get her on the stagecoach, she would fret all the way home knowing she'd have to deliver the sad news to Granny. And she'd hate him. He wasn't sure why he was worried that she would think ill of him, but right now, it was foremost in his mind. *Dang it all!*

Settling his Stetson back on his head, his gaze shifted to his men as he walked pur-posefully toward Rose. He hoped they

35

would understand his reasoning for doing what he was about to do without explanation. He took Rose by the arm, urging her a few feet away, out of earshot of the men.

Before he spoke, he pulled his bandana from his back pocket and handed it to her. "Dry your eyes."

Rose accepted his bandana and held it to her eyes, willing herself to stop crying.

"Miss Langtry, I'll take them back to Whispering Pines and let the judge decide what to do with them. Joseph will come in and tell the judge what he saw. It'll be up to the judge what happens after that. But I tell you right now, I can almost guarantee you will see a hanging one way or the other. You'd best prepare yourself for that outcome."

She looked up at him with pleading eyes. "But he said he purchased those horses from some man. Couldn't you find that man?"

"Do you think any man in this territory wouldn't check the brand before he paid for a horse? Do you think anyone in the territory wouldn't recognize my brand? And do you honestly think there is even a remote possibility that your brother didn't recognize my brand?" He gave her a minute to consider his questions before adding, "Besides, they had no bill of sale. If a man in this country buys a horse off a stranger, you can bet your . . . hat, he'll get a bill of sale."

Rose didn't respond. She couldn't argue that the LeMasters brand was well-known, and certainly Frank would have recognized his brand. And she couldn't argue the fact that most men would think to ask for a written bill of sale. She also knew there had been some bad blood between Morgan and her brother for a long time, but she didn't know the cause. No one ever talked about it at home.

Morgan stared at her. He didn't know what else to say. She obviously believed her brother would never do anything as nefarious as steal another man's property. Was she naïve, or had she chosen to ignore Frank's evil ways? Morgan told himself not to worry about what she thought. One way or the other, Frank was going to hang. Today, or two weeks from now, it was going to happen.

Frank broke the silence when he yelled out, "Hurry up and give him what he wants so he'll let us go!"

Rose glanced back in her brother's direction and frowned. "What do you mean, Frankie?" Before Frank responded, her eyes darted back to Morgan. "What do you want? Money?"

"He wants what every man wants. Just do it and get these ropes off our necks," Frankie shouted.

That did it. Morgan turned and stalked to Frank in a few long strides. He glanced at his man holding the reins of the horse. "Untie him, Grady."

Grady leaned over and pulled the rope off of Frank's wrists and removed the noose from his neck. Frank rubbed his wrists and smirked at Morgan. He missed the murderous look in Morgan's eyes.

Morgan reached up and hauled Frank off the horse by the front of his shirt and slammed his fist in his jaw.

Frank hit the ground hard, dazing him. A few seconds passed before he moved. "You're real brave with my legs gone numb from sitting on that horse."

"Take your time, I'm not going anywhere." Morgan stood over him, waiting for him to react. Part of him wanted a reason to beat him into oblivion. He might not have a hanging today, but he'd have the satisfaction of giving Frank the good thrashing he so rightly deserved.

Within seconds, Frank jumped to his feet and charged Morgan headfirst. Morgan read his intent and braced himself, barely moving an inch when Frank's head slammed against his chest. He grabbed Frank by the front of the shirt and quickly landed another punch to his face. This time Frank went down with blood gushing from his broken nose.

Rose rushed to her brother, who was writhing on the ground holding his nose with both hands. She kneeled down beside him and held Morgan's bandana to his nose to stop the bleeding. "Frankie, are you okay?" When Frank didn't respond, her eyes snapped up at the man looming over them. "Why did you do that? You just said you would take him back to Whispering Pines! What do you want? And how will you ever face my grandmother after this?"

Of all the ungrateful . . . Morgan stopped himself from saying aloud what he was thinking. He glanced at Murph and saw him shake his head. Didn't she have enough sense to know that her precious older brother had insulted her? It took every ounce of effort he had left to be civil.

"It might interest you to know that I spoke to your grandmother before I left Colorado to trail your brother. I've seen her a heck of a lot more than you have over the last several years. She understood what I had to do." He didn't mention that Granny Langtry said something to him before he left that had been nagging at him ever since. She'd told him to make sure he was going after Frankie for the right reasons, and not because he sought vengeance for past deeds. Well, he couldn't think about that now; he had enough Langtrys to deal with at the moment.

He grabbed Faithful's reins, but before he mounted he turned back to Rose, who was mollycoddling her brother. "Like I said, I'll take them back. And I'll do one better than that, Miss Langtry. Your brother can even ride in the stagecoach with you, since I don't want his sorry carcass on one of my horses. But don't get any ideas that he will have an opportunity to take off. We will be right behind you all the way to Whispering Pines." He turned his hardened gaze on Frank. "And you can ask this miserable excuse of a man what he thinks I want from you."

CHAPTER TWO

Two hours later, Morgan was still fuming over Frank's comment. He fought the temptation to pull Frank out of that stagecoach and take his anger out on his face. Once his temper was under control, he pulled his horse beside Murph's. "You said the passengers weren't armed?" Before he'd allowed Frank inside the coach, he'd asked his foreman to check the passengers for weapons.

"They weren't wearing holsters, and there were no rifles inside the coach. One of the men said he had a pistol in his valise, and I put it on top of the coach. That tall fellow looks like he can hold his own if Frank gets out of line. Seems like I've seen him before, but I can't place him."

Morgan thought it odd neither man in the stagecoach was heeled, but then again, they were from back East. "I didn't ask George if he found the problem with the wheel."

41

"He said he didn't see anything wrong," Murph said.

Morgan glanced at the stagecoach in front of them, but saw nothing amiss with the wheel. His thoughts moved to the woman inside the coach. He figured Rose and Frank were having a reunion of sorts. Frank was probably filling her head with more lies. The thought rankled him. Frank had a silver tongue, and more than one person had fallen under his spell, accepting every lying word out of his mouth as gospel. It appeared Rose was one of those who believed his lies. "You think the men understand why I didn't hang him?"

Murph nodded. "The men don't blame you. None of us would have hanged Frank with his little sister watching. It was going to be tough enough to face Granny once we hanged him. We couldn't let Rose witness something like that."

"Yeah." It meant a lot to Morgan that his men felt the same way he did. After all the problems Frank and his gang had caused them, they had every right to demand the satisfaction of a hanging.

"Still, I wish you had beaten him within an inch of his miserable life for being so disrespectful to his sister."

"I considered doing just that," Morgan said.

Murph grinned at him. "Well, I did hear some of his teeth rattling from that one punch."

"I think he spit some out."

Murph chuckled. "His nose will never be the same." He inclined his head toward the stagecoach and said, "She sure turned out to be a beauty. 'Course, she was a pretty little girl."

Morgan stared at his foreman. He was surprised Murph remembered her. "You remember her?"

Murph laughed. "Just because I'm almost thirty-six don't mean I can't recognize a pretty face when I see one. She's the youngest of the three girls, and she was the prettiest little gal I ever saw. I remembered those green eyes of hers. I never saw eyes that color. The other two girls have blue eyes and dark hair."

"How do you remember so much about the girls? They ran every time they saw me."

"Can you blame them? You'd scare anyone to death with that scowl of yours," Murph teased. "When you'd send me over to do some work for Granny, the girls would bring me something to drink. The two older girls would talk to me, but Rose would never say a word. She was real skittish. Don't you remember when we'd sit behind them in church, Rose's pretty blond hair was always hanging over the back of the pew? She would always turn around and stare at you like she thought you might sprout horns."

"Yeah, I do remember that." Most of the time, Morgan wanted to sit behind the Langtrys just to put the fear of God in Frank. Preacher's sermons didn't seem to have much of an influence on him.

"Maybe she'll talk to me now that she's older," Murph said.

Morgan thought he heard more than a passing interest in Rose Langtry. "Whoa, Murph, she's way too young for you."

"I figure she's about nineteen now. I don't reckon she's too young. Some men marry women twenty years younger than they are."

If Murph was right about Rose's age, Morgan calculated she'd left Colorado when she was fourteen if she'd been gone five years. He would have been twenty-six. That must have been why he'd never paid much attention to the girls. He was working nonstop building his ranch back then, and he didn't have much free time for anything else. "How old are her sisters?"

"I think all the kids are a couple of years apart. Seems like Granny told me that her daughter-in-law was having a baby every other year. It darn near killed Granny when her son and daughter-in-law died."

"Yeah, Granny had a tough time." Morgan thought the death of her son seemed to take the life out of her. It was a long time before she started smiling again, and he suspected raising the grandchildren had a lot to do with bringing her back to life.

"I reckon Rose is coming home to take care of Granny now that she's getting on in years."

"Yeah." Morgan was thinking about Rose's age. He was surprised he was only twelve years older, but then, he was always older than his chronological age. Sometimes he felt like he was born an old man. It came from the responsibilities he carried on his shoulders. Even though his ranch was considered a success during these hard times, he rarely took time to enjoy what he had built.

Like most of the men who worked for him, Morgan wanted a wife and kids. But unlike his men, he didn't make much of an effort to find a woman to marry. Of course, there wasn't a wide selection of available ladies in Whispering Pines. His men made it a point to go to Denver at least once a month in hopes of meeting some eligible females, but he rarely joined them. Even though Denver was only an hour away, his days started before dawn, and by the time it ended he needed sleep more than he needed to spend another hour in the saddle. Most of his nights were spent reading about breeding cattle, and doing paperwork into the wee hours of the morning. Not exactly a life conducive to attracting women.

He recalled Granny telling him, after Preacher Langtry died that she wasn't ready to meet her Maker until she saw her granddaughters married, and had a few great-grandbabies to enjoy. If all of his men reacted to Rose like his foreman, he figured Granny's wish would be granted within a year.

"Frankie, why does Mr. LeMasters think you stole his cattle and horses?" Rose asked once they were on their way to Whispering Pines.

Leaning back on the seat, Frank lifted the bandana from his nose. Seeing he was no longer bleeding, he turned to his sister. "You know LeMasters, he thinks he's better than everybody else. Since I was a boy, he was always blaming me for something."

"But why would he do that?" For the first time, Rose started to question her brother's opinion about Morgan.

"You've been gone a long time, Rose. You don't know how things are at home anymore. LeMasters is a rich man now, and everyone does his bidding. Someone's been rustling his cattle and he's pinned it on me. He's had it out for me for years. That old Indian, Joseph Longbow, will say anything LeMasters tells him." He put his arm around Rose's shoulders and pulled her closer. "Granny warned me that LeMasters was out for vengeance. It didn't matter that I didn't do nothing to him, or his cattle." He grinned at her, certain he could charm her the way he charmed all women. "It's a good thing you came along when you did, or me and the boys would be swinging."

"Frankie, Mr. LeMasters said Mr. Longbow saw you stealing."

Frank removed his arm from her shoulders, slid away from her and gave her a mutinous glare. "You mean to tell me you'd believe that old Indian over me?" He looked her up and down and curled his lip in disgust. "I should have known. Look at you. You've changed. Why did you come back here? To show us poor folks how you've lived with all your finery?"

"I think you should show your sister more respect after what she did for you back

47

there," the stranger on the opposite seat said.

Frank's eyes snapped to the stranger. He was a big man, but Frank figured he was just a city man wearing boots. "And I suggest you mind your own business, or I'll give you a reason to keep your mouth shut."

"You talk real brave for a man absent a revolver," the other male passenger said.

Frank looked him over. He'd seen Hank Murphy check to make sure the two men weren't armed. "You ain't heeled yourself."

The man patted his waistcoat. "Who says I'm not armed?"

Frank knew the man couldn't be carrying anything larger than a derringer in the getup he was wearing. "It would take more than a little derringer to stop me if I decide to come after you."

"Frankie! Stop it this minute," Rose insisted. She looked at the gentlemen opposite her and said, "I apologize for my brother's ill manners." The two men had been excellent traveling companions, and she wouldn't allow Frankie to threaten them, no matter how much she loved him.

She glanced back at Frank and lowered her voice. "I'm just trying to understand why Mr. LeMasters would think you stole those animals, and why Mr. Longbow identified you as the thief. Do you know those other men they were going to hang?"

"Yeah, they are my boys."

"What does that mean?"

"We work together on the ranches when we can find work."

Rose was no closer to understanding what was going on. "Why don't you tell me about the trouble you've had with Mr. LeMasters."

A loud cracking sound halted Frank's response. Thinking it was a gunshot, he leaned to the window and looked out just as the stagecoach violently lurched to one side.

"Jump out!" George yelled as he leaped from the driver's seat.

One of the men inside the coach tried to open the door, but it was too late. The coach started to slide down the steep incline, and the momentum prevented the passengers from escaping the plummeting tomb. The big man inside the coach tried to brace himself, and he stretched out his arm in an effort to grab Rose, but he lost his grip when the coach picked up speed.

Within seconds, the coach began to roll over and over, and the passengers were tossed about like rag dolls with each revolution. Trunks were flying through the air, breaking apart on impact as the coach tumbled over the rocky terrain. The dresses and petticoats from Rose's trunk floated through the air, resembling rainbow-colored clouds before they settled in vibrant heaps over the rugged landscape. The ear-piercing roars from the horses were deafening as they struggled against their yokes, trying to escape their certain death. The stagecoach began to splinter apart as it bounced over tree stumps and larger boulders on descent.

Morgan jumped off his horse and shouted orders as he raced down the incline. "Ken, watch those men. Murph, check on George. Dan, you and Grady come with me." As the three men made their way down the slope, half running, half sliding, they saw one of the male passengers fall out when the doors were ripped off the coach. The man rolled to a stop next to a downed tree. "Grady, see to him." Morgan didn't know if it was Frank or not, and he didn't care. It wasn't Rose. He didn't slow down. He'd never experienced such a helpless feeling as he raced after the fast-moving coach. There was no way he could catch the coach as it vaulted down the incline with increasing speed. He reasoned it would be the lesser of two evils if Rose fell out before the coach slammed into the creek bed below. Right before his eyes, the coach started breaking apart, and the horses were freed from their tethers when the frame rolled over a large boulder.

"Take care of the horses, Dan," Morgan yelled above the melee. Within seconds, Morgan heard one shot behind him, and he knew Dan had put one horse out of his misery. Another shot rang out a few seconds later.

Suddenly, the coach slammed against a cluster of rocks mingled with spiky tree stumps and came to a crashing halt. What was left of the structure was little more than jagged fragments. Morgan came to a sliding halt near one of the larger pieces of wood. He started throwing the rubble aside, looking for Rose. Several feet from him, he saw a large slice of one wooden door tossed aside, and Frank rolled from beneath the wreckage. Frank tried to stand, but from Morgan's vantage point, it looked as though he fell back to the ground. Morgan thought he must be injured or dazed. He hurried toward Frank, thinking Rose had to be nearby because he hadn't seen her fall from the carriage.

Before he reached Frank, he saw Rose's hat lying a few feet from him. Blood stained the blue cloth brim. "Frank, where's . . ."

Before he finished his question, Frank

51

stood, holding his sister by the waist. Rose was hanging limply over Frank's forearm, and he had a Remington double-barrel derringer pointed to her head.

"Stay where you are, LeMasters!" Frank shouted.

Morgan could hardly believe his eyes. Even for a lowlife like Frank Langtry, this was beyond reprehensible. Morgan pulled his Colt and aimed it at Frank's head. "Put that derringer down, Frank."

"Holster your iron or I'll shoot her! I swear I will!" Frank threatened. "Now back off."

"How do I know she's not already dead?" Morgan countered.

"She ain't dead," Frank assured him. "She's unconscious."

"There's blood on her hat." Morgan knew he could easily blow Frank's head off, but he didn't know if that cocked derringer had a hair trigger. He couldn't risk Rose getting shot accidentally.

"She's got a gash on her head. Now, for the last time, holster that iron."

"What are you going to do, Frank? Where are you going to go? You know we'll hunt you down."

Frank smirked at him. "Me and my boys are going to ride on down to Mexico and party with some pretty señoritas. No one will find us where we are going. Even if some cowboy was dumb enough to try to find us, the Comancheros would gun them down for us. We keep them supplied with whiskey and guns in exchange for protection."

"What about Rose?"

"What about Rose? I don't care what happens to her. She's been gone a long time. She didn't care about me when she left the farm."

Morgan couldn't say he was surprised at Frank's callous admission. It was clear Frank only cared about himself. The way he'd treated Granny Langtry was proof of that. Granny might make excuses for Frank, but Morgan wasn't that generous, or that forgiving. "You might not care, but she saved your sorry hide today."

Frank shrugged and pressed the derringer against her temple. "Her misfortune." He met Morgan's eyes. "Last time. I don't have nothing to lose."

Morgan had never seen such deadly, soulless eyes, and he holstered his pistol. "Now what?"

"Tell your men we're coming up and don't do anything stupid." He motioned with the derringer for Morgan to precede him up the hill.

"You can't drag your sister up that hill. She probably has broken bones."

"I sure ain't gonna carry her and give you a chance to waylay me."

"Give her to me, I'll carry her."

"Hand over your iron." When Morgan was a foot away, Frank added, "And don't try anything stupid."

Morgan pulled his pistol and handed it to him. He half expected Frank to blow a hole in his chest when he gave him his gun, but Frank tossed Rose's limp body at him. Seeing the nasty gash on her head, Morgan wasn't sure she was still alive. He was tempted to make a move on Frank, but he knew Frank wouldn't hesitate to kill him and Rose.

Spotting one of the men from the stagecoach lying on the ground near Frank, Morgan gently placed Rose beside him. He wanted to make sure she was still alive before he went up that hill with Frank. When he found a faint pulse at her neck, he breathed a sigh of relief. Directing his attention to the man on the ground, Morgan reached out and turned him over. Sadly, the man's lifeless eyes said he was beyond help. He closed the man's eyes before he lifted

Rose into his arms.

"Now that's real touching," Frank said snidely. "Too bad about that city slicker. I owe him for carrying this derringer. Looks like Hank should have checked his vest." He waved Morgan's pistol at him and said, "Get moving, LeMasters."

"Don't you care what happens to your sister?"

"No."

Dan was making his way down the slope, but Frank halted his progress when he turned Morgan's pistol on him. "Far enough. Hand over your gun."

Morgan nodded, indicating Dan should do as Frank instructed.

"What's going on?" Dan asked after he gave Frank his pistol.

"One of those passengers had a derringer," Morgan said.

They reached the top of the hill and Frank said, "Tell your men to throw down their guns and untie my boys."

Murph was helping George, who had suffered a fractured leg when he jumped from the coach, but when he saw Frank with a gun aimed at Morgan, he sprang to his feet.

"Murph, do as he says." Morgan placed Rose beside George before turning to his men. "Let them go."

Morgan's men tossed their guns aside, and untied Deke Sullivan, Dutch Malloy, and Corbin Jeffers.

Morgan kneeled beside Rose while George held his bandana against her bleeding wound. He spotted a canteen near George. "Can you hand me that canteen?"

After Morgan poured some water on the bandana, he handed the canteen back to George. "Put it under you so they don't see it." He expected Frank and his men to take all of their supplies.

George leaned over and whispered, "I had my rifle in my hand, but I don't know where it landed."

Hearing George whispering to Morgan, Frank walked to them and kicked George hard in his broken leg. "What did you say, old man?"

George grimaced in pain. "I said you're a sorry son-of-a . . ."

When Frank pointed the pistol to George's head, Morgan lunged at him, taking him to the ground. They rolled in the dirt and within seconds, Morgan was on top of Frank, trying to wrestle the gun from him. Dutch picked up one of the rifles and cracked Morgan in the head with the butt, knocking him senseless. Murph started to lunge for a gun, but Deke nudged his spine with the barrel of a rifle.

"Frank, I don't know how you managed to get the drop on this big man," Corbin said, pointing to Morgan.

"You see, boys, I told you I have nine lives," Frank bragged as he gained his feet. "Now get those horses ready to go."

The second male passenger stumbled to the top of the incline, and Frank said, "Be sure to check him for a gun."

"I'm unarmed," the man replied.

"Check him anyway," Frank said.

Deke checked the man and didn't find a weapon. Seeing Morgan move, Deke pointed to him and asked, "Should we tie him up?"

"I say we eliminate all of them for good," Frank said.

Corbin Jeffers spoke up. "You mean kill them?"

"You're real quick, Corbin. That's exactly what I mean," Frank replied.

"Wait a minute, Frank," Deke said. "We didn't join up with you to do any killin'. Rustlin' is one thing, but I ain't killin' nobody."

"They didn't mind hanging us," Frank countered.

"We knew what was gonna happen if they ever caught up with us. We wouldn't be in this fix if you hadn't shot at that old Indian. And anyways, what about your sister?" Corbin asked.

"I just wish I killed that Indian," Frank said. He motioned to Rose with his pistol. "We can get rid of her too, for all I care."

"She did us a good turn. Why would you want to hurt her?" Corbin asked.

Frank shook his head. "You men getting skittish on me?" He looked at the one man who hadn't said a word. "Dutch, what about you? You afraid to shoot them?"

Dutch picked up two pistols and shoved them in his belt. "Nope, I ain't afraid to kill. But I ain't never killed an unarmed man. And if we do kill them, Sheriff Roper will keep hunting us down. I say we take off and leave them be. They won't find us in Mexico." He moved closer to face Frank eye to eye. "I can tell you one thing for certain: I don't cotton to killing women. My ma always taught me to respect women. As Corbin said, your sister did us a good turn, and I don't aim to repay her kindness by shooting her. And I ask you, what kind of man would shoot his own sister when she's unconscious? I ain't so sure I'd put much trust in a man who did something like that." Dutch spat near Frank's boot, clearly indicating his displeasure at Frank's cold-blooded plan.

Frank didn't like the look in Dutch's eyes, and he wasn't about to cross him. He wouldn't admit it to another man, but he'd always feared Dutch. The man had an unpredictable side that Frank had not been able to penetrate. He could intimidate the other members of the gang, but not Dutch. "Fine, let's ride then. We'll take their horses. They won't get far without them."

They gathered up the guns, along with the few supplies and prepared to leave.

Morgan's head had cleared enough for him to make sense of their conversation. Though he was having trouble focusing, he managed to stand and face the gang. "I need to get your sister to a doctor. Leave one horse."

"Back off, LeMasters. Be thankful you are still above the daisies. Don't push your luck," Frank replied.

"Frank, we could leave them one horse so he could get her help," Deke said.

"We're leaving them alive, that'll have to do," Frank retorted.

Deke glanced at Dutch and Corbin. They didn't argue with Frank, but Deke could tell they didn't agree with Frank's plan. The three had already discussed leaving the gang because Frank was becoming more and more violent. Deke wished he'd left before they'd rustled Morgan's cattle. Maybe they should have let LeMasters get the best of Frank when they were wrestling for the gun.

"Deke, take hold of LeMasters's horse," Frank instructed.

As Deke took hold of Faithful's reins, he glanced at Morgan and gave him a subtle nod.

Morgan thought Deke might be sending him a signal. Maybe he'd let the horse go, or maybe he would leave Frank's gang and come back with the horse.

Frank reined his horse to stand in front of Morgan. "We don't want to leave that big black stallion behind. Granny always told me vengeance rode a black horse."

Morgan leveled his dark eyes on Frank, his jaw set in grim determination, trying to control the lethal fury he was feeling. If Rose and his men didn't need his help, he would have taken his chances and ripped Frank's head off. He was certain he could snap Frank's neck before his men shot him. "Granny was right. But I won't have a scale in my hand, it'll be a Colt and a rope." He silently swore he would see Frank Langtry swing from a rope if it was the last thing he did on this earth.

CHAPTER THREE

"What happened?" Granny Langtry asked.

Deputy Webb Grainger assisted the diminutive woman into the buckboard and placed her black bag beside her. "We chased those outlaws into Purgatory Canyon, and they were waiting to pick us off one at a time. The sheriff rode in first and was shot right off. Then all heck broke loose, bullets flying all over the place. That place is nothing but a killing trap, not to mention there are still Indians who hide out in that canyon, and only God knows how many outlaws. It was pure luck we all didn't go meet our Maker that day. There were only three of us, since the ranchers had to get back home." Webb walked around the buckboard and climbed in beside her, picked up the reins, and clicked the horses to action.

Granny eyed the tall, lanky deputy. "It wasn't pure luck you were spared, Deputy. I'm confident God was protecting you."

"Yes, ma'am, I reckon so." Webb silently wondered why God hadn't protected Sheriff Roper, but he wasn't about to voice that question to Granny Langtry. He didn't want to hear her preach all the way to town about questioning the ways of the Lord.

"What about Morgan LeMasters? Was he with you?" Granny asked.

"No, ma'am, the gang split up and Mr. LeMasters and his men went after . . . well, he went after Frank." Webb glanced at Granny to gauge her reaction to his comment.

Granny shook her head. "I'm not surprised. I've told Frankie for years he should stop poking that big bear, but he wouldn't listen."

Webb agreed with Granny on that score. If he was in Frank's position and LeMasters was after him, he'd take off to Mexico and never come back. Webb figured that just proved criminals were plain stupid, or in Frank's case, just loco. He'd never seen a meaner-looking man than LeMasters, and while he'd never seen him in action, he'd heard he was one man you didn't want to anger. One thing was certain, LeMasters wasn't going to take any more grief from Frank Langtry.

"Where was Sheriff Roper hit?"

"In the shoulder. I dug the bullet out, but now he has a fever and he's out of his head."

"But he was fine right after you removed the bullet?"

"Seemed to be doing good, but we had a lot of riding before we got back home, and he insisted we keep moving fast. Stubborn fool, if you ask me. I wanted to take him to see the doctor in Denver, but he wouldn't let me. He said you could help him, so I put him in Doc Emmett's old office."

"I wish Preacher was here. He saw a lot of gunshot wounds in his time. He helped the doc out on more than one occasion before they both died."

Webb knew she was talking about her deceased husband. He always thought it was odd how she called her own husband Preacher. "Yes, ma'am, he was a fine man."

"I wish we could find Joseph Longbow. He's good with wounds."

"Yes, ma'am, he is. But Joseph can be difficult to find if he doesn't want to be found."

Granny nodded her agreement with the truth of that statement. "You say those men who rode with Frank got away after they shot the sheriff?"

"Yes, ma'am, they sure did. We got out of that canyon with our hides, and considering the sheriff's condition, we couldn't leave him alone to go back."

It saddened Granny that Sheriff Roper was shot because of her grandson. Like Morgan LeMasters, Roper was a good man. Sheriff Roper and Morgan were good friends, almost as close as brothers. This incident was going to put one more feather in Morgan's war bonnet when it came to his vendetta against Frank. Granny knew Morgan's acrimony wasn't without cause. Frank had done everything he could to provoke him. She had never been able to figure out what Frank had against Morgan, but it had been obvious for years her grandson hated the man.

Morgan had even given Frank an opportunity to work on his ranch some years back. Within two days, Joseph Longbow rode Frank home and all he'd said was *Frank isn't going to work out.* She could tell by the look on Joseph's face that he was angry, and she knew something had gone terribly wrong. She'd never before seen Joseph Longbow angry. He'd always been a pleasant, amiable fellow, but not that day. Frank's entire face was swollen, he had a black eye and his lip was bleeding. When she'd asked him what happened he refused to tell her.

Frank had stayed in bed for a few days after the incident. He wouldn't even allow her to tend to his wounds. When he finally got out of bed, the way he moved told her he might have some broken ribs, but he never told her what took place on Morgan's ranch. Morgan never mentioned it either. But from that day on, Frank was determined to find a way to goad Morgan into some sort of confrontation.

Granny was certain Morgan had tolerated Frank's shenanigans as long as he did because of her. Morgan had always been good to her and Preacher. There were many winters they wouldn't have been able to feed their grandchildren if not for Morgan. She mentioned that fact often to Frank, but it didn't make a difference. Frank detested Morgan, and he'd nursed that hatred over the years until it consumed him.

From the time the grandchildren came to live with them, Frank had been the most rebellious. She carried a lot of the blame for the way he'd turned out. After the children's parents died of the fever, she and Preacher had pampered the children. She understood their pain, and she thought Frank behaved the way he did because he was grieving. The children lost their parents, but she'd lost her only child, Curtis. Curtis was a wonderful son and a good man, and she missed him every day. Her own sorrow had been devastating, and she didn't have it in her to be harsh with her grandchildren. Preacher had been more accepting of their son's death, always reminding her that Curtis was in a better place. Preacher had never asked why such a thing had happened to them. It had been more difficult for her to accept God's plan to take her only son's life. Frank was the spitting image of his father, so she was constantly reminded of her loss. But the similarities between Frank and his father ended there. Curtis had always been a hardworking man of good character, a trait Frank hadn't inherited. As much as it saddened Granny to admit, Frank's character was lacking.

Preacher always told Frank that idle hands were the Devil's workshop, but it didn't faze him. Frank responded by saying that they didn't have much to show for all of their hard work except a broken-down old farm. Determined to listen to his own counsel, by the time Frank was fourteen he was beyond control. After Preacher died, Frank was of no help at all around the farm. He only came around when he needed a place to sleep or eat, and Granny had reached the end of her patience with him.

It'd taken some time, but Granny had to finally accept that Frank was responsible for his own decisions. Good or bad. Morgan and Frankie were only a year apart in age, and Granny had prayed Frank would change, and see what he could do with his life if he worked hard like Morgan. But her prayers went unanswered. After years of making excuses for him, Granny refused to rationalize, or ask for lenience for his actions any longer.

"When LeMasters hears about the sheriff, he will be out for blood, that's for sure," Webb said.

Granny knew Morgan was out for vengeance.

"They forgot about the horses from the stagecoach that weren't injured," George said to Morgan.

"Yeah, I know." Morgan felt like his skull was about to explode, but that was the least of his worries.

"They ran off, but maybe they didn't go too far. I'll look for them," Murph said.

Morgan glanced at the other men, and said, "Check the luggage. Maybe there's another pistol and some water."

The surviving passenger walked up to Morgan and extended his hand. "I'm Clay Hunt. I had a pistol in my luggage, and a canteen inside the coach."

Morgan shook his hand. "Morgan LeMasters." A quick appraisal told Morgan that Hunt was a man who could hold his own. "Mr. Hunt, glad you're okay." Morgan thought the name was familiar, but he didn't think he'd ever met the man.

Clay glanced at the young woman on the ground. "I hope she'll be okay. I traveled all the way with her, and she is a delightful young woman. It's hard to believe she's even related to Frank."

"I had a saddle on top of the coach, along with my valise and saddlebags. There's some grub in there, a coffeepot, coffee, and some whiskey," George said to Morgan.

"Good, you're going to need some of that whiskey when I set your leg." Morgan kneeled beside Rose and patted her lightly on the cheek. "Miss Langtry." When Rose didn't respond, he looked at George. "How far to the next station?"

"It's about twenty miles away. It's a home station with a telegraph. We can lodge there, and there'll be horses we can buy. We can't go back to the last station because they are out of fresh horses." George looked down at the wound on Rose's head. "Looks like she hit her head pretty hard."

Morgan reached for the canteen George pulled from beneath him. "Yeah." He damp-

68

ened the bandana and washed Rose's face, trying to remove some of the blood from her wound.

"I didn't see nothing wrong with the wheel, but I felt like it wasn't right. This is my fault," George said.

"Don't blame yourself, George. Accidents happen." After Morgan finished cleaning Rose's face, he placed the bandana on Rose's wound again. "Keep an eye on her, George. I'll look around for your rifle, and find a branch we can use for a splint."

"Sure thing," George replied.

Morgan pinpointed the location where George had jumped from the wagon, and it didn't take him long before he located the Winchester in the brush.

"Well, at least we won't be unarmed," George said when Morgan came back carrying his rifle along with a sturdy limb for a splint. "You think they are really headed to Mexico?"

"They'd better find a good hiding place in Mexico. I won't bother with a hanging next time. I'll shoot them on sight." Morgan checked the rifle to make sure it was loaded.

Murph returned leading two horses, and the other men joined them, carrying all the luggage they could find.

Clay Hunt handed Morgan his pistol. "I

don't normally carry a weapon."

Morgan thought it was an odd comment, but he didn't question him. "We have one pistol and one rifle if we need to defend ourselves."

George pointed to one of the valises. "That one is mine." Morgan handed George the bag so he could retrieve his whiskey.

"Murph, George said the next home station is twenty miles away. I want you and Grady to go. Send a telegraph to the sheriff's office telling them of our whereabouts, and that Frank and his gang are on the loose. Bring back a buckboard so we can get George and Miss Langtry out of here." He reached in his pocket and pulled out some money. "Take this with you to pay the stationmaster for the horses and the use of a buckboard."

"His name is Ward Barnett. He'll help you any way he can," George said before he took a long draw from the whiskey bottle.

"George, before you start feeling the whiskey, tell the men if there are any areas where they could be ambushed, just in case Frank was lying about Mexico," Morgan said.

After George detailed the route, Morgan walked the men to their horses. "Murph, ride as fast as you dare." He handed Murph the pistol. "Take this in case Frank and his men didn't head to Mexico."

"We'll be back as soon as possible," Murph said. "I'm sorry I took that man's word that he wasn't carrying."

"Don't worry about it, Murph. He paid for his lie with his life."

Morgan asked his men to bury the deceased passenger with rocks while he tended George. It was near dusk when they finished their tasks, and they were preparing a fire when Morgan saw Rose move.

He bent down on one knee beside her and waited for her to open her eyes. "Hello."

Rose blinked several times in an effort to focus on the dark eyes boring into hers. Her head hurt so badly that her vision was blurred. She started to sit, but she clutched her ribs in pain. "What happened?"

"The stagecoach broke an axle and went tumbling over the hill. I'm afraid you have a nasty gash on your head." Morgan pointed to her head. "That's the reason I bandaged your head."

She reached up and felt the cloth, but even that small motion made her grimace in pain.

Morgan was watching her intently. "And judging by the way you're holding your ribs,

I'd say a couple of them might be busted."

Rose looked into his eyes, trying to comprehend everything he was saying. "Frankie?"

"He's alive."

"What about everyone else?"

"George has a broken leg, but he'll be fine. We lost one passenger."

"Pastor Hunt?"

Morgan saw she was getting teary eyed. "Pastor . . ." Clay Hunt hadn't mentioned he was a pastor. He didn't look much like a pastor. "He's alive."

"Thank goodness, he is such a fine man," she said.

"You need to drink some water." Morgan held her head and placed the canteen to her lips.

She took a small sip, then asked, "Where are we?"

"We're about twenty miles from the next station. I've sent my men to get a buckboard."

Rose glanced around, but she didn't see Frankie. "Where's Frankie?"

"I'm afraid your brother got the drop on us, and he took off with his boys." He didn't mention that her big brother had been planning on killing her along with the rest of them.

She tried to sit up, but Morgan stopped her when he saw her wince and clutch her ribs again. "There's nothing to be done about it now. You don't need to be moving about if you have busted ribs."

"But why did he leave? He was going to have a chance to prove he did nothing wrong."

Morgan remained silent, allowing her to think through her question on her own. She hadn't been inclined to take his word about her lying brother earlier, so he didn't think anything he said would make a difference.

"Where do you think they would go?"

"He said to Mexico."

"I guess he thought he wouldn't be able to prove his innocence."

Morgan ground his teeth together to keep from saying what he thought. He couldn't discuss Frank with a woman who refused to face the truth. "We need to get those ribs bandaged."

Her eyes widened. "You can't bandage my ribs."

"Of course I can. I've done it many times." He'd had a few broken ribs and he knew how painful they were.

Rose frowned at him. "I mean, it wouldn't be proper."

"Proper or not, I'm going to wrap those

ribs." He didn't dare mention that he'd already checked her legs to see if she had any broken bones.

"Absolutely not. I can't allow you to do that."

"We can either find a way to get you out of that getup, or I'll cut it off with my knife. Your choice, but I'm going to wrap your ribs. When the buckboard gets here you can't be jostling around without them wrapped, or you could make matters worse. Not to mention, you probably couldn't stand the pain."

She knew he was right; just taking a breath was painful. She looked around and saw the men sitting by the fire not far away. "But they will see."

One side of Morgan's mouth tilted in a half grin. "I assure you they've seen women before."

"Not undressed."

Morgan arched a dark brow at her.

Rose felt her face getting warm. She tried to think of an alternative to Morgan Le-Masters helping her out of her dress to wrap her ribs. "Perhaps you could wrap the bandage over my dress."

"No, that won't work. It needs to be tight."

She reasoned that Pastor Hunt, even though he was about the same age as Mr.

LeMasters, and quite attractive, was a devout man who wouldn't be inclined to have carnal thoughts seeing a woman in a state of undress. Accepting the fact that she agreed with Morgan that it was necessary for her ribs to be wrapped, she said, "Perhaps Pastor Hunt could do it then."

That rankled Morgan. She didn't really know Hunt, so why was she so willing to let him see her undressed? "I'm not sure he's wrapped ribs before, and it's easy to get the bandage too tight. If you do, then you have to do it all over again. You wouldn't want that."

Rose gave him an indignant glare. "I should say not. I just thought that since he's a pastor . . . well, he wouldn't . . ." She had no idea how to explain her thinking, so the words hung in the air between them.

Morgan waited. He knew what she was thinking, and he didn't hesitate to let her know how misguided she was. "He's a man, isn't he?" When she didn't respond, he turned to walk away. "I'll be right back."

He reached the fire and saw George was sound asleep. The whiskey did its job. Maybe he should give some of that whiskey to Rose to calm her down. He asked the men to take a walk for a few minutes while he tended Rose. "And don't mention her brother wanted to shoot her." Considering everything she'd been through today, he didn't want to make matters worse. She probably wouldn't believe them anyway.

The men nodded.

"Do you need help?" Clay asked.

"I think I can handle it," Morgan replied, as he picked up a petticoat from the stack of clothing the men collected earlier.

He walked back to Rose and held up her petticoat. "I'm afraid I had to use one of these when I set George's leg. It was all I could find to wrap the splint."

"I don't mind."

Once he finished tearing the strips of cloth, he said, "Okay, let's get you out of your dress."

Rose still wasn't inclined to undress in front of him. "I am wearing a corset and it is tied quite snug."

Morgan hadn't thought about that. Still, he wasn't sure it would take the place of a bandage. "That might work, but I'll have to make sure it's tight enough."

Rose allowed him to lift her to her feet, and he gingerly removed her jacket. Her dress had tiny little buttons down the front, from the neck to the waist, but she quickly realized it was too painful for her to unbutton them when she tried to lift her arms.

Morgan saw the problem and he said, "Let me." His big hands made it difficult for him to unfasten such small buttons, and he was tempted to use his knife and slice the things off, but he kept at the task, determined to get it done. By the tenth button, he was getting a little faster. He'd placed one finger behind the buttons to keep them from moving, but that also meant he was touching her chemise beneath her dress.

Rose kept her head down, watching his every move. No man had ever touched her, or removed her clothing. It was very disconcerting to feel his large fingers beneath the cloth, touching her skin.

Morgan was just about to reach the buttons at her bust and his fingers stilled. He glanced at her face to see her staring up at him. He wondered what she was thinking. He hesitated. *Go about this like you would if you were tending one of the men,* he told himself. He searched her green eyes another second, waiting for an objection. None came. Refocusing on the long row of buttons, he continued on.

Finally, he unhooked the last button, and he slid her dress from her shoulders, allowing it to drop to her waist. He could see her corset beneath the flimsy material of her chemise.

"Wouldn't my corset work for a bandage?"

Morgan pointed to her chemise and said, "Do you think you could hold this up so I can see how tight it is?"

Rose knew her face was blood red by now. When she saw his eyes on her chemise, she couldn't read his expression. She was so embarrassed she couldn't form a response, so she nodded. Clutching a handful of the soft cloth, she held it snuggly beneath her breasts.

He couldn't really see the top of the corset, but he did notice that it was made in such a way that it cupped her breasts. It was impossible for him to slide his finger inside the top of the corset without touching her breast. Instead, he moved around to her back, and stuck his hand between her skin and the corset. "I don't think it's tight enough." The corset was already tied as tightly as possible, but it was too loose on her. "I don't think this is going to work." Without waiting for a response, he started untying the laces on her corset. He was tempted to ask how she'd tied it behind her back. Once it was untied, he removed the corset and tossed it on the luggage. Again, his eyes were on her chemise. He couldn't ask her to remove the only thing covering her. It was so soft and thin that it was barely covering her at that.

"Okay, if you'll keep that" — he pointed to her chemise — "up under . . . I'll wrap the bandage around you." He saw she had a death grip on the chemise, preventing it from moving an inch.

His fingers touched her skin as he started wrapping the cloth, causing her to jump. Morgan stopped and looked at her. "Did that hurt?"

"No," she whispered.

He made quick work of wrapping the long strip around her, all the while trying not to pay too much attention to her bare skin, or how soft it was. It was proving difficult to pretend she was one of the men. She was so small that he wrapped the cloth around her several times. He tried to think of something to say to put her at ease. "This will keep you from hurting every time you take a breath." He tied the ends of the cloth. "Now tell me if I have it too tight."

Rose took a tentative breath. He had tied it much tighter than her corset. "No, I don't think so."

Satisfied with her response, he helped her slide her arms back into her sleeves and buttoned her up again. "Are you hungry? We have a small amount of food and some coffee."

"Coffee sounds wonderful, if there is enough."

After he helped her to the small fire they'd built to warm the coffee, he placed a bedroll on the ground to make it more comfortable for her. Once she eased down on the bedroll, he placed a valise behind her so she could lean back. From his experience, he knew it was the most comfortable position.

"Thank you."

"Yes, ma'am."

She watched him walk away. She'd recognized him earlier that morning by his walk. He moved like a supremely confident man. It was difficult to believe that she'd just allowed the man who had scared her to death for so many years to not only undress her, but tend to her. He didn't seem to be as terrible as Frankie led her to believe. As a matter of fact, he'd gone out of his way to help her when he could have easily been angry with her over the turn of events today. Oddly enough, he'd been so gentle that she wondered why she'd ever feared him.

As he'd concentrated on his task of wrapping the bandage around her ribs, she'd had the opportunity to get a good look at his face. Once her sisters were old enough to notice the opposite sex, they would always talk about how attractive Morgan was. It wasn't until she was thirteen years of age that she started to agree with her sisters.

She thought he was even more handsome now than he was before she'd left Whispering Pines. His skin was tanned to a dark golden bronze, his square jawline was even more defined, he now had a few wrinkles at the outer corners of his dark blue eyes, and the cleft in his chin seemed to have deepened with age. She remembered asking Granny about the dimple in his chin when she was a girl. Granny told her that was where God had touched Morgan. Just as He'd given her green eyes as His special mark, He gave Morgan his special dimple.

CHAPTER FOUR

Jack Roper glared at Granny Langtry. "You about finished poking on me?"

Jack started to move off the table, but Granny pushed him back down. "Don't be giving me your evil eye, Sheriff. It doesn't scare me."

"Well, what else is there to poke at?"

Granny ignored him. She placed her hand on Jack's head and closed her eyes.

Webb couldn't figure out what she was doing. It was a few minutes before she opened her eyes, and Webb asked, "Is that a new way of taking a temperature?"

Granny frowned at him. "No, that is an old way of asking the Good Lord to help me figure out what is wrong with him."

"Oh."

When Granny turned her attention back on the sheriff, Webb rolled his eyes.

"Don't you roll your eyes at me, young man. Make yourself useful and tell me if you kept the slug you dug out of the sheriff's shoulder."

Webb was still trying to figure out how she knew what he was doing behind her back. "Now why would I want to keep a used slug?"

"I can't find anything wrong with the sheriff, but look at these red streaks going down his arm. I'd say his shoulder is infected. I think part of that slug is still in there. That could be the reason for his fever."

Looking over her shoulder, Webb saw the red lines she was talking about. "What does that mean?"

Granny gave him a sorrowful look. "That means we have to go in there and dig out the piece that is still in there."

Jack didn't like the sound of that. "We'll give it a few days and see what happens. It'll work itself out." He made a feeble attempt to move from the examining table again, but Granny placed her small hand on his chest, halting his progress with surprising strength.

She didn't soft-pedal her words. "I don't have to tell you, in a few days we'll be removing your arm. That is, if you are still alive. You're burning up as it is." She could feel the heat emanating from him before she touched him.

Jack wasn't going to argue with her. Granny had seen her fair share of wounds, and she was a smart old woman. He dropped back to the table on a loud groan. "Dig the dang thing out."

Granny opened her bag and pulled out some chloroform she'd been given by the town doctor before he died. "I'll give you a dose of this."

"No you won't. Just get to it."

Granny started to open the bottle. "You don't have to put on a brave face, this is going to hurt like the devil."

Jack gave her a hard look. "Put that stuff away, grab your instruments of torture, and let's get this over with."

Granny knew that look. "Okay, you stubborn mule." She motioned for the deputy to come closer. "You stand there in case I need you to hold him down."

"Webb, go on about your business," Jack said.

Granny straightened and put her hands on her hips. "Now listen to me, Jack Roper, the deputy stays where he is. I might need his help."

Webb didn't want to go against the sheriff's wishes, but this time he thought Granny was right. "You two are like two bulls squaring off. I'll stay right here."

Jack started to object, but he didn't feel up to arguing. "Do your worst, old woman."

Picking up her probe, Granny immediately stuck it in the sheriff's wound. "I might remind you it isn't polite to call a lady an old woman."

Jack grimaced as she poked around searching for the offending fragment. Instrument of torture didn't aptly describe the tool she was using, in his estimation. "You plan on staying in there all day?"

Granny glanced at him, but she wasn't listening to him. She was concentrating on her undertaking, hoping to feel something that wasn't quite right. Finally, she grazed something that she didn't think was bone. "There it is."

After Granny removed the small metal sliver, she bandaged Jack's shoulder. She waited for Jack to fall asleep before she talked to the deputy. "Webb, would you pull a chair over here by the sheriff? It'll be dawn soon, and I'll sit right here while you go get some breakfast. I'm sure you could use some coffee." While she was doing her surgery on the sheriff's shoulder, she thought she might have two patients to look after. Deputy Webb was as green as the apples on her kitchen table.

Webb glanced down at Jack. As much as he wanted a good strong cup of black coffee, he wasn't sure he could even eat breakfast. Watching Granny poke around in the sheriff's shoulder had made him nauseous. He was amazed how the sheriff stoically withstood the pain. It was more than he could handle. "You sure he'll stay out for a while?"

Granny nodded. "He's worn out. I'm amazed he didn't pass out when I was digging out that slug."

"I know." He headed to the door. "I'll bring you both some breakfast."

When Webb left, Granny sat in the chair, placed her hand on Jack's chest, and started praying.

Before dawn broke over the horizon, Morgan gathered some wood to stoke the fire. It had been a cool night and they had kept the fire going all night. He didn't want Rose to catch a cold, which could easily turn into pneumonia with her lack of movement. Morgan hadn't slept all night; he wanted to be alert if there was trouble, and he was worried about Rose. She was deathly pale, and she hadn't eaten a bite of the food. He couldn't ignore the possibility that she had more serious internal injuries. He'd tried to make her as comfortable as possible by using the seats from the coach to make a bed for her. The men found two blankets from the coach to cover her with, but he was still concerned over her welfare.

Dan joined him at the fire. "You think we can spare the water for some coffee?"

"I think so." Morgan glanced at George and saw he'd opened his eyes. "How's the leg?"

"It feels a lot better this morning. Could you help me up?"

"Sure thing." Morgan helped George to his feet. He kept an eye on him as he made his way to the brush, to make sure he didn't topple over.

Morgan handed Dan the canteen. "I think we should make a couple of traps to catch something for dinner. I don't want to leave camp with our only rifle. I expect we will be out here one more night and we are going to need some food." He hoped Rose would eat something if they were lucky enough to snare a rabbit.

"I'm pretty good with traps," Ken said.

"I'll help," Clay offered.

"Thanks," Morgan responded.

While the coffee boiled, Morgan glanced at Rose to make sure she was still sleeping before he said, "I half expected Faithful would have made his way back by now if Deke let him go."

Dan filled the pot with beans and water. "You think Deke will really let him go?"

"Yeah, I had a feeling he was trying to give me a signal when he took him." If Deke didn't release Faithful, Morgan planned to go after him once he saw Rose to the way station.

"Deke's not a bad sort. I think he wanted excitement more than anything. I think he's afraid to leave Frank," Dan said.

"It wouldn't surprise me. Frank likes to bully people," Morgan replied.

"I listened to what Deke and Dutch had to say when Frank was riding in the coach. They think Frank is getting in over his head. They said he was getting meaner by the day," Dan said.

If Deke did let his horse go, Morgan planned to put in a good word to the judge on his behalf. Deke seemed to care more about the welfare of Frank's sister than Frank. "Too bad he didn't think about parting company with Frank a long time ago."

Dan agreed. "I'm sure Dutch isn't afraid of Frank, but I don't know what he's doing with Frank in the first place. He doesn't strike me as a man to take orders."

"I'll give some credit to Deke, maybe even

Dutch and Corbin, but no quarter will be given to Frank. Though I'm not certain they would have stopped him if he'd been ready to pull the trigger on . . ." Morgan didn't finish his thought. He glanced at Rose, and even though her eyes were closed he didn't want to take the chance she might not be asleep. He saw no reason to tell her how little her brother thought of her.

Dan saw the direction of his eyes and nodded. "I know."

Even though the men were speaking quietly, Rose heard what they said. They thought she was sleeping, but she was in too much pain to sleep. Her pain wasn't the only reason she'd remained awake most of the night. She was trying to figure out what made Frankie leave when he was going to have the chance to prove his innocence. It was difficult for her to come up with an explanation, particularly knowing she was injured when he made his decision to leave. Perhaps he felt leaving was his only option. But if he wasn't guilty of Morgan's charges, why didn't he want to go back to face a judge? She refused to accept the notion that he was guilty. Frankie simply wasn't capable of being an outlaw. Yet it broke her heart that he'd ridden off while she was unconscious, not even knowing the extent of her injuries.

It was upsetting to hear Morgan and his men talk about her brother as though he was an evil person. But on the other hand, Frankie had never had a kind word to say about Morgan. Morgan's kindness had certainly surprised her. He was nothing like the dark ogre she'd anticipated. Actually, she liked him, and she could tell his men liked and respected him. That said more about the man than anything Frank had led her to believe.

When she was young she'd heard Frankie tell Granny that he hated Morgan LeMasters, and he was going to make him pay. She'd asked Frankie what he meant by that statement, but Frankie wouldn't give her an answer. All he said was, "Never you mind, he's gonna pay." She'd never forgotten that day. Frankie's expression had frightened her. It was the first time she'd seen his face so filled with hate.

Her thoughts returned to Morgan LeMasters. Every Sunday, Morgan would sit in the pew directly behind her family. She didn't need to turn around to know he was there because she recognized his footsteps on the plank floor as he walked down the aisle. When she heard the bench creak as he sat down behind her, she always turned around to stare at him. Frankie would never turn around, but she knew by the scowl on his face that he was aware Morgan was behind them.

After church, Rose and her siblings would often have to wait for Granny, who was sidetracked by people discussing their maladies. Rose spent the time people-watching, and inevitably she'd see the single women in town surround Morgan as he made his way to his horse. There were two young widows in particular who vied for his attention every Sunday. Morgan would politely pause to talk to the ladies, and in a gentlemanly manner, remove his Stetson as he gave them his undivided attention. But Rose could tell he was in a hurry, and was just being polite. When he was ready to take his leave, he would put on his hat and tip the brim to the ladies. She'd hear him say, *Nice to see you, ladies,* in his deep baritone voice, and hurry to his horse.

As a young girl she didn't understand why women wanted his attention. In her child's mind, she assumed everyone was afraid of him. She'd even asked her sisters why all the women wanted to talk to him. They'd laughed and said Morgan LeMasters was the most handsome man in town, and he always smelled good. They were right on that score; he did smell good.

She recalled the last Sunday morning she'd seen Morgan in the churchyard after the service. She'd just celebrated her fourteenth birthday, and it was her last Sunday in Whispering Pines before she moved East. She wouldn't have admitted it at the time, but she'd turned around in the pew, waiting for Mr. LeMasters to walk down the aisle. Before he crossed the threshold of the church, he removed his hat and walked straight ahead. He was wearing a blue shirt, and for a brief moment she thought he looked directly at her. She quickly turned around before he made it to his pew. When the service ended that day, she stood by the buckboard waiting for Granny. As usual, she watched the women surround Morgan, smiling and overtly flirting with him. But this particular morning, Morgan smiled at a comment from one woman. Rose was mesmerized. His smile transformed his uncompromising, granitelike features. She'd thought of that moment many times over the past five years. While she was back East there had been a few young men who had asked her to dinner. It came as quite a shock when she realized she always found herself comparing them to Morgan LeMasters. Her sisters teased her that she was going to end up an old maid if she didn't start accepting more invitations, but none of her suitors had interested her.

Rose's thoughts were disrupted when the men started talking again.

"How's the head?" Dan asked Morgan.

Morgan had a good-sized lump on the back of his skull, but at least his head had quit throbbing. "It's fine."

"He cracked you pretty good. Are you sure you don't need some stitches?"

"No, it's stopped bleeding."

Rose didn't know Mr. LeMasters had been injured. She wanted to ask him about it, but then he would know she'd overheard their conversation. After a few minutes, she opened her eyes and found dark blue eyes staring directly at her.

"Good morning," Morgan said. He poured a cup of coffee for her. "How are you feeling?" Aside from the bruising on her face, she still looked very pale to him.

"I'm feeling much better, thank you." She accepted the coffee he handed her. She worried it would be too painful when she was forced to stand and see to her needs, but the aroma of the hot liquid won the battle.

Morgan noticed she hadn't moved all night. "Do you think you can get up and move around?"

"I'll try after I finish the coffee."

Morgan put two and two together and didn't comment further. "I expect we might be here one more night, so the men are setting some traps, hoping to catch something. I thought you might be hungry since you didn't have a bite of food last night."

"I may be able to eat today," she replied. She saw her damaged trunk nearby, along with her belongings stacked on top. "Thank you for collecting my things."

"I'm afraid the lid to your trunk is beyond repair, but we gathered as much as we could find."

"Thank you. Did you happen to see my Bible?"

"Yes, ma'am." When he'd uncovered the Bible in the rubble, he recalled how she'd held it to her when she stepped off the stagecoach. He'd opened the cover and read the inscription: *To our beautiful daughter, Rose. This book will be your source of strength and comfort in your time of need. We love you dearly, Mother and Father.*

Morgan had placed the Bible on top of his saddle behind her. When he handed it to her, he could see the relief on her face that it was not lost.

Rose clutched it to her chest. "Thank you. My mother and father gave this to me when

I was five years old. It's my most treasured gift." She looked down as she ran her hands over the cover. "They both died not long after."

When she abruptly closed her eyes, Morgan thought she might want to be alone. He started to move away, but he heard her softly say, "Amen."

Rose opened her eyes and saw him staring at her. "I was thanking God for you. I don't know what I would have done without you, Mr. LeMasters."

Morgan was caught off guard by her comment, particularly since he was the man who had been about to hang her brother before the stagecoach stopped. "You don't have to worry about me going anywhere."

They looked at each other for a moment, each trying to read what the other was thinking. Rose felt herself starting to blush, so she reached up and touched the bandage on her head. "Do you think I could remove the bandage?"

"I'll take it off for you."

Once he'd removed the cloth, Rose felt the knot on her head.

"You have a nice lump."

She felt the caked blood on her scalp as she attempted to run her fingers through her hair. "I fear I am a mess. Did you happen to find my brush?" She wanted to ask for water to clean herself, but she knew they had little to spare.

"Yes, ma'am." He walked to the trunk again and retrieved a comb, brush, and mirror, which had fortunately escaped damage.

When he handed them to her she said, "It's hard to believe the mirror didn't break." She lifted her arm to run the brush through her air, but it was so painful that she decided not to try.

Morgan recalled his limited movement when he'd cracked his ribs. He reached for the brush. "I'll give it a try." He'd never in his life brushed a woman's hair. "If I hurt you, let me know." Morgan went about the task as if he were brushing his horse's tail, holding it firm at the base so it wouldn't hurt her as he pulled the brush through the length.

Rose didn't know what to think of this big brute of a man kneeling down beside her to brush her hair. He was so close she could feel the heat emanating from him. She almost felt he was doing something too intimate to be seen by others. She glanced around to see if the men were watching him. "What will your men think?"

His hand halted and he cast a glance at her. "I hadn't given it a thought." He resumed brushing as he considered her question. When he picked up a lock of hair, his hand brushed the back of her neck and he felt her shiver. "But now that I think about it, they'd probably say I am the luckiest man alive." The way he saw it, his men would probably volunteer for the job. As a matter of fact, he questioned why he'd never brushed a woman's hair before. He liked the feel of her silken strands against his rough skin. "When the men get here with the buckboard, we'll have some water so you can wash your face."

His comment made her raise the mirror to see what he was seeing. She could hardly believe her own reflection. Her face was covered with bruises and dried blood. The large lump on her head had an ugly lesion that was scabbing over. And her hair was a total disaster. "Oh my, I look worse than I thought."

"After the tumble you took, I think you look fine. That lump will go down in a day or two and your bruises will fade. That cut won't even leave a scar." Morgan figured most women as pretty as she was would worry about having a scar, but in his estimation she would still be beautiful even if she had a few scars. "Those ribs are going to take the longest to heal. You will probably be in more pain today than yesterday."

There was nothing about her that looked fine, but she was thankful that her injuries weren't more severe. "I think you may be right." She'd already noticed that her entire body hurt worse than it did before she fell asleep last night.

Morgan finished brushing her hair just as Ken and Clay walked back to camp with two rabbits on a spit, ready to place over the fire. "Looks like we'll have a feast for breakfast."

Rose thought it was the perfect time to see to her needs. "I think I will go . . ." She didn't know how to tell him she needed some privacy.

Morgan understood what she needed to do. He extended his hand to help her to her feet. "Can you breathe okay?" He wanted to make sure she didn't have a punctured lung.

She nodded. Every breath she took was excruciatingly painful, but it was a comfort to know Morgan knew what to do. It was even more painful to walk, but she had to see to her needs. "Thank you, I'll be back in a moment."

Morgan watched her slowly walk through the brush. He was hesitant to leave in case she needed assistance getting back to the fire, but he wanted to give her some privacy.

He thought he should have another look at her ribs again to see if they were swollen. He'd cared for injured men and animals, but he'd never tended a woman, and he was hesitant to tell her she needed to disrobe again. He glanced up and saw the pastor walking toward him, so he met him halfway.

"How is she doing?" Clay asked.

"I think she's in more pain than she is saying. I hope the men get here by morning so we can get her to a doctor."

Clay read the concern on Morgan's face. "You're worried."

Morgan nodded. "Yeah. She hasn't eaten a bite of food, and she's barely had any water. She's as white as an apparition. I'd like to get a good look at those ribs, but I'm afraid she'd have a fit. I didn't think she was going to let me wrap them in the first place."

"She might let me take a look," Clay said.

Morgan didn't like the thought of the pastor seeing her in her camisole. He arched a brow at him and said, "I'd say she'd let me before she would another man."

Clay grinned at him. "I am a pastor."

"You're a man." Morgan had already decided he liked the pastor, but there was no way he was going to allow him to see Rose half undressed.

99

Clay was just ribbing Morgan to get a rise out of him. Morgan had been more protective of Rose than a mama bear, and in Clay's estimation, that said a lot about the man's character. Judging by what Ken told him when they were setting the traps, Morgan had every right to dislike anyone named Langtry. Being in the coach with Frank Langtry just a short amount of time, it didn't take long to figure out what kind of man he was. Morgan was to be commended for treating Rose with such kindness and compassion.

"You go to church in Whispering Pines?" Clay asked.

"Every Sunday before Preacher died. There will be a lot of folks happy to see you."

"I wasn't always a preacher. I went back East . . ." He didn't finish the conversation because Rose walked from the brush toward them.

Morgan thought she looked ready to pass out, so he scooped her up in his arms and carried her back to the fire. "When you catch your breath, I want to have a look at those ribs."

"I'm fine. I just need to rest." Truthfully, she wanted out of her dress and that bandage wrapped around her ribs, but she didn't dare say that to him.

Morgan thought she looked like she was struggling to breathe. He was concerned he'd tied the bandage too tight. "Do you want me to loosen the bandage?"

She frowned. "I thought you said it had to be tight."

"That is the general idea, but since you are not moving around much, maybe you could leave it off for a while if you think it would feel better." He hoped he was offering sound advice. When he'd broken some ribs, he'd had to continue working on the ranch, so he'd kept his bandaged.

He knew she was considering the idea. When he saw her gaze over at the men, he half expected her to suggest the pastor again. He pointed to some boulders and said, "We can go right behind those rocks and no one could see."

She wasn't sure she could make it to the rocks. When he'd removed her dress the first time, it was dusk and it was difficult to see. Now the sun was shining brightly and he would be able to see every freckle on her skin. But her need to breathe freely was outweighing her modesty.

"Why don't we do this before the meat is cooked. You might be able to eat something if you are more comfortable," Morgan suggested.

"Do you really think I might be able to breathe easier?"

"All we can do is try."

"I think I can get my dress off myself."

"Okay." He helped her to the rocks and stood with his back against the rock. "Tell me if you need help."

Once she made sure she was totally out of sight, she started unbuttoning her dress. It took forever, but she finally made her way to the last button. Problem was, she couldn't get the dress over her shoulders. She had no choice but to ask for Morgan's help. "Mr. LeMasters, I'm afraid I can't take my dress off my shoulders."

Morgan walked around the rock to see her holding her dress together with one hand. "Here, let me lend a hand." He gently pushed her dress from her shoulders, but once he gripped her chemise to raise it under her breasts, she covered his hand with hers. He immediately released the cloth to her. He untied the bandage and quickly removed the cloth. Her entire ribcage was swollen, and her skin was green in large blotches. He looked at her back and was surprised at the amount of bruising everywhere.

"I'm going to feel your ribs." He glanced up at her to see if she was going to object. When she didn't, he gently felt her ribs, front and back. He wasn't sure, but he thought she might have fractured all of her ribs. Knowing it could take weeks for them to heal, he was concerned that if she didn't breathe properly she might develop serious complications. To make matters worse, to get to the way station she would be riding in a buckboard, bouncing around all over the place, then in a stagecoach to get back to Whispering Pines.

She looked down at the top of his head as he was bent over examining her, his large fingers gently pressing on her body. Just like before, she shivered under his touch. "Do you think I can leave it off?"

"Do you breathe easier?" He straightened and watched to see if she was taking deep breaths.

"It feels better to have everything off," she admitted.

Morgan grinned at her comment. "I don't think that would be the thing to do."

She realized what she'd said, and blushed.

Morgan thought her breathing was still shallow. She needed complete rest and something for the pain, but both of those things were not possible given the circumstances. He questioned if he'd done the right thing by insisting she be bandaged in the first place. When he'd collected her clothing he'd seen a white nightgown that was every bit as modest as her dress but wouldn't be as confining. "Wait just a minute."

Rose felt very vulnerable standing there when he walked away, with nothing covering her top half but her chemise. Thankfully, he returned quickly and held the nightgown out to her.

"I think this will be more comfortable to wear."

Rose looked at him as though he'd lost his mind. "I can't wear my nightgown in the daylight."

Morgan frowned at her. "Why not? You can button it up to your chin."

"For one thing, it's thinner than my dress, and it wouldn't be proper to wear in front of gentlemen."

Morgan had to admit if she wore nothing beneath the nightgown it would present a problem. "Keep your underclothes on and it will be fine."

Rose had to agree it would be more comfortable not to have anything binding her. "Are you sure it will be appropriate?"

"It's more important that you breathe

right now than concern yourself with what's proper." Morgan grabbed the nightgown and tossed it over her head. "Raise your arms as high as you can and let's get them shoved through the sleeves." Once that task was accomplished, and the gown was covering her, he tugged on the bottom of her dress and it dropped over her slim hips to the ground. "Just step out of this."

Being dressed by him made Rose uncomfortable, but she had no alternative. "Thank you for your help. I don't know what I would have done without you."

Morgan watched as she tried to close the buttons on her gown. He moved her hands out of the way and buttoned her up to the chin. "You can repay me by taking it easy, and trying to breathe as deeply as you can. And eating a little bit."

She gave him a tentative smile. "I'll try."

CHAPTER FIVE

Before Frank and his men broke camp the next morning, Frank informed them of his change of plans. "Finish your coffee and let's saddle up. We're going to Purgatory Canyon and then back to Whispering Pines."

"Why are we going to do a fool thing like that?" Deke asked.

Frank glared at him. Deke was already on his short list for releasing two of the horses the day before. Deke swore it was an accident, but Frank wasn't buying his explanation. "Why are you questioning my decision?"

Deke looked away from Frank's piercing eyes. "I just thought we were headed to Mexico."

Dutch stood and tossed the remainder of his coffee in the dying fire. "Deke is right. Why would we want to go back to Whispering Pines?"

Frank wasn't going to be able to intimidate Dutch with a silencing glare that worked on Deke. "We'll never find those cattle now and we need money." He jabbed a finger in Deke's direction. "Now that stupid here let those horses go, we need something to sell. In case you boys have forgotten, we don't have money."

"I told you it was an accident. We still have three horses we can sell," Deke said.

Frank narrowed his eyes at Deke. "I wonder why you released LeMasters's horse. Are you afraid of him?"

Deke didn't comment. Frank was right, he had intentionally released the horses. He didn't feel right about leaving LeMasters with no way to get help for Frank's sister. He didn't have a beef with LeMasters, and he didn't think Frank should have left his sister like he did.

"It's done, so let's forget about it," Dutch said, tiring of the conversation. "Can't we find some cattle to rustle on our way to Mexico? LeMasters doesn't own all the cattle in the West."

"I figure the rest of the boys will make their way back to Purgatory Canyon if they got away from the law. I don't want to leave them hanging, not knowing what happened to us. We'll meet up with them and go to

Whispering Pines to get Stevie." Frank didn't really care about the rest of the gang. He wanted to go back to Whispering Pines to take as many cows as possible from Morgan's ranch once again. He needed the rest of the boys to accomplish his goal.

"We'll rustle some more cattle and be gone before LeMasters gets back, if they get back at all. He had four of his men riding with him. I reckon that means he's shorthanded on his ranch, and his cattle will be ripe for the picking. We know all the shortcuts to get out of there in a hurry."

"We could meet you in Mexico," Corbin suggested.

"Is that right?" Frank felt like shooting Corbin on the spot. He was tired of the men second-guessing him. "You could, I guess. But what if the men didn't get away from Sheriff Roper? Stevie and I can't rustle those cattle alone. And if I'm the one taking all the risks, I can guarantee you won't be sharing in the profits. You can go ahead and ride on out of here if you want." He looked at Deke and Dutch. "You boys want to ride out with Corbin?"

"I didn't say I was ridin' out, Frank," Corbin said. Part of him wanted to ride away, but he had a feeling that Frank would shoot him in the back if he tried.

Dutch figured Frank was right about Le-Masters's ranch being the perfect place to strike. If the rest of the gang had evaded Sheriff Roper, they might be able to pull it off without a hitch. It would be a quick getaway since they knew the territory. They needed money in Mexico, and it was better to rustle where you knew the territory. "I'm in."

Deke remained silent as he kicked dirt into the fire. He didn't want to go back to Whispering Pines. The thought of returning made him nervous, and it wasn't something he could explain to the men. Trying to ignore the feeling of doom, he told himself if Dutch was willing to go, he might as well ride with them.

Before they saddled their horses, Frank had another surprise for them. "While we are at Whispering Pines, I figure we have one more piece of business to take care of."

"What's that?" Dutch asked.

"LeMasters said that old man Joseph Longbow identified us that night. That means he's the only witness that can testify against us. I say while we're there we kill him this time. Problem solved."

Corbin shook his head. "I don't know about that. My pa told me that Joseph Longbow has special powers."

Frankie laughed. "What are you afraid of, Corbin? You think Joseph will cast a spell on you?"

"I've heard stories about him," Deke said. "You know he was a medicine man with his tribe before he came to work for LeMasters. Folks say he refused to live on a reservation, and left his tribe. Soldiers came to Whispering Pines to take him, but Le-Masters wouldn't let them. They searched his ranch, saying they had every right by law to take him to a reservation. Joseph hid in the pines, and the way I heard it, some soldiers went missing when they went in there to get him. They never found them, and the other soldiers left without Joseph. Either the soldiers were afraid, or they didn't want to tangle with LeMasters. They never came back to the ranch again."

"I heard a soldier was shot in there," Corbin added.

"Joseph Longbow is nothing but an old man. I can't believe you'd be afraid of him. You're acting like a bunch of old women." Frank had been around Joseph on several occasions over the years, and he had to concede the old man had a way about him that was spooky. He always felt Joseph knew what he was thinking. He'd also heard the stories about Joseph's powers, but he wasn't

110

going to let tales stop him from doing what needed to be done to keep a noose from his neck.

Corbin didn't care if Frank called him an old woman, he was still reticent to kill Joseph. "Frank, you've heard the stories about him. Besides, it's not just Joseph Longbow. You remember what happened in those pines last time we were there. Maybe instead of going through the pines, we could come in another way."

Frank snorted. He wasn't about to admit he'd been as scared as the men the last time they were rustling on Whispering Pines ranch. "Those pines run the entire border between our farm and LeMasters's ranch, and thousands of acres beyond. I don't intend to ride weeks out of the way to get some of his cattle. Besides, we won't know for sure where they're grazing until we get Stevie. I've lived there for years and nothing has happened to me yet in those trees."

"Maybe nothing happened to you, but what about Smiley Benton?" Corbin asked.

They all looked at each other. Finally Frank said, "Smiley was never right in the head. He got lost in those trees. That's all there was to it."

Corbin gave a nervous laugh. "You heard the screams when we were in there. Whatever it was that happened to Smiley, he's never been seen since. He just disappeared. His pa has looked everywhere for him. All I'm saying is we need to go in another way. We shouldn't push our luck taking the shortcut through those pines."

"Those are just stories about the pines, probably made up to keep people off Le-Masters's ranch. Nothing is going to happen to us except we'll make money off the cattle we rustle so we can have a good time in Mexico." Frank shot a glance at Dutch to see if he had the same sentiment about going through the pines. "What do you think, Dutch? You afraid?" Frank threw the last question out as a challenge.

Dutch gnawed on the match he held between his teeth before he spoke. "I've heard the stories like everyone else. Maybe they're all true, maybe not. I heard the noises that night, but I figure it was just the wind, or some animal. None of us know for sure what happened to Smiley. He could have just taken off, or maybe a bear got to him. I'm not going to let stories scare me. Like Frank said, Whispering Pines is the easiest target to get cattle right now, with them being shorthanded. If we need to go through those pines, then I say we go through them, get our business done, and get out."

"It wasn't the wind that day," Corbin said. "I heard voices and screams."

"I did too," Deke said.

"All I'm asking is that we steer clear of the pines and Joseph Longbow," Corbin said.

Frank's eyes bounced from Deke to Corbin. "Not only are you scared of a bunch of old trees, you're afraid of an old man."

They didn't respond, so Frank said, "If it will make you two girls feel better, I'll be the one to pull the trigger on Joseph Longbow."

No one said another word. They saddled their horses and changed course.

"Webb, I think you need to go find Joseph Longbow," Granny said. She'd sat with the sheriff for hours, and his condition was worsening. She couldn't get his fever down.

"Yes, ma'am." Webb didn't argue. If Granny said she needed Joseph, then he'd find him.

She walked to the door with Webb. "Please hurry."

Webb glanced back at the sheriff lying motionless on the table. He felt a lump form in his throat. He'd never met a man he liked more than the sheriff, and he'd never seen him ill one day in the four years he'd worked for him. "I'll ride as fast as I can."

Less than two hours later, Webb walked in the doctor's office with Joseph Longbow in tow.

Granny jumped up and placed her Bible on the chair. For the last hour she'd been reading some of her favorite passages to Jack. She didn't know if he could hear her, but it made her feel better. "I didn't expect you back this soon."

Webb raised his eyebrow at her and inclined his head toward Joseph. "He was waiting for me."

Granny couldn't help but smile at Webb's stunned expression. "Joseph, I'm glad you came."

Joseph approached the table, leaned over and looked at the sheriff. He pulled off the small leather pouch that was hanging around his neck and placed it on the sheriff's chest. He raised his weathered hand and held it a few inches above the sheriff's head, and muttered a few words Granny and Webb didn't understand. When he finished, he turned to Granny and said, "He will live."

Joseph was about to walk out the door but was halted by Webb when he moved in front of him. "Now wait a minute. Is that all you're going to do?"

Joseph tilted his head back to stare at the tall deputy and narrowed his dark eyes. "What would you have me do?"

Tired and frustrated, Webb ran a hand through his blond hair, ripping out a few strands. "I don't know. Maybe something more than putting a pouch on him and saying some gibberish."

Joseph turned his eyes on Granny. "What is this gibberish?"

"Nothing to worry about," Granny said. "Webb is just concerned."

Joseph shrugged. "There is nothing more for me to do. He will live."

"How do you know?" Webb asked.

"Granny's good doctoring skill, and her prayers to her God. I've invited the presence of the Great Spirit for healing."

"But . . ." Webb looked at Granny, silently pleading for her to intervene.

Granny walked to Webb and placed her hand on his shoulder. "It will be okay." She smiled at Joseph. "Thank you. If you come by the house tomorrow, I will have a cake for you."

"What kind?"

"Your favorite."

Joseph nodded and walked out the door.

Webb stared at the closed door, clearly

baffled by what just took place. "Should I take him back to the ranch?"

"He's probably waiting in the buckboard," Granny said.

Webb shoved his hat on his head. "When I got to LeMasters's ranch, he was just sitting on the porch. Before I told him why I'd come, he said, *I've been waiting for you.* I asked him if he needed to bring some medicine with him, he just said, *I have what I need right here.* He pointed to that little pouch around his neck. He didn't say one word all the way to town."

"Joseph knew what was needed. Now go on and take him back to the ranch. I'll sit with the sheriff." She hadn't been surprised by Joseph's methods since they'd tended other sick people together before.

"I don't know why he didn't just give me the dang pouch and be done with it. I could have put the dang thing on the sheriff and mumbled some strange words. All I'm doing is riding back and forth. He better hope the sheriff lives, or he'll have me to deal with." Webb wouldn't hurt the older man, but he'd sure give him a good tongue-lashing if the sheriff died.

"How are you feeling?" Granny asked the sheriff when he opened his eyes less than an hour later. She appreciated Joseph's optimistic prognosis, but it did little to lessen her worry.

"Can't complain, unless I'm dreaming."

"You mean you don't want my face to be the first one you see in heaven?"

Jack grinned at her. "I'd want to see your beautiful face anywhere. But what makes you so sure I'll be in heaven?" He tried to pull himself into a sitting position, but dropped back to the table when Granny shook her head at him.

She gave him a stern look. "Don't flash that handsome grin at me, Jack Roper, it won't work. I'm too old for your shenanigans. You just stay put for a while. It took quite a bit of prodding in that shoulder to find that sliver, and I don't want you to start bleeding all over the place again. I put a couple of stitches in there and I want them to hold. You've been out for a while and had quite a fever."

Jack's smile turned into a frown. "Just how long am I supposed to stay in this position?" He wasn't a man to stay abed, especially when he had criminals on the loose.

"Stay put for another hour, and we will go from there." She placed her hand on his forehead and relief swept over her when she realized he no longer had a fever. She poured some water in a cup and held his head while he took a sip.

Jack saw the leather pouch on his chest. "What's this?"

"I had Webb fetch Joseph when your fever got too high. I thought his skills might be needed."

"What'd he do?"

"He put those herbs on you and said his prayers."

Jack picked up the pouch and twirled it between his fingers. "Hmm. What's in here?"

"My guess would be sweetgrass, cedar, and white sage. Joseph says it cleanses the wearer."

"It must have worked. But my guess is, you were probably doing your share of praying." He saw her Bible on the chair, and he knew Granny well enough to know she was bending the Good Lord's ear on his behalf.

"We always need His help," Granny replied.

Granny held the cup to his lips again, and Jack said, "I think whiskey would be better." His shoulder hurt, but he wasn't going to admit that to her.

"I reckon you're due. When Webb returns I'll have him fetch some." Granny wasn't opposed to spirits when the occasion warranted. After what she'd put him through, the least she could do was allow him a little whiskey.

"I knew I loved you, Granny. Would you marry me?"

"Hmmm. You need to get married, and if I were fifty years younger I might be of a mind. As it is, I think you might want to court my granddaughter when she arrives. She's more your age."

Jack had forgotten one of her granddaughters was coming home. "Which granddaughter is coming home?"

"Rose, she's the baby. Do you remember her?"

"Yes, ma'am. Prettiest girl I ever saw." Jack had only seen her granddaughters a couple of times. He'd just become the sheriff of Whispering Pines a few months before the three girls moved East.

"She's all grown-up now. But I don't think Rose is the one for you. She will make a good match for Morgan. Addie is the one to suit you, and she'll be home in a few months."

Jack chuckled. "You sure Morgan is ready to get hitched?"

Arching her eyebrow at him, she questioned, "Are you?"

"I'm probably a mite more inclined than

Morgan. All he thinks about is that ranch, but he did tell me he would like to have some sons."

"I've yet to see the man who thought he was ready to wed, but mark my words, when Morgan takes one look at Rose, he'll change his mind quick enough. Men will be lining up to court her."

"I didn't think you'd seen your grand-daughters in a long time. How do you know she'll be such a looker?"

"Rose looked just like my mother when she was a girl. My mother was known for her beauty, and Rose is her spitting image."

Jack smiled at her. "You must have taken after your ma. You're a beauty, Granny. I bet you had more men than Preacher chasing after you." He wasn't teasing. For her age, she was still a handsome woman.

Granny found herself blushing from his compliment. "Hush now. You need to save your energy."

"Tell me about Addie."

"She's a school teacher, and now she's teaching orphans. She has a heart for children, so if it's children you want, Addie is of the same mind. I'm sure you under-stand how important it is to those orphans to have people who care about them." Granny knew Jack had lived in an orphanage when he was a boy. She didn't wait for an answer; she continued to tell Jack stories about her granddaughters when they were young girls, until he drifted off to sleep. Seeing he was sleeping comfortably, Granny closed her eyes, gave a word of thanks to God for answering her prayers, and fell asleep.

Hearing the creak of the door as it opened, Jack's eyes snapped open, and he automatically reached for the nonexistent pistol at his side.

Not realizing it was the deputy returning, Granny jumped out of her chair and grabbed Jack's pistol, which she'd placed on the table, and pointed it at the door. Thankfully, she came to her senses and didn't fire the weapon. "Deputy, you scared the daylights out of us."

Webb was stunned to see Granny holding a pistol. "Sorry." He looked at Jack. "How are you feeling, Sheriff?"

It took Jack a minute to get over the shock of seeing Granny grab his pistol and point it at the door. "Not bad."

"I saw the clerk from the telegraph office outside and he gave me this telegram for you." He handed the piece of paper to Jack.

"Thanks, Webb." Jack scanned the contents. He looked at Granny, his expression somber. "I'm afraid I have bad news."

"Is it Morgan?" Granny had tried to talk Morgan out of going after Frank. She was as worried about Frank shooting Morgan as she was about the reason Morgan was adamant about hunting him down.

"It's from Hank Murphy. There was a stagecoach accident and your granddaughter was hurt."

Granny felt her knees go weak, but Webb grabbed her before she hit the floor.

"Put her in that chair, Webb." Jack felt like a fool for blurting out the contents of the telegram like he did.

"She's hurt, Granny, she's not dead," Jack emphasized. "And Morgan is with her."

Granny gripped the back of the ladder-back chair for support as Webb poured her a cup of water. After she composed herself, her first thought was it had to be a mistake. "Hank must be mistaken. What would Morgan be doing with Rose? He went after Frank."

Jack glanced down at the piece of paper. "Here's what it says: 'Stagecoach accident, Rose Langtry injured. Morgan with her. Frank and gang escaped. Will be back at Barnett's station in a few days. Will telegraph then. Hank Murphy.' "

Jack tried to read between the lines. From

the way the telegram sounded, Morgan and his men had caught up with Frank and his gang. But how Rose Langtry came to be with them didn't make sense. He glanced back at Granny's pale, frightened face. "Webb, would you go get us a bottle of whiskey? There's one in the bottom drawer of my desk in the office."

When Webb left to walk next door to the jail, Jack said, "Let's not get ahead of ourselves. Maybe Morgan happened on the stagecoach accident. The important thing is, he is with your granddaughter. He will see to it that she receives proper care. She couldn't be in better hands."

"I just don't understand why Rose is with him," Granny said, her lips trembling.

Jack couldn't make sense of the message either. He was in no condition to get on a horse and ride for days, or he'd already be in the saddle.

They were silent, each trying to figure out what could have put Rose and Morgan in the same place at the same time. They didn't say another word until Webb came in carrying the bottle of whiskey.

"Grab three glasses and pour a generous amount in each," Jack said.

Webb did as instructed, and when he handed a glass to Granny, he half expected her to refuse. Instead she took the glass and emptied the contents in one gulp.

Granny wasn't unfamiliar with spirits. She'd sipped a bit of whiskey in her toddies whenever she was feeling poorly with a cold or sore throat. Preacher never approved, but Granny's mother always said it was the best remedy for several illnesses. Preacher was a teetotaler, but he didn't generally interfere with Granny's prescribed medicinal spirits. She could only remember one time he'd said she shouldn't imbibe when she was ailing, and she reminded him that Jesus turned water into wine at a wedding. After that, he'd never made another comment on her remedies.

Jack couldn't help but chuckle at Webb's shocked expression. "It's good for what ails you." Webb held Jack's head so he could drink, and Jack quickly finished the contents. Webb filled Jack's glass again, and once he gulped it down, he said, "Webb, this telegram was sent from Barnett's home station. Go send them a telegraph and ask for clarification. Why is Morgan with Rose?" He knew none of them would rest until they had some answers.

Granny focused on Jack. She knew the kind of man he was, and he wouldn't think twice about putting his own life at risk to save a friend. "Don't you even think you are going to go riding off after them."

"I'm not thinking about that as long as I know Morgan is handling everything. I just want more information than we have now."

After Jack rested for a few hours in the doctor's office, Webb and Granny helped him to his small, one room house next door to the jail. Once he was settled in bed, Webb left to go to the hotel to get dinner for the three of them. He stopped by the telegraph office to see if they'd received a response from the way station in Kansas.

Entering Jack's home, Webb quickly passed the basket of food to Granny, and handed Jack the telegram. "We received a reply from Kansas."

Jack opened the telegram and read it aloud. " 'Morgan saw stagecoach accident. Miss Langtry has broken ribs. Sent buckboard. They will be back in two days. Will send message upon arrival.' " He finished reading and his eyes met Granny's. "She'll be okay. Morgan's with her."

Granny gave him a tentative smile. While it was certainly good news Rose wasn't injured more severely, broken ribs could be quite dangerous. "I pray she comes home safe and sound."

Jack was pleased to know more about the

events in Kansas, but he had a difficult time believing Frank and his gang had escaped from Morgan. There was nothing he could do; he'd have to wait for their return to Whispering Pines to hear the details. "Let's enjoy our dinner now that we have received good news."

Granny stacked some pillows behind Jack's head. "I don't expect you think Frank escaping is such good news."

"No, it isn't. Let's just hope he doesn't . . . do anything foolish." He almost said *kill someone,* but he caught himself in time. Sometimes it was hard to remember a man like Frank Langtry had such a sweet grandmother.

"I've prayed for the same thing for many years, but the Devil has a grip on Frank and he won't let go. I shouldn't have been so easy on those two boys. I'm afraid Stevie is going to follow in his brother's footsteps. They needed a firmer hand when they were younger. Preacher and I were too easy on them."

Jack knew she blamed herself for Frank taking the wrong road, and he also knew it was nonsense. "You did everything you could for him. It's not your fault Frank made the choices he made. He's a grown man, and he had more than one chance to turn things around."

"Has Morgan ever told you what started this rift between him and Frank?" Granny thought if Morgan ever confided in anyone, it would be Jack.

"No, he's never said a word." Jack always figured that something serious had happened between Morgan and Frank years ago. Morgan wasn't a man to divulge private matters, and Jack wasn't a man to pry. He respected Morgan enough to know that he had to have a valid reason to harbor animosity toward Frank.

"I know Joseph Longbow knows what happened between them, but he won't tell me." She'd asked Joseph several times what happened between Morgan and Frank, but Joseph always told her she should ask Frank.

"Did you ever ask Frank?" Jack asked.

"He would never tell me."

"Granny, if Frank knows what's good for him, he'll go to Mexico and stay. That's the only chance he'll have not to be found. If his bullet had killed Joseph Longbow, even Mexico wouldn't have been a safe place to hide from Morgan."

"I'm afraid Frank never did want to do what was good for him. I think he's always been jealous of Morgan and what he's accomplished in his life."

After they finished their dinner, Granny washed the dishes and checked Jack's wound one more time before she collected her things to leave. "Deputy, I'm ready to go whenever you are."

"Yes, ma'am."

"Jack, I'm not happy about leaving you alone, but I need to take care of the animals."

"Webb will be back soon. I'll be fine."

While she didn't want him riding all the way to the farm, she worried about him staying alone with no one to care for him if his fever spiked again. "I'll come back after I do my chores."

"Why isn't Stevie helping you out?" He spoke before he thought how his question might hurt Granny's feelings. He agreed with Granny that Stevie needed a firm hand, and when he'd caught him stealing in the local mercantile, he'd tried to talk some sense into him. His words had fallen on deaf ears. What he had to say wasn't as important as the promises of infamy Frank put in his head. Jack made an effort with Stevie because he'd been as hardheaded when he was a young man. He had been an orphan with no family, and no place to go when he was young. It was by the grace of God that he hadn't ended up in the territorial prison.

At least Stevie had people who cared about him, a nice home and food on the table. Stevie should thank his lucky stars that Granny and Preacher cared enough to take him and his siblings in when their parents died. Granny didn't need to be doing chores at her age. She deserved someone to take care of her. He'd like to give Stevie a good butt-chewing or -kicking, depending on his willingness to listen.

"I haven't seen Stevie for a few days. He took off and didn't tell me where he was going." She had her own suspicions that he'd left to see if he could find Frankie. Sometimes he would be gone for days and never give her an explanation for his absence. She could never count on Stevie to take care of any chores around the farm.

"You go on home, and stop worrying about me. You've done a fine job, and I'm well on my way to recovery." Jack knew he was speaking the truth. He felt better and he knew he was on the mend.

"Webb can't take care of you and see to his job. Neither one of you can cook, so you keep the hotel in business. And I couldn't help but notice you don't keep much in the way of provisions in here." Granny had snooped around while Jack was sleeping last night, and noticed he had next to nothing to eat in his place. It was her nature to care for people, and she couldn't stop herself from worrying about the sheriff. She wanted to make sure he had the proper nourishment to aid his healing. "I'll bring back some soup for you."

"I'll have Webb pick it up tomorrow if that will make you rest easier. Stay home and take care of your place. You can come back in a few days to bedevil me if I'm not up to par. And feel free to use Webb if you need some help." Granny wasn't one to inconvenience anyone and ask for assistance. Jack knew Morgan and his men usually helped her out, but his ranch was operating with few men right now.

"Morgan's men come over to help me out," Granny said.

"There aren't many men left at his ranch right now, and you need to get everything ready for Rose's arrival." He planned to tell Webb to have a look around for Stevie if he wasn't at the farm. He didn't like the idea of Granny being alone on the farm with Frank on the run. Granny seemed to accept the fact that Frank was dangerous, but Jack didn't think she thought he could be a danger to her.

Chapter Six

The first thing Morgan noticed when his men arrived with the buckboard the next morning was Faithful being led by Murph. "Where'd you find him?"

"I guess you could say he found us. My horse was with him, and they were headed in this direction. Their saddles are in the buckboard. They look spent, and I'm thinking we need to give them a rest before we take off."

Morgan stroked Faithful's neck, grateful to have him back. "I guess I read Deke right." He slapped Murph on the shoulder. "I'm sure happy to see you two. Did you have any problems?"

"None." Murph pointed to the horses he had tied to the buckboard. "I bought these horses from Barnett, and he loaned us the buckboard and some pistols. We have plenty of water and some grub his missus made for us. He said he'd try to have the doctor at his place by the time we get back."

"That was good of him," Morgan replied. His eyes slid to Rose. "I think she could use something for pain."

"How's she doing?"

Morgan lowered his voice and said, "Not good. She hasn't eaten since you left and she's barely had anything to drink. I think every rib in her body may be broken."

Murph grimaced. "That has to be painful."

"She hasn't moved around much and I worry about pneumonia."

"How's George's leg?" Murph asked.

"Good. He's moving around pretty good with a crutch."

Murph took in Morgan's haggard appearance. "You look like you could use some rest."

Morgan didn't mention his own lack of sleep. "I'll rest easier once Rose has seen the doctor. Did you get a telegram off to the sheriff?"

"Yeah, but we didn't wait around for a response."

While they allowed time for the horses to rest, Morgan warmed water so Rose could wash. The men prepared a place in the buckboard to make the journey more comfortable for her.

When they were ready to depart, Morgan told the men he would be driving the buckboard. "I'll be taking it easy so Rose won't bounce around more than necessary." He carried Rose to the back of the buckboard and made sure she was comfortable. He could tell her breathing was still shallow, and he worried if riding in that buckboard was going to be too much for her. "We're in no hurry. If you need to stop for any reason, just say the word."

"I will."

Morgan climbed into the seat, and wasn't surprised to see George pulling himself up beside him.

"Are you sure you wouldn't be more comfortable in the back?"

"I'll be fine. I'm used to handling the team," George grumbled.

"You will be handling the team soon enough," Morgan replied. "Let me know if you need to stop."

"Try not to hit all the ruts," George teased.

Morgan cast one more glance at Rose before he snapped the reins.

When Morgan pulled the horses to a halt for a lunch break, he thought Rose looked like she was barely hanging on. He'd tried to stop several times that morning, but Rose insisted they make no special stops for her. Even though they kept a slow pace, the uneven terrain made it impossible for her to keep from bouncing around.

Exhausted from the pain, Rose chose to remain in the wagon during their break. Morgan offered to assist her from the buckboard, but she declined, saying, "I believe I will stay here, Mr. LeMasters."

"Call me Morgan. We are going to be here for a couple of hours to rest the animals. Are you sure you wouldn't rather get out and change positions for a while?"

"No, I'll be fine right here."

"We'll get some lunch together and make some coffee." Morgan thought she looked completely exhausted. He didn't think it was a good sign that she didn't want to move. He'd noticed she seemed to have a fondness for coffee, and he wondered if she'd object if he laced it with some of George's whiskey. It might help her to sleep so she wouldn't feel every bump in the road.

"If you need anything, just yell out." He pointed to an area just a few feet from the wagon. "We'll build a fire right over there, so I'll hear you."

"Thank you."

"She's not looking too good," Murph said

to Morgan as they were unharnessing the horses.

"I'm thinking of giving her a dose of George's whiskey to help her go to sleep."

"That might not be a bad idea. Do you think she will go for it?"

Morgan had tried to think of a way to politely insist she drink some whiskey, but he didn't know how he'd go about it. "Nope."

Murph chuckled at Morgan's expression. He looked like he'd rather step into a den of vipers than offer Rose a drink of whiskey. "Ladies don't usually partake of hard liquor."

Once the men prepared some lunch, Morgan filled a plate for Rose. He poured a half cup of coffee and asked George to top it off with whiskey.

Morgan walked toward the wagon and saw Rose reading her Bible.

When Morgan reached her, Rose placed her Bible in her lap, and took the plate from him.

"How are you feeling?" Morgan asked.

"I'm fine."

She didn't look fine in his estimation. "You need to eat something."

She looked down at the food on the plate, and while she appreciated how he was looking out for her welfare, she had no appetite. "Thank you, Mr. LeMasters, but I'm really not very hungry."

"Call me Morgan," he reminded her.

"Of course."

He didn't know if he should insist she eat, or if he should leave her alone. He decided it would be better for her to rest than eat, so he said, "I won't badger you about eating if you drink this." He handed her the cup of coffee. "Before you take a drink, I want you to know I put a bit of whiskey in there. I thought it might help you rest a mite easier."

She accepted the cup and gave him a wry smile. "Granny often put whiskey in tea if one of us had a bad cold." She was at the point she would drink anything if it took the pain away. After swallowing a small sip of the laced coffee, she tried not to grimace at the taste. "It's not so bad."

Morgan would have laughed if he hadn't been so surprised. He'd expected a battle to get her to have a little drink of whiskey. "Hopefully, you can sleep the rest of the day."

She handed him the plate of food. "You can eat this."

Morgan grinned at her. "A deal is a deal. Since you're drinking your coffee, I won't argue. But I don't know what the whiskey will do on an empty stomach. Maybe you should have some of the biscuit." Morgan held the biscuit to her.

His smile nearly made it impossible for her to form a thought. It reminded her of the day in the churchyard when she realized why all the women stopped to talk to him. His smile almost made her forget about the pain. She didn't want to get sick, so she took a small bite of the biscuit.

Morgan balanced the plate on the side of the buckboard as he started eating.

"You don't have to stay here and eat your lunch. I promise I will drink my coffee."

"Did you forget I've been sitting all morning? I prefer to stand for a while."

Rose sipped her coffee, and covertly studied his face. She'd never thought a man was as handsome as Morgan. It didn't take long before she was feeling the effects of the alcohol. To her surprise, her pain seemed to be subsiding.

"I guess you will be glad to get home," Morgan said.

"Yes, I'm anxious to see Granny. I've worried about her over the last few years. She always writes that everything at the farm is fine, but I won't be happy until I see for myself."

Morgan didn't want to add to her worries, but she'd been sorely misinformed if she thought the Langtry farm was going well. "She seems to be in good health."

"It's hard to tell from letters how someone is really doing. I thought she sounded lonely." Rose knew Granny would never trouble them with bad news, or want anyone to worry about her, but the tone of her letters over the last six months had been different. Her letters weren't as long, and it seemed to Rose as if Granny had something on her mind that she chose not to share.

"Granny keeps busy. She's basically the town doctor now that Doc died."

"She wrote that Joseph Longbow often helps out with tending to the sick," Rose said.

"He'll venture as far as your farm, but rarely goes to town," Morgan said.

"Were you telling me the truth that Joseph wasn't badly injured?"

"Yes, the bullet just grazed his hard head."

Even though he smiled when he said the words, Rose knew that if anything happened to Joseph, Morgan would be devastated. Joseph had been with Morgan a long time, and Granny always said he was very fond of him. "I knew Joseph rarely left your ranch when I was a child, but I never knew why."

Morgan didn't respond to her subtle inquiry about Joseph. "Are your sisters coming back home?"

She hadn't really expected him to say more about Joseph. "Yes. Addie will be here in a few months when the school period ends. She is a teacher in an orphanage. My eldest sister, Emma, is accompanying a traveling troupe presently. You may have heard she is an opera singer."

Morgan seemed to remember Granny mentioning the opera singer at some point. "I believe Granny told me."

"Emma will be traveling to Denver to perform onstage before the year ends, and we will see her then."

Morgan had heard tales of traveling troupes and the women who chose that lifestyle, but he didn't express an opinion. He looked into Rose's eyes and could see the alcohol was already relaxing her. He thought he would keep her talking so she would finish her coffee. "What did you do back East?"

Rose's ambitions seemed to pale in comparison to her sisters'. All she'd ever wanted was a husband and children. "I was the governess to my great aunt and uncle's two grandsons for three years."

"Do you plan on returning?"

"No. I always planned to come home to

Whispering Pines. I never wanted to live in the East permanently."

"I expect it was difficult to leave your charges after three years."

His statement surprised her. She couldn't fathom a man like Morgan LeMasters loving anyone as much as she loved those two young boys. When the day came that she'd had to leave them behind, she knew she was leaving part of her heart with them.

"It was a difficult decision as I am very fond of them, but Granny needs me more. The boys will be coming with their grandparents to visit next year." She smiled thinking of how excited the boys were when their grandparents made plans to visit the farm. Granny would certainly be surprised. She hadn't seen her brother in over thirty years, but they had always corresponded regularly.

"How old are the boys?"

"Seven and eight, and they are so very inquisitive."

Morgan grinned, remembering what he was like at that age. He wanted to see and do everything. "I imagine it will be quite a journey for them if they've never been west of the Mississippi."

There was that smile of his again. She looked at his mouth and blinked. *What did he say? Oh, the boys.* She gave her head a slight shake. "Ah . . . no, they've never left Boston." She could imagine how thrilled the boys would be to meet a man like Morgan for the first time. They'd been enamored with the stories she often told them about the cowboys of the West. Quite often she realized when she was describing cowboys, she was actually recalling Morgan's physical attributes. They loved to hear the stories of men who slept out on the open range, wore six-guns and Stetsons. She'd told them stories of the Indians, and the tales of Whispering Pines. To boys who'd never known anything other than city life, it all sounded thrilling and quite dangerous. Naturally, their father wanted them to follow him in the study of law, but that profession didn't seem to garner their interest. They dreamed of riding horses, roping cattle, and learning to shoot pistols.

Seeing the smile on her face, Morgan couldn't help but ask what she was thinking.

"I was thinking how excited they would be to see a man like you," Rose answered honestly.

Morgan placed his plate on the floorboard, folded his arms on the rail and leaned closer to Rose. "What do you mean, a man like me?"

Rose could feel a blush creeping up her neck. "Well, a larger-than-life cowboy who wears a pistol and rides a big horse. They've never even been on a horse."

Morgan couldn't imagine boys that age who didn't ride. "How could boys that age have never ridden a horse?"

"Their parents have never been on a horse, and they considered it a dangerous activity. I'm afraid they wouldn't allow me to teach them." The one time she'd arranged to take the boys riding, their parents were quite upset with her. She'd tried to explain that all young men should be able to sit a horse, but they could not be persuaded. She had to respect their decision, but she'd promised the boys when they came for a visit, she would definitely teach them to ride. It was their secret, and she knew it was one the boys would never reveal.

Morgan thought of her other comment. "What do you mean by a *larger-than-life cowboy*?"

She didn't want to insult him by saying dime novels were written about men like him. "I meant your size. You're . . . you're . . . larger-than-life. You can be quite frightening."

The whiskey was working on her. She was much more talkative, and Morgan liked her honesty. Murph always told him he was intimidating to most people. Right now, he didn't want to scare the prettiest little rose he'd ever seen. "Does my size scare you, Rose?"

Rose smiled at him. "When I was young you scared me to death." She didn't know why she'd admitted that to him so easily.

Morgan stared into her eyes. "What about now?"

"I'm not a small child anymore."

He couldn't argue with the truth of that statement. She definitely was no longer a little girl, but a very beautiful woman. And Morgan didn't know quite what to make of the fact that he was very attracted to her.

They gazed into each other's eyes, and didn't hear Murph approach.

Murph held a plateful of food toward Rose. "I saw Morgan eating your food, Rose, so I brought you another plate."

Morgan was caught off guard by Murph's untimely appearance, and he was about half aggravated that he had interrupted them. He'd liked the way Rose was talking so freely. "She wasn't hungry."

Morgan's abrupt tone wasn't lost on Murph. Nor was the blush covering Rose's cheeks. He glanced from Rose to Morgan. "Did I interrupt something?"

Morgan didn't know why he was miffed. He should be thanking Murph. He reminded himself that Rose was Frank Langtry's sister. No matter how beautiful he thought she was, or how much he was attracted to her, he couldn't forget that fact. He picked up his empty plate and turned toward the fire. "Nope. You didn't interrupt anything."

CHAPTER SEVEN

Hobb, the stagecoach driver, slowed the horses when he saw a horse in the middle of the road. Coming closer, he saw the rider was slumped over in the saddle, his arms dangling down, and his hat was lying in the dirt beside his horse. "What do you make of that?" he asked his shotgun rider, Cal.

Cal squinted against the sun shining in his eyes. "Looks like he's hurt."

Pulling the team to a halt, Hobb yelled out, "Hello." When no response came, he looked at Cal. They were on a schedule, and this was time they didn't have to waste, yet he couldn't pass a man by if he needed help. "You better check it out." Hobb had been a stagecoach driver for a long time, and he was by nature a cautious man. He picked up his rifle to have it at the ready if needed.

"Sure thing, Hobb." Cal climbed down from his perch with his rifle in hand. He was just a few feet from the rider when he yelled out, "Mister, you okay?" Met with silence, he looked back at Hobb. "He might be dead, Hobb."

Hobb rolled his eyes. They'd traveled together many times, so they knew each other like brothers. And just like brothers, they got on each other's nerves. Cal was one heck of a shot, and Hobb was always happy to have him along, but sometimes he could be dumber than a rock. "Well, check it out." Hobb was already calculating the time it would take to bury a man. They'd made good time, so he figured he could spare thirty minutes if necessary.

Cal turned around, took hold of the horse's reins that were dangling on the ground, and picked up the man's hat. The man's face was covered by his long dark hair, so Cal gently poked his thigh with the butt of his rifle. "Mister?"

The motionless man came to life. He easily snatched Cal's rifle from him, jumped off his horse in a flash, and had his forearm wrapped around Cal's throat before he knew what was happening. The man threw the rifle to the ground and pulled his pistol, jamming it against Cal's temple. It all happened so fast that Cal didn't have time to react.

Even Hobb was slow to respond, but when

it finally registered in his brain what had happened, he pulled his rifle to his shoulder and took aim.

"Mister, what in blue blazes are you doing? I was trying to help you," Cal managed to ask even though he thought his windpipe was being crushed.

"And I appreciate that, Cal. Now tell Hobb to put his rifle aside and throw the strongbox down. And pass my hat over your shoulder."

Cal held the man's hat over his shoulder. "You mean you ain't hurt?" Cal was dumbfounded at the turn of events.

The man placed his hat on his head and pulled the brim low. "No, Cal, but you and Hobb are gonna be hurt if he don't toss that strongbox to the ground."

"We don't have a strongbox," Hobb said to the man he couldn't see because he was shorter than Cal.

A shot exploded next to Cal's ear, causing him to clutch his head from the deafening sound. At the same moment Cal realized his ear was still attached, he saw Hobb's hat flying through the air.

"Now don't lie to me, Hobb. I know you are carrying an express shipment to Denver. Throw it down, or Cal will be missing one ear the next time I ask."

"He don't listen nohow," Hobb replied.

"What?" Cal yelled. He couldn't hear what they were saying for the ringing in his ear.

Hobb heard the man cock the pistol. "Now wait a minute, mister. Wouldn't we have a lot more firepower if we was carrying money?" He figured most outlaws would know it would be unusual to carry such a shipment with so few gun hands.

"Hobb, I take it you don't think much of your friend. I'm going to start counting, and when I get to one, you're gonna see the insides of Cal's head. Three . . . two . . ."

Hobb held up his hand. "Wait just a dang minute!" Hobb hated the thought of being robbed. He maintained a good reputation as a driver who always made his destinations on time with cargo intact. But he wasn't going to risk Cal's life over a little money. He placed his rifle aside. "It's inside the coach."

"Get it. And leave that rifle on top."

"You know you will be hunted down for this," Hobb said as he climbed from the top of the coach.

"Don't waste your worry on me. Me and my men will take care of any posse that comes after us. Now drop your gun belt."

Hobb turned to face the man, but still

couldn't see anything but his pistol at Cal's scalp. "Your men? I don't see no one but you."

"Maybe you better look more carefully. Left and right."

Hobb looked left and saw a rifle balanced on a large boulder. From the right, another rifle was peeking out through the brush. With that pistol to Cal's head, and two rifles pointed at him, Hobb had no choice. He unfastened his gun belt and let it drop to the ground before he walked to the door of the stagecoach. When he opened the door, he said, "I have to pull it out, unless you want to help me carry it."

"Get on with it. I'm getting impatient, Hobb."

Hobb turned his attention to the inside of the coach, and looked at the man crouched down on the floorboard with a rifle at the ready. He shook his head and whispered, "Boyd, he's a crack shot and he's got men with him, one on the right and one on the left. So lay low right now." Hobb was thankful he had another shotgun rider with him on this trip. It had been a last-minute decision for Boyd to accompany them. It turned out to be a prophetic decision. Boyd was an even better shot than Cal, and the rifle was his weapon of choice. No doubt Boyd could probably handle the two men with the rifles. Now all he had to do was find a way to get Cal out of the man's grip.

Boyd nodded and said softly, "Leave the door cracked open. If I can get a shot, I'll take him first. That'll give you and Cal time to drop to the ground." Boyd removed his hat and leaned across the seat, positioning himself to be able to see the robber unobserved.

"You'll be looking directly into the sun," Hobb said as he pulled the strongbox out of the coach and let it drop to the ground.

"Here it is," he yelled to the outlaw, hoping he could get him to walk to the coach away from Cal. If he took the bait, they might have a chance of getting out of this alive.

"Drag it over here," the man said.

Hobb intentionally pulled the box to the robber at an angle. If the robber turned a few inches maybe Boyd would have a shot. He'd also like to get a look at his face so he could identify him if they didn't find a way to stop him. But his hat was pulled low, and Hobb couldn't make out his features. Hobb glanced down at his boots, thinking he might be wearing something special-made like the pearl-handled Colt he held to Cal's head. No such luck; his boots were nothing special. "You're making a big mistake, mister."

"Open it," the man demanded.

"I don't have the key," Hobb said.

Quicker than Hobb could see his hand move, the man directed the barrel of his pistol at the lock and pulled the trigger. Again, his shot was true, and the lock broke apart. "Now open the lid."

Squatting down, Hobb pulled the lid open. Seeing a large amount of bills, Hobb glanced up at Cal. He could tell by Cal's expression that he was as surprised as Hobb was by the amount of money in the strongbox. Now the question was, how did this hombre know they were carrying the money, and when they were due to arrive in Denver?

"Looks like I was blessed today," the man said. He gestured with his pistol. "Is there money bags in there?"

"Yeah," Hobb said.

"Good. Put the money in the bags and put them in my saddlebags."

Hobb was in no position to argue. The man was good with that pistol, and he had a feeling he wouldn't hesitate to shoot Cal if he didn't comply with his instructions. While Hobb shoved the money inside the bags and stuffed them in the man's saddlebags, he made a mental note of his horse, including his hoofprints. Unless he had a packhorse nearby, the man was traveling light, indicating he might be from around these parts. Of course, his partners could have their saddlebags full of provisions. Speaking of partners, they weren't too keen on showing their faces. Hobb glanced toward the rifles that were still visible. Strange, he didn't think they'd moved an inch. Was it possible the man was bluffing and he didn't have any partners? It might be taking a lethal gamble to make that assumption and make a move on him. But if the man was alone, they might have a chance against him. Hobb turned back to the man. "Now what?"

"You and Cal walk back to the stagecoach. Don't look back."

While the man's attention was on Hobb loading the saddlebags, Boyd planned exactly what he would do. He didn't know if he could shoot them all, but he had to try. He planned to shoot the man holding the pistol on Cal first. The men behind the rocks were farther away, and he had the cover of the coach if they started shooting. If he kept his wits about him, he thought he could take them out before they had a chance to get more than one shot off. He inched his rifle through the opening in the door. If Cal just moved a fraction, he would shoot that no-good son-of-a-gun.

"I have a feeling you're going to shoot us in the back." Hobb wasn't one to trust an outlaw. "If it's all the same to you, I'd just as soon face you if you are going to do me in."

"I got no reason to shoot you, Hobb. You've done everything I've asked. Now turn around and walk." He hadn't made up his mind if he was going to shoot them or not. They hadn't been able to get a good look at his face because he wore his hat low, and the sun was in their eyes. They wouldn't recognize him if they passed him on the street. But there was a part of him that wanted to know how it felt to kill a man.

Hobb looked at Cal and inclined his head toward the coach. Hobb thought he spotted the barrel of Boyd's rifle, and he hoped Cal saw the same thing. Hobb nodded his head, trying to send a silent signal to Boyd that he saw him and knew what he was going to do, just in case he was ready to shoot. Hobb figured the outlaw would fire before they were too far away if that was his intent, so he had to act quickly. He realized his only option was to shove Cal down and pray Boyd didn't hesitate to take a shot. Cal's rifle was in the dirt behind them, so there was no chance he could get to it in time to fire off a round. All he could do was rely on Boyd's true aim, and the Good Lord to protect them. Step one. Step two. His heart was beating so fast that he could hear it pounding in his ears, and he wasn't sure, but he thought he heard the pistol being cocked behind them. He shoved Cal hard, sending him reeling sideways as he dropped to the ground. *Kaboom!* Boyd was ready and waiting! Hobb looked back, saw the robber clutch his arm, and saw his opportunity. As Hobb scrambled on his hands and knees toward Cal's rifle, the outlaw glanced at him and read his intentions. He aimed his pistol at Hobb and fired. Hobb rolled in the dirt, but the bullet found his shoulder. To Hobb's surprise, Cal was right beside him. Cal grabbed the rifle just as another shot rang out. Boyd fired another round, but he missed his target. The outlaw had mounted his horse and was making fast tracks out of the area. Cal fired, but the man had disappeared through the brush.

Boyd jumped out of the stagecoach and hurried to Hobb. "Sorry, Hobb, I tried to shoot him dead center, but he moved just as I shot."

"I'm okay, Boyd. It went straight through." He stood with Boyd's assistance. "I realized he was bluffing about having partners. I guess you figured out the same thing."

"Yeah, after I shot him, I turned to shoot at the man behind the rock, but when no one was shooting, I knew he'd been bluffing. That's what took me so long to get another shot off."

"That was a good shot with the sun in your eyes." Hobb looked at Cal. "Sorry I had to shove you so hard, but there wasn't much time to do anything else."

"I appreciate it, Hobb. You saved our sorry hides."

"Cal, did you get a look at his face?" Boyd asked.

"No, his hair was covering his face when I walked up. Then everything happened so fast that I didn't have a chance to get a look at him. The only thing I know for sure is he stunk to high heaven."

"Stunk?"

"Yeah, I noticed his hair when I first walked up. It was long and greasy like it hadn't had a good scrubbing in a while. Then when he was behind me, I was wishing he was standing downwind."

The situation was serious, but Hobb couldn't help but chuckle at Cal's face. He looked like he'd just sucked on a lemon.

"He was a crack shot, that's for darn sure.

Don't guess you gotta smell good for that."

"Yeah, he was good," Hobb agreed.

"Hobb, let's get you bandaged up and get the heck out of here. We'll be in Denver in an hour and the doc can have a look at you," Cal said.

"I'll go get those rifles," Boyd said.

"Where have you been? I've been waiting forever." Reuben's tone was brusque, and to make his point, the little man pulled his pocket watch out, tapped the face of the timepiece and frowned. He'd been waiting at the designated meeting place between Denver and Whispering Pines. "I should have already been back at my desk fifteen minutes ago."

"Sorry, I let a little thing like getting shot delay me." Stevie Langtry slid off his horse. "Seems like you forgot to tell me there were three men on that stagecoach."

"Three? We were told there would only be two men."

"They had another man inside the coach who took me by surprise. Take a look at my arm."

Reuben stepped away from him. "I don't know anything about gunshot wounds. What do you expect me to do?"

Stevie pulled his bandana from his pocket

and held it out to Reuben. "Just wrap my bandana around it to stop the bleeding. The bullet just grazed me."

Reuben timidly reached for the bandana, as though he were about to grasp a deadly scorpion. "Well, did you get it, or not?"

"As soon as you wrap my arm, take a look in my saddlebags."

The incentive worked. Reuben made short work of tying the bandana around his arm. As he walked to the horse, he pulled out his handkerchief and wiped his hands. He opened the saddlebag and pulled out one of the two large bags of money. After he looked inside, he said, "Perfect." He carried the bag to his buggy, pulled out his valise, and stuffed the bag inside.

"What are you going to do now, Reuben?"

Peering over his glasses, Reuben seemed surprised by the question. "I'm going back to work, of course. I certainly don't plan on calling attention to myself by disappearing right now. You don't plan on taking off, do you?"

"No, I'm going home. If I don't hear from Frankie, I'm going to Purgatory Canyon to see if he's there. If Frank, or any of the gang escaped Roper and LeMasters, that's where they will meet up."

"Do you think Frank will escape?"

"Yeah, I do. Frank is too smart for Morgan LeMasters." Stevie thought Frank was too crafty to be caught. If he ever did get caught, he was certain he'd never be hanged.

"If Frank hasn't been caught, what then?"

"Depends on what Frankie wants to do, but I want to leave Whispering Pines. I don't care if I ever come back. Maybe we'll go to Mexico."

"No one will ever suspect me, so we could do this a few more times and have enough money to travel the world." Reuben was confident that the people he worked with thought him to be too ignorant to plan a robbery. He smiled at the thought. He'd made an effort to appear timid and inconspicuous since he'd arrived in Whispering Pines a few years ago. His glowing recommendation from a fictitious boss in Boston had won him the job working for Mr. Rivers at the bank. His boss considered himself to be an exceptionally intelligent man. But he wasn't smart enough to figure out Reuben had never worked for a bank. Rivers thought his clerk to be so inconsequential that he rarely spoke to him other than to bark orders. Reuben often wanted to tell his boss that he was a bumbling fool, but playacting had its benefits. He'd been wise enough to hold his tongue and plan his revenge. He knew the day would come when he would find a way to rob the bank. Then, totally by accident one day, Reuben found the one person who could help him achieve his dream.

"I'll be in touch." Stevie had to agree, no one would suspect Reuben of robbery. At first, he didn't think Reuben had it in him to do anything that wasn't legal. He'd seen the timid, bespectacled clerk around Denver a few times, but they'd never spoken. They'd struck up a friendship one day when Reuben was out for a buggy ride and happened on Stevie target practicing. They started talking, and before Stevie knew what was happening, Reuben had told him of his plan to rob a stagecoach. Reuben was not at all what he seemed to most people. His frail appearance and unassuming manner certainly belied his cunning mind. Reuben was almost as devious as Frankie. Almost. In some ways, Reuben was more dangerous than Frankie. Reuben was a master at deception, and it appeared he had everyone fooled. Stevie often wondered if Reuben had happened on him that day by accident, or if he'd planned it all along.

"You're too smart to ride with Frank and his gang. Let's keep working together for a few more holdups, and then we could take off together and travel the world." Reuben wanted a traveling companion who could handle a gun. He looked at their partnership as the perfect union: his brains and Stevie's deadly shooting ability. "Wouldn't you like to see what's on the other side of the ocean?"

Reuben's plan did sound appealing. Maybe he could talk Frankie into seeing the world. "I'll be in touch once I find out what happened to Frankie."

Reuben closed his valise and lifted it into the buggy. He tipped his bowler hat. "Until then."

When Hobb pulled into Denver he stopped the stagecoach directly in front of the jail. After they told their story of the robbery, the sheriff had plenty of questions.

"Can you give me a description of this character?" the sheriff asked.

"We didn't see his face, Sheriff. His hat was pulled low, and he'd forced Cal in front of him at gunpoint, so he was well hidden during the holdup," Hobb said. "Boyd was looking into the sun when he winged him. If not for him, we'd all most likely be saying hello to our Maker."

"What can you tell me about him?" the

sheriff asked.

"He was a short fellow. Cal is about six feet, and I'd say he was six inches shorter," Hobb replied.

"Like I told Hobb and Boyd, he had long dark hair, and from the way he smelled, I don't think he'd had a bath in months. But he was mighty fast with that gun, and accurate," Cal added.

"His voice sounded like he was a younger man," Hobb said.

"And you say he was riding alone?" the sheriff asked.

Hobb explained to the sheriff the reason they'd stopped in the first place. He also told him about the hoax with the rifles strategically positioned.

"That sounds like a pretty smart move if you were planning to rob a stagecoach," the sheriff said. "You think a young man would have come up with that scheme on his own?"

"I don't know if he thought of the holdup alone, but it was well planned, and no one was riding with him. If he had a partner or partners, they didn't help him out. He didn't lack in confidence when it came to shooting," Hobb said.

"He was an experienced marksman," Cal said.

The sheriff digested this piece of information before he asked, "Who knew you were transporting that much money?"

"We didn't even know how much there was, and we'll need to send a telegram to find out who was privy to that information," Hobb replied. "But I can tell you one thing, Boyd was added at the last minute to ride inside the coach. That hombre didn't ask what we were carrying, he already knew. But I'd swear he didn't know about Boyd. Everything was planned well, and I figure if he'd known a man was inside the coach, he'd have forced him out."

The sheriff ran a hand over his whiskered face. "So you're saying that he expected there would be just two men on that stagecoach with that much money?"

"That's the feeling I got," Hobb said.

"That would seem to indicate that someone on this end didn't know about the extra man if it was an inside job," the sheriff theorized.

"Well, someone told him what we were carrying. Someone who wasn't aware we had an extra man. Maybe we need to go to the bank, tell them what happened, and see who knew the shipment was due to arrive today," Hobb said.

CHAPTER EIGHT

Morgan was thankful Mr. Barnett had the doctor there to greet them when they arrived at the way station. Rose had slept most of the way, mostly due to Morgan dosing her with a small amount of whiskey every time she awoke. He fully intended to be in the room while the doctor examined her, but the look on Mrs. Barnett's face silently conveyed she wasn't keen on the idea.

"You'll stay with the doctor?" Morgan asked Mrs. Barnett. The doctor seemed like a decent sort, but Morgan wasn't going to take any chances where Rose was concerned.

"Every second," Mrs. Barnett replied primly.

Mr. Barnett understood Morgan's concern, and put his hand on his shoulder. "You can be sure my wife will take care of your Rose. While you're waiting, let's get that telegram to the sheriff."

Morgan didn't correct his reference to *his Rose.* Let them think she was his. But he gave the doc a hard look and said, "You'd better take good care of her."

The doctor looked the big man up and down. He couldn't imagine anyone being so foolish to anger this cowboy. "Mrs. Barnett and I will look after her."

Morgan knew he'd made his point, and he walked away with Mr. Barnett. After he sent his telegram, Mr. Barnett told the men where they could wash.

Morgan stripped out of his dust-covered shirt and tossed it by one of four huge pails of clean water. The pails were situated on top of a long wooden table outside the back door of the house. He was thankful he had one clean shirt in his saddlebag. "I don't think I've eaten so much dust since I drove cattle from Texas."

"It makes you appreciate being at the ranch and bathing anytime you want," Murph said, claiming the pail of water next to Morgan's.

Morgan dipped his hand in the cool, clean water. "This feels good." He picked up the bar of soap, dunked his head and started scrubbing his hair. "Speaking of the ranch, I want you and the men to go on back there. I'll stay here with Rose, and if she's up to it, we'll leave on the next stagecoach in two days."

"You think it will be safe for you two to travel alone?" Murph asked.

Morgan soaped his torso as he considered Murph's question. He knew Murph was asking him if he thought Frank would be back. He didn't really want to talk about Frank Langtry while he was enjoying the first bath he'd had in days. Maybe he couldn't really call it a bath, but it was the next best thing. "I'll be ready for anything. I don't know what Frank will do, but one thing is certain, he didn't care enough about Rose to see if she was seriously injured. I don't think he has a reason to hang around."

"We both know it has been his hatred of you that kept him close to Whispering Pines all these years," Murph said.

Morgan couldn't disagree with Murph. "So you think he'll come back to Whispering Pines?"

"I think Frank hates you so much that he won't be happy until you are dead. He just wanted to draw out the process before he shoots you in the back, or summons the courage to call you out. Unless he gets whiskey brave one day, I don't think he'd ever call you out. That means you'd best watch your back. I wouldn't put anything past Frank. Nothing matters more to him than hurting you; not Granny, not Rose, nothing."

"I should have killed him years ago," Morgan said flatly.

"You almost did." Murph remembered the day he, along with three other men, had to pull Morgan off of Frank Langtry.

The doctor walked out the back door and approached Morgan. "You were right, Mr. LeMasters, your Rose has several broken ribs. She'll be uncomfortable for a few days, but she's going to be fine."

"I was getting worried since she wasn't eating anything," Morgan confessed.

"She's promised she will eat something tonight," the doc told him.

"Will she be able to travel on the next stage?" Morgan asked.

"I think she will be fine. Just make sure she doesn't bounce around too much." The doc smiled at him when he added, "You probably won't even have to give her more whiskey."

"It's all I could think of to help her rest," Morgan said.

"The rest probably helped her more than anything," the doc replied.

Morgan pulled some bills from his pocket. When he handed them to the doctor, he said, "Thanks for being here, Doc."

"If you should need me before you leave, just send for me."

Mr. Barnett joined them and handed a piece of paper to Morgan. "You received a response from the sheriff in Whispering Pines."

Morgan finished reading the telegram and looked at Murph. "Jack was shot and Granny is caring for him, and he says she is worried about Rose. No sign of Frank."

"I'll see them as soon as we get home," Murph said.

"We won't be far behind you. Tell Granny to rest easy, I'll make sure Rose will arrive safe and sound."

When Barnett and the doctor walked back inside the house, Murph looked at Morgan and arched his eyebrow. "Your Rose, huh?"

"He jumped to that conclusion."

"Could be because you hover over her almost as much as you do Faithful."

Morgan chuckled. "Are you comparing Rose to my horse, Murph?"

Murph wasn't about to let him evade the question. "You know what I mean. You've never paid that much attention to any woman."

"I was never around a woman with busted ribs before."

"Busted ribs or not, I think you are sweet on Rose," Murph said.

Morgan toweled off his chest and arms. "Are you forgetting I'm the man who intends to hang her brother?"

"Nope. But where matters of the heart are concerned, logic slips away."

Morgan pulled out his straight razor and soaped up his whiskers. "Murph, if I didn't know better, I would think you are turning into a philosopher."

"I don't have to be a philosopher to see how you watch Rose. You remind me of a hungry wolf every time you look at her."

Morgan didn't have a response to his comparison. He probably did resemble a hungry wolf when he looked at Rose. He hated to admit it to himself, but he was curious about her opinion of him. No matter how many times he told himself it shouldn't matter, it was important to him.

Clay and George walked to the wash table, so Murph didn't say more about Rose. Morgan told the men of his plan to stay behind with Rose until the next stage.

"I guess I'm forced to travel by stage, so I'll be riding with you," George said.

"I can stay with Rose and ride the rest of the way with her. I'm sure you need to get back to your ranch," Clay said.

"I already sent a telegram to Jack and told him I would see Rose home. I gave my word to Granny," Morgan said. He didn't know why he was insisting he would be the one to see Rose home. He had a lot of work waiting for him, and it would be easier to let Clay and George escort Rose to Whispering Pines. But he couldn't bring himself to leave without her. Though Clay hadn't said as much, Morgan thought he was interested in Rose. The way Morgan saw it, Clay had had ample time to get to know her on the stagecoach, since he'd traveled all the way from back East with her. But if Clay liked Rose, and she seemed to like him, why should he interfere? On the other hand, it wasn't Clay who had undressed her and bandaged her ribs. Pastor or not, he didn't want any man to see Rose undressed. But the most important reason he would see Rose to Whispering Pines was that he'd given his word to Granny. At least, that was what he told himself.

Once he donned his clean shirt, Morgan walked to the small room where Rose was resting. The door was open, but instead of walking inside, he leaned against the door frame. Rose was lying on the bed, propped up with two pillows behind her. He thought she looked beautiful lying there with her blond hair fanned out over the pillow. "The men are leaving for the ranch, and I thought you might want to send a message to Granny."

Rose gazed at him. He looked so big and masculine with his broad shoulders filling the doorway that it was difficult to focus on his question. He was such a striking man, it was impossible to keep her eyes off of him. His clean shaven face and wet hair told her he'd bathed. Her gaze drifted down to his clean shirt, and she found herself imagining how he would look without it. His muscles bulging beneath the cloth indicated he would be a sight to behold. "Aren't you going with them?" She didn't know why that was the first question that came to her mind.

He wondered if she wanted him to stay with her. "No."

Her first thought was he was going after Frankie, but she didn't know how to ask him. "Why? Don't you need to get back to the ranch?"

"Yes, I do." He did need to get back to his ranch, and he expected to have long days ahead after being gone so long. He didn't mind the long hours; he loved his ranch and the work that gave his life purpose. Whispering Pines was always first in his mind, and that was what was so surprising to him now.

He found himself in uncharted territory. He wanted to be with her more than he wanted to get back to the ranch. The way she was looking at him, he knew she had something on her mind. She would make a lousy poker player. "Why do you ask?" Before she responded, he realized what she was thinking. "You want to know if I'm going after Frank."

She looked down at the coverlet draped over her and she started twisting the fringe on one end. "I did wonder."

Morgan took a deep breath before he responded. It irritated him that Frank Langtry was included in every conversation. "I'm staying to ride home on the next stage with you, if you are feeling up to it. I sent a telegram and promised Granny I would see to it you got home safely."

Her eyes slowly drifted back to his. "I see. Thank you." She wanted him to stay. It wasn't only because she didn't want him going after Frankie. After spending time with him, it came as a surprise to find how much she really liked him. She didn't want their time together to come to an end. When she got home, she wasn't certain she would see much of him, yet she felt guilty knowing she'd already taken up too much of his time. The last thing she wanted was to be a burden to him. She hoped he wasn't staying simply to honor his word to Granny. "I'm sure the pastor could stay. I know you must have work waiting for you on your ranch."

"Clay said he was riding to Whispering Pines with the men. But of course, if you prefer he stay with you . . ." It wasn't a question, but he waited for her response. He felt like something important was riding on her reply, but he couldn't put into words why he felt that way.

They stared at each other, each waiting for the other to speak.

His dark, intense gaze made her heart beat faster. All she could think about was how handsome he was. Had he asked her a question? She couldn't remember.

Morgan wondered if she was afraid to tell him she wanted Clay to accompany her to Whispering Pines. She'd told him she'd feared him when she was a girl. Did he frighten her now? He might not like her response, but there was no reason for her to think he would be angry with her. Without taking his eyes off of her, he walked into the room and closed the door behind him. When he reached the bed, he leaned over and braced an arm on the mattress beside her head. He lowered his torso until his face was mere inches from hers.

Rose was certain her thumping heart was shaking her whole body. Not from fright, but from the sheer excitement she felt at his nearness. She'd never been alone in a room with a man other than a member of her family. Being alone with any other man would have frightened her. But Morgan didn't. He'd been gentle with her, and cared for her when her own brother took off and left her behind. She didn't want to think about Frankie right now. She didn't want to think about anything other than Morgan. He was so close to her she could smell the scent of his soap, and feel the heat from his body. If she were prudent, she would look away from his midnight gaze, but she couldn't. His eyes were like magnets, pulling her into their depths.

He didn't know what possessed him to move so close to her. Her eyes were huge, and her pupils became larger and darker the longer he gazed at her. The urge to kiss her was almost overwhelming. He knew he was in dangerous territory, but he also knew there was no way he was going to move away from her now. "Are you afraid of me, Rose?"

She shook her head. "Why do you ask?"

"Because you didn't answer my question."

She blinked, but her eyes remained on his.

"What question?"

"Do you want Clay to ride with you?"

Her eyes drifted to his mouth, then to the dimple in his chin. "I know you've been away from the ranch a long time, and you must have a lot of work needing your attention."

"Answer my question, Rose." His words were softly spoken, but the demand for a response was not subtle.

What did he want her to say? She'd taken up too much of his valuable time already. "You've been so kind to look after me, and I've inconvenienced you enough."

Why wouldn't she answer him? He leaned over and braced his arm on the other side of her, forcing the feather mattress to dip under his weight. He was so close to her, he could see the flecks of silver in her green eyes. "You haven't inconvenienced me. If you want Clay to ride with you, I'll leave with my men."

She didn't want him to leave, yet there was that nagging voice reminding her he was the man who wanted to hang her brother. Her conscience wouldn't allow her to forget Frankie. If not for Frankie, she might tell him what she wanted to say. She couldn't deny she was attracted to him, and she wanted to be with him as long as possible, but by saying those words she felt she would be betraying her brother.

Morgan didn't know why he kept asking the question. Her evasiveness gave him his answer. He shouldn't care. It didn't make sense why he was drawn to her. He was going to hang her brother, so she was the last person he should want to be involved with. But for some inexplicable reason, he wanted her. Badly. She didn't say a word, so he straightened and turned to the door. "I'll see you in Whispering Pines."

As he took one step toward the door, Rose said, "No."

Morgan stopped, turned around and looked at her. He raised his eyebrow in question, waiting for her to say more. She didn't say more, so he waited. Perhaps it was his pride, but he was determined she would have to tell him she wanted him to stay. What did the Bible say about pride? *A man's pride shall bring him low.* He may be brought low, but she was going to have to tell him what she wanted. Who was he kidding? He wasn't going to leave her behind with Clay or any other man. But he was calling her bluff. And he was a good poker player. "No?"

"I don't want you to go," she said softly.

Her admission made his heart leap. He

wanted to wrap his arms around her, but he was afraid he would hurt her ribs. Still, he wanted to do more than stare at her. He might not be able to embrace her, so he did the next best thing. He stepped to the bed, lowered his head and kissed her.

Instead of being surprised, Rose expected his kiss, wanted his kiss. When he started to walk away, she thought if she missed this opportunity, she might never have another. She wrapped her arms around his neck and opened her lips to his. Not shyly, but boldly, as if she'd been kissed this way a thousand times before. She hadn't. No one had ever kissed her the way he was kissing her. The bed shifted under his weight when he sat beside her, but his lips didn't leave hers. She no longer felt any pain from her ribs. She felt nothing, but her need for him. She curled her fingers through his dark, damp hair and held him to her. She caressed his neck, his powerful shoulders, and ran her hands over his muscled arms. She'd never touched a man the way she was touching him. It was as if she wanted to commit to memory the very feel of him. He felt so strong and potent, and she wanted . . . she needed much more. She heard his breathing increase, and his skin was blazing under her hands. She didn't want this moment to end. She didn't want him to stop kissing her, and she didn't want to stop touching him.

Morgan hadn't expected such an assertive response from her. He felt like he'd died and gone to heaven. He gently lifted her to his chest, and ran his large hands over her back, caressing her as she was him. His lips left hers, only to plant small kisses on her neck before he sought her lips once again. His breathing was ragged. Over and over, he reminded himself to be gentle and not to lose his head. He didn't want to do anything he would later regret, but her response had him so excited that he could hardly contain his desire.

Her hands moved over his broad back, and she pressed against his chest and uttered a small moan.

Morgan pulled back. "Did I hurt you?"

She couldn't form a thought as her gaze focused on his mouth.

"Did I hurt your ribs?" Morgan asked again.

She shook her head. She felt like pleading with him not to stop kissing her.

Morgan searched her face. Her lips were red and swollen from his kisses, but the way she was looking at him and touching him said she wanted more. He wanted more.

Much more than he could have. Frank. There he was again. If not for Frank, Rose would be his. He cupped her chin in his hand. "Why do you want me to stay? You haven't forgotten what I intend to do?"

Knowing he was referring to Frankie, Rose found herself becoming emotional. She hadn't forgotten Morgan was her brother's mortal enemy. The brother she'd worshipped her entire life. But she wanted this man. She shook her head, and whispered, "I haven't forgotten."

"Then tell me why." The thought crossed his mind that she might think he would change his mind if she gave herself to him.

"I want . . ." She was torn. Was it a choice? Her brother or Morgan? When Frankie thought she was accepting Morgan's word against his, he'd been furious. Was that the reason he'd left her behind? Was Morgan using her to get to Frankie? Tears filled her eyes.

"What do you want, Rose?"

A tear slid down her cheek, but she leaned forward and whispered in his ear, "I want you." Her lips skimmed his jaw, and moved to his lips.

It didn't take but a second for the shock of her admission to sink in before Morgan took charge of the kiss once more. When he was about to lose control, he pulled away. He didn't want to stop, and it took every ounce of mental strength he possessed to take his hands off of her. But he needed to make sure she knew where he stood concerning her brother. "Rose, nothing will change my mind about Frank. If you give yourself to me, it won't change my mind."

Rose was stunned by his words. "I wouldn't . . . I wouldn't . . ." She was so shocked, she could hardly speak. He'd misread her response to his kisses. She wiped the tears from her cheek. She was a naïve ninny, like her sisters always told her. It never occurred to her that when she kissed him he would think she was willing to give herself to him. She was offering to give him her heart despite the situation with her brother, and he thought she was bartering for her brother's life. "I would not give myself to any man without benefit of marriage. You of all people know how I was reared, and the beliefs my family hold dear. I can't fathom how you would think I would abandon my faith."

As soon as the words had left his mouth, Morgan knew they did not convey what he intended. He didn't expect her to offer herself up on a platter to spare Frank. He just wanted her to know whatever happened between them would not change his mind about hanging Frank. It was only fair that he made that point clear. "I didn't mean it that way, Rose." He might have been offended that she would think so little of him. But in truth, he had to admit he was on the brink of succumbing to his baser instincts. "I was only trying to make it clear where I stood regarding your brother. Nothing on earth will change my mind about him." The last few minutes had been nothing short of bliss for him, but reality smacked him in the face. "I can't see how a . . ." He'd almost said *a marriage,* but he quickly amended his words. "I can't see how anything between us would work. You're loyal to Frank, and I want someone loyal to me." Prideful though it may be, Morgan wasn't willing to bend on that point. He stood and walked to the door. "We both just got caught up in the moment. It won't happen again."

Rose refused to cry. She was angry with herself for her own behavior. It was little wonder he'd misinterpreted her response to his kisses. She had no one to blame, but herself. It would be wise to put some distance between them, or she might make a fool of herself again. "Ask Clay if he would stay behind with me, please."

So, she was no longer calling him Pastor. It was Clay now. "Sure thing." He left the room in a huff. Not a chance in Hades was he going to ask Clay to stay with her. He might not see himself marrying her, but he'd be a one-eyed toad before he'd give Clay a chance to make headway with her. Now that they'd shared those kisses, he wasn't about to let any man within ten feet of her. That girl could kiss. She'd had him at her mercy when she ran her fingers through his hair. Maybe when he forgot the way she felt in his arms, forgot the way she caressed his muscles, forgot the way she pressed herself tightly to him, forgot the softness of her lips and how perfectly they molded to his, maybe then, and only then, he might be able to see her with another man. That should only take him — what? — a hundred years or so.

CHAPTER NINE

Frank and his men rode slowly into Purgatory Canyon at midnight. They navigated the terrain easily under the large silvery moon, but they exercised caution, thinking lawmen could be waiting. Riding over the flatlands familiar to Frank, he led the men to the narrow, winding passageway through the dense juniper thicket, headed to the higher elevations. Several years ago when Frank was exploring the area searching for the legendary treasure hidden in the canyon, he happened on a one-room log cabin that the gang now used as a hideout. The area was so isolated, Frank doubted anyone had ever been there other than the mountain man who built it. Frank had spent hours exploring the entire canyon over the years, and he'd found many places he could stay for months with no one being the wiser. Not even his men were aware of the many remote cave dwellings in the canyon bluffs.

Once they'd reached the hidden fork along the path that led to the cabin, a voice rang out in the dark.

"Who goes there?"

Frank pulled to a halt. He recognized the voice. "Walt?"

"Frank?"

"Yeah." They dismounted and made their way through the brush. "I'm glad to see you made it," Frank said.

"We all made it." The remaining two men walked from the rocks.

"Roper chased us in here, but Reb shot him," Walt said.

"Is he dead?" Frank asked.

"I don't know. I took a different route than Reb and Mason, and I made it to the cabin a day earlier."

Reb picked up the story. "The sheriff and his men were on our tail. We arrived at the canyon before them, so we had time to get to the rocks to pick them off. We fired as soon as they entered the canyon. They didn't make it this far. All I can tell you is Roper slumped over in the saddle, but his men surrounded him and they rode out fast. They haven't been back."

"Good job, Reb. We'll find out if he's dead when we get to Whispering Pines," Frank said.

"How did you boys get away?" Walt asked.

Frank told the men about the stagecoach accident, but he left out the part about threatening his own sister in order to get the drop on Morgan.

"If it wasn't for Frank's sister we'd be pushing up daisies," Deke added.

"Why are we going back to Whispering Pines?" Walt asked.

Frank smiled at Walt and slapped him on the back. "We're going to rustle more cattle from LeMasters."

"You don't mean we're going back on his ranch?" Walt could hardly believe they were going to tempt fate by stealing from LeMasters again. He didn't know why Frank couldn't leave it alone.

"That's the plan. Stevie will know what's going on. This time we're going to do it up right. We're going to kill Joseph Longbow. He's the only one that can identify us as the rustlers. And when we leave, we're going to take Stevie with us. Who knows, we might even rob a bank after that."

"Don't you think they will be expecting us?" Walt asked.

"Morgan thinks we're headed to Mexico. He's probably on his way there now." Secretly, Frank hoped Morgan was back at Whispering Pines. He wanted to be a thorn in his side for as long as possible. He planned that when the day came that he left Whispering Pines for the last time, he'd see to it Morgan was dead. Morgan was known as a fast draw, so forcing him into a gun battle was not an option. Frank wouldn't hesitate to shoot him in the back. Of course, it'd be interesting to see if Morgan was a faster draw than Stevie. Stevie practiced day and night. Maybe one day they would have the chance to find out.

All that mattered to Frank right now was to kill Joseph Longbow. With him dead, there would be no one to testify against him, and he would never be hanged for his crimes. It was a bonus that Morgan cared about the old Indian.

"It might be smarter to rob the bank and go on down to Mexico. Forget LeMasters," Walt said. He didn't agree with Frank's plan when it came to LeMasters. He'd never met the man, and he didn't have a beef with him. But Frank had it out for LeMasters for some reason, and he couldn't let it go. Walt had joined the gang because of Deke and Dutch, not because of Frank.

Deke and Dutch exchanged a look. They already knew Frank was not going to be dissuaded when it came to harassing Morgan.

Frank figured he needed to make it clear

who was running things. "I'm making the call." He leveled his eyes on Walt and added, "Unless you think you are smart enough to make the decisions now."

Walt didn't back down. "I'm saying it ain't smart to go back to Whispering Pines."

Taking a step toward Walt, Frank was nose to nose. "Are you saying I ain't smart?"

Walt inclined his head toward the rest of the men and said, "We ain't got nothing against LeMasters. This seems to be personal between you two. I think I speak for all of us when I say we ain't hankering to swing from a rope because you have something to prove to LeMasters. With all the trouble with the Sioux, if we were smart, we'd hightail it out of here and go on down to Mexico."

Frank looked at the other men. He could tell they agreed with Walt since none of them spoke up. He couldn't take them all on. "We have to kill Longbow. We need to create a diversion to get to him. If you men don't care that Longbow can identify us, then we can leave for Mexico right now. But all of us can hang for rustling." His eyes met each man's, but silence ensued, so he continued. "I figure we can rob the bank afterward. Heck, we might even rob a train."

"Like the Reno Brothers gang?" Reb asked.

"Who knows, we might become more famous," Frank said.

"Ain't they all dead?" Dutch asked.

"I think they was lynched years ago," Deke added.

"You make my point for me, Deke. If Longbow is dead, no one can testify against us, and we won't end up swinging. I think we'll be more like Jesse James. No one lives long enough to point their finger at him in court." Frank turned toward the cabin. "You boys have whiskey? I sure could use a drink."

"Stevie, where have you been?" Granny asked when her grandson walked in the kitchen.

"I went to Denver to see a friend of mine." Stevie walked to the stove to see what she was cooking. "Something smells good."

"I'm making some soup for Sheriff Roper. One of the men in Frank's gang shot him."

"He's alive?"

"By the grace of God." When she glanced up at Stevie, she saw how pale he was. "Are you sick, son?" She raised her hand to his forehead, but he jerked away.

"I'm fine. I'm just hungry. You got anything else to eat beside soup?"

"I'll fix you a sandwich." She'd thought once Frank was no longer around to influence Stevie, he might be more like the sweet young man he once was. He'd changed over the last few years, and like Frank, she wasn't able to steer him on the right path.

Granny watched as he walked to the stove and poured himself a cup of coffee. He was moving slowly. When he reached for the cup, she noticed he winced in pain. "Is there something wrong with your arm?"

"I told you, I'm fine. Where was Roper when he got shot?"

"The deputy said they were in some canyon." Granny pulled out some ham and sliced some of her freshly baked bread.

Just as Stevie figured, Frank would make his way back to Purgatory Canyon. "Was Frankie with them?"

"No, Morgan went after him, but he escaped with three men. Somehow Morgan met up with your sister, who was on the stagecoach. There was an accident and Rose was injured. Morgan is bringing her home in a few days."

"Where's Frankie?"

"I don't know." It irritated Granny that Stevie didn't ask about Rose. She placed his sandwich in front of him. "You don't have any questions about your sister?"

Stevie picked up the sandwich and took a huge bite. "You said she was coming home in a few days, so I reckon she must be okay."

Granny pulled a chair out and sat across from him. "Mind your manners, and don't talk with your mouth full. It wouldn't hurt you to say a prayer before your meal." Seeing he wasn't going to listen, she bowed her head and said a quick, silent prayer. She thought she might be wasting her breath, but she wanted to try one more time to save Stevie from Frank's fate. She asked God to help her find the right words. "Stevie, I don't know what is going on, but I don't want you following in your brother's footsteps. I failed him, and I'll always regret that, but Preacher and I did teach him right from wrong. As much as it pains me to say it, he doesn't care about anyone but himself. You know what he's done to Morgan is wrong."

Stevie swallowed another big bite. "You care more about LeMasters than you do Frankie. You never did take Frankie's side, and I don't think that he's done anything wrong."

"I love Frank, but I will not abide his outlaw ways. If that means I take Morgan's part, then you are right."

189

"LeMasters started the feud between them. Why don't you ask him what happened to make Frankie hate him?"

"I'm sure Morgan didn't start their problems." She stood and walked back to the stove. She couldn't reason with him when it came to his brother and Morgan LeMasters. "You don't want to go the way of an outlaw. There will only be heartache and death."

Stevie didn't respond, so she dropped the subject. "You need to start helping out around the farm. All you've done for the past year is target practice, and that's not a useful skill for farm work."

"I don't like farm work," Stevie said.

Granny's patience was running thin. He was a grown man now, and he was acting like a baby. She walked back to the table and waggled a finger at him. "You like to eat, don't you? Farming is hard work, but it's good, honest work. It's nothing to be ashamed of. Your brother would have been a lot better off if he'd spent more time on the farm and in church."

"Frankie doesn't want to be a farmer, and I don't either. Don't think I'm going to stay here. You'll have the girls here, they can help you farm if you want to keep it going."

She was almost afraid to ask him the question. "What do you plan on doing with your life?"

"I'm going with Frankie when he comes back."

She shook her head at him. "Frank is going to be in jail."

"That's what you think." There was no way his brother was going to hang. Frankie was too smart for that. He'd outsmarted all of them for a long time.

"Joseph Longbow said it was Frank and his men who did the rustling. Frank was the one who shot Joseph. Your brother is going to the territorial prison if Morgan doesn't hang him first."

Stevie silently wished Frankie had killed Joseph Longbow. Maybe he should make sure Joseph Longbow was dead so he couldn't testify against his brother. He'd talk to Frankie and see what he wanted to do. He was a better shot than Frankie, so it made sense he should be the one to shoot him. As soon as his arm healed he planned to ride to Purgatory Canyon. He felt confident that's where he would find his brother.

Stevie started to walk out the door, but Granny stopped him when she said, "Stevie, you need to consider your eternal soul." When she saw her words were falling on deaf ears, she added, "Take a bath today, and go see the barber unless you want me to take the scissors to your hair. If you can't do that much, you can stay in the barn."

Stevie walked out, and Granny turned to look out the window at the cloudless blue sky. "Preacher, if you're listening, I could use some advice." She felt like she could hear her husband's voice in her ear saying, *You've done all you can do. Pray.* Granny chuckled. "That was always your answer to every problem."

"Granny, you didn't have to bring this food. I know you don't have time to be babysitting me," Jack said.

Granny removed the jars of soup from her basket and placed them on Jack's kitchen table. "I wanted to see how you are doing, and you need that bandage changed."

"Webb could change this bandage."

"I don't trust him to scrub your wound good. Besides, I made you a pie too."

He was grouchy and bored from staying in bed, but the thought of one of Granny's pies brought a smile to his face. "What kind?"

"Apple."

Jack winked at her. "Marry me, Granny."

"I can see you are feeling better, Jack Roper. You're full of your usual nonsense."

Granny walked to his stove to make fresh coffee. "Do you want some soup now?"

"Some of your good coffee with a piece of pie sounds too good to pass up."

"You have to promise you will have some soup later," Granny said.

"Yes, ma'am."

"Now let me look at your wound while we wait for the coffee." Granny filled a pan with water, grabbed a bar of soap, and placed it on a table beside the bed. She removed Jack's bandage and cleaned his wound. "This looks good."

"Did you give Joseph Longbow his medicine pouch back?"

She reached into her skirt pocket, pulled out the pouch and handed it to Jack. "It's a spirit bag. He said it was for you, and you would need it again."

Jack frowned at her. "Why? Is he trying to tell me I will be shot again?"

Granny shrugged. "He said it will protect you. You know Joseph. He's a man of few words and he wouldn't explain. Most of the time he walks away while you are still talking. He doesn't say good-bye, he just takes off."

Jack chuckled. "Yeah. He doesn't spend a lot of time conversing."

After Granny wrapped a clean bandage

around his shoulder, she cut a large piece of pie and poured him a steaming cup of coffee.

Jack thought Granny looked worried, and he figured it had something to do with Stevie. "Did Stevie come home?"

Granny poured herself a cup of coffee and sat in the chair by the bed. "Yes, he told me he visited a friend in Denver."

Jack took a big bite of pie and chewed in silence, trying to figure out where Stevie was spending his time. "You think he's got a girlfriend?"

"Not on your life. The way he smells, he's not good company for the pigs."

"Not big on bathing, huh?"

"I told him he could stay in the barn if he didn't take a bath."

"Does he have friends that you don't know about?"

"I was just thinking that Stevie doesn't have any friends other than Frank. Sadly, he worships Frank and wants to be just like him. I told him that he needed to quit his target practicing and do some work around the farm. But he told me he wasn't going to stay on the farm."

"Where's he planning to go?"

"He said he will be going with Frank when he comes back."

Jack took a sip of coffee. "I'm sorry to hear that, Granny. I reckon sometimes men just have to learn the hard way."

Granny turned her tired, watery eyes on Jack. "That's the problem. I've treated them like they were boys and they are both grown men. I've prayed and prayed for those boys, but it's out of my hands."

CHAPTER TEN

Rose was waiting by the door as Morgan and the station owner hitched the fresh team to the stagecoach. Morgan hadn't mentioned why he'd stayed behind instead of the pastor. She thought perhaps the pastor was in a hurry to get to Whispering Pines, and Morgan felt an obligation to Granny to see her home. Morgan hadn't been overly talkative the last two days, so the last thing she wanted to do was annoy him with questions.

Two men arrived on the incoming stagecoach and they were going as far as Denver, so she wouldn't be riding alone with Morgan. Rose didn't care for the way the two men watched her every move. Morgan may not be saying much to her, but she was relieved he would be riding inside the coach with her. No matter their differences over Frank, she felt safe with him.

Mrs. Barnett walked up beside Rose and

followed the direction of her gaze. "That Mr. LeMasters sure is a handsome man."

"Hmm," Rose replied noncommittally.

"Does he have a wife?"

"No, he doesn't." It was surprising Morgan had never married. Considering the many women who competed for his attention, it was astonishing that one hadn't talked him into settling down after all of these years. Granny's letters always made mention of Morgan, and included the usual small-town gossip. She would tell her of the women who would sit beside Morgan at church, or what single ladies invited him to a home-cooked meal, or if he escorted a particular woman to dinner at the hotel. Rose never understood why Granny thought she would be interested in Morgan's personal life or romantic interest, but she could recall every name of every woman Granny wrote about.

Mrs. Barnett put her arm around Rose's shoulders. "At first, I thought you two were betrothed. He seems so devoted to you."

Rose thought of the kiss they'd shared and how much she'd liked it. She couldn't stop thinking about her reaction to him. "No, we are not betrothed. We've known each other a long time." She thought perhaps Mrs. Barnett knew why Morgan had stayed instead of the pastor, so she said, "Actually, I thought he was going home with his men and the pastor was going to wait for the stagecoach."

Mrs. Barnett hadn't heard any conversation about Morgan leaving. "I wouldn't know about that." It hadn't escaped her notice that Morgan had more than a passing interest in this lovely young woman. And it seemed that Rose couldn't take her eyes off of him. "Not only is he handsome, he's a hard worker too. I swear that man doesn't sit still. He's been a big help to Ward while he's been here. If I were you, I wouldn't let him get away. I can't believe some woman hasn't roped him into marriage before now."

Rose didn't reply because Morgan was walking toward the house. "Your valises are on the stagecoach. We can pull out when you're ready."

"I'm ready." Though Rose was still moving slowly, she was feeling much better. She stepped on the porch, and Morgan reached for her elbow to assist her.

Mrs. Barnett was right behind them. "Now you take care, and if you need to stop, you just tell the driver. Ward told them to take more rest stops than normal."

Rose turned and squeezed Mrs. Barnett's hand. "You've been so kind. Thank you for your care."

"It was my pleasure." Mrs. Barnett looked at Morgan. "Mr. LeMasters, don't let her move around too much."

"Yes, ma'am."

"Where's George?" Rose asked.

"He says he's riding on top with the driver. I don't think he likes riding inside the coach. I guess he's spent too many years driving the team." Morgan didn't care to be inside the coach either, but he wasn't about to let Rose ride inside with the two strangers. Not only that, but he reasoned she might be frightened riding in a coach again.

The men were already seated in the coach when Morgan helped Rose inside. They were sitting opposite each other, which meant Morgan had to take the seat across from Rose. From the moment the two men stepped off the stage, Morgan thought they looked like trouble, so he wasn't at all happy with the seating arrangement. They watched Rose like a couple of vultures, and he figured he'd have to teach them some manners if they stepped one foot out of line. He couldn't blame them for noticing how pretty she was, but it was one thing to look, but quite another thing to leer.

Once inside the coach, Rose glanced at each man. She chose to sit on the same seat

with the one that looked a tad less dangerous. It was a tough choice.

The man grinned at her. "Looks like it's
my lucky day. It's not often I have a gal as
pretty as you sitting beside me."

Morgan remained silent, but he looked at
Rose, trying to gauge her reaction to the
man's comment. Rose ignored him. She
looked out the window and waved good-bye
to Mrs. Barnett.

Morgan situated his rifle next to the door
before he tapped on the coach door to
signal they were ready to leave. When the
coach started moving, Morgan tried to find
a comfortable position. His legs were so
long that he had to straddle Rose's legs,
basically trapping her between his knees.
He leaned back and pulled his hat over his
eyes, but not so low that he couldn't keep
an eye on Rose. He also kept an eye on the
men as they ogled her. He didn't want to
have a conversation with them, and he
certainly didn't want them talking to Rose.
He hoped he didn't have trouble with them
because he wanted time to think.

Mostly, he wanted to think about Rose
and the kiss they'd shared. As much as he
told himself to put it out of his mind, he
found it impossible. Over the years there
had been many women he could have devel-

oped a lasting relationship with if he'd been so inclined, but no one had tempted him until now. If Frank weren't her brother, Morgan could envision himself married to Rose. He hadn't wavered in his determination to find Frank once Rose was safe in Whispering Pines. He'd hang Frank for sure this time, if for no other reason than the way he'd treated Rose. No matter how he looked at it, Rose would never accept what he had to do. What amazed him was how Frank had fooled her all these years. Of course, it was possible Granny hadn't told the girls the truth about their brother. Whatever the cause, it was obvious Rose wouldn't listen to reason, and Frank would always have her allegiance.

The next hour passed quietly, and Rose was relieved she had been successful ignoring the two strangers. The two men aside, she was already uneasy about being on a stagecoach again. It didn't seem likely that she would be involved in two stagecoach accidents, but that thought did little to allay her fears. The ride was bumpy, and she held on to the side strap for dear life to keep from bouncing around. Her arm was beginning to ache, but she couldn't let go for fear of landing in a heap on the stagecoach floor, or worse, in the lap of a strange man. Suddenly, the coach hit a large rut and Rose lost her grip on the strap, and her worst fears came to life. She went sliding across the seat, and landed right next to the stranger.

The man draped his arm around her shoulders. "Honey, let me hold you in place so you don't have to hold on to that strap."

Rose tried to scoot away from him, but he held on tight.

Morgan tipped his hat back with one finger and stared hard at the man. "Unless you want to lose that arm, I suggest you let her go."

The man held on. "Why don't you mind your own business? I'm just doing her a favor. I don't see you helping her."

Morgan was out of his seat so fast the man didn't have time to react. He wrenched the man's arm from Rose's shoulder and twisted it at an odd angle, causing the man to yelp in pain. "I don't think the lady likes your favor." Morgan heard a pistol cock behind him.

"Let him go," the man with the pistol said.

Morgan didn't have a pistol; his only weapon was his rifle, and it was beside the stagecoach door. "Now why would I let him go? He needs to be taught some manners."

"Mister, my brother has all the manners

he wants. He was just helping your lady friend. We've been without women for a spell, and we'd like to have a little fun. If you don't let go of his arm, I'll have to shoot you."

Morgan didn't like the sound of that. He'd had a bad feeling about this pair from the start. "If you shoot me, your brother will still have a broken arm." He quickly thought about his options. He might be able to kick the gun out of the man's hand, but if the gun went off, Rose might get hit. If he let the man go, he had no idea what they had planned for her.

"Put your gun down," Rose said.

Morgan glanced her way. He didn't know how she'd done it, but she'd managed to get as far away from the man as she could, and somehow she was holding on to a cocked pistol. Her hands didn't look particularly steady as she pointed the barrel at the man who was holding a gun on him.

"Now, honey, you ain't going to shoot me. Just hand me that gun," the man said.

Morgan didn't think Rose had it in her to shoot a man. She didn't sound convincing, and he didn't think the stranger thought she would pull the trigger either. He had to make his move now while the man with the pistol was distracted. Morgan turned slightly as he held on to the man's arm, and quickly kicked the gun out of the other man's hand. The gun hit the floor, and Morgan took advantage of the man's slow response and kicked him hard in the face, busting his nose wide open. The man Morgan was holding on to tried to reach for his pistol with his other hand, but Morgan snapped his arm. Once the man slumped over in pain, Morgan removed his pistol from the holster and stuck it in his belt. He reached over and took the pistol from Rose's hands. "Rose, hand me the rifle."

Even though Morgan thought she looked like she might faint, she managed to grab hold of his rifle and pass it to him. He rapped sharply on the ceiling with his rifle. Within seconds the coach came to a halt, and it wasn't long before George opened the door and stuck his head inside. "Morgan, is everything okay in here?"

Morgan motioned with the pistol for the men to get out of the coach. "George, these skunks need to learn some manners. They will be riding on top with the luggage the rest of the way."

George looked at the men. One was holding his hands over his bloody nose, and the other man was cradling his arm. George figured they'd obviously done something to get on Morgan's bad side. Dang fools. "You want them to walk the rest of the way?"

"If they so much as blink the wrong way, throw them off," Morgan replied.

The man with the broken arm glared at Morgan. "What about our guns?"

Morgan picked up the gun on the floor and handed it to George. "When we get to Denver you'll get them back."

As soon as the men were out of the stagecoach, Rose slumped to the seat and Morgan sat beside her. "Are you okay?"

His big body felt so solid and strong that she could have cried from relief. "It seems you are always protecting me."

He felt it was his duty to protect her. What man wouldn't? "Do you mind if I put my arm around you? I'll keep you from bouncing all over the seat." He knew she'd been scared to death when that man had put his hands on her. He didn't want to do anything that would frighten her more.

"No, I don't mind." Actually, she didn't think she could hang on to that strap one more minute. She relaxed against his muscled chest as he wrapped his arm around her. It felt wonderful to be beside him, to be held by him. She knew she could trust him not to do anything improper. Everything he'd done for her since the stagecoach accident was to protect her. Even her own brother hadn't stayed around to help her. "Thank you."

"Where did you get the pistol?"

"Mrs. Barnett gave it to me."

"Why?"

"She didn't like the looks of those two. She told me she was certain you could protect me, but it didn't hurt for me to be prepared since I was the only woman on the coach."

"I didn't know you could shoot," Morgan said.

"Stevie taught me a long time ago. He was always a good shot."

"Would you have shot that man?"

She wanted to think she would protect the people she cared about if it was necessary, but in all honesty, she didn't know when it came to actually pulling a trigger. "I'm not sure. I've never shot anyone."

"Promise me that when you point a gun at someone you've already made your mind up that you can pull the trigger. Otherwise some man might take the gun from you and you'd be in real trouble."

She looked up at him and nodded. "I promise."

He kissed the top of her head. "Good. Now get some rest."

Rose stared up at him for a long moment. She wished he would kiss her again, not on the head, but on her lips. Her eyes drifted to his lips, and she was tempted to kiss him. If only she could be that bold again. But as he'd made clear, Frankie was between them, and he always would be. "Thank you."

Morgan wondered what she was thinking as she gazed up at him. He came close to kissing her like he had at the way station. But he needed to take control over this attraction, or whatever it was he was feeling for her. There was no sense tempting fate when nothing would change the situation between them.

Rose closed her eyes and within minutes she was asleep. He smiled as he watched her. It made him feel good to know she trusted him to look after her. He leaned over and lifted her legs onto the seat and positioned her head on his thigh. He didn't mind if she thought of him as her protector. He liked the way it made him feel. If she were his wife, he'd always protect her. There was no question he'd lay down his life for her. Heck, she wasn't his wife, and he already felt that way about her. He'd been prepared to kill two men if they'd so much as harmed a hair on her head.

What about the man between them? Frank

had had a chance to demonstrate if he had any moral fiber when she was injured, but he'd only been worried about protecting his own hide. Morgan would never reveal Frank's betrayal to Rose. It was important to him that she form her own opinion about Frank's character. There was no question in his mind that Rose would soon learn of Frank's true nature. He just didn't want her to be hurt in the process.

CHAPTER ELEVEN

"Granny's at the sheriff's house," the deputy said to Morgan and Rose. "She's been mighty worried about you."

Morgan picked up the valises and they walked to the sheriff's house next door. Morgan knocked on the door before he cracked it open. He didn't want Jack to get up if he was in bed.

Granny turned from the stove when she heard the door open. "Rose!" She ran across the room and wrapped her arms around her granddaughter. "How are you, child? The telegram said you were hurt."

"I'm fine. I just have some broken ribs, but thanks to Mr. LeMasters, I made it safe and sound."

Granny held her at arm's length and looked her over with tears in her eyes. "You are a welcome sight. You're nothing but skin and bones, and I think you need some good home cooking." She wiped her tears with her apron. "I'm so happy you are home. I've prayed every night for your safe return. I knew the Good Lord sent Morgan to watch over you."

"Granny, don't cry." Rose found herself tearing up at Granny's emotional outburst. Granny was a stalwart woman, not one given to tears. Seeing her cry made Rose feel guilty that she'd been away so long. She certainly hadn't expected her to look so much older, nor so frail. Granny had always been so healthy and strong, and she realized she'd never thought about her aging. "I'm so sorry I haven't come home before now."

They hugged again. "Nonsense, you're home now and that's what counts. I'm turning into a foolish old woman, crying at the least little thing. Just like Preacher. You remember how the smallest thing would make him cry."

Rose smiled through her tears, thinking of her grandfather. They would always tease him about the way he would become emotional over the least little thing.

Granny moved to Morgan and hugged him. "Thank you for looking after my Rose."

Morgan wrapped his arms around the older woman and held her. He saw how happy she was to see Rose, and it was nice to see her smile. "It was my pleasure." Morgan wasn't exaggerating; he'd enjoyed every moment alone with Rose. He was sorry she'd been injured, but it had given him time to get to know her. It was strange now that he thought about it. He'd known her since she was a little girl, but he'd never expected she'd become the one woman who would capture his attention these many years later.

Granny took Rose by the hand and turned toward Jack who was sitting up in his bed. "I told you she was a real beauty."

"I can't argue with you there," Jack said, thinking she was the loveliest woman he'd ever seen.

"Rose, you remember the sheriff," Granny said.

"Yes, I do. How are you?"

"Granny has been taking good care of me. I'm happy to see you are on the mend."

Morgan walked over and shook his hand. "Jack, glad to see you looking so good."

"Rose, come sit at the table while I finish lunch, and give the men some time to talk," Granny said, taking Rose by the hand. Granny figured Jack would want to hear about Frank's escape.

Jack pointed to the chair next to his bed. "Have a seat, Morgan."

As the women walked to the stove, Morgan overheard Rose ask Granny if she'd met the new pastor, Clay Hunt. He didn't hear Granny's response, but he heard Rose clearly when she said, "He is a wonderful man."

"Aren't you going to sit down?" Jack asked.

"Yeah," Morgan replied, but his mind was on Rose's comment. *So she thinks Clay Hunt is wonderful.*

It was impossible for Jack to have a private conversation with Morgan since his home was only one room, but he wanted to let him know Murph had told him how Frank and his gang escaped the hanging. "Murph came to see me when he rode in."

Morgan nodded in silent understanding. "Who shot you, Jack?"

"I don't know. We rode into Purgatory Canyon and they were waiting for us. We didn't see them, but they saw us." Jack glanced across the room to see if the women were talking. He lowered his voice, and said, "They got away, but we know for sure that's their hideout."

Morgan leaned forward, braced his elbows on his thighs, and quietly asked, "Do you think they might be waiting to meet Frank in that canyon?"

"I wouldn't be surprised. They are probably just one gang out of many hiding out in there. They can see us coming a long way off. It's a real witches' brew."

"Frank said he was headed to Mexico, but I don't believe him."

"When you stopped in Denver did you hear about the stagecoach robbery?" Jack asked.

Rose was sleeping when they stopped in Denver, so Morgan didn't leave the coach. "No."

"They were transporting a lot of money by coach, and they said one man pulled the job. No one saw his face, but they said he was a small fellow, and he sounded very young." Jack repeated everything he'd heard about the robbery from some of the local cowboys who had heard the details in a Denver saloon. "Hobb Devers was the driver, Cal Pickett was riding shotgun, and Boyd Larsen was inside the coach."

Morgan knew the men, and Cal and Boyd's reputations as excellent marksmen. They had a good record dealing with robberies. "And one man got the drop on them?"

"They didn't know it was one man." Jack explained the ploy the man used to make it appear he had accomplices. "But they said he was one heck of a shot. Even carried a pearl-handled pistol, so he must think himself to be a real outlaw."

"He must be pretty good to take those three men," Morgan agreed.

"Devers was winged. I didn't figure it was . . ." Jack turned his head to make sure the women weren't listening before he finished his thought. "I guess it could have been one of his men, because he's not small, and he doesn't sound young."

Morgan nodded, indicating he knew Jack meant Frank hadn't robbed the coach. He leaned closer and said, "They always rob as a group. If you hear any news about him, let me know. Otherwise, I'll ride to Purgatory Canyon soon."

"I may not be able to ride for a while," Jack said.

"Am I still deputized?"

"Yeah."

"Then I'm going after him." Morgan glanced at Rose and saw her carrying two plates in their direction. "I'll tell you more when we can talk."

While they ate their lunch, they discussed what was happening around town with all of the newcomers settling in the area. Not one word was mentioned about Frank, and for that, Morgan was thankful.

■ ■ ■ ■

"Granny, I'll take you and Rose to the farm," Morgan said when they were ready to leave.

"Morgan, the buckboard is out front. Webb picked Granny up earlier. Just bring it back to the livery when you have time," Jack said.

Granny walked to Jack and patted him on the shoulder. "Don't you do too much. I'll be back tomorrow to check on you."

"That's not necessary. I plan to start moving around more tomorrow. You stay home and visit with your granddaughter. If I need anything, I'll send Webb to the farm."

"You have enough food for a few days, so if you promise me you'll take care, I'll trust you," Granny said.

"I'll be in town tomorrow and I'll look in on him," Morgan said. He'd planned on coming back to town tomorrow so he could speak to Jack alone.

Granny trusted Morgan's judgment. "Good. I know you will let me know if he is resting."

Morgan grinned at Jack. "Yes, ma'am, I will."

On the way to the farm, Granny noticed

how considerate Morgan was of Rose's condition. He'd asked her several times if she was doing okay, or if she needed to stop. To Granny's surprise, her granddaughter couldn't keep her eyes off of Morgan. Knowing Rose had always shied away from Morgan when she was younger, she wondered what had transpired between the two. If she didn't know better, her granddaughter had the look of a woman in love. Granny hoped it wasn't because Morgan had been the one to look after her while she was injured. One thing for sure, she didn't want Rose to have her heart broken. As much as Rose adored Frank, Morgan hated him just as much, and Granny couldn't see Morgan changing his mind. Morgan was a good man, but he could be a hard man. Admittedly, it wasn't without cause. But Morgan had harbored this anger a long time, and he hadn't had gentleness in his life. Rose could give him that if he would let her. She wondered if Rose might help Morgan forget about his vendetta against Frank, and allow the law to handle him. It was probably wishful thinking. Perhaps if Rose had been here before Frank shot Joseph Longbow there might have been a chance. Frank's past transgressions might have been forgotten, but shooting Joseph was something Morgan would never get over. No amount of wishing would make it so.

"Have you seen Joseph?" Morgan asked.

"Yes. As a matter of fact, he came to look at the sheriff's wound," Granny replied.

"You mean he actually rode into town?" Morgan knew Joseph liked Jack, but he didn't normally go into town for any reason.

"Yes. I asked the deputy to go get him, and when he arrived at your ranch, Joseph was waiting for him."

That didn't surprise Morgan. Joseph had a sixth sense that no one could explain. "I guess that hard head of his suffered no permanent damage."

"No, he's fine."

"Granny, how's Stevie? You've said very little about him in your letters," Rose asked.

Granny wasn't sure how to respond, but she supposed it was time for truthfulness. "Stevie told me he's not going to stay on the farm. He says he hates farm work."

"What does he plan on doing?" Rose asked.

"You'll have to ask him." Granny wasn't going to bring up Frank's name, at least not for a while.

Morgan pulled in front of the house, and was surprised by the condition of the farm. He figured his men had had little time to come over and help her since he'd been gone. But he didn't comment as he climbed out of the buckboard and helped the women to the ground.

Granny opened the door and invited Morgan inside.

Morgan grabbed Rose's valises from the buckboard. "I'll carry these inside, but I need to get to the ranch."

He set the valises inside the front door and looked at Rose. "Take care of those ribs. It'll take a few more days for them to heal properly."

"Thank you for everything, Mr. LeMasters," Rose said.

Granny glanced from Rose to Morgan. Something was definitely going on there. "Rose, go on and sit down. I'll see Morgan out."

Rose had the feeling Granny wanted to speak to Morgan alone, so she said goodbye to him.

Morgan tipped his hat and walked out the door with Granny.

"Why don't you go ahead and tell me what happened?" Granny asked as soon as they reached the buckboard.

"I'm sure Jack told you Frank got away," Morgan said.

Granny stared up at him. "What I want to

know is how he slipped through your fingers, Morgan. You aren't a careless man, and I think there is more to this story than anyone is telling."

"Your granddaughter was on the stagecoach when they happened on us as we were about to hang Frank. You have her to thank for keeping Frank alive a while longer." Morgan wasn't angry about his decision not to hang Frank in front of Rose. He'd made it, and he would have kept his word to take Frank to jail and let a judge deal with him. But it wouldn't happen the next time.

"God works in strange ways," Granny said softly.

Morgan looked at her. "What do you mean by that?"

"Of all the people to place in your path to keep you from seeking your vengeance, don't you wonder why it was Rose?"

Morgan shook his head. "Granny, you call it vengeance, I call it justice." He took a deep breath and softened his tone. "We've been over this. Why don't we agree to disagree? It was a coincidence Rose was on that stagecoach."

Placing her bony fingers on Morgan's forearm, she said, "I might understand your feelings if you'd tell me what happened between you and Frank years ago."

"Frank can tell you," Morgan said. He didn't want to talk about that day on his ranch. To this day, every time he thought of it, he wanted to kill Frank.

"You're a good man, Morgan. But you've got to let some things go, or they'll eat you alive and keep you from true happiness. You recall the Bible says vengeance is the Lord's and He will repay."

"I won't let this go, Granny. You remember the verse, 'an eye for an eye.' " Morgan had never given much thought as to whether he was a happy man or not. He was too busy working to worry about such things. "Maybe true happiness isn't for everyone."

"You don't believe that, Morgan. What about Rose?"

Morgan arched his brow at her. "What about Rose?"

"I saw how you two were looking at each other. I'm not so old that I can't see that glimmer in your eye when you look at her. I've always thought you two would make a fine match."

Morgan wished it were as easy as Granny made it sound. "Rose is a lovely young woman, but like I said, I won't let this go with Frank. Rose loves her brother, and she would never forgive me for what I will do when I find him." Morgan had a question of his own. "Why is it she doesn't seem to know anything about Frank? She seems to look at him through a child's eyes. I've been wondering why you haven't told her the truth about him."

Granny had often alluded to Frank's darker side, but she'd never told her granddaughters the unvarnished truth about the evil that resided inside Frank's heart. Maybe she'd hoped her prayers would get the Lord's attention and He'd put Frank on the right path. She finally figured the Lord needed Frank's cooperation, and that was one thing Frank would not relinquish. "I didn't know how to tell her the truth. The girls were crazy about Frank, particularly Rose. She worshipped the ground he walked on. I just didn't have it in me to break her heart."

Morgan heard the sadness in her words. He was in no position to pass judgment on Granny's decision. He hadn't told Rose about Frank threatening her life when she was unconscious. He didn't want to hurt Rose if he could avoid it. He understood the reason Granny didn't tell her the truth. "I'm sure she will find out soon enough."

"Sadly, I'm sure she will."

They were silent for a minute, then Granny said, "Since you're going back to see Jack tomorrow, why don't you stop for dinner on your way home?"

Morgan accepted her offer, and as Granny walked inside the house, she started formulating a plan. She might not be able to help Frank, but she would make sure he didn't ruin Rose's chance for happiness. She found Rose in the room she'd shared with her sisters, unpacking her clothing. "You should have waited for me to carry your valise."

"It's not heavy, and I am feeling much better. You don't need to worry about me."

Granny took the dress Rose was holding. "Now sit down and rest. I will put your things away."

Rose took hold of Granny's hand. "I'm not tired. Sit with me a moment so we can chat." Rose had noticed the sad state of the farm as soon as they rode in. Granny had always had a huge garden, but now it wasn't even a quarter of its normal size. "Granny, hasn't Stevie been helping at all on the farm?"

Granny hated to give Rose depressing news on her first day home, but it couldn't be helped. She didn't know if Stevie had left again, or if he would be home later. "I guess you know what Frank has been doing since you were about to see him hang. He doesn't come around much. And Stevie . . .

well, he hasn't been around much over the last year either. He leaves all the time, and won't tell me where he is going. I never know when he will return. When he is here, he doesn't do anything but sleep and eat."

"Granny, is it true what Mr. LeMasters says about Frankie?"

Seeing the hope in her eyes, Granny hated to reveal the truth about her brother, but there was no way around it. "Yes. Frank and his men have been rustling cattle from Morgan for a long time. Oh, no one could prove it was Frank before, but everyone knew it was him. This last time, Frank made a big mistake. Joseph Longbow saw them and Frank shot him. Thankfully, he just grazed Joseph's head."

"Are you sure it was Frankie?" Rose realized she questioned everyone's word when it came to her brother.

Granny squeezed her hand. "Yes, honey, it was Frank. I'm not sure all he's done is rustle cattle. Frank's always got money, and Lord knows he's never worked for it."

Rose's worst fears were confirmed. Deep down she knew Morgan had told her the truth about her brother. Tears streamed over her cheeks. "Granny, what are we going to do?"

"I've tried everything I know to get Frank

to listen to reason, but he refuses. Now, I'll tell you what I'm going to do."

Rose looked at her expectantly. "What? Morgan is determined to hang Frank. He told me as much."

"I know. But we can't continue to worry about Frank, and what might happen. His fate is in the hands of the Lord. What we can do, and what we will do, is make sure he doesn't keep you from your happiness."

Rose was puzzled by her response. "What do you mean?"

"Why don't you tell me what happened in Kansas?"

Rose told her about everything that happened, leaving out the part where Morgan kissed her.

"So you were unconscious when Frank left?" Granny asked.

"Yes."

Granny was furious at Frank for leaving Rose without knowing if she would even survive her injuries. She thanked God for Morgan LeMasters. "So Morgan looked after you the entire time instead of going after Frank when he had the chance?"

"Yes. He was very good to me. After what you've told me about Frank, it's hard to believe Morgan treated me so well. He had every reason to leave me there. I was hoping he was wrong about Frankie."

Granny smiled at her. "Are you in love with Morgan because he was kind and took care of you, or do you love him because he is a good man?"

Expelling a loud breath, tears welled in her eyes again. "Oh, Granny." She wasn't surprised Granny saw right to the core of the problem. "I think I love him because he is a good man. But I can't turn my back on Frankie."

"Frank is not allowed to ruin your happiness. That's where I draw the line."

Chapter Twelve

Joseph Longbow was leading horses from the stable when Morgan reined in at the ranch. Morgan jumped down from the buckboard and took Faithful's reins from him. "How are you, Joseph?"

"I am well. You've been gone a long time."

"Yes, I'm glad to be home. I'm sure Murph told you Frank Langtry is still on the loose."

"He will be back," Joseph said.

Morgan's expression grew grim. "Probably. I want you to be alert at all times. Don't give him another chance to take a shot at that hard head of yours."

"His aim is not true," Joseph said.

"That may be, but don't give him another opportunity to improve. They may be hiding out at Purgatory Canyon. Do you know the place?"

"I have been there many times."

"Can you draw me a map?"

"It is not a place for a man alone," Joseph told him. "He will come to you if you wait."

"I'm not sure I can wait. Frank was willing to kill his own sister to escape." Morgan explained the situation after the stagecoach accident, and Frank's indifference to Rose's condition.

"It will not go well on his next journey," Joseph said.

Morgan figured Joseph was speaking of Frank's journey in the hereafter. "He's a danger to all of those who get in his way, especially his family. I need to find him first, and if that's in Purgatory Canyon, then I'm going."

The two men discussed the drawbacks of entering the canyon. Joseph disagreed with Morgan's plans, but having been with him a long time, he understood his determination when he set his mind to a goal. Joseph owed Morgan his life, and he'd remained his steadfast friend. Joseph had been shot by a soldier when he was out hunting, and he'd ended up in the pines, where Morgan found him. Morgan had cared for him, and he'd lived on his ranch since that day. He didn't want his friend to ride into a trap in Purgatory Canyon. "I will ride with you."

Morgan shook his head. "No way. I can't even believe you rode into town. It's not safe now for you to be away from the ranch. If soldiers see you, they may shoot first and ask questions later. After what happened at Little Bighorn, no one is going to listen to reason. All sides have dug in their heels."

"I was not there," Joseph said.

"That will make little difference to some."

The next morning, Morgan drove the buckboard back to town, and stopped to visit with Jack to discuss his plans. They could speak freely without Granny and Rose present. Even though Granny knew of Frank's outlaw ways, Jack worried that she might accidentally let something slip in front of Stevie about their plans to capture his brother.

"Joseph hasn't been to Purgatory Canyon in years, but he told me as much as he remembers. Tell me how you rode in."

Jack took a piece of paper and drew their route the day he was shot. "Morgan, you can't go in there alone. If Frank is hiding out there, you can be assured he knows the area like the back of his hand. Even if you know where you're going, I think it's almost impossible not to be seen."

Morgan stood and started pacing the room. "I'll get in. I'm going to find Frank. He's not going to get away with what he's done this time."

Jack watched Morgan pace the room for a few minutes. Morgan seemed edgy, and that was out of character for him. Ordinarily, he was cool and calm even in the midst of the most challenging circumstances. He had a feeling something other than finding Frank was on his mind. "Murph told me Frank threatened his sister's life, and that was how he got away."

Morgan stopped moving, faced Jack and shook his head. "He actually pointed a gun to her head and said he would shoot her if I didn't drop my gun. Can you believe that sorry . . ." He didn't finish his thought, he just shook his head. It was still difficult for him to believe the depth of Frank's cold-heartedness.

"You think he would have done it, or was he bluffing?"

"He wouldn't have hesitated. I could see it in his eyes." He'd seen that look in Frank's cold eyes once before.

Jack gave a low whistle. "That's one callous man. What did Rose say?"

"She was unconscious at the time. I didn't tell her, and I told the men not to tell her. Even Deke Sullivan and Dutch Malloy didn't agree with Frank. I'm sure Deke let our horses go so we could get her to a doctor. I'll tell the judge what he did, so he may not hang. I was willing to bring Frank in to stand trial, but not now. Not only did he shoot Joseph, who's done nothing more than try to help Frank through the years, but he threatened to kill his own sister after she'd just saved him from hanging. Frank's a dead man."

"Don't you think Rose has a right to know what he did?" Jack thought if a family member had threatened him, he'd want to know.

Morgan started pacing again. "She's crazy about Frank. I don't think she believed one word when I told her he'd rustled my cattle." He ran a hand over his face. "I just didn't want to hurt her when I wasn't even sure she was going to make it. She looked pretty bad the first few days."

There was something about Morgan's expression when he talked about Rose that made Jack think he had more than a passing interest in her.

"She sure is a beautiful woman, and sweet too."

Morgan nodded. That was the problem. Rose was too beautiful and too sweet. He couldn't get her out of his mind. Maybe he wanted to go after Frank right away and get it over with so he would stop thinking about her. Rose would never speak to him again once he killed Frank. The way he saw it, there was no reason to delay the inevitable. But why did he accept Granny's invitation to dinner tonight if he wanted to push Rose away? He could easily avoid her if that was what he really wanted. Who was he kidding?

"You two spent a lot of time together," Jack commented.

Morgan heard Jack speak, but he wasn't paying attention. "Huh?"

When Morgan glanced at him, Jack raised a brow. "I said you two spent a lot of time together."

"Yeah."

"Well, how did you two get along?"

"Fine."

"You couldn't keep your eyes off her yesterday," Jack said.

Morgan shrugged. He sat back down in the chair across from Jack. "I seem to recall you gawking at her a time or two."

"What man wouldn't?"

Morgan conceded that point. But that didn't mean he liked it, or would ever get used to men staring at her if she was his wife. "Yeah, when she marries, her husband will have his hands full keeping the men away."

"Since you don't seem too interested, I

guess you wouldn't mind if another man courted her."

Morgan glared at him. "*Another man —* meaning — you?" Jack wasn't the only man who would be chasing after Rose. The *wonderful* pastor came to mind.

Jack grinned. "Yeah."

Morgan found himself getting riled. "I didn't say I wasn't interested."

"Are you — interested?"

"You serious about courting her?" Morgan countered.

"I could be," Jack said, still smiling from ear to ear. "But I'd want to know your intentions. After all, you two already spent a lot of time together."

Morgan gave him a look like he thought he was the dumbest son-of-a-buck alive. "I'm going to hang her brother, Jack."

"Yeah, there is that." Jack couldn't stop grinning. "I guess that's not the perfect way to start a relationship."

Despite the situation, Morgan let out a chuckle.

"Of course, you could wait for me to be able to ride, and I'll hang him, so you could pin it on me."

"I already told her I am going to hang him."

Jack knew he was getting to the bottom of

what was really on Morgan's mind. "If it wasn't for the small matter of hanging her brother, would you be interested in being husband material?"

Morgan stared at him for a long time before he expelled a loud sigh. "I would have found a preacher before we ever got back to Whispering Pines."

Just as he suspected, Rose Langtry was what was really on Morgan's mind. Jack thought he'd never see the day when Morgan would have his tail tied in a knot by a woman. Through the years, Jack had seen all the single women in town tempt Morgan with their flirtations and fine meals, but he had never taken the bait. Morgan was a man who had a lot to offer a woman. He was a hard worker with a beautiful ranch to show for it. And he was a man of integrity, a man who stood for something. After Jack took one look at Rose yesterday, he understood why his friend was smitten. No woman in town could compare to her beauty.

Even though Morgan was in an untenable situation, Jack couldn't help ribbing him just a little. "Seeing as how it couldn't work out between you two, I guess I can ask Rose to dinner on occasion."

Morgan didn't like the sound of that. He'd been told by some of the ladies that they considered Jack quite handsome. And he knew Jack received as many dinner invitations as he did. On the other hand, Rose would be getting a good man if Jack was really interested. At least, she'd have a man who could protect her, and that was important given Rose would always draw unwanted advances simply because she was beautiful.

When Morgan didn't respond, Jack said, "Morgan?"

"Yeah, I guess you could invite her to dinner."

Jack was not expecting that response. "You know Granny said she thought Rose was perfect for you."

Morgan's head snapped up. "What? She told you that? I hadn't even seen Rose in five years, and when she left Whispering Pines she was a young girl."

"While Granny nursed me along, she talked to me about the girls. She said Rose was perfect for you, and Adelaide was meant for me. I just wonder if Adelaide turned out as pretty as Rose."

Morgan didn't say it, but he didn't think any woman would be as pretty as Rose. "The way you're talking, you sound ready to get hitched."

"I'm not opposed to the idea. We aren't

getting any younger, and I'd like some boys. If you grew up like I did, then you'd understand what having a family of your own means."

Morgan remembered Jack telling him he'd spent time in an orphanage, and had never met his real family. His life in the orphanage hadn't been an easy one. He was subjected to routine beatings for small infractions of the rules. At twelve years of age, he had decided there had to be a better way of life, so he ran away. He'd lived by his own wits from that day on. For Jack to have made something of himself, and become a lawman instead of an outlaw, was a tribute to his strong character. "You'd make a fine father."

"Thanks." He waited a beat, then said, "I'd say it'd be a real pleasure to have kids with Rose." Jack half expected Morgan to throw something at him for the way he was baiting him.

That did it. Morgan jumped up and started pacing again. Morgan felt like pounding his friend's face for even thinking of having kids with Rose. If Jack was thinking about that, then he knew what else he was thinking. "You got any whiskey in the place?"

"Nope, I drank it all. For the pain."

"Dang it, Jack!"

"You can run down to the saloon if you want a drink of whiskey that badly."

Morgan stalked to the stove and tossed some beans in Jack's coffeepot. "You know it's not that."

"Then what is it?" Jack was beginning to take pity on his friend.

"This is driving me crazy."

Jack wanted to laugh. "What's driving you crazy?"

"Rose."

"Why don't you compromise and bring Frank in if you're all-fired set to go find him now? That way, Rose wouldn't hold it against you when the judge sentences him to the gallows."

Morgan couldn't say that alternative hadn't entered his mind. But he'd lived his life by his code of right and wrong. Frank had been a thorn in his side for too long. "I just can't do it, Jack. I made my mind up a long time ago what I was going to do to Frank if he ever harmed anyone I care about. Trying to kill Joseph was the last straw. I'm not changing now. He's going to get what he deserves. I owe him for . . . well, let's just say, I should have taken care of him before he shot Joseph. I don't think Rose would think much better of me, knowing I had a hand in his demise one way or the other."

The coffee started bubbling and Morgan poured two cups. He decided to stop thinking about Rose once and for all because he was unwilling to change his mind about Frank. It was best that he just move on. He handed Jack a cup of coffee.

Jack took a sip and said, "You make good coffee."

"I've had years of experience." They sat in silence for a few minutes. Morgan's mind kept drifting back to Rose, and Jack was giving him time to talk if he wanted. Seeing the pain etched on Morgan's face, Jack didn't have the heart to badger him further.

Finally, Morgan asked, "Have you met the new preacher?" Morgan thought of Rose's description of Clay Hunt. "Rose traveled with him, and she says he's a wonderful man."

Jack thought he heard a hint of jealousy in Morgan's voice, but he let that pass. "Yeah, he came here to meet me. Granny was here, so we had a nice talk. I like him."

"Yeah." Morgan hated to admit it, but he liked him too. "His name seems familiar, but I'm certain I've never met him before."

"I'm not surprised his name is familiar; he used to be an outlaw." Jack told him about Clay Hunt's past, but he was convinced the man had changed, and was now the man of faith he claimed to be.

Morgan agreed with Jack's opinion. Clay seemed sincere in his beliefs. "He had a gun in his valise, but he told me he never carries one."

"I imagine he'd use it if necessary," Jack said.

Morgan's thoughts seemed to be flitting all over the place, but somehow they all revolved around the Langtrys. "What's going on with Stevie? Granny said she doesn't see much of him. He told her he doesn't plan on staying on the farm."

"I'm not sure. I haven't seen him in a long time. Granny told me all he does is target practice. From what she said, he's going to ride with Frank when he comes back."

Morgan hated to hear that news. He'd hoped one of the Langtry boys would turn out to be a good man like Preacher. "He thinks Frank is going to go free?"

"Sounds like it. Granny said he's not helping at all on the farm."

"I'm planning on doing some work over there tonight after dinner. It's really run-down."

"I'm sure she'll appreciate that. I think Granny is a lot more worried than she's letting on. It seems like she's come to terms with Frank's fate, but she was hoping it wasn't too late for Stevie."

Morgan had tied Faithful to the back of the buckboard on the way to town, so he was happy to be back in the saddle again. He couldn't remember a time in his entire life he'd gone so long without being on horseback. Riding Faithful felt like home to him. It seemed to him that he did his best thinking on horseback. He'd allowed plenty of time to ride to Granny's, and it gave him time to think about finding Frank.

After what Jack said about Stevie, Morgan wondered if Stevie knew where Frank and his gang were hiding out. Instead of riding on a wild-goose chase, it might prove to be a wiser course to follow Stevie and find out how he was spending his time. Granny said Stevie was often gone for days at a time. Stevie could be riding to Frank's hideout to see if he'd made it back.

Morgan was about to take the turnoff on the trail leading to the Langtry farm when he saw a man on horseback about a hundred feet off the trail to Denver. The man on the horse was talking to someone inside a buggy. As Morgan rode closer, he recognized the horse and rider. The very man he'd been thinking about: Stevie Langtry. Morgan rode slowly in their direction, and they were so engrossed in their conversation that they didn't hear him approach.

When Stevie realized someone was behind him, he drew his pistol and turned to point it at the rider. Immediately recognizing Morgan, he quickly holstered his weapon.

"LeMasters," Stevie said.

Morgan thought Stevie's target practice was paying off by the speed with which he drew his pistol. A pearl-handled pistol. "Problem?"

"Nope. I was headed to the farm when I saw this gentleman stopped here. I thought maybe his horse threw a shoe. Turns out he was just out for a ride on a pretty day."

Morgan looked inside the buggy at the spectacled man wearing a bowler hat. He didn't recognize him, so he said, "Morgan LeMasters."

The man smiled. "Pleasure. Well, I must be on my way. I'll say good-day to you gentlemen."

As the man rode away, Morgan took note of the horse harnessed to the buggy. It was hot and lathered. The man had pushed him hard for some distance, certainly not out for a leisurely ride. "I don't believe I've ever seen him before. Who is he?"

"I don't know. I've never seen him before either. We were just passing the time."

Though Morgan couldn't prove it, he didn't think Stevie's words rang true. The two of them were having a serious conversation. That pearl-handled pistol had his mind racing. Stevie was a little man, and he sounded younger than he was. *No way,* Morgan thought. Stevie wasn't smart enough to pull off a robbery like that on his own. He couldn't judge Stevie by his brother's criminal ways. "You say you were headed to the farm?"

"I figure I'll get there just about suppertime."

"Looks like we are going the same way. Granny invited me to dinner." From the sour look on Stevie's face, Morgan didn't think he was too pleased about the invite. That was just too bad. "Have you seen your sister?"

"Not yet."

So Stevie wasn't home last night. "She was in a nasty accident."

"Granny told me. I reckon she's okay if she made it here."

Morgan didn't care for Stevie's callous tone. Stevie sounded as ruthless as Frank, and that made Morgan want to knock him off his horse. "She's better now, but she still has a ways to go."

"So how did you end up bringing her home?"

"I was with her and your brother when the accident happened. You haven't seen your brother, have you?"

"Nope. I expect he's in Mexico by now."

"Why do you say that?"

"Why should he hang around here in this no-nothing town? I don't reckon he's hankering to get hung."

Morgan had to give him credit. Not only was Stevie evasive, he was a pretty smooth liar. "I guess you know the sheriff was shot."

"That's what Granny said. Guess he shouldn't have gone in that canyon. I hear a lot of outlaws hide out in there."

"Maybe it's time someone cleaned it out." Morgan clicked Faithful into a full gallop. He couldn't take more of Stevie's attitude, or he might be inclined to follow through on his instincts and knock him off his horse. He figured that wouldn't be a wise course if he didn't want to be disinvited to dinner.

CHAPTER THIRTEEN

Dinner was an interesting affair with Morgan, Granny, and Rose conversing pleasantly, and Stevie sitting like a sullen child, not uttering a word. Even though Stevie hadn't seen Rose in years, he'd had very little to say to her. Morgan was relieved when Stevie finished his dinner and left the table.

"Granny, thank you for dinner. I don't think I've ever eaten so much," Morgan said.

"It's a pleasure to have you here," Granny said. His pleasant company aside, Granny planned to make sure Rose and Morgan were together as much as possible until they figured out a way to work out their differences regarding Frank. "I know how much you like fried chicken. I hope you saved room for some of Rose's cobbler. You were always partial to her blackberry cobblers, and she made one especially for you to-night."

Morgan looked at Rose and smiled. "Thank you. I always did like blackberry the best. But if it is okay with you, Rose, I'll have a piece after I've done some work. I want to get some things done before it gets dark."

"Of course, but it's not necessary that you do any work. I'm sure you've already had a full day. I'll be able to help out in a few days." Rose planned to speak with Stevie tonight to insist he do some work around the farm. She'd already made a list of things that needed to be done.

"Rose is right, Morgan. You are our guest. I didn't invite you here to make you work."

Morgan winked at Granny. "Granny, if I don't work off some of this dinner, Faithful will refuse to carry me home. Besides, I want to be able to do justice to that cobbler." He excused himself from the table and walked out the back door.

The first thing he did was check on Faithful to make sure he was still grazing. Seeing his horse was enjoying himself, he headed to the stable to get some tools to repair the fence around Granny's garden. After that, he planned to repair some boards on the stable that were barely hanging on. If he had time tonight, he planned to build Granny a handrail on her porch stairs. He'd noticed she had difficulty negotiating the steps without a rail.

As soon as he entered the stable he saw Stevie's horse. He hadn't removed his saddle when he rode in. Morgan was tempted to go in the house and drag Stevie to the stable to care for his animal properly. The only reason he didn't was because of Granny and Rose. Morgan removed the saddle and blanket from the horse, and grabbed a brush. The horse hadn't been groomed in days, maybe even weeks. The poor animal had sores on his back from lack of care. Once Morgan brushed off the grime, he washed and applied ointment on his sores. Seeing the condition of the filthy stalls, Morgan led the horse outside, gave him some fresh water and let him graze with Faithful. He went back inside the stable and mucked out the four stalls. Since Frank was no longer at the farm, Morgan figured they only had the one horse, but at least all of the stalls would be clean. After spreading hay, and pumping fresh water for the stalls, he searched for some grain. The longer he worked, the angrier he became. Stevie was just like his big brother. He didn't have a care for anyone or anything but himself.

Morgan didn't like the way Stevie spoke to Granny and Rose during dinner, but he didn't think it was his place to say anything. If Stevie had been as rude at his dinner table, he'd set him straight in a second. And he couldn't tolerate any man who would abuse an animal.

Morgan was leaving the stable with a hammer and some nails to work on the fence when Stevie walked toward him. Stevie passed him without saying a word, so Morgan turned around and followed him back inside the stable.

Stevie reached for his saddle, but Morgan slammed the hammer down so close to his hand that Stevie jerked away. "You're not taking that horse out tonight."

"This ain't your ranch, you don't give orders around here," Stevie said.

"Maybe not, but you're still not saddling that animal." Morgan glared at him, almost hoping Stevie would take a swing at him, or draw that fancy pistol. "You've abused that animal and he needs rest."

"What I do with my horse ain't none of your business," Stevie snarled. With his sore arm, he was in no condition to fight Morgan. And even if he was, Morgan was a big man, and Stevie was smart enough to know he couldn't take him in a fair fight. He'd never seen Morgan draw, but he'd heard he was fast. Still, Stevie was proud of his quick draw, and he told himself he could take Morgan.

Morgan could see in Stevie's eyes he was calculating his next move. Morgan correctly assumed Stevie was trying to figure out if he was faster. "If you are looking for something to do, there's plenty of work that needs to be done around here. If you're determined to leave, you can walk wherever you are going. Your choice." It came as no surprise to Morgan that Stevie decided to walk away. He walked toward the pine trees on the boundary of his ranch. Morgan didn't think Stevie had a destination in mind, he was just trying to put some distance between them. When Stevie veered away from the pines, Morgan chuckled. Most people avoided the area, either because of firsthand experience with strange incidents they'd encountered, or because of the stories they'd heard. He wondered what Stevie heard in the pines.

While Rose was washing the dishes, she saw Morgan lead Stevie's horse from the stable. She'd noticed how good he was with animals, but she didn't know why he was caring for Stevie's horse. Then she saw Stevie walking toward the stable. "Do you think Stevie is going to help Morgan?"

Granny looked out the window. "I hope so."

"He shouldn't have let the place get so run-down." Rose had been looking forward to seeing her brother, but he'd given her a cool reception tonight. She thought it may have been because Granny invited Morgan to dinner. Stevie knew his brother hated Morgan, so it was possible he felt disloyal, the same way she had felt initially. Judging by the few comments Stevie made tonight, he seemed to resent her for being gone for so many years. She felt as though she no longer knew her two brothers. "Stevie wasn't happy to see me. He certainly didn't like having Morgan to dinner, but that doesn't give him the right to be rude."

"I know he didn't want Morgan here. Don't let it trouble you, honey. I don't think anything makes Stevie happy." Granny had tolerated his surly attitude for a long time. "Frank has filled Stevie's head with lies about Morgan, but it is still my home, and I invite whom I please." As soon as Morgan left tonight, Granny planned to have another talk with Stevie. No matter how much she loved him, she wouldn't allow him to be rude to guests in their home.

"Do you think Stevie will go to church

tomorrow?"

Granny shook her head. "He has no interest. I don't even think he's read his Bible in years."

Rose and Granny exchanged a look when they saw Stevie walk away from the stable. They continued to stare out the window until Stevie was out of sight. They saw Morgan walk to the garden and start working on the fence.

The women finished cleaning the kitchen, and decided to sit on the porch and chat while they waited for Morgan, who had finished the garden fence and moved on to work on the stable. Rose couldn't keep her eyes off of him as he worked, and she was disappointed when he walked inside the stable. They could hear him sawing wood, and about thirty minutes later, he exited the barn and walked toward the porch carrying some wood and tools. "Ladies," he said as he started digging a hole in the dirt by the front porch.

"Morgan, it's going to be dark soon. What in the world are you doing?" Granny asked.

"Putting up a handrail."

Granny was so moved by his thoughtfulness that she found herself near tears.

Rose couldn't believe Morgan had been so considerate. "Thank you. I was thinking this morning that Granny needed a railing for those stairs."

"I really appreciate this, Morgan. It will make climbing those stairs a lot easier," Granny said as she stood. "I'll put on some fresh coffee to go with that cobbler. If you two young people don't mind, I'm a bit tired and I think I'll go to bed. The new pastor was kind enough to say he would come out early to pick me up for his first sermon. Are you going to church in the morning, Morgan?"

"No, ma'am, I have a lot of work to catch up on tomorrow." Morgan wondered if Rose was going to church with Clay and Granny.

"Remember, tomorrow is the day of rest, Morgan. Your work will wait until Monday. But I told Rose she should stay home tomorrow and rest instead of riding in the buckboard. She'll probably be feeling more like herself next week." She stood and kissed Rose's cheek. "Keep an eye on the coffee."

Morgan stopped digging long enough to say, "Thank you for dinner."

Granny surprised him when she walked to the edge of the step, leaned over and gave him a kiss on the cheek. "You've earned enough dinners for a month. Good night."

"Night." Morgan watched her walk in the house. Granny made him feel like a little boy who had done something good. He saw Rose watching him, and he said, "She's some lady."

"Yes, she is." She waited for him to say more, but when he didn't, she asked, "Where did Stevie go?"

Morgan scooped up another shovelful of soil. "I don't know. But I wouldn't let him take that horse out tonight. He's in bad shape. And if you have any say over Stevie, don't let him take that animal out for a few days. Stevie doesn't need to be on a horse until he learns how to respect them."

Rose never expected her brother would abuse an animal. But she didn't doubt Morgan's word. "I'll speak to him."

It was dark by the time Morgan finished his work. Rose had kept the coffee warm, and when he came inside, she placed a huge piece of cobbler in a bowl.

"Does coffee keep you awake at night?"

"No, ma'am. After a full day on the ranch, nothing could keep me awake."

She placed a steaming cup in front of him. "You must be tired." After spending time on the road with him, she'd noticed he was up before dawn each morning and went to bed late.

"I won't have trouble sleeping tonight."

He took a bite of cobbler. "This is really good."

"Thank you." She sat across from him.

He noticed she wasn't eating. "Aren't you going to have a piece?"

"No, I get tired of eating my cobblers."

Morgan raised his brows at her. "Really?" He didn't know how anyone could get tired of eating something so good.

Once Morgan finished his dessert, he stood and reached for his hat. He hated to leave, but it was late and he needed to get home.

Rose walked outside with him, hoping he might kiss her again. "Thank you for everything, especially for the rail."

"Thank you for the cobbler." Morgan told himself to step off the porch and put some distance between them because he really wanted a taste of her for dessert. He didn't listen to his little voice; instead he turned to face her. "How are the ribs feeling?"

"I'm already moving much better."

"Good." He took a step closer. She looked so pretty in the moonlight. Why couldn't he listen to himself and stay away from her? He stepped back and settled his Stetson on his head. He removed his Stetson again. "Rose."

She looked up at him. "Yes?"

He stopped thinking about why he shouldn't do what he wanted to do, and took her in his arms and kissed her. He purposefully kissed her in a way that let her know she was his, in a way he didn't think the *wonderful* pastor would kiss her. It wasn't a first-kiss kind of kiss, and her response to him numbed his mind. Just like that day at the way station, she threaded her fingers in his hair, and held him to her as tightly as he was holding her. They were so caught up in the sensations of their bodies melded together that they were oblivious to the world around them. With some difficulty, and fighting against his own desire to continue, Morgan forced his lips from hers. He needed to put a halt to what was happening before he couldn't stop.

His mind was struggling against his desire, but a sound behind him brought him to his senses. He heard someone walking near the porch. In one quick motion, he pushed Rose behind him and pulled his gun. His pistol was aimed directly at Stevie's nose.

Stevie smirked. "Looks like I interrupted something."

"Yes, you did," Morgan said, holstering his gun. "That's a good way to get shot."

Stevie didn't move. He stopped on the step and stared at them with undisguised hostility.

Morgan saw the hate in his eyes. Ignoring Stevie, Morgan turned back to Rose. "Thank you for dinner, Rose. I especially liked dessert."

"Thank you for all of your hard work," Rose said. She was sorry Stevie walked up when he did. Not only did she want more of Morgan's kisses, but she felt things were left unsaid between them.

Morgan started to step off the porch, but Stevie didn't move. Morgan brushed against Stevie's left arm and saw he noticeably winced. He'd just taken a few steps from the house when he heard Stevie say to Rose, "What are you cozying up to him for? You better be doing it to keep the rope off Frankie's neck. Aren't you smart enough to know he's just hanging around to get what he can off you, and to get to Frankie? Or don't you care about Frankie anymore?"

Morgan turned around and stalked back to Stevie. "Whatever happens between us is our business, not yours. If you have any questions or comments, you can say them to me. But I better never hear you speak disrespectfully to your sister again."

"You like to give orders, don't you?" Stevie said.

"If that's how you want to take it, that's

fine. Just remember what I said." Morgan turned around and walked away. He heard the door open and close, but he knew it was Rose who had walked inside. There was no doubt in his mind that Stevie was still watching him. He didn't like leaving Rose alone with Stevie, but he couldn't exactly pick her up and cart her off to his ranch. He didn't know Stevie well, and that was what troubled him. Rose had been away so long that she didn't know him either. Morgan had a feeling Stevie could be every bit as dangerous as Frank, but not as overt in his actions. He wondered if Granny was afraid of her grandsons.

Granny said she was going to church in the morning, and Morgan figured Stevie wouldn't be going with her. That meant he'd be in the house alone with Rose if he didn't take off to look for Frank. Morgan didn't like the thought of Rose being alone with him.

Pulling aside the lace curtain on her bedroom window, Rose saw Morgan light the lantern by the stable door. He led Stevie's horse inside before he saddled his horse. She'd been so shocked by Stevie's outburst that she didn't remember if she'd even said good-bye to Morgan. She could see Stevie standing on the step, so she wouldn't go back outside. She didn't understand what was wrong with Stevie, but tomorrow morning she planned to have a talk with him. If his attitude today was an indication of what she would face come morning, he probably wouldn't stand for her butting into his business. But one thing was certain: She was going to demand he help Granny on the farm, whether he liked it or not. He wasn't going to come and go without a by-your-leave, not offering a fair day's work. He was a man, and it was time he started acting like one and assume some responsibilities. Obviously, Frankie would never be around again to lend a hand. Granny had cared for all of them in their time of need when she could have easily sent them to an orphanage. Now Granny was the one needing help, and Rose was going to see to it that her life was easier now. She deserved to enjoy her waning years. It was difficult for Rose to believe her brothers cared so little for Granny and didn't respect the sacrifices she'd made for them.

The light by the stable was extinguished, and Rose saw Morgan ride in the direction of the pines. It didn't surprise her that he wasn't afraid to ride through there even in the dark. It occurred to her she'd never asked him what he heard when he rode through the trees.

Thinking of the many hours she'd searched for the people who sang the songs she'd heard as a child brought a smile to her lips. She wondered if she would still hear the songs these many years later.

Rose dropped the curtain, walked to her bureau, and picked up her Bible. Granny said Stevie no longer read his Bible and that troubled her. Hopefully, she could find a way to get through to him. She prayed it wasn't too late to keep him from following in Frankie's footsteps.

CHAPTER FOURTEEN

By the time Morgan got home and finished taking care of Faithful, it was near midnight and he was yawning. He still needed a bath, so once in the kitchen he warmed some water and filled the tub he'd carried from the back porch. He relaxed in the water and sipped his glass of whiskey. When he almost fell asleep in the water, he knew it was time to finish up and go to bed.

He walked upstairs in the buff with his holster slung over his shoulder, carrying his boots and hat. If he ever got married, he figured he wouldn't be able to walk around as he pleased anymore. Small price to pay to have a family. As he hooked his gun belt over the bedpost, he glanced out the window. It was a cool night, so he opened the window and looked out at the bright stars lighting up the dark sky. Everything looked peaceful, and the only sounds came from cattle lowing in the distance, and the occasional hoot of an owl.

When he climbed into bed, he stretched out on the feather mattress, appreciating the comfort it provided. He wondered if the bed would be large enough for two people. Why was he thinking about that? He knew why. He couldn't stop thinking about how Rose's body felt pressed to his tonight. He envisioned her snuggled up to him in his bed. The cold winter nights would be more enjoyable with her beside him.

He closed his eyes, willing himself to stop thinking about how it would feel to have Rose next to him. Problem was, he couldn't stop thinking about her. He was driving himself crazy. When he was finally able to get his mind off of Rose, he thought about Frank and Stevie. He was aware of Frank's ruthless character, but it came as a surprise that Stevie was an exact replica. He'd always thought of Stevie as a young boy, but he had to be about twenty-two by now. No longer a boy, but a man. And he was a man Morgan found wanting in character, just like Frank. He'd never spent much time around Stevie, but he seemed to harbor a man-sized animosity toward him. It wasn't much of a stretch to think Frank had poisoned his brother's mind against him.

Morgan thought he should have paid

more attention to Stevie over the years. It may not have made a difference, but there was a chance a man could have made a difference in his life. Now that he was paying attention, he didn't like what he saw. After the way Stevie spoke to Rose, Morgan feared he could be a danger to her.

By four in the morning, Morgan knew sleep was a lost cause tonight. He figured if he wasn't sleeping, he might as well be working. He got out of bed and walked to the kitchen to make some coffee. He wished he had some of Rose's blackberry cobbler to go with it. When his coffee was hot, he poured a cup and carried it to his desk. It was a good time to catch up on his ledgers while he waited for daylight. His work required concentration, and maybe it would take his mind off of Rose.

He was on his third cup of coffee, and adding a column of numbers in his ledger, when out of nowhere, he remembered it was Sunday morning. And Mr. Wonderful was going to be at the Langtry farm this morning to take Granny to church. The pastor had made it a point to meet Granny when he first got to town. Probably thought he would get in good with her to make some headway with Rose. He wondered if Granny had invited the pastor to breakfast. He envisioned Clay sitting in the same chair he'd sat in last night. Rose would probably give him some blackberry cobbler. *His* cobbler. Granny said Rose had made it for him.

Morgan threw his pencil down and watched it skitter across his desk. He glanced at the clock. Time to feed the animals. He walked out the door and saw some of his men already at work. When he walked inside the stable, Murph and Joseph were opening the stalls, and he nodded his good morning.

Murph took in Morgan's haggard appearance. He thought his boss looked like he wanted to chew through nails this morning. Normally, Morgan was cheerful in the mornings, so he knew something was wrong. "You okay?"

"Yeah." Morgan headed to the first stall. "Just got an early start this morning."

"You might not scare the men if you shaved," Murph teased.

Morgan ran a hand over his face. Murph was right, he hadn't even given a thought to shaving this morning. "Dang." He wasn't going to go back to the house now. The men always told him he looked like one mean son-of-a-gun when he didn't shave. Too bad. He'd just have to look mean today.

They finished caring for the horses, and

Morgan saddled Faithful. "Murph, I'll be back in a few hours."

"I'll keep an eye on the house," Murph said.

Morgan was grateful Murph didn't ask where he was going. He couldn't explain what he was doing because he didn't know. Who was he kidding? He knew exactly where he was going. He rode through the pines toward the Langtry farm. He figured he'd get there in time for breakfast.

As Morgan expected, there was a buggy in front of the Langtry house as he reined in. He dismounted and loosened his horse's girth, and as he passed the buggy, he stroked the horse's neck. Clay had been here long enough for the horse to cool down. He stood there with his hat in his hand, trying to decide how he could explain being at their door so early in the morning.

Granny opened the door when he knocked. "Good morning, Morgan."

"Morning."

"You're just in time for breakfast, and the coffee is hot." She motioned him inside as though she had expected him. "Come on in the kitchen."

Morgan followed her through the house, half expecting her to ask why he'd come by. "Something smells good."

"Rose and I are cooking flapjacks this morning."

Morgan's eyes landed on Clay, sitting in the chair where he'd sat the night before.

Clay stood and stuck his hand out. "Morgan, it's good to see you again. I'm happy you and Rose arrived safely."

Morgan shook his hand. "It didn't take you long to find the best food in the territory."

Rose turned from the stove and looked at Morgan. She thought his tone sounded abrupt. His appearance stunned her. He looked like he hadn't slept, and it was obvious he hadn't taken the time to shave. She wondered why he was visiting so early. Did his visit have something to do with Frankie? "Hello."

"Rose." Morgan noticed she was wearing a pretty yellow dress, and her long hair was arranged in a braid hanging down her back. It seemed to him she'd gone to a lot of trouble to look nice for *Mr. Wonderful.* The way she was staring at him, he thought his scruffy appearance might scare her, or perhaps she was comparing him to the pastor. Clay definitely looked spit-shined this morning, and he was clean shaven.

Clay thought Morgan didn't sound too friendly this morning. He wondered if the sheriff had shared his past with Morgan, and that was the reason for the less than sociable greeting. "The sheriff told me Granny was an excellent cook, and Granny just told me Rose is just as good. I couldn't resist when they invited me to have breakfast this morning. Flapjacks are my favorite."

Morgan figured Clay arrived so early to pick Granny up specifically to be invited for breakfast. "You arrived pretty early to go to church." Morgan pulled out the chair next to the one where Rose sat during dinner. Maybe she would sit by him and not Clay. Morgan wondered who invited Clay to have breakfast — Granny or Rose.

Granny placed a cup of coffee in front of Morgan. "Did you change your mind and decide to go to church this morning?" Granny had a feeling Morgan was concerned the new pastor might take an interest in Rose. Good. A little competition for her granddaughter couldn't hurt.

"No, ma'am." What could he say? He'd told her last night he had too much work, and now here he was sitting in their kitchen getting ready to share their breakfast. "I'm not dressed for church. I've already been working this morning." He glanced across the table at Clay. "Ranchers have to get up early and work, even on Sundays."

"The Lord doesn't care how we come dressed, as long as we come," Clay told him.

Morgan had no retort; he couldn't argue with the truth.

Rose was stacking the flapjacks on the plates, and Granny carried them to the table. She placed a huge stack in front of Morgan, and an equally huge stack in front of Clay.

"These look delicious," Clay said.

"Thank you," Rose replied, placing two more plates with smaller stacks on the table.

Morgan saw Rose glance at the empty chairs. Instead of sitting, she walked back to the stove and poured two cups of coffee.

When she returned to the table, Granny had taken the seat beside Morgan. Clay stood and pulled out the chair next to him. Morgan could have sworn that Clay pulled her chair closer to his.

"Thank you," Rose said, and smiled at the pastor.

Morgan glared at Clay, but he was mad at himself for his own bad manners.

"Would you like to say grace?" Granny asked Clay.

"Certainly."

After Clay said amen, Granny said, "What a lovely prayer."

"Yes, it was," Rose agreed.

"Thank you, ladies. And may I say these are the best-looking flapjacks I've ever seen."

Morgan picked up his fork and started eating without remarking on the prayer or the flapjacks.

Clay took a big bite, closed his eyes, and smiled like it was the best food he'd ever tasted. "It's been so long since I've had flapjacks, but these are the best I've ever had."

Morgan thought the pastor was putting on a great performance for Rose's attention. But when he glanced at Rose, she was beaming at his compliment. He wanted to kick himself for not telling her how good they were before Clay told her.

"Do you like the flapjacks, Morgan?" Granny asked.

"Yes, ma'am, I do." Morgan continued to shovel forkfuls in his mouth. Actions spoke louder than words was his motto. He intended to show Clay that he could eat more flapjacks than Clay could, any day of the week. Rose would have no doubt who liked them better.

Rose had taken a few bites when she noticed Morgan's plate was empty. "Would you like some more?"

"Yes, I would. Thank you."

Rose stood, and Clay held his plate to her.

"Since you're making more, could I have another plate?"

"Of course." Rose carried both plates to the stove and started ladling more batter into the skillets. She'd never seen anyone eat flapjacks so quickly. While she was busy cooking, she heard Granny and Clay talking, but she didn't hear Morgan join their conversation.

Morgan kept his eyes on Rose's every move. She looked beautiful this morning. And he didn't like her sitting next to Clay. But the day he couldn't outmaneuver the pastor was the day he needed to be six feet under. He stood, grabbed his cup of coffee, and walked to the stove.

As he poured a fresh cup, Rose glanced up at him. "Why didn't you say something? I would have brought the pot to the table."

"You have your hands full. Making flapjacks is not as easy as it looks."

Rose had one plate stacked full, and Morgan picked it up. "I'll help." He walked to the table and slammed the plate in front of Clay and glared at him. "Here you go."

Rose carried the second plate to the table and placed it in front of Morgan. Morgan made sure he remained standing until Rose took her seat.

"Pastor, have you met most of the folks in

267

town?" Granny asked.

"I think I have. I expect to have a full house this morning if everyone shows up. I know I will have a difficult time filling your husband's shoes. Everyone in town has praised his sermons. I just hope they will give me a chance."

"The folks here are good people. We've looked forward to your arrival, and everyone is excited. Rest assured, you will be warmly received."

"I'm thankful you are so accepting of a new preacher." Clay was sincere. He was excited to begin his new life in Whispering Pines with his new church family.

Morgan was too busy stuffing more flapjacks in his mouth to make a comment.

"Morgan, Rose said she may feel up to going to church with us," Granny said.

Clay smiled at Rose. "Do you enjoy attending church, Rose?"

"Very much. I don't think I ever missed a Sunday. I have a sense of peace talking to God in His house," Rose replied.

"I always thought it was easier to talk to God alone out under the blue sky, or at night on the range under the stars," Morgan said.

Rose studied Morgan, thinking he was a man full of surprises. What he said sounded lovely, but she'd never slept out on the range at night.

"I thought you attended church, Morgan," Clay said.

"I do, but that doesn't mean it's the only place to converse with our Maker," Morgan replied.

Clay couldn't argue with the logic of his statement. He turned his attention back on Rose. "Rose, I'd be delighted to have you in the front pew during my first sermon."

Morgan saw red as he chewed the last of his flapjacks. The only way Rose was going to get in that buggy next to Clay was over his dead body. "Rose, could I have some more flapjacks?" He looked at Clay, and lifted his dark brow in a challenge. He almost laughed when Clay filled his mouth with a huge bite in an effort to keep up with him.

Rose stood and walked back to the stove. She hadn't realized Morgan ate so much. After she poured more batter in the skillet, she picked up the coffeepot and carried it to the table. She poured Morgan another cup before she filled Clay's. "Granny, more coffee or flapjacks?"

"No thank you, honey."

"Rose, I think I can eat some more," Clay said, handing her his plate. He glanced at

Morgan and smiled wide.

Morgan's mouth tilted in a half grin. Mr. Wonderful didn't know who he was challenging. Morgan could eat more than any two men on his ranch on a bad day. Clay was tall and lean, but Morgan was sure a pastor didn't put in a day's work before sunup.

The men started on their third helping while the women watched in amazement. Morgan was finished in no time, and he was ready to ask for more when Clay stopped eating. "I think I've had enough."

Morgan looked at Clay's plate. He hadn't eaten half of the stack. Morgan reached over to grab Clay's plate. "No problem, I'll finish them so they don't go to waste."

Granny laughed. "Rose, let's clean the kitchen so we won't be late."

Morgan swallowed his food and said, "Granny, I'll help Rose. You two go ahead. If Rose decides she wants to go, I'll take her."

"Thank you, that is nice of you, Morgan," Granny said, smiling. Things had a way of working out just as they were supposed to. Her prayers were reaping some rewards. She'd give proper thanks to the Lord in church this morning.

Morgan stood, hoping to hurry Clay out

the door. "See you later, Clay," he said, slapping him on the back. He was much more affable now that he was going to be alone with Rose. Granny and Clay walked out the door, and Morgan picked up the dishes from the table. "Your flapjacks were great."

"You seemed to like them better than the cobbler last night," Rose replied.

"I wouldn't say that. They were both great." Morgan realized he hadn't seen Stevie this morning, so maybe he hadn't wanted to be around the pastor either. "Where's Stevie this morning?"

"I don't know. I was going to have a talk with him before I cooked breakfast, but he wasn't in his room. I checked the stable and his horse was gone."

Morgan thought he should have taken the horse home with him last night. "Granny has no idea where he goes?"

"Stevie doesn't seem to tell her anything. I was hoping he might talk to me, but he's not giving me much of a chance." Rose was disappointed Stevie had left so early. He was making it clear that he didn't want to be around her.

"Morgan, why did you come by so early this morning? Did you want to see Stevie for some reason?"

"No, I didn't come here to see Stevie."

How could he tell her he thought of nothing else but her all night? That thinking about her was making him daft.

He didn't say why he was here, but Rose decided to wait for him to tell her. She washed the dishes and Morgan dried. When they put the final dish away, she said, "I would never imagine you helping out in the kitchen. My brothers always said that was women's work."

"Your brothers aren't too bright. It's a nice way to pass the time with a pretty lady." He didn't want to talk about her brothers.

Rose wondered if he'd helped other ladies with the dishes after they'd prepared him dinner.

Morgan thought he might stay a little longer, so he said, "Let's go outside." Then he thought she may have decided she wanted to go to church. "Or did you want me to take you to town?"

"No, I think I would rather stay home this morning." Rose was finally alone with him, and she wanted to know what was on his mind.

Morgan held the back door open for her. "Do you feel better, or did you do too much this morning?" He was starting to feel guilty for making her cook so many flapjacks.

"I'm much improved." When they stepped

on the back porch, Rose said, "It's a lovely morning."

"Yes, it is." Morgan pointed to the swing. "Let's sit."

Rose sat down and Morgan sat a few inches from her. Her internal dialogue continued. Did he sit on porches with other women, and kiss them the way he'd kissed her last night? Did the women kiss him the way she'd kissed him? These were questions she wanted to ask, but she didn't. She turned slightly so she could look at him. Even with his scruffy beard and dark circles around his eyes, he was still the most handsome man she'd ever seen.

Morgan leaned back and placed his arm along the back of the swing, and unconsciously picked up her braid and ran the silky length through his fingers. He remembered how he'd felt brushing her hair the day she was injured. He envisioned her sitting in his bedroom by the fireplace while he brushed her hair. What was he waiting for? Last night he'd realized that before his next birthday, he wanted to be married and maybe even start family. He could tell Rose liked him, and he liked her. She certainly seemed to like his kisses. They had that much in common.

He was probably rushing his decision to

get married, but after his last encounter with Stevie, he wasn't comfortable leaving the women alone with him. If Rose married him, he would also be taking on the responsibility for Granny, and that was fine by him. He wanted them both to live on his ranch. He'd take care of the farm if they wanted to keep it for the other girls, but he wanted Granny and Rose at home with him where he could keep them safe. It was a good plan. They needed a man to look after them, and he wanted a family.

"Rose, if not for Granny, would you stay in Whispering Pines?"

Rose stared at him, her eyes wide with fear. "Granny's not ill, is she?"

Morgan held up his hand. "No . . . no. I was just curious if you would stay here if you didn't have Granny."

"Yes. This is home. My sister Adelaide is coming home to stay too. And I hope one day, Emma will return permanently. We planned to live here the rest of our lives. Why do you ask?"

Morgan dropped her braid and leaned forward, bracing his elbows on his thighs. "I just thought . . ." He straightened and faced her. "Rose, do you trust me?"

Staring into his dark eyes, she wondered what was on his mind. He had to know she trusted him. She could go through her whole life and not meet another man with such a sterling character. "Yes."

He thought that was a good start. "And I have a feeling you like me." His eyes drifted to her lips, and he thought of the kisses they'd shared. "In some ways, we seem to suit well."

She felt a blush rising from her neck to her cheeks. She wanted to tell him she more than liked him. She loved him. While she might not understand how it had happened so quickly, there it was. She loved everything about him. If only Frankie didn't stand between them, she might be tempted to tell him her true feelings. "I like you very much." She still didn't know where he was going with this conversation.

Morgan liked that response, but he thought about Clay. She'd said he was wonderful. "Are you interested in another man?"

His question confused her. "What do you mean? Are you speaking of my brothers?"

"No, I mean are you interested in any man courting you? A man like . . . well, a man like Clay. You seem to think he is *wonderful.*"

She did think the pastor was a wonderful man, but she didn't think of him as a potential suitor. "I think he is wonderful for the town, but no, I didn't even think that he might be interested in courting me."

Her response didn't answer his question. "If he wanted to court you, how would you feel about that?"

"Did he ask you to put these questions to me?" she asked suspiciously. "Why didn't he ask me himself?" She'd given the pastor no reason to think she wanted more than his friendship.

"I'm asking, not him. Are you interested in him as a husband?"

She couldn't deny the pastor was an attractive man, and a good man, but she didn't think of him in that way. "Heavens no."

He smiled at her response. So, Pastor Clay wasn't all that wonderful. "What about me?"

Rose felt her heart start to thump in her chest. What was he asking her? Surely he wasn't asking her to marry him. "What are you asking?"

Morgan didn't look away, didn't blink. "Would you consider me a suitable husband?"

Rose nodded.

"Is that a yes?"

Before she was definite in her response, she had to ask an important question. "But what about Frankie?" she whispered, almost on the verge of tears. If he was asking her to marry him, she couldn't ignore his hatred for her brother.

"Rose, we may never agree about Frank. You and Granny may not want to admit it, but you are not safe here alone. Frank and his gang are dangerous men." He held up his hand when she started to speak. "I know you don't want to believe that about your brother. But I'm asking you to trust me on this. If you aren't afraid of Frank, think about his gang. These are men with nothing to lose. I want you and Granny to live with me on the ranch. Stevie doesn't want to stay on the farm, and you and Granny can't handle it alone."

As far as proposals went, he thought he could have done a lot better. But if he vowed undying love, he wasn't sure it would be honest. "I want a family, and I will be good to you and Granny. I will keep this farm going for your sisters if they want to live here. But if Stevie stays, he'll have to work. I think that's fair."

Rose was overcome with so many emotions she couldn't think straight. The most amazing man she'd ever met was asking her to marry him. He hadn't professed love for her, yet he was welcoming Granny into his home. That alone meant more to her than he could ever imagine. She had worried how she would keep the farm going alone, and how she would care for Granny as she aged. They were not wealthy people, and it would be up to her and her sisters to provide care for Granny.

She wasn't so naïve to think people always married for love. Many people in these difficult times married for convenience, as a way to survive. Granny had already told her if not for Morgan providing beef every winter, they might have starved. But her one major concern was Frankie. She feared Morgan would begin to resent her for her belief in Frankie. She was in love with Morgan, but Frankie was her blood. "But what will you do if you find Frankie?"

To his credit, Morgan didn't even consider telling her Frankie had threatened her life when she was unconscious. He hoped in time she might come to care for him the way she cared for the brother who wasn't deserving of her love. "I won't kill him if I find him; at least, not unless I have no choice. You have my word on that."

Rose gazed at him as she thought about his response. She didn't question his word. But she had another question. "You asked me if I liked you. I'd like to know if you like me."

Morgan wasn't about to say he cared so much that he didn't want her in another man's bed. "I like you very much, and I do want a family. I think we can make a good marriage based on trust and friendship. I will provide for you and our children as long as I live. You will never want for anything if I have a say in the matter."

They were both silent for a minute. Morgan figured she was weighing her options. He knew he was getting the best end of the deal. There would be plenty of men in line waiting to marry her in no time if she didn't accept his offer. But he was also confident no man would care for her and Granny as well as he would.

Rose had always planned to marry for love. If she said yes, she would be marrying for love, but the groom didn't feel the same way. She didn't know if Morgan would ever love her the way she loved him, but she would make certain he never regretted his decision to take her for a wife.

"What do you think? Do you want to marry me?"

"Yes, I do."

Chapter Fifteen

"I don't know if Granny will want to leave the farm," Rose said.

Morgan had a feeling Granny had already come to accept that she would never be able to depend on Frank or Stevie, and she might be more willing to leave the farm than Rose believed. "I'll go home and get the buckboard to pick Granny up after the service. We'll ask her how she feels about living at the ranch. If she is okay with everything, I want you two to move in today."

"When do you want to marry?" Rose asked.

"What do you think about a few weeks from now?" Now that they had made the decision, Morgan didn't want to wait too long.

"We shouldn't move in until then. It wouldn't be proper," Rose said.

"Hogwash. Granny will be our chaperone.

Everything will be proper. I refuse to let you two stay here alone another night." Morgan knew he would be losing more sleep from worrying about them if they didn't come home with him.

Rose started to tell him they had Stevie, but Granny said he was rarely there at night. And she had a feeling Morgan was worried about their safety with Stevie. "I guess that would be fine since Granny will be there. Would you mind if we marry outdoors?" There was a special spot in the pine trees that Rose thought was particularly lovely, and the perfect place for a wedding.

Morgan laced his fingers through her and brought the back of her hand to his lips. "Whatever makes you happy."

Rose didn't want him to leave. "Must you go home now?"

Morgan didn't want to leave her alone, but he'd ridden his horse to the farm. "Do you feel like sitting in front of me on my horse? You can go with me."

Morgan rode slowly on the way to the ranch simply because he enjoyed having Rose ride in front of him with his arms wrapped around her. Once he reined in at the porch, he helped Rose to the ground. "Come inside. I want you to see your new home."

After he showed her around the lower level, he led the way upstairs so she could see the bedrooms. He first took her to the bedroom he thought Granny would like. The furnishings were sparse — a bed, a bureau, and a chair — but it had the makings of a very nice room. "We'll need to get some things, but the fireplace keeps it nice and cozy in here. We can ride to Denver when you feel up to it to buy what we need."

"It's a lovely room. I'm sure Granny would be comfortable here." Rose noted the room was much larger than Granny's bedroom at the farmhouse. She silently prayed that Granny would agree to move in with Morgan, but she was skeptical since the farm held so many fond memories of her life with Preacher. If Granny objected, Rose didn't think she could leave her alone. Granny had spent too much time alone over the past few years.

"Our room is down the hall." He took her hand and pulled her into his bedroom. Rose's eyes immediately zoomed in on the large bed. "That bed is huge."

Morgan pulled her into his arms. "I promise not to lose you in there. I'll keep you close to me." He saw a blush rising on her cheeks, and she looked so delectable he wanted to kiss her. He didn't talk himself out of it. When his lips left hers, he said, "I plan on doing that a lot for the rest of our lives."

Rose didn't want him to stop, but she knew they had to get to town. "This is a lovely room."

"You can do whatever you want in here. I want you to be comfortable."

His generosity brought tears to her eyes. "Thank you."

"This is your home now. I want you and Granny to make it your home." He reached for her hand again. "Let's go get that buckboard." Now that she had agreed to become his wife, he wanted to tell everyone as soon as possible. His excitement surprised him, and he couldn't stop smiling.

Joseph appeared as Morgan was harnessing horses to the buckboard. Rose approached him to say hello. "How are you, Joseph?"

"Well. Morgan said you were injured."

"I'm much better. I wanted to tell you I am sorry my brother shot you."

Morgan overheard what Rose said to Joseph. She must believe what he'd told her about Frank, and he couldn't help but wonder why she'd changed her mind.

"Joseph, Rose and I are to be wed in a few weeks. Would you mind if we married in the pines? Rose has a spot she is partial to in there." Morgan might be the owner of the land by law, but he always thought of Joseph as the caretaker of the pines.

Joseph smiled. "I know this place. I do not object."

"Thank you." Rose turned to Morgan and said, "Joseph showed the place to me a long time ago." She had so many fond memories of talking with Joseph when she was a young girl. He'd always been patient with her many questions about the Sioux. Before she'd left Whispering Pines, she'd visited the altar one last time. Joseph was there, and she remembered saying to him that when she found a boy who heard the same sounds in the pines as she heard, she would marry him when she grew up.

"It is the place where I speak to the Great Spirit. I showed you a long time ago," Joseph reminded Morgan.

Morgan knew the place. "It is beautiful there."

"You don't mind being married there?" The fact that Morgan wanted Joseph's consent for them to marry at the sacred place said so much about the kind of man she was marrying.

Morgan put his arm around her. "I can't think of a better place."

"It is good you take a wife, Morgan. About time," Joseph said before he walked away.

"I had to wait on the right one," Morgan yelled after him. He turned to Rose and laughed. "We seem to have his blessing."

Rose smiled. "I'm glad we do."

Granny was at the door of the church speaking with Clay when she spotted Morgan and Rose. Clay took her by the elbow and they were making their way to the buckboard when another parishioner stopped the pastor. Morgan jumped down from the buckboard to assist Granny.

"What are you two doing here?" Granny asked.

"We came to pick you up. We have news to tell you," Rose said.

Granny looked at her smiling face. "It must be good. You're both smiling from ear to ear."

"Morgan asked me to marry him," Rose said.

Granny clasped her hands together. "Oh my, that is wonderful news. I knew it would happen."

Clay walked up and overheard Granny. "What's wonderful news?"

"Morgan and Rose are going to need your services soon," Granny replied.

"Really, why is that?" Clay asked.

Morgan put his arm around Rose's shoulders. "Rose and I are going to marry." He felt his chest swell with pride when he said those words.

"You work fast, Morgan," Clay said, extending his hand in congratulations.

"We plan to marry on the ranch. Can you come out and perform the ceremony?" Morgan asked.

"I'd be honored," Clay said.

Morgan looked at Rose. "Honey, what time do you want to get married?"

She was so stunned he'd addressed her as *honey* that she could hardly think of a reply. "Anytime."

"Noon sounds good to me," Morgan said. "We'll let you know the exact date when it's decided."

"We'll have a nice lunch afterwards," Granny said. "I'm sure all of Morgan's ranch hands will be there." She glanced at Morgan to see if she had overstepped her bounds. "Would that be okay with you, Morgan?"

Morgan smiled at her. "Granny, that sounds good."

Granny became emotional and her voice cracked when she said, "Morgan, you've made me so happy. There isn't a better man for my Rose. I know you will take good care of her."

Morgan found himself getting choked up at her confidence in him. "Yes, ma'am, I promise you, I will always take care of her."

"And I know she will make you very happy."

They said their good-byes to the pastor and left for the farm. Morgan drove slowly so they could discuss their plans with Granny.

"I would love to live on your ranch . . . if you're sure you want me," Granny told them.

Rose was relieved Granny had so readily agreed to uproot her life.

"We definitely want you," Morgan assured her. "I've already got your bedroom picked out. If it doesn't suit, you can choose another one. There's plenty of room."

"I'm sure it will be fine. I expect you two to start working on giving me great-grandbabies before I am too old to enjoy them," Granny informed them.

"Granny!" Rose was appalled Granny would say such a thing.

Morgan laughed. "You can bet we will get to work on that, first thing."

Rose was turning a nice shade of pink.

"I think four sounds like a good number;

two boys and two girls," Granny said, enjoying Rose's embarrassment.

"I can't guarantee boys or girls, but as many as Rose wants is fine with me." Morgan glanced down at Rose and grinned. "How many children do you want, honey?"

"We have time to think about that," Rose said, ready to die of embarrassment. She couldn't believe these two were discussing something so personal.

Morgan winked at her. "Yes, ma'am, we have a lifetime." Morgan was thankful Granny didn't mention Frank or Stevie. He'd expected one of them to ask if Stevie could live at the ranch. He'd already decided Stevie could work for him, and bunk with the men, but he wasn't going to allow a man not to work for his keep. But Morgan figured if Stevie really wanted to work, he'd stay on the farm. The property could be his one day. If Rose was right, and the sisters came home, Morgan felt sure men would be lined up to court them. They'd find themselves married in no time. Stevie could start a family of his own if he was interested in that kind of life.

They reached the farm and Morgan was helping Granny to the ground when Stevie walked out of the house.

"Good morning, Stevie. We have some

288

wonderful news," Granny said, still beaming with excitement.

"Yeah?" Stevie stared hard at Morgan.

"Rose and Morgan are planning to marry in a few weeks. The new pastor will perform the ceremony."

Morgan was lifting Rose to the ground when he caught the look on Stevie's face. It was not a look of joy, but rather one of disbelief.

Stevie took a step forward, bringing him within inches from Rose's face. "What is wrong with you, Rose? He's the man that is going to make sure Frankie hangs!"

"Stevie . . ." Rose started, but was interrupted by his ongoing tirade.

"You're no sister of ours. You're nothing but a . . ."

Morgan grabbed him by the collar and pulled him away from Rose. "Watch your mouth. I warned you about the way you speak to your sister."

"Stevie, Rose's relationship with Morgan has nothing to do with Frank. What your brother has chosen to do is not going to ruin our lives," Granny said firmly.

Stevie started in on her. "What do you know, old woman? You're no better than her." He pointed his finger in Rose's direction. "You always take Morgan's side against

Frankie. All of you make me sick."

Rose stepped forward and slapped Stevie hard across the cheek. "Don't you dare speak to Granny like that! She's the one person who doesn't deserve your wrath. I don't know what's happened to you, but you've changed. And the change is not a good one." Rose had never struck anyone in her life, but she was shaking with anger.

Stevie's face was so twisted with rage Morgan thought he might strike Rose. He stepped between them. "Stevie, you may not like Rose becoming my wife, but you're going to have to get used to the idea."

"You don't care about Rose, you're just trying to make Frankie come home so you can set him up to hang. You're using Rose to get to him. You know if Frankie hears you are going to marry her, he'll come for you."

"I don't think Frank is man enough to face me. If he was any kind of man he wouldn't rustle cattle in the middle of the night like a coward."

Smirking, Stevie said, "Frankie's not afraid of you, if that's what you're saying."

"That's exactly what I'm saying. Your brother is a coward, plain and simple. Like the rest of his gang, they don't have the nerve to face a man. If they can't shoot you in the back, they hide in rocks waiting to waylay a man, just like they did when they shot Jack. Now if you want to end up like your brother, that's your business, and nothing anyone can say to you will change your mind. You're a man, and you'll make your own decisions. You should have been taking care of Granny instead of letting her take care of you. A real man cares for the women in his life. If you want to do the right thing, you're welcome to work on my ranch for wages like the rest of my men. Whatever you decide, just know, if you can't keep a civil tongue when you speak to Granny or your sister, then you'd best keep your mouth shut."

Stevie spat on the ground near Morgan's boot. "You're gonna pay, LeMasters. When Frankie hears about this, all of you are gonna pay." He glared at Granny and Rose one last time before he stalked toward the stable.

Morgan spotted Stevie's horse still saddled outside the stable. He knew Stevie hadn't bothered to care for him when he arrived at the farm. "I'll be back in a minute." He quickly caught up with Stevie. "I warned you about taking care of that animal."

"And I told you to mind your own business. You don't own this farm, and I'm telling you to get out of here."

Morgan grabbed the reins of the horse. "You're not riding this animal."

"Get out of my way," Stevie yelled.

Morgan didn't move. He saw in Stevie's eyes that he was going to draw on him. Before Stevie had a chance to pull his gun all the way out of his holster, Morgan punched him hard in the jaw, knocking him to the dirt. Stevie's gun fell a few feet from him, and Morgan kicked it out of the way. "The horse is going to my ranch until he heals. If you want to file a complaint, go to the sheriff."

Turning, Morgan led Stevie's horse to the buckboard and tied the reins to the back. After he removed the saddle and blanket, he threw them in the buckboard. When he looked up, Granny and Rose were staring at him. "I told him last night this animal was in bad shape, so he's staying at the ranch until his sores are healed. I told Stevie he can talk to the sheriff if he has a problem with that."

"Thank you, Morgan. I had no idea Stevie wasn't caring for that animal. I own the horse, and you have my permission to care for him," Granny said. She wasn't angry at Morgan for punching Stevie. She'd felt like doing the same thing several times lately.

Maybe this would be Stevie's wake-up call. She'd thought for a long time he needed to answer to a man for his bad manners.

"I want you two ladies to show me what you want to take to the ranch and I'll load the buckboard right now."

"Granny, do you think it will be proper to live with Morgan until we are married?" Rose asked.

"I foresee no problems with that. As Morgan said, he has enough bedrooms, and with me there, no one will say a word," Granny replied. She had to face the fact that it might be dangerous for Rose to stay at the farm now that she was marrying Morgan. Just as Stevie said, Frank would be furious once he got word of their impending marriage.

Worried about Stevie staying alone on the ranch, Rose almost balked, but if Granny wasn't protesting, she thought it best to go with Morgan.

Morgan had a hunch Rose was thinking about Stevie. "Rose, he's a man, and he needs to act like one. He can cook his own meals and look after himself for a change. If he's man enough to draw a gun, then he can darn sure work like a man."

Granny placed her arm around Rose's waist, urging her to the house. "Morgan's right. Let's pack our valises and show Morgan what he can load on the buckboard."

Once they had ridden away with a full buckboard, Stevie walked in the house. The first thing he did was walk in his bedroom to make sure everything was as he'd left it earlier. Seeing nothing out of place, he went to the kitchen and looked around for something to eat. He'd never even prepared a sandwich. He considered cooking women's work, and he cursed Granny and Rose all the more for taking off with Morgan. Judging by the many things Morgan had loaded into the buckboard, they would be staying at his ranch permanently. That was fine by him. After he cut some bread and slapped a couple of pieces of ham on it, he carried it through the house to see what they'd left behind. He walked in Granny's room and saw her favorite rocker was gone, along with her daguerreotype of Preacher. He wanted to find Frankie and tell him what was going on, but he had no way of getting to Purgatory Canyon. He took solace in the fact that Frankie would make sure Morgan paid for everything he'd done. All he had to do was wait. Frank would come to him.

CHAPTER SIXTEEN

Two days later, Stevie was still without a horse. He considered walking to town and buying one, but word was sure to get back to Granny. He didn't need anyone questioning where he got the money. That was another thing he hated about small towns: Everyone wanted to know your business. He couldn't raise suspicions now. If he could get to Denver, where no one knew him, he could buy a horse there. He couldn't just sit at the farm and do nothing. He needed to find Frankie and tell him what was going on. But to find Frankie, he had to have a horse. After pacing for an hour, he decided there was nothing he could do tonight. He knew Granny well enough to know she would give him a few days to calm down and see the error of his ways. There was no way she'd leave him without a horse for long.

He walked to his bedroom and moved a

table in the corner of the room to get to his hiding place. After he pried open one of the wooden slats in the floor, he retrieved one of the bottles of whiskey he'd purchased in town. He uncorked the bottle and took a drink before he pulled out the bag of money he'd stashed in the hole. He sat on the floor and counted his money again. He couldn't wait to tell Frankie what he'd done. Frankie would be proud of him. He placed the money back in the bag and stuck it back down in his secret hidey-hole.

Frankie rode to the farm in the middle of the night. He was near the stable, watching the farmhouse for over an hour to make sure no one was waiting for him to appear. He'd left his men a few miles away at the old Conner place. It was an abandoned log home whose occupants were long forgotten. Their old homestead was nothing more than a dilapidated dwelling fading into the wild brush. No one would ever know he was hiding out so close to the farm.

"Stevie, wake up," Frank whispered.

Stevie's mind was still foggy from the bottle of whiskey he'd consumed. He thought he was dreaming about his brother. "Huh?"

"Shh, wake up and talk to me."

"Frankie?"

"Keep it down." Frank sat in the chair next to the bed. "Where's Granny?"

Stevie slowly moved to a sitting position. He wiped his eyes, trying to clear his vision. It wasn't a dream, Frankie was sitting in his chair. Fumbling for a match on his bedside table, Stevie finally put his fingers on one. Striking the head on the wooden table, he held the flame to the kerosene lamp. "Frankie, what are you doing here?"

"Turn that low," Frank said. "What do you think I'm doing here? I came to see what's going on."

He dimmed the light as Frankie instructed. He couldn't have been happier to see his older brother. "What happened in Kansas?"

"We got away from Morgan, and hid out at Purgatory Canyon. I thought you might be there."

"I was going to ride to Purgatory, but Morgan's got my horse. Frankie, you are not going to like what's going on here."

"Why does Morgan have your horse?"

"That's what I'm trying to tell you. But first, I don't think it's safe for you to be here."

Frank grinned. "I'm smarter than all of these yokels. Now tell me what I'm not going to like to hear."

"The sheriff ain't dead. I heard talk around town that they are going to go looking for you as soon as he's able."

"They've tried that, and see where it got them — nowhere. What else is going on?"

"Rose is going to marry Morgan LeMasters in a few weeks. The new pastor is going to perform the ceremony."

Frank stared at him so long Stevie was beginning to wonder if he'd heard him.

"So she's alive," Frank finally said.

"Yeah, she had busted ribs, but she came home with Morgan. You'd think he was some kind of hero the way Granny is treating him."

Frank smirked. "Well, that hero is not going to marry a sister of mine."

"I knew you wouldn't let that take place."

"I promise you, that ain't never going to happen. Langtry blood will never be mixed with LeMasters blood. Now get dressed so we can get out of here. The gang is holed up at the old Conner place." Frankie pointed to the whiskey bottle on the floor by the bed. "Any left in there?"

Stevie tossed the bottle to him. "LeMasters took my horse and he hasn't brought him back."

"Why did he take your horse?"

"Said I was abusing it."

Those words sounded familiar to Frankie. He knew Morgan would die protecting animals. Frank intended to be the man to see that he did. He opened the whiskey bottle and took a long swig.

"Granny didn't say a word. I told her she cared more about Morgan than she did you," Stevie said.

"Granny always did take his part. Where's Rose and Granny now?"

"They're staying at his ranch. Did you see the house? They moved most of the stuff out. Granny is going to live with Rose and Morgan."

"Granny is going to leave the farm?" It was difficult for Frank to believe Granny would leave her home.

"Yeah. LeMasters said I could come work for him. Can you believe he thought I would work for him? Anyway, that's not all I have to tell you." Stevie got out of bed, walked across the room, and moved the table once again. He lifted the wooden slat and pulled out the bag of money, carried it across the room, and dropped it in Frankie's lap. "I robbed a stagecoach." He sat back down on the bed and told Frankie how he pulled off the stagecoach robbery, and about his partner in Denver. "I got shot in the arm."

He removed his shirt and showed Frankie his wound.

"Why didn't you duck?" Frankie teased.

"I didn't know another guard was inside the coach. Reuben didn't either, but he was right about everything else, including how much money they were carrying. We can get out of here and go to Mexico. Just you and me, like we always talked about. We can start our own place now." Stevie had never forgotten the plans they made when they were younger. Frankie always said he wanted to see the country, and not stay in one place and get old before his time, like Preacher.

Frank lifted the bag. "How much is in here?"

"Me and Reuben split the take. There's two thousand in there." Frankie wasn't as excited as Stevie expected him to be. "Aren't you happy I got us some money so we can leave here and never come back?"

"Yeah, Stevie, I'm real happy about that. But tell me more about this Reuben fellow. He could be very useful to us." Frank was already considering how he could use Reuben for a bigger payday.

"You mean you don't want to go to Mexico?"

"Stevie, we'd need a lot more money than

this to survive and buy our own spread. After we get even with Morgan, I'm thinking about robbing a bank. I want to set us up so we never have to come back here again." What he left unsaid was he didn't plan on leaving Whispering Pines for good until Morgan LeMasters was dead.

Stevie wasn't going to argue with his big brother. Frankie had always outsmarted everyone. "Reuben works in the Denver bank; he's been there over two years. That's how he knew that stagecoach was carrying the money. Reuben's smart, and he knows everything going on in Denver. He's not the kind of fellow who is good with a gun, he's more of a tenderfoot, but he can give us the information. We'd have to split the money with him. That was how we struck our deal."

"How did you meet him? You go to Denver often?"

"I don't go there much. I was out target practicing, and he was out for a ride one day and stopped to talk. We talked for a long time about my shooting, and he told me about his job. We became friends, and before I knew it, we were planning the robbery."

"Friends or not, he shouldn't get half of the take. He doesn't take any risks, he just told you what stage the money was on. You took all the risks."

"But, Frankie, I wouldn't have known about the stagecoach in the first place if not for Reuben. He's so smart that he planned the whole thing. He staged the rifles on the rocks, and told me exactly what to do. He felt real bad about me getting shot."

Frank laughed. "Yeah, I bet he did. But you were getting shot while he was nice and safe sitting on a soft chair in the bank. The man taking the risk always gets the biggest cut."

"Is that how you do it with your gang?"

"If my boys don't risk as much as me, then they don't get a share."

"I don't know if Reuben would agree to anything if he didn't get half. He's risking losing his job. And I like him, Frankie, he's a real nice fellow. He even told me I could travel the world with him."

Frank stood. "Well, we'll just have to make him see things our way. Did you two plan anything else? You sure as heck couldn't travel the world on a measly two thousand dollars."

"No. I told him I didn't think we'd be interested since I thought we were going to Mexico."

"How do you get in touch with him?"

"We usually meet once a month at the

place where I target practice. But we met just this past week so he could let me know if anyone talked to him about the robbery. Morgan happened along and saw us talking on the road."

"Did Morgan know him?"

"Nope, and Reuben didn't mention his name. I told Morgan I didn't know him."

"Good. Now let's go get that horse from LeMasters."

"We'd have to go through the pines to get it," Stevie reminded his brother.

"Don't tell me you're afraid to go through there." He'd heard enough whining about the pines from his boys.

Stevie didn't readily admit that he was afraid, but he did everything he could to avoid riding in there, particularly after dark. "Frankie, even if we get to Morgan's stable, you know Joseph or one of the other men will be on watch and will hear us," Stevie said. "Not only that, but everyone is expecting you to come back here, or to be in Purgatory Canyon. I know LeMasters will shoot you on sight, and I'd bet he's told all his men to do the same thing."

Frankie hadn't consumed enough whiskey to do something foolish. When he went back on Morgan's ranch he wanted to take more than one horse. "Yeah, you're right. It's not like we can't afford to buy a horse. I'll send Walt to town to buy one. No one knows him in Whispering Pines. We might even rob a bank before we rustle again. Then we can sell what we rustle on our way to Mexico." Frankie planned to send Walt to Denver to find out everything he could about Stevie's friend Reuben. He had a feeling robbing a bank was going to be a reality real soon.

"Yeah, we'll get the horse when we rustle. LeMasters thinks he runs everything. I guess he thinks he'll have this farm now, since I ain't staying."

Frankie had already figured that out. "That'll never happen. Just like he ain't gonna marry Rose. I'd rather see her dead before I let her marry him, and I'll burn this place to the ground before he gets it."

"Yeah," Stevie agreed.

"Stevie, I promise you, LeMasters will pay for everything he's done. Now let's go meet up with the boys. You keep the stagecoach robbery to yourself. We ain't sharing this money." Frankie opened the bag and pulled out a handful of bills before he stuck the bag back in Stevie's hiding place. "This will get you a horse and tide us over until we get a plan together. We'll keep the money right here for now and come back for it later."

Stevie and Frank rode double to the Conner place, arriving just before dawn. Frank took Walt aside and pulled out some bills. "I want you to go to town and buy enough supplies for a week, and buy a horse. Bring back several bottles of whiskey. After you come back, I want you to ride to Denver and check out a man for me." Frank told him where he could find Reuben. "Don't say anything to the other men about this Reuben fellow, but find out what you can about him."

"Who is he?" Walt asked.

"Never you mind who he is. Just watch him for a couple of days. I want to know everything he does. See who he talks to, where he goes, if he's got a girlfriend, or a sister. You understand? I want to know everything about him."

"Sure thing, Frank." Walt didn't ask more questions. He was happy to go to Denver for a few days and get away from the rest of the men.

Just because Stevie trusted his friend Reuben, Frank didn't have the same inclination. He wanted to know more about Reuben in case he needed leverage to make sure Reuben saw things his way. Reuben had told Stevie he was going to travel the world, so it sounded like he was planning on a few more jobs, or something big. Frank was curious to find out what he had in mind. "Walt, don't forget to keep this between us. Some of the boys ain't too smart, and the less they know, the better."

"Understood. Listen, if you are planning on robbing the bank in Denver, I know a place near town where we can hide out. It's a lot like this place, well hidden, off the main trail, and no one even remembers it's still there."

Frank liked the sound of that. The Conner place was too close to Whispering Pines to make a safe hideout for long. "That's good to know, Walt. It might be smart for us to go there while we figure out our next move."

Frank walked inside the cabin to get Stevie. "I want you to take my horse and go back home."

Stevie shook his head. "I thought I was going to ride with you."

"Now listen to me. You've got to go back and act like nothing is going on. I don't want them to get wise to us. Keep the horse out of sight, don't put him in the stable. I need to plan our next move, and it's important that you know what's going on at Le-Masters's ranch. We're going to rustle his cattle one last time, but we're also going to get rid of Joseph Longbow. Can you do this for me?"

Stevie wasn't happy about going back to the farm, but if it would help Frankie, he would do it. "Yeah, I can do it."

"Good. If Morgan comes around, be friendly. Make them all think you've had a change of heart about staying on the farm."

"How long am I going to have to do this?"

"Not long. We'll figure something out."

Chapter Seventeen

"You think you'll be feeling up to coming to the ranch in a few weeks?" Morgan asked Jack.

Jack was already behind his desk at the sheriff's office. "What's happening?"

"I'm getting married."

Grinning, Jack stood and stuck out his hand. "Congratulations. I guess I don't have to ask who you're marrying."

Morgan shook his hand. "I doubt that you would."

"It's pretty fast, isn't it?"

"Yeah. But Granny and Rose need a man to look after them. I don't think it's safe for them to stay on the farm, and I figured there was no reason to wait."

"Not to mention the fact that you are getting one beautiful bride."

Morgan laughed. "There is that."

"So I take it that means Granny is going to live with you?"

"They already are. I moved them to my house on Sunday. We're in town today so they can pick up a few things that they need."

"This is a big change, Morgan. Having women living in your house when you're not used to it could be difficult."

"I'm enjoying it. I know I'm eating a whole lot better." He found himself looking forward to coming home at night and talking with the women. Their conversations were different than the ones he had with the men, but he enjoyed them all the same. He noticed all the little things they had done around the house in just a short time. His home was tidier, the wood floors were shined, pretty dishes were on the shelves in the kitchen, flowers were on the tables, and everything smelled nice and fresh. "To tell you the truth, I think I'm getting spoiled."

"If Granny has anything to do with it, I wouldn't be surprised. She thinks the sun rises and sets on you."

"I feel the same way about her. She's a fine lady."

Jack looked at his friend and asked the question on his mind. "And what about Rose?"

Morgan frowned at him. "What do you mean?"

"Are you in love, or do you just want to take care of them?"

"I care a lot about Rose." Morgan hadn't thought much about love; he thought highly of Rose, and he wanted to take care of her and Granny. It'd been difficult for him to say good night at Rose's door each night since she'd moved into his house. He couldn't wait to have her in his bedroom permanently. That was something he wasn't going to discuss with Jack or anyone. "You hear anything about Frank?"

Jack knew when a door was closed on a conversation. "Nope. But I was thinking about putting a posse together soon and taking a ride to Purgatory Canyon. Since you're getting married, I don't expect you'd want to go."

"I'll go." Morgan fully intended to keep his promise to Rose and not kill Frank if he could help it, but he still wanted to be there when he was captured. He'd make sure he got to jail without anyone else being shot.

"I'm hoping we will have some word on his whereabouts by then."

"Joseph keeps telling me Frank will come here."

"I wouldn't argue with Joseph."

Morgan agreed with Jack. If anyone had a handle on people, it was Joseph.

■ ■ ■ ■

Morgan pulled the buckboard in front of the mercantile, and when he jumped down from the seat he noticed one of the horses tied to the rail. It was a flashy palomino gelding with a white mane and tail. Out of habit, he stopped to admire the horse, and noticed he looked well cared-for. When he walked inside the mercantile, a man carrying several large burlap bags filled with supplies passed him on the way out the door. Morgan spotted Rose and Granny at the counter and headed in that direction. "You ladies have everything you need?"

"Yes," Rose said, giving him a wide smile. She pointed to a bundle on the counter. "This is ours."

Picking up the bundle, Morgan tucked it under his arm. On the way out the door, he noticed the man from the store loading his supplies on the palomino.

The man turned and stared at Rose as they stepped off the sidewalk. He tipped his hat and said, "Morning."

Granny said good morning to the stranger, and Morgan nodded. Morgan placed the bundle in the back of the buckboard, and assisted the women to the seat. Out of the corner of his eye, Morgan could see the stranger was still staring at Rose. He was tempted to tell him to put his eyeballs back in their sockets, but he figured unless any man said or did anything improper, he'd have to get used to men looking at his lovely bride-to-be. Judging by the supplies the man had purchased, he was probably passing through town. On the heels of that thought, Morgan wondered: If the man was traveling a long way, why didn't he have a packhorse?

"Since you were so kind to take time out of your day to bring us to town, we are cooking you a special dinner tonight," Granny said, taking Morgan's mind off of the stranger.

"Sorry, it'll have to wait until tomorrow night because I'm taking you to the hotel for dinner." He'd planned to take them to dinner when they told him they needed to make a trip to the mercantile. Not having the time to court Rose properly, he wanted to be seen with her around town. Part of the reason was to show her he knew how to treat a lady, but he also wanted to make sure every man in town knew she was taken.

"Oh, I haven't eaten at the hotel in years," Granny said. "That will be lovely."

"Morgan, you already charged all of these

things on your account. You shouldn't spend so much money," Rose said.

"Honey, I didn't court you, so consider this courting. You two have been working hard at the ranch, and you're due a break."

The man continued to stare as Morgan took his seat beside Rose and picked up the reins. "That's a fine-looking animal, mister." He congratulated himself for sounding affable as he let the stranger know he was aware he was gawking at his wife, or soon-to-be wife.

"He's a good horse, but he don't compare to a beautiful woman," the man said, his eyes remaining fixed on Rose.

Morgan gave him a hard look. "Like my horses, I take care of what's mine. You'd be wise to be respectful."

Walt had never met Morgan LeMasters, but he didn't need an introduction. He'd heard about him from Frank and every man in the gang. There was no doubt the woman with LeMasters was Frank's sister. Deke had described her perfectly, except she was even more beautiful. He couldn't keep from staring at her, but he wasn't foolish enough to anger LeMasters, so he wisely mounted the palomino and rode away.

Rose saw the look Morgan gave the man. His jaw was still clenched after the stranger rode away. She knew Morgan well enough to know that he was keeping a tight rein on his temper. She was curious if he knew the man, but she didn't want to say something to ruin their evening. Placing her hand on his arm, she said, "Did you just compare me to a horse?"

"Honey, I don't think there's a horse on this earth as pretty as you."

"Thank you . . . I think," Rose replied.

"I'd take that as high praise coming from Morgan. He places great value on his horses."

Laughing, Morgan put the stranger from his mind and headed to the hotel.

As Morgan assisted Rose from the buckboard, she brushed off her skirt, wishing she'd worn a different dress today. She wondered if they would see some of the women who used to flirt with him after church and cook him dinner. At that thought, she automatically touched her hair, hoping the ride to town hadn't done too much damage. She wanted to look her best so Morgan wouldn't be ashamed to be seen with her.

Granny leaned over and whispered in her ear, "You look lovely, dear. Stop worrying."

Rose smiled at her. Granny always knew what she was thinking. "Thank you."

Morgan held the door for the ladies, and when they walked into the restaurant, his arm was firmly planted around Rose's waist. Every head in the place turned to stare as they walked across the room to a table by the window. Before they could even order their dinner, five men stopped to speak to Morgan. Politely, he introduced them to Rose, making sure they knew the lay of the land by saying, "Meet my future wife." Like Morgan, Granny knew everyone in the restaurant, and many of the ladies made a point of stopping at their table to speak with her.

By the way the women eyed Morgan, Rose knew Granny wasn't the only reason they'd stopped at their table. She recognized some of the women from the past, and her presence didn't prevent the women from asking Morgan where he'd been keeping himself. To Morgan's credit, he didn't hesitate to mention his impending marriage. There was no doubt by sundown everyone in town would know they were going to be married.

By the time the dinner ended, Rose was on top of the world. Morgan was polite and attentive, and seemed genuinely proud to introduce her to everyone. Even though she was irritated that so many women flirted with Morgan, she thought it was one of the best evenings of her life.

Granny was delighted with the way the relationship was developing between Rose and Morgan. She thought they were crazy about each other, though they might not even understand the depth of their feelings. Granny was amused by the way Morgan let every cowboy know Rose was his.

Once they reached the ranch, Morgan still had work to do, and he left Rose and Granny in the kitchen discussing Rose's wedding dress. It was late by the time he returned to the house, and he thought the women had retired for the evening. He was disappointed he'd missed out on his goodnight kiss at Rose's bedroom door, but when he walked upstairs he heard laughter coming from Rose's room. The door was ajar, and he peeked inside to see Granny and Rose laughing at something. He stood there as though his feet had taken root to the floorboards. Rose had removed her dress, and she was standing there in her camisole, corset, and bloomers. Her hair was seductively draped over one shoulder, and he didn't think he'd ever seen a more beautiful sight. He couldn't force his eyes from her, thinking he hadn't seen so much of her bare skin since the day he'd wrapped her ribs. And he wanted to see more. As much as he hated to make his presence known, he tapped lightly on the door. "I wanted to say good night."

Rose reached for her dress, which she'd dropped on the bed. "Just a minute."

Granny walked to the door and opened it wide. "I was just going to bed. We were looking at my old wedding dress, and having a few laughs over some pleasant memories." She patted Morgan's shoulder. "I'll be saying good night, and thank you for a wonderful dinner. Preacher and I didn't often go to town for dinner, and it was a real treat."

"We'll do it more regularly now that you and Rose are here," Morgan promised. He waited until Granny had entered her bedroom before he turned back to Rose. She was holding her dress in front of her. He was tempted to run across the room and take her in his arms. Trying to maintain what little control he possessed, he walked into her room and slowly closed the door behind him. "Did you have a nice dinner?"

"Yes, I had a lovely dinner." Her eyes widened as she watched his every step in her direction.

"Good. I enjoyed the company." He stopped directly in front of her.

"I think a lot of women had broken hearts

tonight." Rose felt herself blushing as she stared into his dark, penetrating eyes.

Morgan crinkled his brow. "How so?"

"I don't think they thought you would be marrying so soon. Or perhaps they were surprised that you were marrying me."

Morgan took the dress from her fingers and tossed it on the bed, his eyes slowly drifting from her mouth down her body. "Marrying you shouldn't surprise anyone. There isn't another woman as beautiful as you."

Rose's breathing picked up speed as his eyes devoured her. "It's probably not wise for you to be in here with me dressed like . . ." That was the problem, she wasn't properly dressed.

"Probably not." Morgan reached out and picked up a lock of hair hanging over her shoulder, and the back of his hand grazed her bare shoulder.

Rose shivered. Not from lack of clothing, but because she was reminded how his strong hands felt when he'd bandaged her ribs. Every night she'd been in his home, she thought of nothing else but the way it felt to be touched by him.

Morgan wound her hair around his hand and gently tugged her to him, and once she was close, he wrapped his arms around her.

"I can't wait until I don't have to leave you at night, and you can climb into my big bed with me."

His words were provocative, and they made her tremble with excitement. Rose felt the same way, but she didn't know if she should tell him she was counting the days until she would be with him at night. She'd never felt tempted by another man, never even thought about making love with another man. The thought of making love the first time with him thrilled her, yet frightened her. She wasn't experienced, and since he was older, it was likely he'd been intimate with other women. The way he kissed, the way he held her, the way his hands moved over her bare skin, staying within the bounds of propriety but suggesting he wanted to do more, spoke of his experience. He displayed gentlemanly restraint, yet at times, the look in his eyes said he was on the precipice of losing control. She didn't want him to be disappointed when they made love the first time. She wanted to make him feel like he made her feel — desired.

Morgan watched her eyes, desperately wanting to know what she was thinking. He didn't want to leave her tonight. He wished she would say something so he would know how she felt.

Rose couldn't say what she was feeling, but she stood on her tiptoes and placed her lips on his. Morgan thought that beat the heck out of words any day of the week. He crushed his lips to hers and cradled her tightly to him. His lips left hers only to move to her ear, her neck, as he slid the straps of her chemise off her shoulders. He wanted to taste as much of her bare skin as he could find. Caught up in the pleasures of his lips, Rose dropped her head back, allowing him free access to her neck and shoulders.

Morgan's fingers found the ties to her corset, and he untied the bow. Rose didn't stop him. But his fingers stilled just as he was about to loosen the ties and strip the corset from her. What was he doing? Her grandmother was down the hall, he reminded himself. He couldn't bring dishonor to Rose, no matter how much he wanted her. And he wanted her like he'd never wanted another woman. He pulled back from her and held her at arm's length. Her heavy-lidded eyes told him she had a longing that matched his own. When his breathing slowed, he said, "I need to say good night before I do something I shouldn't." The way she was looking at him, he couldn't help but kiss her one last time, but he kept it brief. "I'll be riding to Denver tomorrow, so I won't be back until late."

It took Rose a moment before she grasped what he'd said. "Oh." She was surprised he hadn't mentioned this during dinner. "Why do you have to go to Denver?"

"Business. I want you and Granny to stay close to the ranch. Did you need me to pick up anything for you?"

She wondered why he hadn't asked her and Granny to accompany him. He probably figured it was too much trouble to take them, unless . . . No, she refused to think he might be seeing another woman. But why hadn't he mentioned this trip earlier tonight? "You didn't mention your trip at dinner. Was it a sudden decision?"

He was puzzled by her question. "I hadn't thought to mention it. Are you going to miss me?"

Rose didn't answer his question, but asked, "Will you be back for dinner?"

Morgan felt like he must have said something that displeased her, but he didn't know what it was. He didn't think it was his imagination that there was a sudden coolness in her voice. Was she angry with him because he'd stopped kissing her? If he hadn't put a halt to things when he did, he might not have left that room until morning. "I'm leaving early, so I should be home for dinner." He kissed her on the forehead. "I'll take Stevie's horse to him on my way out in the morning." He didn't want to return Stevie's horse, but he held out a thread of hope that he'd learned his lesson.

"Thank you."

Rose stood there staring at the closed door after he left her room. On one hand, she was thankful he'd pulled away from her when he had, because the situation could have easily gotten out of control. Her willpower seemed to be nonexistent around him. Her attraction to him was electrifying, and his touch evoked new sensations for her. She thought he felt the same way.

On the other hand, his sudden trip to Denver raised questions in her mind. She hadn't asked him if he was seeing another woman before she agreed to marry. Maybe he was seeing someone in Denver. Why was she even thinking such things? She knew why. Women were very attracted to him, and she hadn't even realized how many wanted him until tonight at dinner. Women obviously recognized that he was a virile, passionate man. Had he been as passionate with some of the women she'd met tonight? She couldn't seem to control her errant thoughts. Maybe he had a woman in Denver, and he needed to end that relationship before their marriage. It was ridiculous even to think such a thing. What on earth was wrong with her?

She'd thought her biggest worry would be how they would keep Frankie from coming between them. But that was before she thought Morgan might be seeing another woman. She'd heard of men who were not faithful to their vows. No matter how much she loved him, she couldn't be married to a man who wouldn't be committed to their marriage. Trying to end her wayward thoughts, she told herself Morgan had given her no reason to think he would be unfaithful. He'd asked her before if she trusted him, and she did. Though tempted to rush down the hall and ask him not to go to Denver, or to take her with him, she didn't think either choice was wise. She decided to remove her undergarments and go to bed before she did something she would later regret.

Once in bed, she turned to gaze at the moon shining through her window. Her mind was racing in a thousand different directions. She told herself the wiser course would be for her to pray over the situation, and ask for guidance. She closed her eyes and prayed. When she finished, she listened for that small, still voice that seemed to be silent tonight. She waited. Nothing. In frustration, she pulled the covers over her head. Sometimes the wiser course was a difficult road to follow.

CHAPTER EIGHTEEN

Reaching the Langtry farm just after dawn, Morgan was surprised to find Stevie wasn't home. Considering Stevie might not return for a few days, he was hesitant to leave the horse. He decided he could check on the animal on his way back from Denver, and if Stevie hadn't surfaced by then, he'd take the horse back to the ranch. After he filled the water troughs, he put the horse in the corral.

Finally, Morgan was on the road to Denver, but his thoughts centered on Rose. He was still trying to figure out what he'd said last night that upset her. He didn't really have time to take away from the ranch to ride to Denver today, but he wanted to buy Rose a wedding ring. It was important to him for her to have a symbol of their union. He remembered he'd never seen his mother without her wedding band. He figured it would also ensure that every man would know she was a married woman. But he had the feeling Rose didn't want him to go to Denver, and he couldn't help but wonder why. Was it possible she thought Frank could be in Denver? As far as Morgan knew, Frank hadn't committed any crimes in Denver, so maybe he wouldn't be recognized there. It was possible he had a hideout there, and Rose had a way of communicating with him. He didn't want to believe she would know Frank's whereabouts and not tell the law, since he was a wanted man. But he reminded himself she didn't have to be in contact with her brother to know where he might be lying low until the law gave up. While she might not be directly helping Frank, her familial ties might prevent her from divulging information that might help the sheriff apprehend him.

Walt arrived outside of Denver in the early morning hours. He rode to the abandoned two-room farmhouse he'd mentioned to Frank, several miles from town. Off the trail by several hundred yards, deep in the woods, the place was as eerie as he remembered. Years ago he'd heard a tale of an old woman who went insane living out here in the middle of nowhere after her husband and children died of cholera. She'd died addlepated and alone, and it was weeks before someone found her body. Local folks said she still haunted the place. People were too afraid, either of disease or ghosts, to come out here and scavenge what was left behind. Walt hoped the old woman didn't mind sharing the place for a few days.

He dismounted and walked around the house looking for signs of recent visitors. Aside from being more dilapidated, everything looked as it had when he'd hid out here a few years back after he'd done some rustling in New Mexico Territory. In the weeds, he found the mound of empty tins of food that he'd left behind, but there were no signs of more recent visitors. The rickety old lean-to, where he could shelter his horse, was still standing at the back of the house.

Once his horse was settled, Walt walked inside and looked around. As he swiped at the cobwebs, he thought it was too bad the spiders and other critters weren't afraid of ghosts. There was still an old broom in the corner that he'd used to sweep the place free of dust before, so he figured that was the first order of business. He didn't mind sharing his accommodations with a crazy old woman he couldn't see, but he drew the line at spiders. He hated the darn things.

He'd get the place clean enough to live in for a couple of days, then go to town and find this Reuben guy Frank was so interested in.

He laughed out loud thinking about Frank. Frank had a big problem, and that was thinking he was smarter than every other man. Walt read him like a book, but he'd let Frank go on thinking he didn't have the brains to think for himself. He didn't know how Frank had found out Reuben worked in the bank, but he'd bet his intention was to blackmail the clerk into helping him rob the bank. It was a certainty that Frank intended to double-cross Reuben if he could. Walt hadn't trusted Frank from the moment they'd started rustling together. After Deke told him the truth of what happened in Kansas, that Frank had been willing to kill his own sister to escape, Walt decided he'd best be watching his own back as long as he rode with him. He'd play this out, see what he could find out about Reuben, and then make up his own mind about whether to stay with the gang or not. The way he saw it, he didn't have anything better to do for a few days, and it was better than staying at the Conner place with the entire gang. They got on his nerves with their whining and bickering. He didn't mind

Deke and Dutch so much, and if he decided to break away from Frank, those two would probably go with him. They agreed with him; rustling was one thing, but he didn't abide killing. He figured if he went his own way, he might even go to the Black Hills and pan for gold. Seemed like a lot of folks were headed that way. Looking for gold sounded a whole lot better than rustling for a living.

When Morgan reached Denver, he took Faithful to the livery and walked to the jeweler. Inside the small shop, Morgan found some lovely rings on display, but he thought they all looked too large for Rose's small finger. He explained his dilemma to the store proprietor, Mr. Talmadge, telling him Rose's ring finger wasn't as large as his smallest finger. The man assured him any ring he selected could be sized to fit.

"Wait just a moment, I may have the perfect ring in my safe," Mr. Talmadge said as he walked through a curtain to a back room. He returned within minutes and handed Morgan a gorgeous sparkling diamond ring. The ring had one large diamond in the center and two smaller diamonds on each side. "This is one of my finest pieces. I'm sure your lovely lady would be thrilled to receive such a ring on her wedding day." As Morgan inspected the ring, the man discussed the quality of the stones as well as the price.

Morgan placed it on his little finger and he couldn't get it past the tip. He thought it would be perfect for Rose. He hadn't considered purchasing a ring with diamonds, but it was so beautiful he couldn't resist. He felt guilty that he'd asked her to marry him without giving her an engagement ring as was the custom. The ring was expensive, but he could afford the price, and he wanted her to have something beautiful. He'd saved for a lot of years, and he didn't squander his money. This was something Rose would have for the rest of her life. Morgan had noticed Granny still wore her wedding band, even though Preacher had been gone for a few years. That told him how important a symbol it was for a woman. He didn't want Rose to think another man might provide her with something better. "I'll take this one."

The man beamed. "You've made an excellent choice, and I'm sure your wife will be delighted."

Tucking the small box in his pocket, Morgan left the jeweler and decided to have lunch before he headed back to Whispering

Pines. He walked into the hotel restaurant, which was located directly across the street from the bank. The restaurant was nearly full, but he found a table near the back of the room. After he ordered, he glanced around the room, and his eyes landed on the man he'd seen before in front of the mercantile in Whispering Pines. He was the man who couldn't take his eyes off of Rose. The man was sitting by a window drinking coffee and staring out at the street.

Morgan watched the man while he ate his lunch. When the waitress came to collect Morgan's money, he pointed to the man. "Do you know who he is?"

The waitress eyed the man sitting alone. "No, sir, I don't think I've ever seen him before. Just passing through, I reckon."

Before Morgan finished the last of his coffee, the man jumped up and walked out the door. Morgan was curious what had made him take off in such a hurry, so he left the restaurant and stepped out on the sidewalk. He spotted the man walking down the street, so he decided he would follow him at a safe distance. The man was headed in the direction of the livery. As Morgan walked along the sidewalk, he spotted the man's palomino tied to a rail in front of a saloon. The livery was coming into view, and the man passed it by, so Morgan slowed. Fewer people were on the streets at this end of town. The way the man was walking, then stopping and waiting, made Morgan think he was following someone. Morgan stepped into the street to see what was ahead of the man he was stalking. He saw a man in a bowler hat walking some distance ahead. Morgan crossed the street, and stopped by the last building where he would have some cover to watch both men. The man Morgan was following stopped behind a tree. The man with the bowler hat stepped inside a gate and proceeded down the pathway to a small house.

Morgan waited for several minutes, but the man in the bowler hat didn't leave the house, unless it was through a back door. But he couldn't just stand there all day and watch the man, so he decided he'd go to the saloon where the palomino was tied. He'd have a beer and wait to see what happened. Less than an hour later, Morgan was sitting in the saloon by the window, drinking his second beer, when the man in the bowler hat came strolling by. Morgan noticed he was a small man, very tidy in his suit, certainly no cowboy or farmer. He watched the man enter the bank. The man following him stopped a block from the bank and sat in a chair in front of the barbershop. Morgan was curious what he was up to. If the man saw him and remembered him from the mercantile, he couldn't see why it would matter. Since Morgan had an account with the bank, he decided he'd go inside and see if he could find out the identity of the man in the bowler hat.

Inside the bank, Morgan stepped up to the counter. The man who had been wearing the bowler hat was sitting at a desk in the corner. If Morgan wasn't mistaken it was the same young man who had been talking to Stevie that day on the trail. The man in the buggy who didn't offer his name.

Douglas Rivers, the bank president, walked up to Morgan and stuck out his hand. "I thought that was you, Mr. LeMasters. I haven't seen you in a long time."

"Mr. Rivers, it's been a while since I've been to Denver." Out of the corner of his eye, he saw the young man look up at him. "How's the banking business?"

"Good." He pointed to two men sitting at desks, and added, "So good, in fact, I've hired more employees. How may we help you today?"

Morgan didn't really need anything, but he quickly made up an excuse for his presence in the bank. "I came to Denver to buy a present for my fiancée, and I need some cash."

"So you're getting married. When is the big day?"

"In a couple of weeks."

"Congratulations. Now, how much cash will you require?" Mr. Rivers moved behind the counter to help Morgan personally.

Morgan gave him a figure, and as Mr. Rivers was pulling the cash from the drawer, Morgan addressed the young man in the corner, who was looking down at a ledger in front of him. "I believe we met not long ago."

Reuben looked up at Morgan and nervously pushed his glasses up from the tip of his nose. "No, I'm sorry, I don't think so."

"Reuben, this is Morgan LeMasters. He owns Whispering Pines ranch," Mr. Rivers said.

Reuben nodded his head at the introduction. "Sir."

"Yes, I'm sure we met the day you were talking to Stevie Langtry," Morgan said.

"No, you must be mistaken. I don't know anyone by that name."

Morgan could read the lie on Reuben's face, just as he could see his hands were shaking.

"Well, perhaps it was a relative."

"Reuben is from back East, and he doesn't have relatives here," Mr. Rivers offered.

"Have you ever been to Whispering Pines, Reuben?" Morgan asked.

Reuben pretended to be very interested in the ledger in front of him. "No, I haven't had the time to explore the surrounding towns. Denver has everything I need right here."

Morgan accepted the money from Mr. Rivers and put it in his pocket. He tipped his hat and said, "It was nice to see you again, Mr. Rivers." He glanced in Reuben's direction. "Good to meet you, Reuben."

"Likewise," came the weak response.

Morgan hesitated, debating whether or not he should tell Reuben about the man following him. Finally, he thought he should give him fair warning in case the man had nefarious intentions. "Reuben, one more thing. I was having lunch in the hotel when I noticed a man following you once you left the bank. It may be a coincidence, but I thought I would mention it to you." Morgan certainly wasn't mistaken when he thought Reuben turned as white as an apparition.

Reuben swallowed and said, "I can't imagine why anyone would follow me."

Morgan smiled. "Must be a coincidence

then. If you're curious, he was sitting in a chair in front of the barbershop when I came into the bank."

Morgan walked out the door, and he could see the man was still sitting in the chair in front of the barbershop. There was no doubt in his mind Reuben was already at the window. Morgan crossed the street to make his way to the livery.

On his way home, Morgan thought about Reuben, and the day he saw him with Stevie Langtry. Why didn't Reuben want to admit he'd met Stevie? Unless . . . Stevie might not be smart enough to pull a robbery alone, but what if Reuben helped him? Stevie was a small man, carried a pearl-handled pistol, and Morgan had noticed Stevie seemed to be favoring one of his arms the other night. Had he been shot? Perhaps suspecting Stevie of a robbery wasn't as far-fetched as Morgan first thought. He planned to stop and see Jack before he went to the ranch. He'd tell him what he knew and see if he thought it was all a coincidence.

"Rose, are you feeling poorly today?" Granny asked when she placed their sandwiches on the table. She'd noticed Rose had been unusually quiet all morning.

"No, I'm feeling fine." Rose poured coffee

in their cups and took her seat.

Granny clasped Rose's hand and started praying. When she finished, she glanced at Rose. "What is troubling you?"

"Granny, do you think Morgan was seeing another woman before I returned?"

"He was not serious with anyone, if that is what you are asking. Why?" Granny was aware of every woman Morgan had been seen with, but he'd never seriously courted anyone.

"This trip to Denver seemed to come up suddenly," Rose replied.

Granny had heard Morgan leave very early this morning. "Why did he go to Denver?"

"He said it was business." Rose picked at her sandwich. "It's just that he didn't mention it at dinner earlier, and he only told me last night before he retired." She plopped the sandwich back down on her plate. "I may be jumping to conclusions, but he seemed to be secretive when I asked why he was going. He'd mentioned he would take us to Denver, yet last night he didn't ask us to join him."

"Did you tell him you wanted to go?"

"No. I didn't think he wanted us to go. I thought he might be seeing a woman in Denver."

Granny reached over and patted her arm.

"Dear, I don't think Morgan ever had time to go to Denver to see a woman and take care of his ranch."

"I suppose you are right. He's given me no reason to mistrust him."

"No, I should say not, and I don't think he ever will. Morgan is a wonderful man, and you should give him the benefit of the doubt. Don't prejudge him. Why don't you ask him when he gets home and get this all out in the open?" Granny was confident Morgan had nothing to hide and there was a perfectly reasonable explanation for his going to Denver without notice.

"Thanks, Granny, you always give good advice." Rose felt relieved. She would take Granny's advice and speak to Morgan later tonight.

"Now, how are we going to alter that old wedding dress? We need to do something to it to make it stunning. You are getting a handsome groom, and I want you to knock his eyeballs out," Granny said, smiling. "That old dress was the style of the day, but I much prefer the fuller skirts today."

Rose laughed. "That's the reason I purchased so much satin. The bodice of the dress is lovely, but I think we should make a very full skirt." Rose discussed her ideas for restyling Granny's wedding dress.

"Oh my, that sounds like a Southern belle dress. It should be beautiful," Granny said.

Rose found her mood improving the longer she discussed her impending wedding. "Now that we know how we are going to design my wedding dress, we need to work on a dress for you. I think that pink fabric we purchased is going to be lovely on you, Granny."

"It's a beautiful color. The last time I had a pink dress, I was a young girl. Preacher's favorite color was blue, so I often wore that color to please him."

"Blue does look lovely on you, but I thought you might like something different." Rose knew she would do the same thing if Morgan said he preferred one color over another. He always told her she looked beautiful in whatever she was wearing.

"And I do want something different. Rose, your marriage is a wonderful new start for you. And in some ways, it is a new start for me. I'm thankful Morgan wanted me to live with the two of you. And when you give me great-grandbabies, it will be the highlight of my final years."

Rose left her seat and put her arms around Granny. "Of course Morgan wanted you with us. It wouldn't be the same without you. And don't talk about your final years.

You will be with us for a long time. You'll want to see Addie and Emma married with babies too."

Granny smiled. "It is up to the Good Lord when our time is up. But I would like to stay with you for a long time. I do want to see Addie and Emma back home and happily married, as you will be soon."

Rose hoped Granny was right about her being happily married. She wanted that more than anything.

CHAPTER NINETEEN

Walt was sitting in the hotel restaurant by the same window when the bank closed and Reuben walked across the street and entered the restaurant. Since Reuben had been in the bank all day, other than during his lunch break, the day had been uneventful for Walt. As far as he could see, Reuben was just a little mouse of a man who had nothing exciting going on in his life. He didn't strike Walt as the kind of man who would do something illegal. If Frank approached Reuben to be his inside man at the bank, Walt thought the little man might die of fright. But there was always the possibility Frank had some knowledge about Reuben he could use to blackmail him. Frank could be one devious son-of-a-gun. Any man who was willing to kill his own sister, particularly a sister as pretty as Rose, had to be a man without conscience. Frank was an outlaw on a whole different level.

Reuben took a seat at a table beside Walt's. He was so close, Walt could hear what he ordered for dinner. He hoped Reuben was supposed to meet someone so his day wouldn't be a total loss. So far, he'd learned nothing about him, and the little man hadn't done more than work and eat. But no one met Reuben for dinner, and the waitress didn't spend time in idle chitchat with him like she did with some of the other patrons. When Reuben finished his dinner and left the restaurant, Walt motioned for the waitress.

"Would you like something else?"

Walt pointed to the table where Reuben had been sitting. "Do you know the man who was sitting there?"

"Reuben? He's just a clerk at the bank. He don't talk much, a bit odd if you ask me. Always orders the same dinner, and drinks hot tea even if it's a hundred degrees outside. And he never says thank you for nothing, even though he eats here every night."

Walt smiled when she finished ranting, thanked her and left the restaurant. He spotted Reuben and followed at a safe distance. Reuben walked into the home on the outskirts of town, just as he had earlier in the day. Walt found a grassy spot under a tree where he could watch the house until dark.

When Morgan walked through the door he smelled dinner cooking. He ran upstairs and put Rose's ring in his bureau drawer under his shirts before he hurried downstairs. It would be difficult not to give her the ring before their wedding day, but he wanted to surprise her.

"Hello," he said when he strolled into the kitchen.

Rose turned at the sound of his voice. "Hello. How was your trip?"

"Fine." He walked across the room and poured a cup of coffee. "By the way, Stevie wasn't home when I left for Denver this morning, but I left the horse in the corral. I stopped back by on my way home, and he hadn't returned, so I brought the horse back with me. I wasn't going to leave him there with no one to care for him."

"I wonder where Stevie is, with no horse to ride," Rose said.

"I doubt he's walking, wherever he is going." Morgan had ridden around the farm, and he found fresh hoofprints but no sign of Stevie.

During dinner, Morgan talked about Denver, and how it was bustling with people and new shops all over town.

"Emma's troupe is supposed to perform in Denver before the year is out," Granny said.

"Maybe you ladies would like to go see her perform," Morgan suggested. "We could spend a few days in Denver so you could do some shopping."

Rose had to bite her tongue to keep herself from asking why he hadn't invited them along today.

Granny glanced at Rose, and said, "That would be lovely. Don't you think so, Rose? I would love to see Emma perform."

"Yes, lovely." Rose looked at Morgan. "Did you do anything exciting in Denver today?"

Morgan hesitated, thinking the cool tone was back in Rose's voice. "No."

Granny noticed his hesitation, and was wise enough to change the subject.

After Granny and Rose finished cleaning the kitchen, Rose decided to sit on the front porch so she could talk to Morgan when he returned from the stable. She didn't have to wait long before she saw him exit the stable, talking to Murph. They chatted for a few minutes, then Murph turned toward the bunkhouse and Morgan headed toward the house.

It was Morgan's intention to talk some business with Murph tonight, but he saw Rose sitting on the porch when he left the stable and decided he'd rather talk to her. She'd been acting strangely, and he wanted to know what was wrong. "What are you doing out here?"

"I wanted to talk to you."

He wondered if she was having second thoughts about marrying him. He pulled a chair up beside her. "Okay."

She took a deep breath and forged ahead. "I was thinking last night that we haven't really known each other . . . we didn't know each other well before we agreed to marry."

Morgan looked at her and nodded.

"Well, I was thinking . . ." She paused.

"What were you thinking? Do you want to call off the wedding?" If that was what she had to say, he didn't want her to waste time trying to find a nice way to say it.

Her eyes widened. "Oh no. I was just wondering if you had been seeing someone else before I arrived."

Morgan felt a sense of relief. "By seeing, do you mean courting?"

"Yes. I didn't know if you had a serious relationship with someone before me."

Did she not know him at all? He'd done nothing to make her think he had an interest in someone else. "Rose, if I'd been courting someone, I would have ended the relationship before I asked you to marry me. No, I wasn't serious about anyone, and by asking that question, I'm not sure what kind of man you think I am." He was offended, and he didn't try to hide it. He knew women were interested in him, and he could have married over the last few years if that had been his aim.

Rose hadn't considered that her question might insult him. "It's just that so many women stopped to speak to you the other night, and I hadn't even considered you may have had someone else in your life."

"If you're asking if I've spent time with several women, the answer is yes. But I've never asked one to marry me."

"I'm sure if you did, they would have said yes." Rose knew without a doubt any of those women would have loved to be married to him.

"I'd like to think so. But I asked you, and I want you. Not someone else." Here he'd ridden to Denver to pick out a wedding ring for her, and she was basically calling him a scoundrel.

"But last night, you seemed to want me, and then you just stopped. And I thought when you suddenly said you had to go to

Denver, you were planning on seeing another woman."

What in the world was she talking about? First, she wanted to know if he was courting another woman, and now they were discussing last night. "Rose, what are you talking about?"

Rose's face turned red, and she was thankful it was getting dark so he couldn't see how embarrassed she was. "I thought you wanted to be with me last night."

"In your room? Is that what you are talking about? I did want to be with you. But what has that got to do with me courting another woman?" She was confusing him.

Rose looked down. How could she possibly ask this question? She'd started this conversation, so she was determined to see it through. "If you wanted . . . me, why did you stop last night? Do you have a woman in Denver that you went to see to . . ." Under no circumstances could she finish that question, no matter how much she wanted to know.

Jumping from his chair, Morgan started pacing in front of her. Surely, she wasn't asking what he thought she was asking. "Let me get this straight. Because I stopped kissing you and . . . because I stopped, you think I am so weak at controlling my urges

347

that I found it necessary to go to Denver to see some woman to seek companionship?" He was proud of himself for asking such a question in a gentlemanly way.

Rose was sure her entire body was beet red. Now that he'd summarized what she was thinking, she was beyond embarrassed. "It's just that I didn't know why you stopped."

Morgan threw his hands in the air. The woman was infuriating. "Of all the hare-brained comments." He leaned over, placing his palms on the arms of her chair, his nose just inches from hers. "I stopped because I wanted you. I stopped because in another second we would have been in your bed. I stopped because I respect you. I stopped because I thought you were a lady. I stopped because Granny was just down the hall. But most of all, I stopped because I'd like to think I have some character, and I can control my baser instincts." He wasn't about to admit that last night he'd been holding on to his control by a very thin thread.

Rose blinked. He was angry, very angry. She didn't know what to say. She hadn't intended to make him angry.

Morgan scooped her up in his arms and carried her to the door. "But since you are obviously no lady, and didn't want me to stop my advances, we can take care of that right now."

Rose was stunned. "What do you mean?"

Morgan opened the door, walked through, and kicked it shut with his boot. He walked to the staircase, hesitated as he looked at her, and said, "I mean we are going to do what I wanted to do last night, since you have no objections."

"But . . ."

If he hadn't been so angry he might have laughed at her stunned expression, but he set her on her feet instead. He started unbuttoning his shirt as he turned to walk up the staircase. When she didn't move, he turned around. "Aren't you coming?"

"But . . ."

He raised one eyebrow at her. "Well?"

"I didn't mean . . . well, I meant . . ." She had no idea how to explain her feelings.

Morgan unbuttoned his last button, pulled the shirt from his pants, stripped it off, and tossed it on the banister. "I thought you'd be in a hurry since you want me to prove to you that I wasn't with another woman in Denver."

Rose couldn't have said another word if her life depended on it. When he removed his shirt, her eyes were riveted on his rippling muscles, and she forgot all about their conversation. His bronzed torso was magnificently formed, and her desire to touch him was almost overwhelming. She couldn't imagine another man on earth as handsome as the one in front of her.

Morgan leaned over her and stared into her eyes. "You know I can't control myself, so you should hurry and get that dress off before I rip it off." His hand moved to the top button on her dress.

She slapped his hand away. "I didn't mean you couldn't control yourself!"

"Really? Well, what exactly did you mean?"

Rose backed away to put a few feet between them. "I just saw how those women looked at you." Her eyes were fixed on his broad shoulders and bare chest, and she almost lost her train of thought again. "Then, when we were . . . well, last night after you stopped . . . well, you suddenly mentioned a trip to Denver. I thought it was possible you were going to see another woman."

Morgan grabbed his shirt and shoved his arms through the sleeves. "Yeah. You said that." He was reading between the lines. She didn't trust him. That was the bottom line. Since he didn't finish what he started last night, she thought he had a backup woman waiting. He distinctly remembered asking her if she trusted him before he'd asked her to marry him. She just confirmed she believed all the lies Frank had told her about him. "The way I see it, Rose, you think I'm as lacking in character as your brother. Maybe I should live up to your expectations." That being said, he walked out the door and slammed it behind him.

Morgan stalked to the stable, saddled Faithful and slowly rode toward town. He thought of the women he'd spent time with over the past few years. He knew he would be welcomed if he stopped at any of their homes. Maybe he should go visit one of them, since that was what Rose expected him to do. He didn't question whether he could spend the night with another woman; he knew he could.

He couldn't keep from asking himself what would have happened if she hadn't slapped his hands away from her buttons. What if she'd allowed him to remove her dress? She was making him crazy. He didn't stop until Faithful was in front of the saloon. Morgan wasn't one to visit the saloon often, but he didn't care tonight. He needed a stiff drink.

Morgan sat in the corner of the saloon, sipping whiskey. Once he calmed down, he tried to think through his conversation with Rose. He couldn't figure out another way to show her that he deserved her trust. To him, trust was the very foundation for a good marriage. Perhaps it wasn't enough.

One thing was certain: He wasn't going home tonight. He looked around at the gals in the saloon. He could always spend the night here in one of their rooms. If he wanted company, it wouldn't be difficult to come by. He finished his drink, walked out the door, untied Faithful, and headed to the livery. He was tired, and he was determined he wasn't going to ride all the way back home tonight. He'd sleep at the hotel, and let Rose think what she wanted.

Rose left her bedroom door cracked open, waiting to hear when Morgan returned. She'd gotten out of bed at least a dozen times to look out the window to see if there was a light coming from the stable. He hadn't returned. It hadn't been her intention to insult him, or to imply that she didn't trust him. At first, she couldn't understand why he'd jumped to that conclusion. Now that he'd explained why he had stopped his amorous advances, she felt guilty for thinking there was someone else. He respected her, and she'd thrown his good intentions back in his face. He had every reason to be angry with her. She trusted him. It was all of the other women she didn't trust.

She may not have wanted him to stop last night, but if he hadn't she would have been upset that he wasn't treating her like a lady. She was so confused that she didn't know what she wanted. She was certain of one thing: She wanted him to come home. Where was he? Had she driven him to another woman's arms? Loving him was driving her daft. She reminded herself of Preacher's favorite three words: Love never fails. Problem was, she loved Morgan, but he wasn't in love with her. He'd made it clear from the start that he was basing their marriage on friendship and trust. Marriage was a sacred union before God, and she felt Morgan would honor his commitment once they married. Problem was, they weren't married yet.

Walt watched Reuben's home until the wee hours of the morning before heading back to the little shack. He didn't have much to report back to Frank yet, so he'd stay another day, but instead of wasting his time while Reuben was at work, he planned to find a more pleasurable way to spend the afternoon. He was due a little fun while he was in Denver. That big, fancy saloon was near the bank, and the perfect place for what he had in mind. He wondered how a man like Reuben could go to work the same time every day, get off at the same time, following the same routine, day in and day out, without allowing himself some pleasant pursuits at night. Walt would go nuts, just like the old woman who'd lived in the house he was occupying. Sometimes a man had a need to get on his horse and take off, or visit the saloon and tie one on. In his estimation, ranch work was a better alternative than living in the city with a bank job. Of course, even if a man had a job in the city, he could always have a little fun at night. But then, Reuben didn't strike him as the kind of man who would darken the door of a saloon. What did a man like Reuben do for entertainment? Probably had his nose stuck in a book every night. Walt reached for the whiskey bottle he'd placed on one of the shelves. Reuben might not enjoy what Denver had to offer, but he wasn't about to make the same mistake.

Rose left her bedroom early the next morning to prepare breakfast. When she passed Morgan's bedroom, the door was open and she noticed his bed covers had not been disturbed. She hoped she might have fallen asleep sometime during the night and didn't hear him return.

While she kneaded dough, she kept waiting for him to come walking through the door. She heard footsteps, but when she turned around, it was Granny joining her.

"You are up early," Granny said.

"I couldn't sleep." She turned back to the stove, trying to hide her misery from Granny.

"Didn't he come home?" Granny asked.

Rose was surprised at Granny's question. "How did you know he wasn't home?"

"I heard him leave. I imagine all of heaven heard the front door rattling on its hinges." Granny figured they'd argued, but she decided not to meddle in their business.

Rose's eyes filled with tears. "No, he didn't come home."

Granny hurried across the room and took Rose in her arms. "There, there, honey. He'll come back soon. This is his ranch."

Rose couldn't help but laugh through her tears. "But he was so angry with me. I made a mess of things."

"He won't stay mad. Just give him time. You two will work everything out."

"I'm not so sure. He was very upset. I'm

afraid I pushed him into another woman's arms."

"Rose, it would take more than one argument to send him to another. Morgan is not that kind of man."

"That's what he said. He thinks I don't trust him because I asked him if there was another woman in his life."

Granny looked into her eyes. "Don't you trust him?"

"He's never given me a reason not to trust him. But where is he? You saw how those women flirted with him."

"Yes, I did. But I also noticed he introduced you to each one of them as his future wife. He certainly didn't behave like a man trying to hide something. Remember the Good Book says love endures all things."

If only Morgan loved her, then perhaps they would survive their argument. "I wanted to know why . . ." She paused. She didn't know how to tell her grandmother what had provoked their argument. She was angry because Morgan had been a gentleman.

They heard a horse ride in, and men's voices outside. Rose ran to the window and looked out. "He's here." She watched him as he spoke with Joseph and Murph for a few minutes. Then he led his horse to the stable. When he exited the stable he was riding another horse, and rode away with Murph by his side.

"Where were you all night?" Murph asked. He'd seen Morgan leave the ranch late and not return until morning.

"At the hotel."

Murph knew something was on his mind. "What's wrong with you this morning?"

"Nothing."

"You and the little woman have a fight?"

"Something like that."

"You better treat her right, or some hombre might take her away from you."

Morgan glared at him. "Yeah? I'd like to see him try."

"Did you go to the saloon last night? You hungover?"

"Yeah, I went to the saloon. No, I'm not hungover. I only had one whiskey."

"Is that the reason Rose is mad at you?"

"No, she doesn't know where I was. But I bet she thinks I was with a woman last night."

Murph was beginning to understand the reason for Morgan's bad mood. "She thinks you are seeing another woman?"

"Woman, or women. I'm not sure. All I

357

know is she basically said she doesn't trust me."

Murph knew how much Morgan valued trust. It didn't make sense to him why a woman wouldn't trust the man he would trust above all others. "Why did she agree to marry you if she doesn't trust you?"

The situation was as confusing this morning as it was last night. "Now there's a question. Beats the heck out of me."

CHAPTER TWENTY

Having watched Reuben go back inside the bank after his lunch break, Walt walked into the saloon. He had the entire afternoon to have a little fun. Reaching the bar, he threw some coins down and told the barkeep to leave the bottle of whiskey after he filled his small glass. Walt turned around as he sipped his whiskey and glanced at the three women in the room. One gal was playing cards with four men, and Walt thought she was a real looker for a saloon dove. At the same time Walt was admiring her, she looked up at him and smiled. He was tempted to sit at the table and play poker, but he had to keep an eye on the bank.

He glanced at the other two gals in the room. They were hustling drinks to three cowboys who didn't appear interested in anything other than getting drunk. Walt grabbed his bottle and walked to a table near the window. He'd keep an eye on the bank just in case Reuben decided to shake up his routine and do something unexpected. It didn't take long before one of the women who had been hustling drinks strolled over to his table and asked if she could join him. He was disappointed it wasn't the pretty one playing cards.

They had nearly finished off the first bottle of whiskey, and Walt gave the woman money to buy another bottle. He didn't figure he'd wasted time because he'd questioned the woman about Reuben. She knew Reuben was a bank clerk, but she said he never frequented the saloon. When the woman returned to the table, she convinced Walt they would have more privacy upstairs. Walt didn't object, and she reached for his hand and led the way upstairs to her room.

Waking up with a start, Walt looked around the room. It took a minute for his whiskey-soaked brain to clear. He realized he'd fallen asleep, and one glance at the woman lying next to him said she was passed out. He looked her over, from her made-up face down to her slippers. Having consumed a good portion of whiskey, she wasn't nearly as handsome as he'd first thought. He fished out his pocket watch from his pants pocket and snapped open the cover. Dang. It was quitting time for Reuben. He didn't feel like leaving the comfort of the soft feather mattress, but he had to go. He picked up the bottle on the side table and swallowed the last drop of whiskey. He had just enough time to go to the hotel and order a cup of coffee. If the waitress was right, Reuben would be dining in a few minutes.

Walt's first cup of coffee was just beginning to work on his pounding head when Reuben walked through the door. The little man sat at the same table as the day before and ordered the same meal. By his third cup of coffee, Walt wanted nothing more than to go back to the shack and sleep until daylight. He saw no point in following Reuben home again tonight. This was not a man who did anything out of the ordinary. Walt couldn't imagine leading a more boring existence. When the waitress came by to refill his cup, Walt decided he'd order some pie before he headed out to the cabin.

The waitress brought his pie, and then stopped at Reuben's table to collect his money. Reuben stood and picked up his hat from the table, but instead of walking out of the restaurant, he approached Walt's table and sat in the seat opposite him.

Walt stared at him. This was certainly an unexpected move from the little mouse of a man. Maybe Reuben did occasionally vary his routine.

Reuben removed his round glasses and started to clean the lenses with his handkerchief. "I'm thinking either Stevie or Frank Langtry sent you here for some reason. I would venture to guess it was Frank. I think you and I should have a talk."

Morgan and Murph rode back to the ranch at lunchtime, mostly because Morgan was hungry. When they reined in at the stable, Morgan spotted Rose at the corral. He jumped off his horse and strode toward her. "Stay away from that horse!"

Rose turned at the sound of his angry voice. "But . . . I was just talking to him."

"I said to stay away from him. As long as you are on my ranch, you'll do as I say with my animals."

His tone frightened her, and she stepped away from the corral. "But . . ." She hesitated. Morgan hadn't even given her the courtesy of an explanation. He turned his back and stalked toward the stable. If he had given her the chance she would have told him why she was with the horse. She'd watched him in the corral alone for over an hour, and she felt sorry for him. She thought the poor thing looked as lonely as she felt, so she sliced an apple to take to him. At a distance he was a beautiful animal; a shiny black coat with four white stockings, and long, flowing black mane and tail. As she approached, she was shocked to see the large animal had large raised scars covering his body. She didn't know what had happened to him, but he seemed quite tame and docile. When she held her hand out to him he came over and sniffed her. He took the apple from her hand gently, and allowed her to stroke his neck as he ate.

Confused, she stared at the stable door a minute before turning back to the horse. "Good-bye, I'll come back again." She wouldn't touch him without Morgan's approval, but she had every intention of asking him why she shouldn't be around that horse.

As soon as she walked in the kitchen she started preparing a sandwich for Morgan. When he came through the door a few minutes later, he was silent. He walked to the stove and poured himself a cup of coffee.

"Would you like more than one sandwich?" Rose asked.

"I can fix my own sandwiches." He was still angry over last night, and seeing her with his horse opened up old wounds.

Wounds that he wore on the inside, not the outside like his horse.

Rose placed the plate on the table in front of him. "Why can't I be around that horse? He's gentle and tame. I've been around horses all my life."

"Leave it alone, Rose." Morgan realized he didn't even know if Rose could ride a horse.

"Are you going to tell me why you are so angry with me?"

Morgan wasn't willing to give an inch. "I think we said enough last night."

She'd told herself she wasn't going to ask, but she found herself asking anyway, "Where were you all night?"

"Didn't you assume I would live up to your expectations?" he replied curtly.

Even though he was angry with her, Rose hadn't expected that response. "Are you saying you were with a woman?"

So he wasn't wrong last night. That was what she was thinking he would do. Morgan jumped up so fast his chair skidded on the wood floor. He grabbed two pieces of bread and slapped a hunk of meat in the center, then picked up the sandwich she'd made and stuffed two apples in his pocket. He walked out the door without saying another word.

It angered him each time she let him know how little she thought of his character. Well, she could just stand in that kitchen and talk to herself, because she wasn't going to insult him again. What did the woman want from him? He helped her when she was injured, protected her from her brother, he'd seen her home safely, he'd offered her and Granny the security of his home, and promised to take care of them. What more did she want?

Rose watched Morgan from the kitchen window. He stopped at the corral as he ate his sandwiches, and it looked like he was talking to the black horse. After he ate, he pulled a knife from his pocket and started slicing an apple. He held the slices out to the horse. When the horse finished the first apple, he sliced the second one for him. Morgan braced both arms on the top rail, and the horse nudged his shoulder. He stood there for a long time stroking the animal's neck. Rose could tell Morgan was indeed talking to the animal, and it looked as though the horse held his head close to Morgan's and listened.

"Did you talk to him?" Granny asked over her shoulder.

Rose jumped a foot off the ground.

"Granny, I didn't hear you."

"No, you were busy watching your man."

"I don't think he's mine. He said he was with another woman last night."

Granny could not believe Morgan would do such a thing. "Now, Rose, I'm sure you misunderstood."

Rose repeated their conversation and Granny said, "He didn't say he was with another woman. He said that was what you expected of him. Is that what you truly believe he would do?"

"I don't know what to think. My emotions seem to be getting the best of me."

"Rose, Morgan could have had another woman long ago if he wanted. You need to trust in God's plan."

Rose wasn't sure she knew God's plan, but she was willing to trust Him. "I'll try."

"Good. You'll never be disappointed when you give your trust to Him. I'm confident He wouldn't have brought Morgan to you if he wasn't the one."

Rose couldn't seem to pull her eyes away from Morgan as he talked to that horse. "Morgan told me to stay away from that horse. Do you know why?"

Granny looked out the window. "I don't know. Morgan used to ride that horse years ago. I remember thinking it was the most beautiful animal I'd ever seen."

"You can't see them from here, but he has a lot of scars over his body."

"Maybe he had some sort of accident," Granny said. "That's a shame, he's so beautiful."

"He's still beautiful, but it comes from the inside."

Rose left her bedroom door ajar again so she would hear Morgan when he came home. He hadn't come home for dinner, and they'd waited for him for two hours before they ate. Finally, she heard his footsteps on the staircase. She listened as he walked in his bedroom and quietly closed the door. She glanced at the clock on the mantel. It was almost midnight. He kept mighty late hours for a rancher.

Nothing changed over the next few days. Morgan left the house before dawn and didn't come home for lunch or dinner. Occasionally, Rose would see some men ride in midday, but Morgan was never with them. Joseph was always around the ranch, caring for the animals or working on anything that needed repair. Rose was devastated, and she didn't know how to repair their relationship if Morgan wouldn't meet her halfway. They needed to talk if they were going to go through with their marriage. She thought perhaps he was trying to tell her he no longer wanted to marry her. If that was his aim, she needed to find out soon.

Rose and Granny were eating lunch, and Rose was tired of sitting around waiting on Morgan to get over his anger and talk to her. "Granny, Stevie's horse is still here, so I'm going to take him to the farm to see if Stevie needs him. I'm worried about him."

"I'm worried about him too. I'll go with you." Even though the farm was just a few minutes away through the pines, Granny didn't want Rose to go alone. She felt sure it would upset Morgan even more. She'd hoped she would have a chance to speak with Morgan on Rose's behalf, but since he wasn't coming home, the opportunity hadn't presented itself.

Rose led Stevie's horse from the stable, and she and Granny walked through the pines. Stevie was not home, but they could tell he'd eaten there recently. They washed all of the dishes and straightened the house before they went outside to care for the garden.

"Rose, I need to start canning some of these vegetables," Granny said.

"I was thinking the same thing. Do you think we should do it here, or take them to Morgan's? I hate to do something without asking him. Since I haven't seen him, I'm wondering if he's trying to tell me he'd like to call off the marriage."

"I'm sure if he felt that way, he would let you know." Granny had faith in Morgan, but even she was disappointed that he was avoiding them.

They heard a horse behind them, and when they turned around, there was Morgan glaring at them. "I thought I told you two not to come here without me."

"It's difficult for us to tell you anything when you are never around," Rose snapped before turning her attention back to weeding the garden.

Granny looked at Morgan and raised her gray eyebrows at him. "We haven't seen much of you the last few days. We brought Stevie's horse back, but he's not here. We need to start some canning soon, and Rose and I were just discussing if we should do it here."

"We'll take what you need to the ranch," Morgan said. His eyes were fixed on Rose's backside as she was bending over, pulling weeds. She was ignoring him. He couldn't blame her, he'd been acting like an idiot.

And he was the one getting the worse end of the deal. Instead of kissing her good night and climbing into his nice soft bed, he was bedding down with his horse and sleeping on the hard ground. Every bone in his body was aching. "We can come back tomorrow with the buckboard."

Morgan heard a sound at the side of the house and was about to draw his gun when Stevie came strolling around the corner.

"Stevie, we brought your horse back," Granny said.

"Thanks." Stevie remembered Frankie wanted him to pretend he was staying on the farm. "I was just out walking. I planned on coming to the ranch to ask what you wanted me to do with the vegetables."

Granny was pleased that he was offering to help. "Rose and I are going to start canning, but you can gather the ripe vegetables and we'll pick them up tomorrow."

"Sure thing." Stevie looked at Rose. "So when's the big day?"

Rose glanced at Morgan. She had no idea what to say.

"In two weeks," Morgan said. "You're welcome to join us."

"Thanks, I will."

"If you ever want to join us for supper, you're welcome anytime," Morgan added.

"I'm sure Granny and Rose would like the company."

Morgan wasn't fooled by Stevie's sudden interest in the farm, or their marriage. Something was up, he just didn't know what it was yet. He sure as heck wasn't out for a walk. He started to tell Stevie about meeting Reuben in Denver, but he didn't want to tip Stevie off if Jack was looking into the stagecoach robbery.

Rose felt a surge of relief at Morgan's response, and that he was trying to be cordial to Stevie. After Stevie's past behavior, Morgan was more forgiving than she expected.

Stevie wanted them to leave so he could take Frankie's horse back to him. "Well, thanks for bringing the horse home, and I'll get the vegetables together."

"Do you want to come to dinner tonight, Stevie?" Rose asked. She thought he probably hadn't had a good meal since they'd left. Granny was right, he needed to work if he was going to eat, but she couldn't help feeling sorry for him.

"No thanks, I'd best get to work," Stevie said.

"As I said, you're welcome to work on the ranch," Morgan said.

"I'll think about it."

"We'll come back in the morning for the vegetables," Granny told him.

Morgan dismounted and offered to let Rose and Granny ride his horse, but they said they preferred to walk. The three of them walked through the pines back toward the ranch.

When they reached the house, Morgan said he was going to take a bath in the bunkhouse and would be home for dinner.

As soon as he was out of earshot, Granny said, "You see, he is still planning on marrying. He told Stevie when the wedding would be."

"Yes, he did. I still think we need to talk." Rose would see what kind of mood he was in before she tried to have a discussion with him tonight. She didn't want to ruin another evening and have him take off. Particularly since she didn't know where he'd been spending his nights.

That night, after Granny retired, Morgan walked in the kitchen and told Rose he'd like to talk to her. Rose removed her apron and walked with him to the parlor. He sat on the settee and asked her to sit beside him.

"Rose, I've had a hard time understanding why you don't trust me. What you said the other night about me having another woman didn't make a bit of sense."

Rose looked into his eyes. "I do trust you. I explained things badly the other night. It felt so good when we were kissing and then you just stopped." Rose hesitated as she tried to put into words what she felt. She looked down at her hands folded in her lap. "I think I was afraid you didn't want me as much as I wanted you. I'm not experienced, and I know you are, and I felt inadequate." She couldn't be much more honest. Plain and simple, she was worried she couldn't please him.

Morgan couldn't have been more shocked if she'd pointed a pistol at him. "You must be out of your mind to think you want me more than I want you." He pulled her on his lap. "Honey, I've never wanted anyone as much as I want you."

Rose rested her head on his chest. "I loved the way you made me feel."

Morgan took her chin in his hand and kissed her. He kissed her so long and so thoroughly they were both breathing hard when they pulled apart. "I love the way you make me feel too." He lowered his lips to hers and kissed her again. Like before, his lips moved to her ear and he whispered sweet words to her.

Rose wrapped her arms around his neck

and whispered in his ear, "You are so beautiful without your shirt."

Hearing those words from her excited him beyond belief. He held her to him and continued to kiss her. It was apparent that she didn't want him to stop. But he had to stop. "Rose, we need to stop."

Rose pulled back and looked at him. Her eyes were glazed over, just as they had been the other night. "Rose, I don't want to stop, but we have to. Do you understand?" He wanted to explain this time so she wouldn't get the wrong idea.

"I'm trying to understand."

The way she was looking at him nearly made him forget his vow to wait until he married her. "Honey, there's a point when a man has to stop, or he risks losing control."

"I'm not sure what you mean," Rose said.

"I mean if we keep kissing like this, I'll want to take you to my bed. I don't want to lose control of the situation. It's been a long time since . . ." He thought it might not be wise to finish that thought.

When he didn't finish his sentence, she said, "It's been a long time since what?"

He took a deep breath, hoping she would figure it out.

She did. "Oh." His words meant the world to her, and she wanted to be equally honest with him. "Thank you for explaining. I've been jealous since that day in town when I saw how all those women flirted with you right in front of me. You are so handsome, and I was afraid you might want someone else if I didn't live up to your expectations."

"I don't want another woman. I want you."

Rose hesitated to ask a question about another matter that had troubled her, but she thought they needed to clear the air. "I have another question. Why did you get angry with me for touching that horse? You know I would never hurt him."

"I know. It's just, that horse can be skittish, and I don't want you in danger if he acts up."

"He seemed very gentle when I fed him the apple."

"Some particular sounds make him nervous, and he might rear unexpectedly," Morgan warned.

"What happened to him?" She remembered Granny told her Morgan rode that horse years before.

"It's not important. Just be careful around him."

She could tell he didn't want to discuss it further. "Does he have a name?"

"Judge."

CHAPTER TWENTY-ONE

Stevie rode to the old Conner place, back-tracking several times to make sure he wasn't being followed. He thought Granny and Rose bought his act, but he couldn't be sure about Morgan.

"What are you doing here?" Frankie asked, stepping from the brush before Stevie reached the cabin.

"I brought your horse back."

"So Morgan returned your horse?"

"Yeah. I did like you told me and made them think I would do some work around the farm. They even invited me to their wedding in a couple of weeks."

"The wedding that won't take place. Do you know where the cattle are grazing?"

Stevie knew Frankie was talking about Morgan's cattle. When he'd left the farm, he'd seen Morgan's men moving cattle. "Yeah, I saw them moving part of the herd to the west. Are you planning on rustling soon? I wanted to tell you that I'm meeting Reuben tomorrow at the same place, if you want to come along."

"I do want to meet him." Frankie expected Walt to show up soon, and hopefully he'd have some information to share about Reuben. "What time are you meeting him tomorrow?"

Stevie gave him the time and place. "I'll ride this way and we can ride together."

"No, you go on your own just in case someone is watching you. I'll meet you there."

"Okay. I've got to go back now. I told Granny I'd do some work in the garden before tomorrow. Frankie, I still wish we could take that money from the stagecoach robbery and head on down to Mexico now."

"I told you, we need a lot more money. Are Granny and Rose coming to the farm often?"

"Not much, but they're coming back tomorrow morning for the vegetables."

Stevie mounted his horse, and Frankie said, "I'll see you tomorrow."

Not long after Stevie left, Walt returned and Frankie walked outside to talk to him privately. He hadn't told the other men why Walt was in Denver. "Did you bring more whiskey?"

Walt pulled four bottles from his saddle-bag. "That should hold you over."

Frank opened a bottle and drank greedily. He wiped his mouth with his sleeve. "That's good whiskey. What did you find out about Reuben?"

Walt shook his head. "Frank, that fellow don't do nothing but work. He goes to work, goes home for lunch, eats dinner every night at the hotel, and then goes home. I don't know if you've seen him, but I can't imagine him being a help if you plan on robbing the bank. He doesn't have family in Denver, and no friends according to the waitress at the hotel. Nobody knows much about him."

That wasn't the news Frank wanted to hear. He needed somebody on the inside if he was going to rob the bank. He didn't want to pay Reuben half the take, but if he didn't have someone or something to hold over his head, Reuben might not agree to help him. "Does he go to the saloon? Does he drink? He's got to do something besides work at the bank."

"He doesn't go into the saloon." Walt shook his head and smiled. "Frank, you have to see this guy to understand. He orders hot tea with his meals." Walt held his hand in the air four feet off the ground.

"He's about this tall, and I doubt he weighs much more than a baby calf."

Frank smiled at Walt's description of Reuben. He figured a man like that would be easily intimidated. "Walt, I don't want you to say anything to the men about Denver. I've got a lot to think through, and I don't need their opinions on what I'm planning. I don't want anyone running their mouths if they get a little liquor in their gut."

Walt wondered if Frank would even include the boys in what he was planning. Walt nodded. "No problem. What about Stevie? Does he know what is going on?"

"Yeah, but I'm thinking the two of us could handle the bank robbery. We have no reason to split the money, not even with Stevie." He inclined his head toward the cabin. "Remember if you get liquored up, keep your mouth shut."

"Yeah." Walt figured he just needed to watch his back and make sure Frank didn't try to double-cross him, or eliminate him. If Frank was willing to double-cross his own brother, he wasn't above shooting him in the back. He'd been smart to listen to Reuben last night at the restaurant.

Stevie waited until LeMasters, Rose, and Granny left with the vegetables the next

379

morning before he left to meet Reuben. Frank had been watching all of them from his usual hiding place. He'd timed his trip to the farm hoping to see Stevie leave. After Stevie rode away, Frank waited a few more minutes to make sure no one was coming back. He left his horse out of sight, grabbed his saddlebag and quickly ran inside the house. In Stevie's room, he wasted no time removing the loose board in the corner. He pulled the money bag from the opening, removed half of the contents, and stuffed it into his saddlebag. He replaced the money with old newspapers he'd removed from the walls at the Conner place. He palmed the bag to feel its weight, and then placed it exactly as he'd found it in the cubbyhole. Stevie would be none the wiser unless he looked inside the bag.

"Did you have any trouble?" Stevie asked when Frankie reined in at the designated area.

"No, I was just being real cautious." Frank looked at Reuben. "I'm Frank Langtry."

Reuben removed his glasses and peered at Frank. "I've heard about you."

Frank didn't like the sound of that. "Who's been telling you about me?"

"Stevie, who else? He was quite concerned

about you being hanged."

Frank's first thought was that Walt's description of Reuben was dead-on. He couldn't see how tall he was since he was seated in his buggy, but he was definitely a little fop of a man. This was going to be easier than he thought. He didn't waste time getting to the point. "Stevie's told me about the stagecoach robbery, and how you planned everything out. I think you could be very helpful with what I'm planning."

Reuben glanced at Stevie. "Are you making plans to rob the bank?"

Stevie shook his head. "This is Frank's idea."

Reuben took his time responding as he settled his glasses on his nose. "I don't think I'm interested in robbing the bank. I would be inside at the time, and that sounds very dangerous. It's not like planning a stagecoach robbery out in the middle of nowhere. We have a sheriff and deputies, and I am told they are quite accurate shots."

Frank felt like laughing. "No one would know you are in on it. We would point a gun at you like we would the others. All you need to do is tell me what would be the best day to rob. The day the vault is full."

"And what would be in it for me?"

There was the question Frank had been

expecting. "I'm sure you understand that it can't be the same deal you had with Stevie. We have too many men and we all will split it equally."

"That would not make it worth my time," Reuben said.

Frank dismounted and walked toward the buggy. Reuben slid back in the seat. Frank leaned close to him and spoke in a low tone. "Let's put it this way. If you don't, we'll shoot you when we rob the bank, because we are going to rob it one way or the other."

Reuben's eyes widened. Frank had the coldest blue eyes he'd ever seen. He felt as though he was looking into the depths of a soulless creature. "I could tell the sheriff what you are planning."

Frank grinned. "Yeah, you could. But then I reckon someone could inform the sheriff how you robbed the stagecoach."

"But I didn't rob the stagecoach," Reuben said.

"You had a hand in it. Oh, you might not get as many years in the territorial prison since you didn't rob it yourself. But how do you think you would do in prison for five years or so?" If Frank wasn't mistaken, Reuben paled a bit.

"I guess I see your point."

Smiling wide at him, Frank said, "I

thought you would. Now why don't you tell me about the next shipment the bank is expecting?"

Reuben stared at him a minute, then said, "We are expecting a large shipment by Friday and the money will be at the bank for ten days."

Frank and Stevie listened as Reuben explained the details of the shipment.

"Frankie, our take would be enough money so that we will never have to pull another robbery," Stevie said.

Frank slapped his brother on the back. "Stevie, you may be right. Now let's plan how we can pull this off."

They sat for two hours discussing how and when to rob the Denver bank. Reuben was impressed with Frank's devious mind and his thorough planning. He was not a stupid man, but Frank had weaknesses. Reuben thought two of those weaknesses would eventually destroy him: his greed, and his hatred for Morgan LeMasters.

They were riding back to the cabin when Frankie told Stevie of his plans to rustle cattle tonight.

"I already told the boys not to drink too much because we're going to have a long ride after we get those cows. We're going to drive them down to New Mexico Territory to sell. That'll give us some money to tide us over."

Stevie had hoped Frankie was going to change his mind about rustling on Morgan's ranch. He hadn't forgotten what had happened to Smiley. Sometimes he still had dreams about the screams they'd heard the last time they rustled on Whispering Pines. He knew the other men felt the same way about riding on LeMasters's land.

"Frankie, we can use some of the stagecoach money. There's more than enough to get what we need. If the bank holdup don't pan out, we will still have enough to make a start somewhere else."

"Stevie, I want us to keep that money just in case we can't pull off this bank job. I'll be in Denver watching Reuben for a few days. I want to make sure your friend can be trusted."

"Reuben can be trusted," Stevie insisted.

"As long as you were the one actually robbing, he didn't have much at stake. If you got caught and said he was involved, it would have been your word against his."

Stevie didn't comment, but he thought Frank was being paranoid.

"But tonight we are going rustling. LeMasters needs to know he will never be safe from me." Knowing Stevie was probably thinking about Smiley, Frank grinned and said, "Don't worry about no spooks. We'll ride in from the cabin after midnight. We won't be in the pines that long if we go in from that direction."

"Can I go with you to sell the cattle?" Stevie asked.

"I don't plan on going with the boys to sell them. I'm going to stay here with you and Walt. If I decide to rob the bank, the three of us can handle it. They won't have more than three employees there at any one time. You heard what Reuben said, Mr. Rivers isn't hiring extra guards. I want you to stay around the farm until we decide when we are going to rob the bank."

"What happens after the holdup?" Stevie asked.

"I'm going to tell the boys we'll meet them in New Mexico territory. A town called Las Vegas. You remember I told you about that town. The men want some female company, and there's no better place to get what you want than in that wild town. But don't slip up and talk about robbing the bank. We ain't sharing that money."

Stevie remembered the stories about the lawless town where every outlaw in the West hid out in plain sight. He'd been wanting to go to Las Vegas and meet some of the fast guns. Maybe he could even call one of them out to see who was the fastest. "I can't wait to see that town."

"You'll see it soon enough," Frank promised.

"Frankie, we should rustle in the morning," Stevie said.

Frank gave his brother a hard look. "You wanting to run the show now, little brother?"

"No, I was just saying we should wait until tomorrow morning because Morgan said they were all going to church. They invited me to go along. A lot of his men go to church, so I figured they'd be shorthanded. I'd bet no one would be on that west range if we strike before dawn."

"Well, that's good to know. Pretty smart thinking, little brother. Maybe the boys won't be as skittish as little girls, riding through those pines in the morning. We can ride out a lot faster in daylight hours."

"It's a rustler's moon tonight," Deke said when Frank and Stevie arrived at the cabin.

"It's a good night to be seen," Corbin grumbled.

Frank looked at them and snorted. "Stevie had a good idea. Tomorrow is Sunday, and

Stevie said most of the ranch hands go to church, so that's when we are going to hit them. They'll be shorthanded. And you girls may not be as scared to ride through the pines in the daylight."

"Makes sense," Walt said.

"Sounds good to me," Dutch said.

"Okay, gather around, we'll lay out the plan for tomorrow." After Frank planned the rustle, he told them he would be meeting up with them later in Las Vegas. "You know where to sell the cattle, and I figure you boys deserve a rest. I know how you love that town."

"What do you mean? You usually handle the sale of the cattle," Deke said.

"I won't be leaving with you. Me, Walt, Stevie, and Corbin are going to stay behind," Frank said.

"Why are the four of you staying behind? That don't sound like a smart thing to do," Reb said.

"When the time is right we're going to take care of LeMasters and that Sioux. I know you men don't have nothing personal against LeMasters. So I trust you to sell the cattle and take the money to Las Vegas. You understand how important it is for Joseph Longbow not to testify against us?" He looked from man to man as they all nodded in unison. "Well, I'm going to make sure he don't."

"Why can't I go with the boys to sell the cattle?" Corbin asked. "I ain't got nothing against LeMasters."

"I'm going to need you for a diversion when I go after LeMasters and Longbow." Frank figured Corbin was the most expendable man in the gang. He wasn't a good shot, and he was stupid enough to believe anything Frank told him. Frank needed someone he could sacrifice, and he nominated Corbin.

"How many cows are we going to take?" Deke asked.

"I'm hoping we can get at least fifty head," Frank said. "Now I trust you boys not to spend all that money on whiskey and women. We're going to need some of that money to get us to Mexico when the time comes." He slapped Stevie on the back. "And Stevie will want to spend some of it when he gets there. He's never been to Las Vegas, so find him a good-looking woman."

The four men laughed. They were all relieved they wouldn't be involved in killing LeMasters or Longbow.

"Sometimes the women ain't bad looking," Mason said.

"Yeah, especially after that first bottle,"

Reb joked.

"How long should we wait?" Dutch asked.

Frank turned his eyes on Dutch. "You don't expect us to be killed, do you, Dutch?"

"You never know. If we get down there and wait two or three weeks, more than likely you won't be coming," Dutch replied.

"Dutch, I thought you knew me better than that. I told you boys it'll take more than these locals to do me in. We'll be there. But if you boys get nervous after ten days, then take off to Mexico if you want."

Dutch looked at Walt and Stevie. They were both quiet . . . too quiet. Dutch had a feeling something else was going on. He'd never trusted Frank, and he thought he could smell a double cross a mile away. But since they would have the money from the sale of the cattle, it was hard to figure out what Frank was plotting. "You ain't planning on robbing a stagecoach without us, are you, Frank?"

Frank should have known it would be Dutch who would question him. "Why would you think that? If I was planning something like that, every man would be needed."

Dutch saw the look exchanged between Stevie and Frank. "We'll wait ten days, no more."

"We'll plan our next move when we get to Las Vegas," Frank said. "Now let's get some shut-eye. We'll be pulling out early in the morning."

CHAPTER TWENTY-TWO

Frank led the way through the dense pine trees with the cattle and men following in a single line. This rustling job had gone much easier than he'd expected. He was disappointed he hadn't had the opportunity to take another shot at Joseph Longbow, but he'd have his chance. The next time he planned on being more accurate. Frank wasn't worried about anyone picking up their trail when they noticed cattle were missing, because he'd chosen a route that was difficult to maneuver with cattle. And if they got lucky it would be days before Morgan's men took a head count.

Now all he had to do was concentrate on driving the nervous cattle through the pines. The eerie sounds were spooking them, and the men were doing their best to keep them from bolting. Just like the last time they rustled on Morgan's land, the sounds in the pines started when they rode into the trees before dawn. Frank always heard whispers when he rode into the pines, and today was no different. It almost sounded like people were surrounding them, whispering loudly. But now, the deeper they rode into the pines with the cattle, the sounds had changed to screams. Just like the night that Smiley went missing. Before long, the spine-chilling shrieks were deafening. The men were as spooked as the cattle. Frank didn't laugh this time. His heart was racing, and he kept looking back to make sure no one was coming after him. He wanted to ride like the Devil was on his heels to get out of those trees, but it was slow going as they snaked their way to the clearing.

When Frank rode through the western boundary out of the trees, he breathed a sigh of relief. Just a few feet from the boundary, he no longer heard anything but the panicked bawls of the cattle. After twenty head appeared through the trees, Stevie and Walt emerged behind them.

"I ain't never heard anything like that in all my life," Walt said, sounding out of breath.

"Me neither," Stevie said, wiping the sweat from his face. "What do you make of that, Frankie?"

"I don't know what to think." Frank

didn't bother to deny he'd heard the same thing they had. The night Smiley was with them was fresh on his mind. He'd laughed at the men for getting so frightened that night. He'd laughed until Smiley didn't ride through the trees.

Deke and Dutch came riding out behind another twenty head of cattle. Neither man said a word, but their tense expressions said they were as terrified as the other men.

More cattle appeared through the clearing before Reb rode out. "I ain't never going back in there. Did you hear those screams?"

The men nodded.

"Scariest thing I ever heard," Reb continued. "Who was that screaming?"

No one had an answer.

"Let's count how many we have," Frank said, trying to think of something other than the mind-numbing fear he'd felt moments earlier. His heart was still pounding as though he'd been chased by renegade Indians.

A few more cows scurried from the trees, but there was no sign of the remaining two men, Corbin and Mason.

"I count sixty-seven," Frank said.

"Yeah," Walt said.

Stevie nodded. "Me too."

Corbin emerged from the trees with his

pistol drawn, looking behind him. "Mason was right behind me, but I don't see him now. I stopped to wait, but he didn't show."

No one responded; their eyes remained fixed on the eerily silent forest before them.

They waited for several minutes for Mason to appear, but Frank started getting antsy. He pointed to Dutch, Deke, and Reb. "You three go ahead, we can't waste more time. We'll wait here for a few more minutes."

"What if he don't show up?" Deke asked.

"I ain't going back in there to look for him," Reb said. "That was worse than the night Smiley was ridin' with us. And no one has seen him since that night. I figure Mason's a goner."

"If he don't show up, then he don't show up. You've got sixty-seven head right there to sell, and you know where to go," Frank said.

"What if it was him screaming?" Stevie said.

"We can't do nothing for him now," Frank countered. "We ain't got time to go back in there."

Deke and Dutch glanced at each other, both wondering if it was one of them left in there, if anyone would go back to find them. They looked one more time into the trees before they started moving the cattle.

"Stevie, you go on back home and get your horse in the stable. If they stop by on the way home from church, I want you to be there," Frank said.

"I don't feel right about leaving Mason. If he's found by Morgan's men, they will figure out it was you rustling," Stevie said.

"Smiley was never found," Frank replied.

Stevie looked at Walt. "What do you think?"

"If you want to ride back in there, I'll go with you," Walt said. He didn't care much about Mason, but he figured he'd want someone to go back for him if he was the one who was missing.

Frank moved his horse to face them. "I give the orders around here, and I'm telling you to go home, Stevie." He glared at Walt. "We need to get back to the cabin right now."

When neither man moved, Frank added, "You know I'm right. We can't take a chance on getting caught."

Stevie looked back at the trees before he turned his horse toward the farm. Frank and Walt rode in the opposite direction without looking back.

Three days later, Murph found Morgan repairing one of the railings surrounding the paddock. "We got about seventy head missing."

Morgan stopped what he was doing and gave Murph his attention. "What range?"

"West. They could have been rustled days ago. We didn't find a trail."

Morgan didn't figure it was Indians. If they rustled, it was generally only one or two cows. While he didn't like people stealing, he understood they were starving, so he was apt to forgive that theft. This was someone rustling to sell what was his, and he wasn't willing to overlook that transgression. "You think it could be Frank?"

Murph shrugged. "That would be pretty gosh-darn brazen since everyone is looking for him."

Morgan knew Frank was just that brazen. "Just like something he would do."

Murph nodded his agreement. "Frank thinks he's invincible."

"Let me get saddled." Morgan walked to the stable to get his horse.

When Morgan and Murph reached the western range, they rode for over an hour, but they found no trails. "Well, they didn't just disappear." Morgan looked across the range at the pine tree boundary. "After the disappearance of Smiley, I can't see the rustlers going through those trees again.

That incident scared the daylights out of everyone."

"And it would have taken a long time with seventy head," Murph added.

"Likely they did it on Sunday morning. Might as well take a look." Morgan didn't share his thought with Murph, but he had a gut feeling Stevie was involved. He wasn't buying his change of heart to stay on the farm. And if Stevie was involved, it followed that Frank was calling the shots.

They rode the line of the pine-tree range until they found an area where tree limbs were broken off. They followed the trail of damaged trees, and Morgan had no doubt this was the area where the rustlers led the cattle off his land. Having made their way through the trees, they rode for several miles before they stopped.

"They aren't going in the direction of Purgatory Canyon," Murph said.

"Nope, probably headed to New Mexico Territory."

"You think that means it wasn't Frank?"

Morgan had been thinking about that as he rode through the trees. "I'm thinking it was Frank."

"How so?"

"Like you said, Frank has made it his purpose to hurt me as much as possible. As long as he's not in jail, he's going to be a thorn in my side. He knows he can't stay at Purgatory Canyon because we know that's where they've been hiding out."

"Yeah, but it's still a great place to pick off a posse if they go in after them."

"True enough. Let's head back to the ranch. No sense in following them tonight." Morgan wanted to think about the situation. More than anything, he wanted to go after them, but it was going to be dark by the time he got to the ranch to ready supplies for a few days. "I'll take off early in the morning and follow the trail."

"I'll go. Don't forget you're getting married soon," Murph said.

"I'll be back in time, but I'm going. Keep a close eye on the women. And I'll tell them I don't want them riding to the farm without one of the men with them."

"You want me to ride to town and tell the sheriff what's going on?" Murph asked.

"I don't want to waste Jack's time. We don't know how much of a head start they have. I may not find anything."

"It could be someone else rustling, thinking we would blame it on Frank," Murph said.

"Could be," Morgan said, but he didn't believe it for a minute. His intuition told him this was Frank's doing.

Murph read Morgan's expression. Morgan wasn't buying his theory. "Watch your back."

Morgan was a little late for dinner, but Rose and Granny were waiting for him. He waited until they finished dinner and were sitting in the parlor before he told them he was leaving in the morning. "We've had some more rustling."

Rose and Granny looked at him, waiting for him to say the words they feared.

"I'll be riding out early and following the trail we found."

"Alone?" Rose asked.

"Yes. The men will help you with anything you need. I'd prefer you stay on the ranch, but if you have to go to the farm, one of the men will take you."

"Morgan, do you think it was Frank and his gang?" Granny asked the question they were all thinking about.

"I can't be sure, but since he's not in jail, I think it's highly likely."

"But what will you do alone? Shouldn't someone go with you?" Rose hated feeling torn between her brother and her future husband. She couldn't help worrying about both of them. Frankie was her blood, and she didn't want him hurt. But she would soon share a bond with Morgan, a bond that was supposed to run deeper than blood.

"I can't afford to take my men from their work. We're behind on ranch work from the last time we chased them to Kansas. We have a lot to do before winter sets in." Morgan wondered if Rose was worried he would string Frank up if he found him.

Granny stood, but before she walked upstairs, she turned to Morgan. "I no longer think you feel the vengeance in your heart now that you are to marry Rose. I expect you will do the right thing if you catch up with them."

Morgan didn't respond. He hoped he could live up to her expectations. He hadn't forgotten everything Frank had done to provoke him. He told himself he could control his anger if he ever caught up to Frank, but there were times he wasn't as confident.

Rose waited until Granny left the room before she expressed her concerns. "I'm afraid for you to go after so many men alone."

"Are you worried about me, or about Frank?"

Rose wouldn't lie to him. "Both. Is it

wrong of me not to want either one of you hurt?"

Morgan appreciated her honesty. "No, it's not wrong." He stood and held out his hand to her. "I have to turn in since I'll be leaving early."

When they reached Rose's bedroom door, Morgan said good night and kissed her lightly on the lips.

"Please be careful."

"I'll be back before the wedding." He knew she was upset over what he was going to do, but he wouldn't allow her feelings to deter him.

Rose watched him walk down the hallway. "Morgan," she said before he opened his bedroom door.

Morgan turned around and looked at her.

Words seemed to fail her. She ran to his open arms and kissed him again.

"That will have to hold me until I get back," he said when he released her.

She looked up at him with tears in her eyes. "You will come back."

He hugged her one last time. "Nothing could stop me, knowing I'll be getting kisses like that every night."

Before dawn, Morgan had reached the area where he'd turned back the day before. He wanted to know if Frank and his gang were responsible, and he wanted to know who was buying his cattle. The buyers had to know they were buying stolen cattle since his brand was on every animal. He couldn't shake the feeling Frank was behind this, even though he couldn't prove it this time. If Frank had a lick of sense, he'd ride down to Mexico and hide out for a few years. But Frank wanted to make a point, and he wasn't going to ride away until he had accomplished that goal. He was allowing his personal feelings to get in the way of good judgment. Morgan wasn't going to make the same mistake. Morgan sensed one of them would be dead before their feud ended. He was determined it wasn't going to be him. The way he saw it, he had a lot to live for. He felt very fortunate to be marrying Rose and starting a family. Indeed, fortune had smiled on him, and he wasn't a man to take his blessings lightly.

Rose was in the kitchen helping Granny cook vegetables when she looked out the window and saw Murph leading the big black horse to the paddock. She grabbed two apples and sliced them into pieces. "Granny, I will be back in a few minutes."

When she reached the paddock, she

started talking to Judge. He ambled over to her and nudged her hand with his muzzle.

Murph was filling the water troughs, but he was keeping a close eye on Rose and the horse. It surprised him that Judge had taken to her so quickly. He was actually behaving affectionately, much as he did with Morgan. "Morgan is the only one that horse usually likes."

"He's so sweet," Rose said as she held out her slices of apple to the horse.

Sweet wasn't the word Murph would use to describe Judge, but he was being very gentle with Rose. "Sometimes he can be as rank as a wild mustang, but now I'm beginning to think the apples are the secret. Morgan feeds them to him all the time."

Rose thought her heart would break each time she looked at the raised scars over his body. She stroked his powerful neck, and Judge leaned into her. "What happened to him?"

Murph stared at her. "Morgan didn't tell you?"

"No. Granny said Morgan used to ride him years ago, but she hadn't seen him in a long time."

Murph figured Morgan wouldn't care if he told her about Judge. The only thing Morgan had told him and the other men not to tell Rose was that Frank had threatened to kill her. The way Murph saw it, Rose had a right to know what a low-down skunk she had for a brother.

When Murph didn't respond right away, Rose turned to him. "Don't you know what happened to him?"

"Your brother Frank did that to him."

Morgan followed the trail for two days, and just as he suspected, they were going into New Mexico Territory. There were only three men with the cattle, and Morgan figured the gang split up for some reason. Morgan hoped Frank was one of the three men; he didn't like the thought of Frank being in Whispering Pines. But he was confident Murph and his men would see to the safety of Rose and Granny. They were all aware of the lengths to which Frank would go to hurt him. By the third day, Morgan knew he had to turn back. If he didn't head back now, he wouldn't get home in time for his wedding.

CHAPTER TWENTY-THREE

"Joseph, would you go to the farm with us?" Rose asked when she found him in the stable. She hated to ask him to leave the ranch, but he was the only man around. She wanted to talk to Stevie, and Granny wanted to pick up more vegetables.

"Yes. I'll get the buckboard ready."

On the way to the farm, Rose decided to talk to Joseph about Judge. She'd already discussed it with Granny the night before. Granny told her she didn't doubt Murph's account of what Frankie did to the beautiful horse. Granny recounted the day Joseph brought Frankie home from Morgan's ranch. He hadn't said anything other than Frankie wasn't going to work on the ranch anymore.

"Joseph, do you know what Frankie did to Judge?" Rose asked.

"Yes."

"Why didn't anyone tell me?" Granny asked.

"It wasn't for me to say," Joseph answered.

"Is that why you brought Frank home that day, Joseph?" Granny asked, remembering Frank had been nineteen when Morgan gave him a job on his ranch.

"Yes."

Murph had told Rose that Frank had taken a whip to the horse, nearly killing him. Morgan nearly killed Frank. Once the men pulled Morgan off of Frank, Joseph got Frank in the buckboard and took him back to the farm. Murph thought it was best to put the horse down, but Morgan wouldn't hear of it. Morgan had helped foal Judge, and he was determined to nurse him back to health.

"Why would Frankie do such a thing?" Rose asked, not really expecting an answer.

"Bad spirit."

Rose and Granny stared at Joseph. His comment seemed to sum up Frankie's life. What else could be said? When Murph told Rose the truth about Judge, she didn't want to believe Frankie could do such a thing. But too much evidence was mounting against him. She wanted to speak with Stevie to find out how much he knew about Frankie. She hoped she could convince him not to follow in his brother's footsteps.

"This explains so many things. Little wonder Morgan carried so much vengeance in his heart," Granny said.

They reached the farm, and Stevie met them on the front porch. He seemed surprised to see them. "I didn't know you were coming back today."

"I need to talk to you, Stevie," Rose said.

"Joseph and I will load the vegetables while you two talk," Granny said.

Rose and Stevie walked inside to the kitchen and sat at the table. "Stevie, do you know where Frankie is hiding out?"

Stevie made an attempt to feign surprise at her question. "No, why are you asking me that?"

Rose had always been able to tell when Stevie was lying, and she thought he was lying now. "Someone rustled cattle at the ranch."

"When?"

"I'm not sure, but it had to be recent. Are you sure you don't know where Frankie or members of his gang are hiding?"

"I told you I don't know where he is. How should I know?" He jumped up and walked to the stove and poured himself a cup of coffee. "Is Morgan trying to find the rustlers?"

Suddenly, Rose became suspicious. She wasn't sure how much she should reveal out of fear for Morgan. "He's talking about it."

"Why does everybody think it has to be Frankie when cattle are rustled? I expect he's probably in Mexico having a fine old time."

Stevie was talking to her, but he wasn't looking her in the eye. "You told me you thought Frankie would come back here for you. Why do you think he is in Mexico now?" she asked.

"I was hoping he would come back, but he won't."

"Stevie, he should pay for his crimes. Maybe if he turned himself in, he might not hang."

Stevie grunted in disgust. "I don't think he's done half of what everyone says. If he turned himself in, Morgan would make sure he hangs. You know the sheriff is Morgan's best friend."

"Stevie, did you know what Frankie did to Morgan's horse years ago?"

He turned to walk back to the table, but he didn't sit down. "What are you talking about?"

After relating everything Murph had told her, Stevie said, "Did Morgan tell you that pack of lies? I can't believe you would listen to anything he has to say. Frankie wouldn't do that."

"Frankie, Morgan didn't tell me. I'm afraid it is true."

Stevie narrowed his eyes at her. "No wonder Frankie hates you. You've let Morgan turn you against him."

The undisguised hatred in his eyes forced Rose to lean back in her chair. Unlike the last time, she thought she was prepared for anything he said to her. But she wasn't prepared for the look of sheer hate on his face. "Stevie, you know more than you're saying. You know Frankie is guilty of rustling, and a lot worse. He tried to kill Joseph Longbow. Joseph Longbow would never tell a lie. Don't you see Frankie could kill someone? If you know where he is you should tell me. I don't know what's happened to him, but he's dangerous. You can't trust him, Stevie."

"I hope he kills Morgan," Stevie growled.

"How can you say such a thing to me? Don't you understand Frankie has lied about Morgan?"

Stevie hated her all the more for her defense of the man he hated. "Maybe Frankie will kill both of you."

Tears filled Rose's eyes at his words. "I was hoping to talk some sense into you, but

I think it's too late. You've become as wicked as Frankie." She turned to leave, but before she walked out the door, she said, "Stevie, evil deeds cannot escape His judgment. I'll pray for your soul."

As soon as Rose reached the buckboard, Granny saw the tears running down her cheeks. She walked to Rose and put her arms around her. "Don't cry, honey."

Stevie walked outside and yelled, "Rose, don't come back here."

Granny turned to face Stevie. "Stevie, I will remind you this is my farm. Rose will come and go as she pleases. We were going to invite you to the wedding on Saturday, but I think it's best if you stay away."

"I don't want to come to their wedding. I bet it won't even take place." Stevie knew he shouldn't have said that, but he was angry. He wanted them to worry about what could happen.

Before Rose climbed in the buckboard, she wiped the tears from her face. She wouldn't allow Stevie to ruin her special day. She turned to confront him. "The wedding will take place. I am proud and honored to become the wife of a man with sterling character, who works hard for a living, and doesn't steal from others. And you can tell Frankie what I said. If you are helping Frankie steal, you are no better than he is."

Granny was heartbroken her youngest grandson would not listen to reason. "Stevie, I'm sorry to say your brother betrays everyone. What makes you think he won't betray you? How do you know that you can trust him? A man who breaks all of God's commandments will not come to a good end. And if you've helped Frank rustle, just remember the Good Book says 'Treasures of wickedness gain nothing.' "

Stevie grunted. "I'm tired of hearing what the *Good Book* says." He stalked inside the house, slamming the door behind him.

Rose cried all the way back to the ranch. She cried for the brothers she'd lost forever. She cried over not trusting Morgan from the moment the stagecoach stopped on that road in Kansas. She cried for Granny. This wonderful woman had given so much of her life to caring for her grandchildren, and she was heartbroken over Frankie and Stevie. "Granny, I am so sorry about my brothers. You've sacrificed so much for us."

"Rose, it's not your fault. They made their own choices. Now they will have to live with the consequences. If not on this earth, then they will surely pay when they meet their Maker."

■ ■ ■ ■

Stevie thought about Granny's question as he saddled his horse. Reuben had asked him the same question the last time he saw him before Frankie arrived for their meeting. Reuben tried to tell him Frankie was going to double-cross him. Stevie refused to believe Frankie would ever betray him. Everyone was wrong about his brother. Right now, what he needed to do was get on his horse and ride to the Conner place. He had to tell Frankie the wedding was going to take place tomorrow.

The cabin was empty when Stevie arrived, so he walked inside to wait for them to return. He thought it was possible Frankie was in Denver watching Reuben. Stevie waited over two hours before he decided to go home. On his way, he thought about taking the money he had stolen from the stagecoach and leaving Whispering Pines for good. He could take Reuben up on his offer and travel with him. Even if Frankie did go through with the bank robbery, he would probably stay around Whispering Pines to cause Morgan more trouble. Frankie seemed to live for seeking retribution against Morgan.

If Frank didn't come by the farm tonight, Stevie figured he'd ride back out to the cabin tomorrow. The money was due to arrive at the bank, and it would be nice to know one way or the other what day they were going to stage the robbery.

Morgan made it back to the ranch at dinnertime on Friday. Rose saw him ride in, and by the time he'd cared for his horse, she was waiting for him on the front porch. Seeing her standing there waiting for him lifted his mood. He was tired, dirty, and hungry, but seeing her made him forget all about the way he was feeling, and he picked up his pace. He liked knowing this was what it was going to be like in the future each time he came home. What man could ask for more than a beautiful woman waiting for him with a smile?

Morgan picked her up and held her to him. He'd missed her more than he imagined he would. "I'm happy to be home."

She looked up at him and said, "I missed you."

He kissed her, then said, "And I've missed your kisses." After tomorrow he would be free to take her to his bedroom and show her how much he'd missed her in the most intimate way. He was a lucky man.

"You're just in time for dinner."

"Good, I'm starving. I found out I can't cook as good as you." He placed his arm around her waist as they walked into the house.

While he was away, Rose had thought of the many things she wanted to say to him. She wanted to tell him how sorry she was that Frankie had hurt Judge so many years ago. She was sorry she'd ever doubted his word when he'd tried to tell her about the crimes Frankie had committed. She wanted to tell him she would make him a good wife, and he'd never have a reason to regret marrying her. Since he was tired and hungry, and dinner was waiting, she decided to wait until later for that conversation.

Morgan noticed how she suddenly grew quiet. She was probably curious if he'd found the rustlers. "I didn't catch up with them. They were headed to New Mexico Territory, but I had to turn back or I would have missed our wedding."

"I don't think it was Frankie," she said.

Just a moment earlier he was thrilled to see her smiling face. But now he found himself getting irritated that she was still intent on defending Frank. He tried not to take it personally, since Frank was her blood, but it was becoming more difficult to be tolerant of her unwillingness to accept the truth. "Rose, I know you don't want to believe your brother is responsible . . ." He stopped midsentence when she turned to face him and placed her hand on his chest.

"No, I mean I don't think Frankie is on his way to New Mexico Territory. I went to see Stevie." She saw the disapproving look on his face, and quickly added, "Joseph took us to the farm. I asked Stevie if he knew where Frankie was hiding and he said he didn't. But I know he was lying, I could see it on his face. Stevie was never a good liar. I think Frankie is still near Whispering Pines."

"That doesn't mean it wasn't Frank I was following," Morgan told her.

"No, it doesn't. But Stevie said something else that made me think Frankie is nearby."

"What did he say?"

"Granny told him he should stay away from our wedding, and he said he didn't want to come *if* it did take place. Something about the way he said it made me think Frankie would do something to try and stop us from marrying."

Morgan thought he saw fear in her eyes. "Honey, don't you worry about that. Frank is not going to stop our wedding."

"I'm afraid he will do something to you," she admitted.

Morgan was surprised she finally seemed to believe everything he'd told her about Frank. "Don't worry about me, I can handle Frank." He leaned over and kissed her again. "What made you accept the truth about Frank?"

"So many things. I remember being very young, and Frankie was always telling me not to go near you. He told me no one trusted you. He told me so many things, and that's why I was frightened of you. He filled my head with lies. I'm sure he's done the same thing to Stevie. Granny and I have talked about some of the terrible things he has done. Deep down, I know he's guilty." She was crying now and Morgan was holding her close. "I'm sorry I didn't believe you. It was so hard for me to believe the worst of my own brother."

"I know, honey. Don't cry." As much as he wanted her to face the truth about her brother, he hated to see the pain it caused.

He held her as she cried. She said something else, but he couldn't understand what she was saying for her sobs. "What? Honey, it's okay. Stop crying so I can hear you."

"I'm so sorry about Judge."

Morgan stiffened. He hadn't wanted anyone to mention the horse to her and cause her more heartache. "Who told you?"

"It doesn't matter. You should have been the one who told me." She wasn't angry he hadn't told her. She knew he did it to keep from hurting her.

"Would you have believed me?"

She saw his point, and it upset her even more that she'd ever doubted him. "I'll never doubt your word again."

"Honey, what happened to Judge was a long time ago. We can't do anything about it now, and it wasn't your fault." He handed her the bandana from his pocket. "Dry your eyes, and tell me if you finished making your wedding dress."

She wiped her tears away. "It's finished."

"Will you show it to me?"

She shook her head. "It's bad luck. You can see it tomorrow."

He kissed the top of her head. "It's probably a good thing, I'm not sure I could control myself."

"What do you mean?"

He leaned down and kissed her ear before his lips moved to her neck. "You know what I mean," he whispered.

She shivered. "Oh." He'd made her completely forget about Frankie.

He pulled his lips away from her ear. "Now before you can't control yourself, could I talk you into feeding a starving man?"

Rose blushed at his words. "I was just making some coffee when you rode in. There's fresh water on the back porch if you want to clean up first."

Remembering how she'd reacted the last time he'd stripped out of his shirt, he leaned down and whispered in her ear, "Do you want to watch me take off my shirt?"

"Morgan LeMasters, you are incorrigible." The truth was, she did want to see him without his shirt.

CHAPTER TWENTY-FOUR

Corbin lifted the whiskey bottle to his lips, draining the last drop. "I'm glad we came to Denver."

"Walt can come and go here since no one knows him. It's safer here for all of us than at Whispering Pines," Frank said, opening another bottle and passing it to Corbin.

"It's better than staying around Whispering Pines," Corbin slurred. As he took a drink from the new bottle, he thought about the screams he'd heard in the pines. He was hoping the more he drank the quicker he would forget about those sounds. He didn't want to think about it, but he couldn't help himself from saying, "I wonder what happened to Mason."

Frank wanted to forget what happened in the pines. "It's best we all forget about Mason. What's done is done."

Walt didn't comment, but if Frank thought he was going to go back to that ranch so

Frank could exact whatever revenge he wanted on LeMasters, he was in for a surprise. After they robbed the bank, Walt had plans of his own, and they didn't include riding with Frank.

"Frank, it's hard to forget those screams," Corbin mumbled.

"Drink up. Whiskey will do the job," Frank said.

Frank and Walt were waiting for Corbin to pass out. They were visiting Reuben later, and Corbin was in the dark about the robbery they were planning. Frank was beginning to think it would have been faster to crack Corbin in the head with the butt of his pistol than to wait for him to succumb to the liquor. Corbin finally passed out before he finished half of the second bottle.

"Who would think he could drink that much?" Walt asked.

"Yeah, I imagine his head will be throbbing in the morning when I send him back to the Conner place."

"What reason are you going to give him to go back to Whispering Pines?" Walt asked.

"I don't have to give him a reason. And I ain't about to take him with us to rob the bank. We don't need him. I just didn't want him staying at the Conner place in case Stevie came back. He'd tell him we were in

420

Denver, and little brother doesn't need to know everything we are doing." Frank walked to the door. "Let's get out of here."

Walt led the way to Reuben's home. It was three o'clock in the morning, and the streets were empty, but taking no chances, they tied their horses in the trees near the back of Reuben's home, and slipped in his back door.

It was dark and Frank stopped in the doorway until his eyes adjusted to his surroundings. He made his way deftly across the room to the bed in the corner of the room. He stopped cold in his tracks when he heard someone cock the hammer of a revolver.

"What are you doing in my home?" Reuben asked.

"We want to talk," Frank responded.

Reuben swung his legs over the side of the bed and lit his lamp. "What do you need to talk about at this hour?"

If Reuben hadn't had a derringer Frank might have laughed at his nightclothes. He was wearing a nightshirt that stopped just below his knees, and Frank thought he'd never seen such white, bony legs. "We decided we're gonna rob that bank Sunday during church instead of waiting until next week. So we are going to be spending today with you."

Reuben looked from Frank to Walt. "Where's Stevie?"

"He'll be along," Frank lied smoothly.

"I always attend the church service," Reuben said. "I'm sure people will notice when I'm not there."

"All the better to make people think you were forced at gunpoint, and had no hand in the robbery," Frank countered.

Reuben had already thought about that angle. He just didn't want to be found dead inside the bank after Frank got the money. Reuben had no choice but to agree to the new plan. After they discussed the details of the robbery, Reuben told them the best place to leave their horses for a quick getaway.

Walt had already found the perfect place for the horses, but it was good to know Reuben agreed on the spot. "We will leave Stevie with the horses."

Reuben didn't believe for a minute that Stevie would even be in Denver. "I will meet you in a week for my share. I can't keep money with me in case the sheriff gets suspicious and searches my home."

"That sounds like a good idea." Frank couldn't believe any man could be as gullible as Reuben, not even Corbin.

"This is going to be a lot of money. Where are you and your men headed from here?" Reuben asked.

"We haven't decided yet," Frank said. "What about you?"

"I'm undecided as well," Reuben said, being as cautious as Frank about his future plans.

Frank figured they'd spend the rest of the night with Reuben, and he would leave early in the morning to tell Corbin to go back to the Conner place. He wasn't going to need him until he got back to Whispering Pines.

Early Saturday morning, Stevie rode back to the Conner cabin and found it empty. He saw nothing to indicate Frank had been there since yesterday. He didn't know how he was supposed to tell Frankie that Rose's wedding was at noon if he had no idea how to find him. He thought Frankie was probably in Denver. Frank should have told him where he was going and when he would return. Stevie paced the floor. Something told him he was the only one who didn't know what was going on. He had a feeling Frankie was going to double-cross him and rob that bank without him. Problem was, he didn't know what to do about it.

■ ■ ■ ■

Clay Hunt arrived at Morgan's ranch an hour before the wedding. When Morgan opened the door, Clay said, "I hear there's a wedding today."

"You heard right. Come in and have a cup of coffee while we wait for my bride." Morgan ushered Clay into the kitchen and poured him some coffee. "How are you enjoying Whispering Pines?" He pointed to the table and added, "Have a seat."

"It's a fine little town, and all of the folks have been more than generous to me. I swear I don't ever have to cook my own meals. The ladies see to it I eat hearty."

Morgan refilled his own cup and sat down. "I bet the single ladies are trying to outshine each other." He'd been on the receiving end of all that attention, and he knew how the women openly competed with each other, showing off their culinary skills.

Clay laughed. "Sounds like a man speaking from experience."

"Yessir, I've been there."

"And not one tempted you before now?"

Morgan shook his head. Even though he wanted a family, it wasn't until he saw Rose that he felt the urgency to marry. "No, I didn't give it a lot of thought before Rose stepped off that stagecoach."

"I'm glad we have a moment to talk alone. I've heard a few interesting stories about your ranch, and to be honest, I'm not quite sure what to make of them. Several of the parishioners mentioned they wouldn't attend this wedding if they were me. For some reason they seem quite frightened of riding on your land. Can you tell me if they are just having sport with me?"

Morgan explained the history of the pine-tree range as explained to him years ago by Joseph. "You will meet Joseph Longbow soon."

"Did a man really get lost in there and was never found?" Clay asked.

"That's the story. I'm sure you are referring to the man who was rustling cattle with Frank and his gang. They told folks he never came out of the pines. Joseph tells me the same thing has happened to many men over the years. As you will see, those pines cover a large territory, and it's easy to lose your sense of direction. A man could get lost in there and never find his way out if he's not careful. A soldier was lost in there a few years back, and never seen again."

"Tell me, do you really hear screams in there?"

Morgan smiled at him. "You will see for yourself today."

"I have to admit, I'm nervous and curious at the same time."

"Just so you know, people hear different things in the pines."

Clay gave him a skeptical look. "I'm beginning to think this is a joke you locals play on the newcomers."

Morgan chuckled at his comment. "As I said, you will see for yourself today."

There was a knock on the back door, and Jack stuck his head inside before Morgan reached the door. "Am I in time for the wedding?"

"I was hoping you would make it," Morgan said, shaking Jack's hand.

"Clay," Jack said, acknowledging the pastor.

"Good to see you, Sheriff," Clay said.

The last time Morgan saw Jack he'd discussed his suspicions about Stevie. He thought he'd ask Jack about it before Granny and Rose came downstairs. "Did you hear any more about that stagecoach robbery?"

"Yeah. From all accounts that clerk fellow is a good employee, and no one thinks he would be involved in anything like that."

"Maybe so," Morgan said.

"But one of the guards winged the man who did the robbing," Jack added.

Morgan arched his brow at him. "Is that so?"

"Yeah. Now enough business. Where's the beautiful bride?" Jack asked.

"We're waiting for her," Morgan said.

"I was just about to say, Morgan seems very calm for a man who is about to change his life," Clay said.

"I look forward to the change. I've been alone a long time." Truthfully, Morgan hadn't expected he would be as excited as he was to marry. He hadn't been able to sleep last night for thinking about today. He planned to do his best to make many happy memories with Rose. Of course, they would have some hardships, that was life, but with a woman like Rose at his side, he could deal with anything. He'd be working for a family now, and that made him more determined than ever to leave something behind for his children. He hadn't asked Rose, but he hoped she wanted to start a family right away.

"You are getting a beautiful woman," Clay said.

"Yes, I am." Morgan raised an eyebrow at

him. "Did you know she has two sisters who will be home soon?"

"I think I heard something about more sisters," Clay replied.

Morgan was telling him about Rose's sisters when Granny walked in. "I was just telling Clay that Adelaide will be home soon."

"Yes, she will, but don't get your hopes up, Pastor. Adelaide is perfect for the sheriff," Granny said.

Jack rolled his eyes. "Granny already has me married off."

"How do you know Adelaide is the one for Jack?" Morgan asked.

"The same way I knew Rose was perfect for you. I think it will be Emma who will interest the pastor."

Morgan and Clay exchanged a look. They weren't about to argue with Granny's intuition.

"Emma's the opera singer," Morgan said.

"She will be coming to Denver with her troupe by the end of the year, and Morgan has promised to take us to hear her. You should join us."

Granny looked at Jack and said, "Of course, you and Adelaide will be going with us."

Morgan grinned at Jack and slapped him

on the back. "Granny has everything planned out."

"As I told her, if Adelaide is as pretty as Rose, she can marry me off any day," Jack said.

"Granny, that is sure a pretty pink dress you are wearing," Morgan said.

"Thank you. I told Rose I hadn't worn a pink dress since I was a young girl."

"You're still young and beautiful," Clay said.

Granny leaned over his shoulder and poured him another cup of coffee. She gave him an affectionate tap on the top of his head. "And you, Pastor, are a sweet-talker just like the sheriff. You should do very well with my Emma." Rose walked into the room and all conversation stopped.

Morgan stood, but he didn't move from his spot. He simply stared. She reminded him of an angel standing there in her white dress. A fancy fanlike comb that resembled a crown held her hair on top of her head. An angelic princess, Morgan thought.

"I knew she would take your breath away, Morgan, but I didn't know you would be speechless," Granny teased.

Rose couldn't take her eyes off of him. He looked so handsome in his black suit, and his white shirt emphasized his darkly tanned skin. In a few short minutes this wonderful man was going to be her husband. God had truly blessed her with a remarkable man.

"You're beautiful," Morgan finally said as he walked to her. He didn't think his words adequately described what he was thinking.

"Thank you. You look very handsome in your suit."

Morgan took her hand. "Are you ready to get married?"

"I am." Rose put her arm through his, and they turned to the others in the room.

"You are such a lovely couple," Granny said with tears in her eyes.

"Granny, just think of the great-grandbabies they will give you," Clay said.

Morgan brought Rose's hand to his lips. "Let's go."

They walked out the door to see the ranch hands were waiting for them. Morgan introduced the men to Clay. "Where's Joseph?"

"He's waiting for us there," Murph said. "You know Joseph. He wanted some time to talk to the Great Spirit."

"It's a perfect day for a wedding," Granny said, looking up at the vivid blue sky.

It took them fifteen minutes to walk to Rose's special spot in the pines. It was the most beautiful area on Morgan's land, where Rose and her sisters spent a lot of time when they were young. It was a small clearing with a raised grassy plateau, and in the background the trees had grown to form an archway. The backdrop always reminded Rose of an altar, and she'd pretended to have a marriage ceremony. She'd never told her sisters, but when she was older, she'd often envisioned herself as the bride and Morgan LeMasters as the groom. Adelaide pretended she was standing on the platform in front of her classroom instructing children. Emma used the area as her stage, entertaining her audience of two: Rose and Adelaide.

When they entered the pines, Clay heard the soft whistling sounds of the wind in the trees. As they approached the plateau, they saw Joseph standing with his arms raised to heaven, speaking in his native tongue. Joseph turned when he heard them and said, "We are ready."

Rose whispered something to the pastor and he nodded. Morgan pulled him aside and spoke to him quietly before everyone took their positions at the altar.

Clay started to speak about the sanctity of the marriage vows, but stopped in midsentence when he thought he heard people laughing. It almost sounded as if the sounds were coming from heaven. He looked at the wedding party and guests, but they didn't appear to think anything was amiss, so he continued on.

Clay reached the point where Rose was going to place a ring on Morgan's finger, and Morgan was surprised when she took his hand in hers and slid a ring in place. It had been her grandfather's ring, and Rose worried that it might be too small for Morgan's large fingers. To her surprise, it fit perfectly. She looked into Morgan's dark blue eyes, trying to convey the love she felt for him.

Morgan took her hand in his, and from his pocket pulled out the diamond ring he'd purchased in Denver. Rose gasped when she saw the glittering ring he'd placed on her finger. Seconds later, Clay pronounced them man and wife, and Morgan took Rose in his arms and kissed her. When the kiss ended, the men applauded before they stood in line to kiss the bride and shake the groom's hand.

Joseph approached Morgan and Rose and took their hands in his. He looked up to heaven and said, "Great Spirit, direct the four winds to guide them as one on this earth, together in harmony."

It seemed to everyone at the gathering that

the winds picked up after Joseph spoke.

Clay shook Morgan's hand. "You were right about this place. Did you hear laughter?"

Granny heard Clay's question, and she hooked her arm through his. "I'll explain on the way to the house. We are going to have wedding cake."

Morgan had his arm around Rose as they walked back to the house. "Was this Preacher's ring?"

"Yes. Granny gave it to me. We were worried it might not be large enough for your finger."

"I'm honored to wear it, and it's a perfect fit," Morgan assured her.

Rose held her hand up and looked at her diamond ring. "I'm afraid it's much simpler than this one. It's such a beautiful ring, I never expected anything so lovely." Actually, Rose hadn't expected Morgan would think to give her a ring.

"It's not nearly as beautiful as you." Each time he looked at her, he could hardly believe his good fortune. "That was the reason for my trip to Denver."

"You certainly surprised me," Rose said, feeling guilty at the memory of her questioning his trip to Denver. "Did I ruin your surprise because I thought you were seeing another woman?"

Morgan squeezed her to his side. "Honey, you could never ruin anything for me."

Everyone walked into the house for cake, but Morgan noticed Joseph walking toward the bunkhouse. Instead of following the others through the door, Morgan held back. He pulled Rose into his arms and kissed her again. Their kiss ended and he whispered, "Are you happy, Mrs. LeMasters?"

"Very. Are you happy?"

"Yes, and I'll be even happier tonight when I have you all to myself."

Rose didn't think Morgan was the type of man who would ever say he loved her, but she knew he cared for her. She loved him, but she didn't want him to feel obligated to say words he didn't feel. She'd wait, and pray one day his feelings for her would evolve into love. "Am I going to see you without your shirt?"

Her teasing surprised him, and he arched a brow at her. "Can you wait until tonight?"

Rose started to blush. "Behave yourself."

Morgan kissed her again. This time he held her tightly to him without worrying about doing something improper. Hearing someone walk up behind him, he turned around to see it was Joseph.

"Ready for some cake?" Morgan asked.

"Yes. Here is wedding blanket," Joseph said, holding out a folded blanket.

"Oh, Joseph, you didn't need to give us a gift," Rose said.

"It is for you," he said.

Rose took the beautifully woven blanket from him. "Thank you."

Joseph looked at Morgan and gave him a little smile. "This will give you many children."

Morgan raised his brow at the little man. "I'll put it to use first thing."

Rose kissed Joseph on the cheek. "It's beautiful. Thank you."

"My bride and I would like you to take two head of cattle in celebration of our marriage," Morgan told him.

Joseph nodded. "As soon as I try wedding cake."

Morgan picked Rose up in his arms and carried her over the threshold. "Welcome home, Mrs. LeMasters."

The day was filled with laughter, no one mentioning Frank or Stevie. Later that night when Morgan and Rose retired to their bedroom, Morgan pulled off his jacket and hung it over the back of a chair. He pointed to the corner of the room and said, "I put the dressing screen in here if you aren't comfortable undressing in front of me." He hoped she wouldn't use the screen, but she was young and inexperienced, so he would be patient and give her time.

Rose hesitated. She was shy about undressing in front of him, but she knew she would overcome her shyness eventually. She decided to talk to him for a few moments to see if that would put her at ease. "Why did you give Joseph two cattle?"

"Not all of his people are on the reservation, and they don't have enough to eat. I imagine the women worked many hours to make that blanket. The cattle will show our appreciation for their special gift."

"But aren't they all supposed to go on the reservations?"

"I've been free to roam this country my whole life, just as they have. I wouldn't want to be on a reservation, so why should we ask that of them? This was their land before we were here, and they are allowing me to use it. A couple head of cattle a few times a year is hardly payment enough."

She was learning her new husband had unusual views on the subject. As Granny had told her, there was more to Morgan than met the eye. "Thank you for including me in the gift." She sat on the bed and started to remove her shoes.

Morgan kneeled on one knee, took her

foot in his hand, and removed her shoe. "You are part of my life now, and that includes anything that happens on this ranch. What is mine, is yours." He removed her other shoe before reaching under her skirt. He found her garters above her knees, and removed them one by one. Then he slowly rolled down her stockings.

The way he deftly handled her stockings, Rose figured he'd removed ladies' garments before. She refused to allow jealousy to creep in her mind. He was her husband now, and she trusted him. By the time he finished, she was shivering from his touch.

Morgan was tempted to do much more, but he forced himself to take it slow. He stood, unbuttoned his shirt, stripped it off, and tossed it on the nearest chair.

Rose stood in front of him. She didn't know if a man should be called beautiful, but he was so perfectly formed it was the only way she could describe him.

Morgan saw how she was staring at his chest. He took her hand in his and kissed her palm. "Touch me, Rose."

Rose slowly ran her hands over his massive chest, much like she'd wanted to do the first time she saw him without his shirt. She caressed his shoulders, then moved her hands over his torso again before gliding down past his stomach to his waist. When Morgan couldn't take much more, he reached for her hands and brought them to his lips. His dark eyes bore into hers, and he whispered, "My sweet Rose."

"I could go ask Granny to unbutton my dress . . ." She turned her back to him. "But if you wouldn't mind."

Morgan glanced at the long row of buttons down her back. Why did women have all those tiny buttons on their clothing? He remembered the day of the stagecoach accident when the buttons were down the front of her dress and it had taken him forever to get the darn thing off.

He thought his heart might give out before he got this dress off of her. He took a deep breath, and started with the first button at the back of her neck. He was sweating by the time he finished. He pushed the dress from her shoulders and it dropped in a puddle around her ankles, but she was still wearing a corset, chemise, and bloomers. He unlaced the ties on her corset and tossed it on top of his shirt. He didn't see buttons on the chemise, so he figured it buttoned in the front. To his delight and surprise, he knew when she lowered her head she was unbuttoning her chemise. When she finished, with her back still to him, he gently slid the straps down her arms and let it drop to the floor.

Standing there in nothing but her bloomers, Rose was trying to muster the courage to turn around and face him. Before she did, Morgan slid his arms around her waist and held her. He ran his lips over her shoulder, progressing leisurely to her neck. Rose gripped his arms and leaned her head to one side and closed her eyes, forgetting all about her inhibitions. His chest felt so warm and solid against her back, and his tender kisses made her mind race with images of what was to follow tonight.

"You are so beautiful," Morgan whispered.

She turned around in his arms.

Chapter Twenty-Five

Reuben insisted Frank and Walt hold him at gunpoint as they made their way from his home to the back door of the bank, in the event anyone was watching. They didn't see one person as they hurried along the back of the buildings.

But there was someone who caught a glimpse of the men through an alleyway. Stella Wood, a soiled dove at the Crystal Saloon, was sitting on the second floor balcony, scantily clad and drinking a whiskey-laced cup of coffee. It was her Sunday morning ritual to listen to the church bell ringing. The other girls were still in bed, and Stella enjoyed her quiet time alone on Sunday mornings. She hadn't been inside a church since she was a young girl, but she'd never forgotten the peaceful solitude of the small church she'd attended. The soiled doves knew they weren't welcome in church, and most of the girls didn't care one way or the other. They didn't bother to even get out of bed before noon on most Sunday mornings. Oftentimes, Stella wished she was brave enough to put on her most demure dress and go to church just so she could listen to the old hymns. Not wanting to be shunned by the towns-folk, she'd never summoned the courage to give it a try.

Stella's musings were interrupted when she glanced across the street and saw three men walking behind the buildings. When they crossed a wide alleyway, she realized the man leading the threesome was the strange little clerk who worked at the bank. It looked to her like the man behind him was wearing a bandana covering most of his face, and he was holding a gun in the clerk's back. There was no doubt in her mind they were making their way to the bank. She thought about raising an alarm, but she'd seen the sheriff lock his office and head to church earlier. There was no way she'd walk in that church to fetch the sheriff, not even if the entire town was burning down.

If those men were robbing the bank, the way she looked at it she didn't have a horse in that race. It wasn't as if she had money in the bank, and she didn't expect she would ever earn enough money to save. It was her opinion the Denver Bank had made more than their fair share of money by selling the farms and ranches they'd foreclosed on during these hard times. Nor did she feel any particular concern over the bank clerk's welfare. He wasn't one of her customers, and she'd never even seen him in the saloon. She'd passed him a time or two on the sidewalk, but he'd never looked at her, not even to offer a polite nod like most men. When his boss came into the saloon, he didn't give her the time of day either. So why should she get all hot and bothered about these men sticking up the bank?

Frank and Walt pulled their bandanas away from their faces once they were inside the bank. Walt locked the back door as Frank lowered the shades covering the front windows.

Reuben took both of their saddlebags. "Both of you keep your eyes on the street while I fill these up." He knew the combination of the vault by heart, and he quickly opened the safe.

Frank and Walt took their positions by the windows where they could peek through the shades and watch the street in both directions.

"It's a quiet street on a Sunday morning,"

Frank whispered.

Walt saw the woman sitting on the balcony above the saloon. It was the pretty dove who had been playing cards the day he'd been in the saloon. She was the one who'd smiled at him. He wouldn't mention her to Frank, because if she saw them enter the bank, she wasn't doing anything about it. He saw no reason to put her life in jeopardy by telling Frank. Frank wanted to kill Joseph Longbow because Joseph could identify him as one of the rustlers. It stood to reason Frank wouldn't hesitate to kill that woman if he thought she could pin the robbery on him.

After a few minutes passed, Frank walked around the counter near the vault door. "You about finished?"

"Yes, just keep your eyes on the front," Reuben said. "I can handle this."

Frank didn't like Reuben giving instructions, but this wasn't the time to set him straight. The little man could pull the door of the vault shut, and they would walk away with nothing. He walked back to the window and looked out. He'd take care of Reuben later.

Stella watched as the shades lowered at the bank. They were definitely robbing the bank. Maybe she could work this to her benefit. She walked into her room and grabbed her robe.

Walt saw the gal sitting on the balcony walk inside. He had a feeling she'd been watching the bank. Still, he wasn't going to say anything unless he saw her leave the saloon and head for the sheriff's office. He waited and watched the front door of the saloon. He figured she could leave by a back door, but something told him to remain quiet.

Reuben walked from the vault and handed the men their saddlebags. "I'll stay here until you have time to get out of the area."

Frank looked out the window one last time. "Let's get out of here, Walt."

"I'll see you in a week," Reuben reminded him.

"Sure thing." Frank opened the back door and started running toward the brush. He didn't look back once he entered the trees, until a shot rang out. He stopped and looked back toward the bank, but he was already too far into the trees to see anything. He listened, thinking he would hear Walt running behind him. Nothing. Where was Walt?

Walt ran from the bank with his saddlebag over his shoulder when he skidded to a halt. Standing at the corner of the building was

444

the woman who had been sitting on the balcony. Walt was face-to-face with her. Up close, she was even prettier than he remembered. She wasn't wearing makeup today, and she looked young and innocent. He couldn't explain what happened to him in that moment, but a strange feeling came over him. He nodded.

Stella smiled at him.

Walt stared at her. She was smiling, but there was something about her, maybe the lonely look in her eyes, or perhaps it was the haunting look of hopelessness. Whatever it was, Walt had an overwhelming urge to grab her and take her with him. If someone had asked him yesterday if he'd ever settle down with one woman, he'd have told them they were crazy. He was a drifter, a loner. There'd been many a time he'd felt emptiness of his solitary life, but those were the times he'd pick up and move on to the next town.

He'd already planned on leaving Frank and his gang after this holdup. He didn't trust Frank, he was evil through and through, and the farther he got away from him, the better. The money he was carrying was the means to a whole new life. Why keep drifting? Why not try something totally new? Suddenly, he could see himself settling down with a woman. This woman. He opened his saddlebag and removed a stack of bills. He held the money out to her.

Stella recognized Walt immediately. She didn't know his name, but she remembered the day he'd walked into the saloon. When he smiled at her, she thought he was the most handsome man she'd ever seen. She remembered thinking she wished she wasn't playing cards with other customers because she wanted to talk to him. The other gal who'd drank with him said he treated her real nice. Stella took the money from him. "Which way are you going?"

"South," he replied.

"I'll tell them you rode north."

Walt glanced around and listened. Hearing nothing, he holstered his pistol and snaked an arm around her waist, pulling her close. He kissed her with a longing he didn't know he possessed. When he released her, he said, "I'm Walt. I'm meeting Reuben in a week. If you're interested, come with him and I'll take you with me."

For the first time since she was a young girl, Stella felt hope rising up in her soul. "I'm Stella, and I'll be there."

"Stella, you're beautiful." He tipped his hat and then ran for the trees.

Frank stepped out of the dense thicket.

"Who fired that shot?"

Walt had his pistol in his hand so he wasn't worried about Frank getting the drop on him. "Reuben pulled his derringer. He was going to double-cross us. Keep going, I'll see you at the Conner place."

Frank turned around and ran for his horse, jumped in the saddle, and didn't wait around for Walt before kicking his horse into a gallop.

By the time Walt got to his horse, Frank was out of sight. Frank was headed back to the Conner cabin, so Walt rode south.

"Reuben, what in the world happened here?" the sheriff asked.

"Two men were waiting for me as I left my home to go to church this morning. They forced me at gunpoint to the bank." Reuben played his role well. Walt had only grazed his upper arm with his shot, but it appeared to the sheriff that Reuben had put up a struggle. "I'm sorry they got away with the money, Sheriff. I tried to stop them."

"You did what you could, Reuben." The sheriff was surprised Reuben had even made an attempt to stop the bank robbers.

Stella kept her promise to Walt, saying to the sheriff, "I saw them riding north. I was sitting on the balcony when I heard the

447

shot." She realized people would come running when they heard the shot, so she'd stuffed the money down her chemise and tied her robe tightly around her. By the time the sheriff arrived at the bank, Stella was banging on the front door. The sheriff forced the door open, and they found Reuben lying on the floor. "I'll take care of him, go on after them, Sheriff."

"Thanks, Stella," the sheriff said. "You say there were only two of them?"

"That's all I saw," Reuben said, clutching his arm.

"I only saw two men riding away," Stella added.

"Reuben, did you know them, or ever see them before? Can you describe them?" the sheriff asked.

"They had their bandanas over their faces. I didn't see anything other than their eyes. I don't think I've ever seen them before."

"Okay, Stella will help you," the sheriff said on his way out the door.

Stella knew Reuben was lying. The man who had given her the money, Walt, didn't have his mask on when he left the bank. Walt was meeting Reuben because they were partners in the robbery. She helped Reuben to his feet. "Come on, I'll help you home. I don't think the doctor is in town."

"Thank you. I don't think it's serious. Perhaps you could bandage it for me."

"Of course." Rarely did men surprise Stella, but today, she'd had two of the biggest surprises of her life. This timid little man was a bank robber, and in a week she would be meeting a handsome cowboy and leaving behind the life she hated. Maybe dreams did come true. As soon as they were out of the bank, Stella said, "Reuben, I will be riding with you next week to meet Walt."

Frank stayed off the trail the entire trip to Whispering Pines, and reined in at the Conner place two hours after the robbery. He hadn't even stopped to count the money. When Walt shot Reuben, all he could think about was getting out of the area. He hadn't even slowed down for Walt to catch up with him.

Corbin walked out of the cabin. "Did you bring any whiskey?"

"No."

"Where's Walt?"

"He should be here soon," Frank said.

They heard a horse riding in, and Frank pulled his pistol. When he saw it was Stevie, he holstered his gun.

Stevie jumped from his horse. "Where've you been?"

"Denver," Frank said, dismounting.

"Why didn't you tell me? I've been out here several times looking for you."

"We wanted to check out the town," Frank said. He glanced at Corbin. "You got any coffee on the stove?"

"I'll get some going." Corbin walked back inside the cabin.

Frank waited until the door closed, then said, "We wanted to see what time was best to rob the bank."

"I don't see why I couldn't have gone with you. Anyways, Reuben already told you the best time to pull the robbery." Stevie looked around for Walt's horse. "Where's Walt?"

"I expect him any minute," Frank said.

Stevie was angry he was the one always staying behind. Reuben had told them everything they needed to know about the bank robbery. "You and Walt ain't planning on robbing that bank without me, are you?"

Frank glared at him. "You'd ask your own brother that? We've planned it together, haven't we?"

Stevie hung his head. "Sorry, Frankie, I'm just tired of staying at the farm and not knowing what is going on."

Frank shook his head as if he was disappointed in Stevie. "Why were you coming out here? Did something happen?"

"I came out to tell you that Rose was marrying Morgan on Saturday."

"Next Saturday?" Frank asked.

"No, they married yesterday," Stevie said. "You're too late to stop it now."

Frank's face twisted in rage. "You were supposed to let me know before it happened!"

"I rode out here twice to tell you, but you weren't here. How can I tell you when I don't know where you are?"

Frank's mind was racing. He couldn't believe his own sister had married his enemy. Morgan was going to pay for this. Frank was certain Morgan had only asked Rose to marry out of spite. Rose was going to pay too. He needed time to think. "Stevie, go home. I'll be there in a couple of hours."

"What are you going to do, Frankie?"

"Right now I'm going to make a plan. Do as I say and go home."

Frank watched Stevie ride away before he led his horse to the back of the cabin. He needed to hide his saddlebags in case Corbin got nosy. He wanted to take time to count the money, but right now it was more important to find a secure place for the cash. He walked through the trees until he found a perfect spot beneath a large tree, where he could bury his saddlebags under rocks.

When Frank returned to the cabin, Corbin said, "I thought you said Walt was right behind you?"

"I thought he was." Frank wondered what was keeping Walt. What if he got caught? He didn't know if Walt had killed Reuben, and he didn't care one way or the other. That was one killing they couldn't pin on him. He wasn't planning on meeting Reuben in a week anyway. There was no way he was going to split the money with him.

Corbin handed Frank a cup of coffee. "Where do you think he is?"

"How do I know? Maybe his horse threw a shoe. Maybe he stopped for a nap."

"You want me to go look for him?" Corbin asked.

"No. I want you to sit down. I want to tell you what we are going to do today."

When Stevie reached the farm, he stabled his horse, but he didn't take the time to remove his saddle. In a huff, he yanked off his saddlebag and stalked to the house. Once inside, he threw the saddlebag in a chair. He was tired of being taken for granted. There was no reason for Frankie to be in Denver, other than . . . no, he didn't want to think that of his own brother. On the other hand, Reuben's words kept playing in his mind. Reuben told him Frankie was going to double-cross all of them. And where was Walt? Did Frankie do something to Walt? He'd planned to meet Reuben in a few days, so he'd have a chance to ask him if he'd seen Frankie in Denver.

To be on the safe side, he thought he'd find a new hiding place for his money. If he didn't like Frankie's plans, he'd just take off on his own. That thought spurred him into action. He'd get his things together and hide them in the stable just in case he needed to go it alone. He grabbed his saddlebag from the chair and carried it to the bureau, then yanked a couple of shirts and socks out of a drawer and stuffed them in his saddlebag. He walked to the corner of the room and pried up the floorboard. Once he tossed the bag on the bed, he realized the bag was stamped with the name of a bank in St. Louis. He needed to get rid of that bank bag. He stuck his hand in the bag to pull the money out, but he came out with a handful of old newspapers. He emptied the bag on the floor and saw that more than half of the money had been replaced with newspapers. *Frankie.*

Stevie was distraught over what Frankie

had done. He'd worshipped his big brother his whole life. How could he betray him like this? When had he taken the money? Frank was late the day they'd met Reuben. That had to be the day he took the money.

Realizing he didn't have time to sit there and think about Frankie's deceit, he jumped up and grabbed what money was left and shoved it in his saddlebag. He filled the bank bag with the newspapers and placed it back in the hole. He ran to the stable and hid the saddlebag beneath the hay in one of the stalls. He'd just made it back inside the house when Frankie slipped through the back door.

Frank took a seat at the kitchen table. "I figured out a way to get to LeMasters. I've sent Corbin to ride on Morgan's property to create a diversion."

Stevie found it difficult to be civil. He thought he was a faster draw than Frankie, but before he did something stupid, he wanted to know if his brother had already robbed the Denver bank. "What do you have planned?"

"Corbin is going to set a fire in the north pasture. I figure that will draw Morgan and his men to that area. Then we are going to set a fire here, and I know Rose will come running."

"Then what?" Stevie didn't care one way or the other if he burned the farm down.

"Then I'm taking Rose with us. I'll have the very thing Morgan wants, and he will come to me."

"What if Granny comes with her when they see the fire?" Stevie asked.

"Too bad for Granny. She always cared more about Morgan than she did us."

"You're going to take Rose to Denver with us to rob the bank?" He watched Frankie's face carefully to see how he reacted to his question.

"We'll have to put the robbery off for a few weeks," Frank answered. "We'll take the money you stole and head on down to Mexico."

Stevie walked to his bedroom to get the bank bag. He had his answer. There was no way Frank would put off that bank robbery. Not after he'd already gone to the trouble to meet Reuben and planned the whole thing. Frank had already held up the bank, and Stevie figured it was likely Walt had been shot during the robbery. But what had happened to Reuben? If they'd robbed the bank today, Reuben wouldn't have been working. Stevie retrieved the money, and when he turned around, Frank was standing in the doorway. He threw the bag on the bed. "There you go."

Frank thought Stevie seemed jittery, but he read it as fear over what he had planned for Rose and Morgan. "It'll take a while for Corbin to get there and get the fire started. You got any whiskey?"

"Yeah." Stevie knew Frankie wouldn't look in the bag since he'd already removed most of the money.

Frank grabbed the bag of money off the bed and walked toward the kitchen. Obviously, Stevie had never looked inside the bag and found most of the money missing, so Frank was going to keep it within his grasp and make sure he didn't open it now.

Stevie pulled out a full bottle of whiskey from the cabinet, and Frank filled two glasses.

"Here's to paying Morgan LeMasters back," Frank said, holding his glass in the air.

Stevie clinked his glass to Frankie's. "Yeah."

Frank could tell Stevie was upset. "I thought you would be happy to finally show LeMasters that he don't run things around here."

"I just wanted to rob that bank and get out of here for good," Stevie replied before he downed his whiskey.

Frank looked at his brother over the rim of the glass as he drained his whiskey. He picked up the bottle and refilled both glasses. "That bank won't be going anywhere."

"But Reuben may leave. He wants to travel," Stevie said, and took another long drink.

"We can do it without Reuben." Frank filled Stevie's glass again. He knew Stevie couldn't handle his liquor any better than Corbin. He wanted to leave him behind, and what better way to do it than get him too drunk to know what was happening. He didn't want to split the money with him any more than he did the rest of the gang. "Drink up. Everything will work out well."

They drank several more glasses in silence, and Frank thought Stevie was about ready to pass out until he started talking again.

"Reuben's my friend," Stevie slurred. He hadn't had many friends in his life. Reuben had kept his word about sharing the money after he planned the stagecoach robbery. Stevie thought Reuben was smart, and he trusted him. That was more than he could say about his own brother. All Frankie ever did was use him to get information on where Morgan's cattle were grazing. Frankie always left him behind. He didn't know why he expected things to be different this time. "You don't know what it's like to have a friend you can trust."

Frank laughed. "You think he's a friend? He'd double-cross you in a heartbeat."

Stevie drank some more. "Reuben's not the one who would double-cross me."

"What are you saying, Stevie?" Frank asked.

Stevie stumbled to his feet. "I'm saying I think you're the one who double-crosses everyone."

"You better watch it, little brother," Frank said in a threatening tone. He poured more whiskey in his glass. "Drink your whiskey and let's talk about Mexico."

Slumping back into his chair, Stevie grabbed the glass and threw the contents back.

Frank poured the remainder of the whiskey into his glass. "Looks like we might need another bottle."

Stevie took another large swig before he dropped his head to the table. "I know you took that money," he mumbled.

"What?" Frank wasn't certain he'd heard him correctly.

"Money. Gone."

Frank heard him this time. "Do you have another bottle?"

Stevie tried to stand, but it took him a few times before he stopped wobbling. "It's . . . bedroom." He stumbled across the room.

When Stevie left the kitchen, Frank walked to the window. He saw a thin plume of smoke in the distance. Corbin had started the fire. A few seconds later, he saw another plume of smoke. Good for Corbin. He figured he'd set the fire at the farm in a few minutes. He wasn't going to concern himself if Granny came with Rose. He'd have to improvise. He really didn't care one way or the other what happened to Granny or Rose.

Hearing a crash from the hallway, Frank walked from the kitchen to see Stevie slumped to the floor. His holster and two bottles of whiskey were on the floor beside him. It looked like his little brother went in the bedroom for more than his whiskey. He tucked the bag of money under his arm and threw the holster over his shoulder. He picked up the whiskey bottles and walked to the front door. On the way out, he grabbed two kerosene lamps and smashed them on the floor. Glancing at the sky over Morgan's ranch, he counted four plumes of dark smoke in the distance. It was time to execute his plan. He struck a match on the sole of his boot and threw it inside the house. The wood ignited quickly, and Frank walked slowly to the back of the house to wait.

CHAPTER TWENTY-SIX

Morgan and his men saw the rising smoke in the northern range of the ranch. Every available man rode in that direction to see what was going on.

Rose was outside at the paddock feeding apples to Judge, telling him about her lovely wedding as if he were a trusted friend. As Judge munched on the apples, Rose thought of her wedding night. Those were memories she would never share with anyone, not even Judge. At first, she'd been too shy to turn around after Morgan unbuttoned her dress and removed her undergarments. But when she summoned the courage, it had been well worth her embarrassment when she saw the look in his eyes. At the thought, she felt herself blushing, just as she had last night.

She was jarred from her reverie when Judge nudged her arm. "So you want another apple, huh?" She smiled as she reached inside the bandana to pull out the remaining slices. As Judge ate from her palm, she looked out over the ranch and noticed smoke rising to the sky. She couldn't imagine why anyone would build a fire at this time of day, so she ran to the stable to see if anyone was there. She found one man changing horses, and she told him about the smoke. He jumped into the saddle and rode out fast. She ran back to the paddock and gave Judge the last of the apple. "Granny is napping, so I have to go prepare dinner now," she said, giving him one last rub on the neck.

On her way to the house, she thought she smelled smoke, but it had to be her imagination since the fire was so far away. But when she looked around, she saw a large black cloud rising from the direction of Granny's farmhouse.

There were no men at the ranch to go with her, but she couldn't stand there and do nothing if something at the farm was burning. Stevie might need help trying to put it out. She took off running through the trees in the direction of their farm. The winds were high and Rose didn't hear the usual sounds in the pines. But she thought she heard someone saying *turn back.* She turned around but no one was there, so she didn't heed the warning. She kept running until she cleared the trees on the boundary of their farm. She couldn't believe what she saw. The farmhouse was ablaze. She clutched her skirt in her hands and ran toward the house as fast as she could, shouting Stevie's name. Seeing the entire front of the house was engulfed in flames, she headed to the back. She rounded the corner of the house straight into the barrel of a gun.

"Hello, Rose. Or should I say, Mrs. Le-Masters."

Rose could barely speak. Her heart was pounding from exertion, and from fear. The last thing she expected was to see Frankie. "What's happened? Why are you here? Where's Stevie?"

Frank didn't answer her questions. "Where's Granny?"

"At the ranch, why?" She jumped when the fire exploded to the center of the house, and she felt the heat of the flames on her skin.

"Come on." Frank stepped away from the house, and motioned with his pistol for her to walk in the direction of the stable.

Rose didn't move. "What are you doing, Frankie? We need to see if Stevie is inside before the whole house burns."

"He's not there."

"How do you know he's not in the house?" She tried to walk around him to get to the back door, but he pushed the gun in her ribs. "Why are you holding a gun on me?"

"I told you to walk," he repeated, nudging her again with the pistol.

The flames consumed all but the back part of the house. Surely, if Stevie was in there when the fire started he got out, but she had to make sure. If Frank shot her, then he shot her. She darted around him and headed to the back door. She never made it. Frank cracked the back of her skull with the butt of his pistol.

Frank left Rose lying on the ground as he ran to the stable to get Stevie's horse. He led the horse to the back of the house, where he threw Rose over the saddle. He didn't see Stevie's saddlebags, so he wrapped the money bag and whiskey bottles in the bedroll. Mounting behind Rose, he rode to the area where he'd left his horse. His first stop would be the Conner house to get his saddlebags he stashed under the rocks. If Corbin had returned, then he could go with him. If not, he didn't care. Frank had the one thing Morgan wanted, and there was no doubt in his mind Morgan would come after her.

■ ■ ■ ■

There was nothing Morgan and his men could do to fight the blaze. Morgan knew the fires had been intentionally set because of the distance between them, and he smelled kerosene. After they got the cattle to safety, they would start digging trenches and chopping down trees to contain the fires.

Morgan and Murph were moving the cattle when Murph pointed toward the sky. "Looks like we are going to get a storm. Thank God, that'll help us out."

Morgan didn't notice clouds earlier, and he gave a word of thanks for all the help he could get. "Divine intervention." As the words left his mouth, a loud crack of thunder rocked the earth.

"Whatever it is, I'm grateful for it," Murph said. "Now let's just hope these cattle don't bolt in the wrong direction until that fire is doused. I'd bet this was Langtry's doing."

Morgan did a quick head count of the men to make sure all of them were accounted for. Morgan knew Frank was responsible — whether he'd lit the fires or directed someone to do his dirty work for him, he was behind it. He'd spotted Joseph earlier, so he knew he was safe. Suddenly, the hair rose on the back of his neck. Rose and Granny were alone. "Murph, no one is at the house."

Before Murph could respond, Morgan had already urged his horse into a gallop. Murph raced after him. They raced to the house, and Morgan jumped off his horse and ran inside. Granny met him in the kitchen. "Morgan, there's smoke coming from the farm."

"No, it's on the ranch," Morgan said. "Where's Rose?"

"I don't know. I was napping, but I saw smoke coming from the farm," Granny insisted.

Murph ran inside the house. "Morgan, there's a fire coming from the farm."

"Check to make sure Rose isn't in the house," Morgan said as he ran outside and looked toward the farm. Black smoke was rising from that direction. "Murph, check the stable to see if Rose is in there."

Granny looked through every room before she hurried out the front door. "She's not inside. Something's wrong because she told me she was going to prepare dinner."

Murph ran from the stable. "No one's here," he yelled.

"Morgan, what is going on?" Granny asked.

"Someone set fires on the ranch," Morgan explained.

"Rose must be at the farm," Granny said. "Help me up on your horse. You're not going without me."

Morgan didn't argue. He lifted Granny on Faithful and mounted behind her. "Murph, go with us." He wasn't going to take any chances where Rose was concerned. If Frank had his men with him, they could be riding into a trap.

As soon as they exited the pines, they saw the farmhouse was nothing more than charred timber.

"Dear Lord," Granny said on a sob.

Morgan and Murph exchanged a look. Morgan helped Granny to the ground. "Stay put." The men pulled their guns and rode closer to the house. They dismounted several feet away from the still smoldering structure. They made their way around the perimeter of the remains, praying they wouldn't find anyone who had been inside. Morgan stopped and stared hard at the burned-out contents of the home. He smelled the unforgettable odor of burned flesh. Giving no heed to the smoke and the small flames which hadn't yet burned out, he walked inside to the interior of the house.

"Morgan, it's too hot to be in there," Murph called out.

Morgan didn't hear him; he was focused on a burning board that was at an odd angle in the middle of the house. When he reached the board, he kicked it aside and it broke in half. That's when he saw the small burned body beneath the board. Without thinking, he tossed aside the smoking debris. He didn't feel the flesh on his palms burning for the gut-wrenching pain that had seized his heart. He dropped to his knees in the hot rubble, looking to see if this could be anyone but Rose. The body was burned beyond recognition. Everything burned away; flesh, clothing, hair . . . everything. If it wasn't Rose, it was Stevie. That thought spurred him to action. He jumped up and ran to the stable. If Stevie had been home, his horse would be in the stable.

Murph was yelling at him, asking him what he was doing, but he didn't stop to explain. Murph walked to the spot where Morgan had kneeled down, and saw what he saw. "Dear God," he whispered.

Murph ran toward the stable, but stopped short when Morgan stumbled out and dropped to his knees. Silently, he watched his best friend bury his face in his hands and let out a scream so filled with anguish that he drowned out the thunder overhead. Murph stood there helpless. The only other time he'd seen Morgan break down this way was the day Frank nearly killed Judge. Granny walked up beside him, and together they approached Morgan.

Gently placing her hand on Morgan's shoulder, she whispered, "Is it Rose?"

Morgan tried to compose himself for Granny's sake. "Stevie's horse is gone."

Both Granny and Murph knew by that statement that it had to be Rose's body in that rubble.

Knowing he had to be strong for Granny, Morgan stood. When he saw the tears flowing from Granny's tired old eyes, he pulled her into his arms and let her cry on his chest. No matter how he tried to control his emotions, he couldn't stop his own tears.

"Why did this happen to my sweet Rose?" Granny wailed.

Morgan wasn't able to respond. His heart felt like it had splintered into a thousand pieces, and he'd never be able to put it back together. He wanted to scream until he was too exhausted to feel the pain. But Granny needed him, he couldn't break down in front of her.

Murph walked away to get their horses as

he wiped tears from his eyes. He knew what would happen next. This was Frank's doing, and Morgan would show him no quarter this time. He feared not even Granny would sway him from that path. Morgan's vengeance would be relentless this time, but Murph didn't feel an ounce of sympathy for Frank.

Murph led the horses to Granny and Morgan. "Morgan, it will take some time for this to cool down. I'll come back later and take care of things. We should get Granny home."

Morgan nodded. He prided himself on being a man who could handle most things, but he didn't think he could collect the charred body of his wife. "Granny, none of your belongings will be salvageable."

"No matter. Nothing really matters now." Granny didn't think she'd ever feel the pain of losing another child she loved so dearly. After losing her son, she wasn't certain she now had a reason to go on.

They were silent riding back to the ranch, each grieving in their own way. Morgan's emotions were at war. Heartbreak and rage. He had to stay here to see to Rose, but everything inside of him wanted to go after Frank. He figured Frank wanted him to come after him. Frank was going to get his wish. As soon as he buried his wife, Frank was going to see that vengeance did indeed ride a black horse.

Before they got through the trees, the rain came down so hard that they were soaked by the time they reined in at the house.

Morgan glanced at Murph and nodded. Murph understood without words what his friend was saying. With the rain, the farmhouse wouldn't take as long to cool down and he could get to Rose.

"See to your hands, Morgan." Murph grabbed Faithful's reins and led him to the stable.

Morgan assisted Granny inside. "Go change your clothes while I make us some coffee."

"You sit down and let me see to your hands," Granny said, her voice lifeless.

Morgan walked to the stove. "My hands are fine."

Granny followed him to the stove and reached for one of his hands. Her sharp intake of breath expressed her surprise at how badly he'd burned them. "My goodness, Morgan, this must be hurting like the devil."

"I'm fine."

Granny took him by the arm and led him to a chair. "Sit."

He was too tired to argue with her. He sat in the chair as she washed his hands. Afterwards, she slapped some grease on his palms before she bandaged them.

Joseph lightly tapped on the back door before he walked inside. Without a word, he walked to the stove and started making coffee.

"I guess I should get dinner started," Granny said absently.

"Granny, no one wants dinner. We'll grab a sandwich later if we get hungry. You go ahead and change out of those wet clothes and get some rest." Morgan thought she might want to be alone to do her grieving. She looked lost, much like she did after Preacher died. He figured he looked the same. Lost. That word perfectly described the way he felt.

Granny nodded and left the room.

The coffee started boiling and Joseph poured two cups. The two men sat at the table in silence. Morgan appreciated Joseph's calming presence. After their second cup of coffee, Morgan heard the buckboard pulling out. He didn't want to think about how he'd found Rose. He couldn't. "Thanks for the coffee, Joseph. I'm going upstairs for a while."

When he reached his bedroom, the first

thing he did was grab his bottle of whiskey. He pulled the cork out and didn't bother with a glass. He sat in his leather chair, the same chair he'd sat in the night before with Rose in his lap. He'd only had one night with his bride, but it was the best night of his entire life. Happiness consumed his every thought last night. Just knowing he would have his entire life with her made everything he would accomplish more meaningful. He'd always heard never leave anything unsaid to the people who mean the most to you because no one was promised tomorrow. He wished he'd told Rose that his wedding day was the best day of his life.

Morgan took another swallow of whiskey, leaned back and closed his eyes as he replayed his wedding night in his mind. Rose had allowed him to undress her even though he knew she was embarrassed. Once he'd removed her chemise, she'd waited for what seemed an eternity before she'd turned in his arms. He'd never seen a more beautiful sight in his life. She'd reached up and removed the comb in her hair, and the golden strands dropped over her soft, smooth shoulders and covered her breasts. He knew he would carry that memory to his deathbed. Tears streamed down his face.

Morgan sat there for hours thinking of every tender moment of their wedding night. He cried. He drank. And he cried some more. He didn't know how people went on after such a painful loss. He hadn't even realized how much he loved Rose, until his wedding day. He knew he was very fond of her, and he admired her character, but it wasn't until he was standing on that altar looking into her beautiful green eyes that he realized his true feelings. He loved her passionately, and he hadn't professed his love to her. He had a lot of regrets in life, but nothing compared to this.

There were many things that happened in life he didn't understand, but having such a short time with Rose made him question why. Was he being punished for harboring hatred against Frank for so long? How could God take away the most precious thing in his life? Not only take her from him, but from Granny. Granny had barely survived the death of her son, she didn't deserve to experience another devastating loss. Granny's heart was full of love and forgiveness; she'd never done an evil deed in her life.

It was still raining when Murph and the two men riding with him reached the farmhouse.

Murph couldn't help but wonder why it hadn't started raining earlier, in time to save Rose. Some questions just didn't have answers. He reached under the tarp and pulled out two blankets. Slowly, he made his way to Rose. He couldn't bear to look at what was left of her body, so he covered her with one blanket and gently lifted her to the other blanket. The two men tossed back the tarp so Murph could place her in the buckboard, and they quickly covered her.

Morgan didn't know how long he sat in that chair thinking about Rose. How she looked that day when she got off the stagecoach holding on to her Bible for dear life, and giving him the devil. How fragile she looked when she thought he would hang her brother. The surprise on her face the first time he kissed her. How he felt when she kissed him back. The look in her eyes when he asked her to marry him. How beautiful she looked as he held her in his arms while she slept last night. So many moments passed through his mind, and the moments he longed to see in the future. He wanted to see her carrying their child, giving birth to sons and daughters. Life would go on, he would go on, but he would never be the same.

Hours later, he quietly left the house and walked to the stable. The men had already built a box and had it loaded on the buckboard. Morgan knew Rose's body was inside, so he climbed in the buckboard and sat beside her. Rationally, he knew Rose was not there, but it comforted him to be by her side right now.

He'd heard many of Preacher's sermons about rejoicing when a loved one died, knowing they were going to a better place. Right now he couldn't find it in his heart to be happy. Maybe if he'd spent the next fifty years with Rose, he might be more inclined to accept her death. Even then, he would have prayed he went before her. One thing he knew for sure: God received a beautiful angel today.

CHAPTER TWENTY-SEVEN

Rose awoke with her hands tied, lying on her stomach over the back of a horse. Her head was throbbing, and she had a difficult time forming a thought. Not knowing where she was, or why she was tied, she didn't speak as she tried to get her thoughts in order. The last thing she remembered was Frankie holding her at gunpoint as she was trying to see if Stevie was inside the burning house. She didn't remember going inside. Frankie must have hit her on the head with something.

It dawned on her the horse wasn't moving, and she didn't hear any sounds, so she looked around. She was tied to Stevie's horse. There was another horse beside her, but no rider. The horses were tied to a rail in front of an old ramshackle house, but it didn't look familiar. Thick weeds surrounded the house, and she figured this must be one of Frank's hideouts. But where was he? Why did he bring her here? Her mind cleared, and she realized what Frankie wanted. He was using her to lure Morgan to him.

Corbin was not at the Conner place by the time Frank arrived with Rose. He quickly ran to the back of the house where he'd hidden his saddlebags. He was curious about how much money he had, but he didn't take the time to look because he feared Corbin might arrive any moment. He'd decided to wait on Corbin, not out of allegiance but because he might need an extra gun once Morgan arrived. It was possible Morgan wouldn't come alone.

Too bad Walt hadn't made it back, he was a better shot than Corbin. Frank shook his head. He was still angry that Walt had half the money in his saddlebag. At the time, he didn't even think to tell Walt to give him both saddlebags. That was a mistake he wouldn't make again. Hearing someone riding in fast, Frank threw the saddlebag over his shoulder, pulled his gun and walked to the front of the house.

Rose thought she heard someone walking through the brush, so she remained silent until she saw it was Frankie. "Frankie, where are we? Why do you have me tied like an animal?"

"It doesn't matter where we are. We'll be leaving here soon." He aimed his Colt and waited to see who was going to appear through the brush.

"Did you see that, Frank? I did just like you said," Corbin said, reining in beside Frank's horse.

"Yeah, Corbin, that was real good."

Corbin glanced at Rose. He remembered her from the stagecoach. "Why is she here?"

"I told you I was gonna get to Morgan." He motioned toward Rose. "Here's my guarantee he will come to me."

Corbin was surprised by the way Frank had Rose trussed up like an animal. "You shouldn't tie your sister up like that."

Frank's lip curled in disgust. "She was my sister before she married LeMasters. She ain't nothing to me now."

"Couldn't you have taken care of LeMasters on his ranch?" Corbin asked in an unusual moment of clarity.

"Not with all of his men around. This way will be more fun."

Rose knew in that moment that her brother was insane, or just truly evil. "Where is Stevie?" Rose asked.

"You don't have to worry about Stevie no more," Frank said.

"Frankie, what did you do?" Rose's voice

479

cracked with emotion.

Ignoring her question, Frank said, "Get her off that horse, Corbin. I figure we need to stay here tonight and leave at dawn."

Corbin untied Rose and helped her off the horse. He saw blood oozing from the back of her head. "What happened to you?"

Rose swayed when Corbin helped her to the ground. She reached out to hold on to the horse to steady herself. "I don't know." Lifting a hand to the back of her head, she felt a gash. Frank must have hit her with something and that was the reason she couldn't remember everything.

Corbin handed her his canteen. "Drink some water."

Rose started to refuse, but she didn't know if she would be offered water again. She hadn't had a drink since earlier in the day, and that must have been hours ago, because the sun was drifting slowly into the horizon. She lifted the canteen to her lips and drank as much as she could.

"Let me help you inside," Corbin said, taking hold of her elbow.

Rose allowed him to assist her. "Thank you."

"She can get inside by herself. You need to get those horses to the lean-to," Frank said.

Corbin opened the door to the cabin before he walked back to get his animal. He was beginning to see why Deke and Dutch didn't want to ride with Frank anymore. Frank wasn't even grateful to his sister after what she'd done for them. As a matter of fact, Corbin thought Frank could be downright cruel for no reason. But he'd have to play this out if he wanted to get his share of the rustling money. He'd collect his share of the loot and take off.

When Corbin grabbed the reins of Stevie's horse, he looked at Frank. "This is Stevie's horse."

"Yeah." Frank stared at him, waiting for him to ask the question.

Corbin didn't ask. He took hold of the reins and led the horses to the back of the cabin. After he cared for the animals, he walked inside the cabin.

Frank led his horse to the back of the cabin and removed the bottles of whiskey from his bedroll. After he unsaddled his horse, he stashed his saddlebags and his bedroll under his saddle on the ground before he led his horse into the lean-to.

"I got two bottles of whiskey," Frank said when he entered the cabin. He knew as long as Corbin had whiskey he would do anything he asked.

"Good. I sure could use a drink. Where are we going when we leave here?"

"I was thinking about Purgatory Canyon, but that will take too long. I want to get this over with."

"Are we going back to Denver and rob the bank?"

His question caught Frank off guard. He didn't realize Corbin had picked up on so much of his conversations with Walt. "We might go to Las Vegas first and meet up with the boys."

"I don't understand why Walt hasn't made it back," Corbin mused.

"You know Walt. He probably met up with some woman." Frank always figured women were Walt's main weakness.

Rose heard what Frank was planning. If he took her to Purgatory Canyon, then he'd shoot Morgan as soon as he rode in, just like his gang had waited for the sheriff. She had to find a way to escape, or Morgan would be riding to his own death. The thought made her sick with fear.

Frank walked to the table and grabbed two tin cups. He uncorked one of the whiskey bottles and filled the cups.

Rose prayed they would drink so much they would pass out and not wake until tomorrow. She'd have to wait until it was light enough outside so she could figure out what direction she needed to go. She didn't want to talk to Frankie, but she wanted to know what he did to Stevie. "Where's Stevie?"

Frank chuckled. "I imagine he's saying hello to Satan about now."

"Frankie, what did you do?"

"Shut up, Rose," Frank said, gulping his cup of whiskey. "I don't feel like listening to your whining."

Rose dropped her face in her hands so he wouldn't see her tears. But Frank was watching her, and his eyes landed on the twinkling ring on her finger. He jumped up and grabbed her hand. "What's this?"

She tried to pull her hand from his grasp. "What do you think it is?"

Frank backhanded her across the cheek. "Don't sass me."

Corbin jumped up. "Frank, you shouldn't hit a woman."

Frank glared at him. "This ain't none of your concern."

"But she's hurt," Corbin said.

Frank ignored him. He twisted Rose's hand at an odd angle. "Did LeMasters give you this?"

"Yes."

Frank smirked at her. "I'm glad to hear it.

At first, I thought he might be marrying you to get to me. But since he gave you a ring like this I'd say he actually wanted you."

"We married so we could both have what we want."

"What's that?"

"A family. We both want children."

Frank released her hand and grabbed the whiskey bottle. "Now ain't that sweet." He poured another full cup, and handed the bottle to Corbin. "Did you hear that, Corbin? They want a family." He pulled a chair next to Rose's and sat down. He leaned in close to her face. "Here's the problem, Rose. You had a family, and it didn't mean nothing to you. You took off and left your family."

Rose shook her head. "Frankie, what has happened to you? Listen to yourself. I always planned to come back home. Adelaide and Emma will be home this year. Granny couldn't afford to see to our education, and our great aunt and uncle told you they would see you were educated, but you refused. You wanted to rob! That was your choice."

Frank sipped his whiskey and stared at her. His eyes landed on her ring again. "I think Morgan wants you."

"Like I told you, Morgan married me for

children. Lots of people marry for that reason. Was Stevie in the house?"

"Yeah. He'd had too much to drink and he didn't make it out."

Rose gasped at his words. Frank knew his brother was in that burning house and he did nothing to try to save him. Tears streamed down her cheeks. Whatever Stevie had done wrong, he didn't deserve such a fate.

Corbin didn't know Frank had planned to kill his own brother. That could only mean one thing: He'd kill anyone who stood in his way. He'd kill his sister too. She knew too much. Corbin didn't know if he could allow Frank to kill such a pretty little lady. Sharing in the loot from a robbery wasn't that important to him. And he was smart enough to know if Frank would kill kin, then he wouldn't hesitate to kill him.

When Rose could speak again, she said, "I don't think Morgan will come for me."

"Oh, he'll come. He was ready to follow me to the end of the earth over a few head of cattle. I'd say his wife is more important to him than that."

"Frankie, did you even think it might be Granny who finds Stevie's body?" Rose asked.

"Why should I care?"

Rose looked him in the eye, and she knew what it felt like to look into the eyes of pure evil. "How do you know Morgan won't think I may have gone with you willingly? We argued over my devotion to you." She didn't want Morgan to come for her and ride into the same trap as the sheriff. She wanted to put doubt in Frankie's mind, praying he would end this madness.

Frank hadn't thought Morgan would refuse to come for her, but maybe he should have considered that possibility. He reached out and snatched Rose's hand, and roughly yanked off her ring. "I guess there is only one way we will find out what your husband will do. If he doesn't come for you, I will sell you down on the border. You know what you will become, don't you?"

"Give me my ring," Rose demanded.

"You won't be needing it where we are going," Frank said, tucking the diamond ring in his shirt pocket. Too bad he would have to forfeit it. He imagined he could get a lot of money for a ring like that. But he wasn't worried about money right now. He had all the money he would need for a long time in his saddlebags.

Corbin refilled his glass. He didn't like what Frank was planning to do with his sister, but he was too afraid of him to raise a ruckus. He'd seen what happened to men when they challenged Frank.

It wasn't long before Frank realized Corbin was already drunk. He had planned to ask him to make one more ride tonight, but he knew if he wanted the job done right, he'd have to do it himself. Corbin would most likely be caught, and while that didn't bother Frank, he didn't want him telling anyone of their whereabouts.

Corbin's head dropped to the table, and Frank grabbed him by the hair and lifted his head to see if he was really passed out. When he released his hold, Corbin's forehead hit the table hard. Frank figured he was out for the night. He grabbed the rope he'd used on Rose and reached for her, but she stumbled to her feet and backed away. "Unless you want another crack on your skull, hold out your hands."

Rose saw no way out of the situation. She held her hands out to him. "What are you going to do?"

"I'm going to leave your husband a present, and I ain't taking the chance of you trying to find your way out of here."

"I don't even know where we are. There's no reason to tie me. Where am I going to go in the dark?"

"I've made it this far because I don't take

stupid chances," Frank boasted as he wrapped the rope around her wrists.

"You're making a mistake now if you think Morgan will come after me."

Frank shoved her into a chair. Once he tied her ankles, he wrapped the rope around her waist, securing her to the chair. He pulled his bandana from his pocket and tied it around her mouth so she couldn't call out and try to wake Corbin. "I'm not the one making a mistake. You made the biggest mistake of your life when you married Le-Masters."

When Frank pulled out his knife, Rose had no idea what he intended to do. She couldn't scream, she couldn't fight him, and she couldn't run. Her heart started thumping rapidly, and she held her breath as he bent over to cut a strip of cloth from the hem of her dress.

Rose's eyes followed him as he walked out the door. Minutes later she heard him ride away. Terrified Frankie might be riding back to hurt Morgan, Rose couldn't stop the tears from coming. She struggled against the rope wrapped around her waist until she was exhausted. She was helpless. The only hope she had was if Corbin woke up before Frank returned. At least Corbin seemed to have a conscience. He might be an outlaw, but she didn't think he was a killer. She prayed she would be able to talk him into releasing her. If Frank was going back to the farm, she reasoned they couldn't be that far away.

The thought of losing Morgan was more than she could bear. Though they had only spent their wedding night together, it had been more magical than she'd even imagined. He had been gentle and loving, but it was his patience she appreciated the most. He understood her inexperience, her nervousness, and he didn't rush her. He proceeded slowly, his every touch tender as he masterfully prepared her for the night to follow. The night was one she would always cherish. She'd fallen asleep in his arms thanking God for sending Morgan to her. Thinking she might never share another night with Morgan brought fresh tears, but also a determination to act. She tried scooting the chair across the room, trying to make as much noise as possible. And she prayed. She prayed like she'd never prayed before, asking God to send his angels to protect her husband.

Joseph walked into the stables before dawn and saw Morgan sitting beside Rose's coffin. He approached the buckboard and said,

"You need to help Granny."

Morgan didn't want to leave Rose, but he knew Granny needed his strength right now. The thought seemed absurd. He didn't feel like he had any strength left. He felt lost, but he had to summon the strength to help Granny through this. He looked at Joseph and nodded. "Joseph, if it's okay with you, and if Granny agrees, I'd like to bury Rose at her altar." He wasn't sure how he could put his sweet Rose in the earth, but it had to be done.

"It is good," Joseph said. "You go. I will stay with her."

Morgan jumped down from the buckboard. He wanted to thank Joseph, but he was too emotional. He put his hand on Joseph's shoulder and squeezed before he walked away.

Granny was sitting in the kitchen when Morgan walked in. He could tell she hadn't slept. "I don't know what I'll do without my Rose."

Morgan leaned over and kissed the top of her head. He knew how she felt, but he didn't want to add to her burden. "Your other granddaughters will be home soon. You need to be strong for them."

"How will I ever tell the girls what happened to their beloved sister?" Morgan was right, she'd have to go on for the girls. "If Preacher were here he'd tell me God had a plan, and to keep the faith."

Morgan didn't comment. He was too upset with God right now. He walked to the stove and pulled out a skillet to cook breakfast. He looked out the window while he was cooking and saw the rays of the sun peeking up over the horizon. The last time he saw Rose they were standing in this very spot, and he'd kissed her before he left. He'd whispered in her ear, telling her what he was going to do to her when he got her alone in their bedroom that night. She'd looked up at him with those beautiful green eyes and said, "I can't wait." He'd ridden off feeling like a new man, even though he'd had only an hour's sleep. But the way he saw it, he'd have a lifetime to sleep, he'd only have one wedding night. He wanted to make it memorable. Little did he know that one night would have to last him a lifetime.

He placed a plate of eggs and bacon and a steaming cup of coffee in front of Granny. "We both need to eat something." As they ate, he told Granny where he'd like to bury Rose, and Granny thought it was a lovely idea.

Granny tried to keep from crying again and upsetting Morgan. "That was her favorite place. I think she would like that."

"Granny, I'm sorry if this happened because of my need for revenge," Morgan said. Through the night, he'd questioned God about taking Rose from him. He'd wondered if God was angry because he wouldn't let go of the vengeance in his heart. Granny had told him several times God would deal with Frank, and to leave it up to Him. "You were right, Granny, I should have let it go. I'm so sorry I didn't listen."

Granny placed her hand over his. "Morgan, this wasn't your fault. That's not the way He works. He wouldn't hurt you by taking Rose. Don't even think that. Men like Frankie make their own choices, and sometimes good people get in the way."

Joseph walked in the back door without knocking. "No ring."

Morgan gave him a questioning look. "What?"

"No ring on finger," Joseph said, making a circle design around his own ring finger.

Morgan realized Joseph must have opened the coffin to include a gift, or herbs for Rose's departure to the spirit world. Jumping from his chair, he said, "I'll be back." He hurried to the stable, threw the saddle over Faithful, and rode through the pines in record time.

He reined in, in front of the burned-out farmhouse. He didn't know what he would find, but he had to look for Rose's ring where her body had been. He'd only taken a few steps when he saw something that hadn't been there the day before. Right in the center of the rubble was a wooden cross. Morgan walked through the debris to the cross. Nailed in the very center was a piece of cloth. Morgan recognized the cloth; it was torn from the pink dress Rose was wearing yesterday when he'd kissed her at the stove. He plucked the cloth from the nail and was overcome with emotion when he saw what was beneath the material. Rose's diamond wedding band was hanging over the nail. He pulled the cross out of the ground and saw the words that had been etched in the wood. He held the wood to the morning light and read: *Purgatory Canyon. Alone or she dies.*

CHAPTER TWENTY-EIGHT

Corbin awoke before dawn with a splitting headache. He looked around the room for Frank, but saw Rose lying on the floor, tied to a chair. He stumbled from his seat and pulled the bandana from her mouth. "Where's Frank?"

Rose had rocked the chair back and forth over the wooden floor trying to wake Corbin. After several futile attempts, she fell on her side. She was so exhausted she could barely speak, and when she did, her voice was raspy. "I think he went back to the farm. He rode out a long time ago." Through the dark hours of the night, she'd thought of a plan if Corbin awoke before Frank returned, so she put the plan in motion. "Could you untie me so I can go outside?"

Corbin understood what she was asking. He was needing to do the same thing. She'd been tied up for hours with no water or food, and he felt sorry for her.

Once he freed her hands, he used his knife to cut the rope at her waist and feet. Rose fell to her knees when she tried to stand, but Corbin helped her to her feet. She managed to stumble out the door.

Corbin exited the house behind her and walked in the opposite direction. He thought Frank had taken off for good, and in a way, he was relieved. If not for Frank's sister, he would get on his horse and take off. He didn't like the way Frank treated her, and it didn't bode well for her future if Frank did come back. Once he finished his business, he walked back inside to look for some coffee while he evaluated his situation. Finding none, he took a swig of whiskey.

Rose heard Corbin go through the bushes at the front of the house as she staggered to the back of the house. She made her way to the lean-to and waited until she heard him go back inside the cabin. She didn't have the strength to lift the saddle, and even if she did, it would be impossible for her to throw it over the horse. There was no option other than to ride bareback. As she was reaching for the bridle, she heard a horse approaching. Frank. She ran for the brush.

"Where have you been?" Corbin asked,

meeting Frank at the front of the house.

"I had to leave a message for Morgan," Frank said.

"What are you talking about?"

"It doesn't matter. We need to get out of here now. LeMasters will be riding to Purgatory Canyon soon, and we need to get on the trail and get ready." Frank walked around Corbin into the house. He spotted the ropes on the floor. "Where is she?"

"Doing her business. You left her tied up all night, and she ain't had food or water. Nothing. I don't think you should treat a lady that way."

"You ain't here to think," Frank shouted, and stormed from the cabin.

Rose hadn't moved for fear Frank would hear her. She heard him as he walked to the back of the house.

"Rose, come out now. If you don't, we'll leave you here. You don't know where you are, and we are a long way from any town. You'll die of thirst and starvation."

Rose was paralyzed with indecision. She didn't know if he was telling the truth, but even if she went with him, she felt certain she was going to die. That didn't matter if Frank would leave Morgan alone. But after what he'd done to his own brother, she knew no one was safe from his evil plotting.

"If you don't come out, I promise you I will kill Morgan."

She didn't have a choice. Her only hope was to find a way to escape before Morgan reached Purgatory Canyon. She wondered if she could kill her own brother if she got her hands on a gun. To save Morgan, she knew the answer to that question.

Morgan ran into the house and found Granny sitting at the table reading her Bible. He was rejoicing that Rose wasn't dead, but now he realized what this news meant for Granny. She didn't lose a granddaughter, but she'd lost a grandson.

Granny closed her Bible and looked at Morgan. His face no longer held the haunted expression of a grieving man. "What is it?"

"Frank's taking Rose to Purgatory Canyon. He told me to come alone, or he would kill her. I'm sorry I can't stay with you right now, Granny, but I've got to go."

Granny clutched his arm. "How do you know he has Rose?"

Morgan held the ring and the piece of cloth for her to see. "He left me a message."

"It was Stevie," Granny whispered.

Morgan nodded.

Granny understood what Morgan had to

do. "I'll be fine, Morgan. Go. I'll pray for you."

He kissed her cheek before he ran for the stairs to stuff his saddlebags with clothing, another pistol, and extra cartridges. Suddenly, he came to a halt. Why would Frank ride all the way to Purgatory Canyon? It would take days to get there. Frank didn't have much of a head start if he was near the farm during the night. Morgan was sure he would catch up to him in a matter of hours since he would be riding alone. Frank had to know that Rose would slow him down. Morgan guessed Frank wasn't really going to Purgatory Canyon. He just wanted him to follow in that direction so he could be ambushed. There were many places along the way where Frank could accomplish his goal. Understanding Frank's plans that didn't alter Morgan's decision. If it saved Rose's life, he would gladly sacrifice his own. Morgan turned to leave, but he spotted Rose's Bible on the bedside table. He opened his saddlebag and placed it inside.

When Morgan came downstairs, Granny had already bundled some food for him, and filled two canteens. She handed them to him and said, "Bring her home, son."

Morgan was touched by her confidence in him. "Granny, I'm sorry about Stevie." He gave her a hug before he grabbed his rifle and headed out the door.

Joseph and Murphy saw Morgan riding away and they ran to the house to ask Granny where he was going.

"Purgatory Canyon. Frank left a message for him. Told him to come alone or Rose dies."

"I better go tell the sheriff what is going on," Murph said. "I know Morgan wouldn't want us to take a chance with Rose's life, but we all know this is a trap."

Before Murph walked out the door, he turned to Granny. "Granny, is it Stevie we need to bury?"

Granny nodded. "We'll bury him next to Preacher at the farm." Granny thought that would be the proper place for Stevie.

"Whenever you are ready, just say the word," Murph said.

"I'll be ready as soon as you get back. We can't wait on Morgan and Rose, not with the heat."

She spoke with such certainty that Morgan and Rose would return that he wasn't about to mention all the reasons it might not happen.

Murph and Joseph left the house together, and Murph asked him to send men to the farm to start digging the grave for Stevie.

"We'll take Granny as soon as I get back from town."

Frank tied Rose's hands to the pommel once she was in the saddle. He threw the reins to Corbin for him to lead the animal.

"What's your plan, Frank?" Corbin asked.

"We're heading to Purgatory Canyon, but that's not where we are going. Tomorrow morning you are going to take Rose and ride to New Mexico Territory. I'm going to wait for Morgan. Once I take care of him, I'll catch up with you, and we'll meet up with the boys in Las Vegas. If Morgan gets me before I get him, then you can do what you want with her."

"Purgatory Canyon makes no sense," Jack said when Murph told him the events of that morning. "Morgan will catch up to them in one day."

"I didn't think about that," Murph said. "But Frank said to come alone, or he would kill Rose. I don't think Frank would hesitate to keep that promise."

"Yeah. All the same, I'm going that way. I'll try to stay out of sight. But you can bet Morgan is riding into a trap."

"I'll go with you," Murph said.

"I appreciate it, Murph, but you'd best

stay at the ranch. You might be needed there in case there's more trouble."

As much as Murph hated staying behind, he knew Jack was right. "I don't like this one bit."

"Me neither. I'm sorry for Granny losing Stevie, but I'm happy it wasn't Rose." Jack couldn't imagine how Morgan could deal with such a loss.

When Murph arrived back at the ranch, Joseph had hitched the team to the buckboard and it was in front of the house. Joseph was sitting with Granny on the porch waiting for him.

Murph told them Jack was going to follow Morgan. "He doesn't think Frank is going to Purgatory Canyon. He thinks Morgan will be waylaid on the trail."

"I hope he's wrong," Granny said.

Joseph jumped up, nodded to Granny, and headed toward the stable.

Granny looked at Murph and said, "I guess it's time."

Murph helped her into the buckboard and they rode in silence to the farm to bury Stevie.

Knowing Morgan would gain on them, Frank had only allowed one brief stop during the day. He was going to have to stop soon because the horses couldn't keep going at the pace he was setting.

Corbin was tired, and he was fed up with Frank's breakneck tempo, particularly since Corbin was leading the horse Rose was riding. His arm was beginning to ache from having to ride with it stretched out behind him. "Frank, we need to stop and let these horses rest. Besides, I'm getting hungry, and I know your sister needs to eat."

"Yeah, I know." Frank pointed to the trail ahead. "There's a creek ahead where we can fill our canteens. There's also a turnoff where you can pick up the trail to Las Vegas. We'll stop there, and at dawn, you and Rose head in that direction, and I'll keep going west. I'll probably catch up to you before you get to Las Vegas."

"Why is your sister going with me?" Corbin asked.

"I don't want her slowing me down. I know the place where I'm going to wait, and I'll have to ride fast."

Corbin didn't mind taking Rose with him, and he darn sure wouldn't ride like the devil was on their tails. Once they were far enough away from Frank, he might untie her and let her go. If he did decide to release her, he'd better have someplace to go, because if Frank showed up in Las Vegas and he wasn't there with Rose, he'd be looking over his shoulder for a long time.

Morgan made good time, and tried not to think about being shot out of the saddle at any moment. His size made him an easy target, but he couldn't let that worry him. By the time darkness surrounded him, he had to stop for a few hours to allow his horse a rest. He pulled out the bundle of food Granny had packed. He couldn't say he was hungry, but he would eat. He'd need his strength to deal with Frank. He pulled out some biscuits and cooked bacon. He wanted coffee, but he didn't think it prudent to build a fire. He wasn't going to make it easy for Frank.

Jack had left Whispering Pines soon after Murph left his office. He couldn't sit back and do nothing, not while his best friend was in danger. There was no doubt in his mind Morgan knew he was riding into an ambush. Frank was holding all the cards, but Jack hoped to come up with an idea to make the odds a bit more even.

Hearing a sound behind him, Jack rode into the brush on the side of the trail and waited. He didn't know who would be out on the trail in the dark. He dismounted and held his horse's muzzle. He listened, but didn't hear anything.

"Do you see someone?" a voice in the darkness asked.

Jack nearly jumped out of his skin. Thankfully, he recognized the voice. "Joseph, what in the heck are you doing out here?"

"Came to help you," Joseph said.

"I thought I heard a horse and rode in here," Jack said.

"I was following you and saw you ride in here."

Jack didn't even know Joseph was following him. "I guess we might as well let the horses rest for a couple of hours. Do you think we are far behind Morgan?"

"Not far," Joseph said.

Before dawn Frank told Corbin and Rose to get in the saddle. Rose's wrists were bleeding from the rope, so Corbin wrapped a bandana around each wrist to prevent further injury. "I'm sorry I have to do this, but we won't be with Frank much longer," he whispered.

Rose could hardly believe she'd heard him correctly. His words gave her hope that if he let her go, she could help Morgan before Frankie killed him. She'd paid careful attention, and she knew she could find her way back if she stayed on the trail.

They rode for almost two more hours before Frank came to a halt. He pointed south, and said, "Corbin, the trail is less than a mile in that direction. Do as I say and get to Las Vegas. The boys will have money when you get there." Frank figured that would be incentive to make sure Corbin stayed the course.

Before Corbin led Rose away, Frank had one parting comment. "You better have her with you when I get there. Don't force me to come looking for you because I promise you, it won't go well for you."

"Frankie, I beg you, don't hurt Morgan." She could barely speak above a whisper from her raw emotions.

Frank curled his lip in disgust as he looked at her. "What are you willing to do to keep me from killing him?"

"What do you want? Kill me instead if you are so determined to hurt one of us."

"Rose, I can't kill you right now. You're going to make me some money." Frank turned his attention on Corbin. "Now get out of here."

Corbin couldn't get away from Frank fast enough. He could tell by the look in Frank's eyes that he would indeed track him down if he didn't go to Las Vegas with Rose. Soon he was questioning his own plan to release her. What was the worst that could happen? He'd take Rose to Las Vegas, and either Frank showed up or he didn't. He wouldn't have long to wait since Frank thought LeMasters was just a few hours behind them. Corbin had seen how Frank went after LeMasters time and time again. If Frank didn't kill Morgan today, there was no doubt in his mind that Frank wouldn't stop unless Morgan killed him. Corbin didn't know what had started this bad blood between Frank and LeMasters, but whatever the reason, Frank had allowed his hatred to consume him.

Frank found the most advantageous spot where he could wait for Morgan. Once he positioned his rifle on a rock, he decided he'd have time to finally count his money. Maybe it would be enough to buy a huge spread in Mexico. Who knows, he might put some of it in a bank in Las Vegas. He laughed at the thought. If he wasn't still angry with himself for letting Walt take one saddlebag, he'd be even happier right now. Walt had obviously been caught or shot, and all of that money probably went back to the bank. Frank didn't think Walt double-crossed him. Walt was smart enough to know that he'd track him to the ends of the earth if he'd pulled a fast one.

He pulled his blanket and saddlebags from his horse. Hovering over his booty, he sat down and rubbed his hands together in anticipation. Once he opened the first flap on one side of the saddlebag, he pulled it wide, but he couldn't believe what he saw. Nothing but a bunch of wadded up paper was inside. "What the . . ." He opened the other flap and again pulled out more paper. No money! He couldn't believe it. Had Reuben double-crossed him? He replayed the robbery in his mind. Reuben was the only one in the safe, and the saddlebags were empty when they gave them to him. After Reuben tossed the saddlebags to Frank and Walt, he'd closed the safe. Frank left the bank first, thinking Walt was right behind him. But he wasn't. He'd reached the trees when he heard the shot. When Walt finally reached the trees he'd said Reuben pulled a gun and he shot him. Had Walt figured out what Reuben had done before he rode away? It was possible Walt went back to the bank to see if he could get into the safe. Was that why Walt had never shown up at the Conner place? Frank figured Walt was dead.

He threw the saddlebags aside and started

pacing. *That double-crossing little weasel.* If Walt hadn't shot Reuben, Frank would have ridden back to Denver and put a bullet between his lying eyes. Stevie had told him Reuben was smart. Well, Frank didn't think he was smart if he thought he could get away with double-crossing him.

Frank stopped pacing. Thank goodness he'd had enough sense to take the rest of Stevie's money. He pulled the bank bag from his blanket and opened it to count what was left. He stuck his hand inside and pulled out a handful of newspapers. He turned the bag upside down and shook it until all the contents emptied on the blanket. Nothing but newspapers. Frank was furious, cussing and stomping around in a circle like a caged animal. What had Stevie done with the rest of the money? *Well, you got yours, little brother. Just like that little weasel friend of yours. You both got what you deserved. And in a little while, Morgan Le-Masters will get what he deserves.*

CHAPTER TWENTY-NINE

Morgan was exhausted, and it was difficult to stay alert in the saddle. He'd only slept one hour before he got back on the trail. His mind drifted back to the last night he'd spent with Rose, and he was lost in the memory of that perfect evening. He rounded a bend and was moving fast when out of the corner of his eye he caught a glimpse of something shiny. Pistol? It was too late. He barely had time to lean forward when a shot rang out as he passed by, and a bullet grazed his head. Dazed, he wasn't quick enough to keep the second bullet from slamming into his back.

Frank was smiling as he shoved his rifle into the boot and jumped in the saddle. He'd finally done what he set out to do. He'd killed Morgan LeMasters. It took less time than he expected, and it wasn't even a challenge. Kicking his horse into a gallop, he rode south. He would catch up with Corbin and Rose before midnight. He could hardly wait to tell Rose she was now a widow.

Jack and Joseph heard the gunshots. They rode into the trees to avoid being seen, keeping the trail in sight. Joseph reached over and touched Jack's arm, and they stopped and listened. They heard a horse snort.

"Morgan's horse," Joseph whispered, slipping out of his saddle.

Jack followed Joseph's lead and dismounted. They tied their horses to a bush and crept quietly through the trees. Spotting Morgan's horse on the side of the trail, Jack pulled his revolver as they ran toward him. When they got closer, they saw Morgan slumped over the horse's neck.

Jack reached Morgan first, and placed his finger on his neck. He nodded at Joseph that Morgan was still alive. Together they lifted him from the horse and placed him on the ground. "A bullet grazed his head, but it's not serious." Jack ripped Morgan's blood-soaked shirt down the back to see the wound. Thankfully, the bullet had missed his spine. "Let's get him off the trail."

Joseph quickly set up camp and rolled out Morgan's bedroll. After they carried Morgan to the blanket, Joseph started a small fire to heat some water from his canteen.

Jack wiped the blood away from Morgan's back and examined the wound. Once he stopped the bleeding, he said, "We need to get the bullet out."

Joseph placed his knife over the fire, and as he waited for it to sterilize he unsaddled the horses.

Jack pulled a bottle of whiskey from his saddlebag, along with the medicine pouch Joseph had placed on his wound when he was shot. He remembered Granny said Joseph told her he should keep it because he would need it again. Jack held it up for Joseph to see. "How did you know I would need this again?"

Joseph shrugged. "It is good to keep."

Morgan woke when Jack was digging out the bullet in his back. "Are you ever going to find the darn thing?"

"How were you so stupid to let yourself get shot?" Jack asked.

"Good question." Morgan groaned when Jack pushed against the bullet. "I thought you were trying to get it out."

"It's not smart to criticize the man with the knife." Jack wiped the sweat from his forehead with his sleeve. "The darned thing is being stubborn. You need some whiskey?"

"Not yet." Morgan wanted to stay alert. When he was bandaged, he was going after Rose.

"Don't move, I think I've finally got it," Jack said. He expelled a loud sigh when he pulled the bullet out.

"Get me bandaged so we can get out of here. They are not that far ahead of us," Morgan said.

"You're not going anywhere," Jack said. "I've got to sew this up, and you need to stay put for at least a day."

"I don't have a day. Every minute Rose is with him is more dangerous for her."

Joseph walked over and looked at the hole in Morgan's back. "He is right. I'll go." He picked up the spirit pouch and mumbled some words. After he handed the pouch to Jack, he walked away to get his horse.

Before Joseph rode away, Jack said, "At least take a pistol with you."

"No need. I have help." Just then, two Sioux braves rode through the brush. They were carrying rifles, along with their bows and arrows.

Jack nearly drew his pistol, but Morgan said, "Don't." Morgan knew Joseph stayed in contact with the members of his tribe who refused to go on reservations. He figured they were aware he was Joseph's friend.

"You mean those two braves were behind us the whole time?" Jack asked Joseph.

"Yes." Joseph looked at Morgan. "We bring Rose here."

Morgan tried to get up, but Jack held him down. "Morgan, you've lost a lot of blood, you'd only slow them down."

Deep down, Morgan realized he was in no condition to ride, but he had to get to Rose. "I have to go."

Joseph slid off his horse and kneeled before Morgan. He placed his hand on Morgan's shoulder. "We bring Rose back. Stay."

Morgan stared into his friend's eyes, and he saw his determination. There wasn't a man he trusted more than Joseph. If Joseph had asked these two braves to help, he thought they could get the job done. Unlike Joseph, the braves were men in their prime, and they had a fearsome countenance. "Don't let them see you, Joseph, and don't kill Frank unless it's necessary. I don't want the soldiers getting wind of this." Morgan saw the braves exchange a look as though they understood what he was saying. If they didn't, Joseph would tell them. Morgan looked at the two braves as he spoke. "Joseph, let them know their families will be fed all winter for their bravery."

Joseph nodded his agreement, and translated Morgan's words to the braves. Both men acknowledged Morgan's promise with a nod.

"We'll wait for you until morning. If you are not back we'll head in that direction." Before Joseph mounted his horse, Morgan added, "Joseph, make sure Rose sees you first, or these fierce-looking braves might scare her to death."

Joseph smiled a rare smile before he turned to ride through the brush with the braves following.

"Are you saving Frank for yourself?" Jack asked.

"That wasn't my reason. I was thinking of Granny and Joseph. Granny buried one grandson yesterday, and I don't think she could handle another loss so soon. She knows what's in store for Frank, but she needs some time. I'll change my mind if he's hurt Rose. And I don't want Joseph to do anything that would bring attention to himself."

Morgan didn't mention his agreement with God. He'd made a bargain with his Maker that if He'd keep Rose from harm he'd leave it up to the justice system to deal with Frank. He didn't care what Frank had done on the ranch as long as Rose was safe. She was too important to him. He'd live up to his end of that bargain. But like he'd told God, if Frank tried to hurt Granny or Rose, or tried to kill anyone on his ranch, all bets were off. "If I'm forced to kill Frank one day, it won't trouble me."

"Let's get you stitched up."

While Jack worked on sewing him up, Morgan said, "Thanks for coming to help me out."

"When Joseph returns with Rose, we'll get out of here. I'll round up a posse and go after Frank and his gang."

Morgan couldn't deny he'd like to ride with the posse, but he would stay at Whispering Pines to make sure Rose was safe.

"Do you think Stevie dying in that fire was an accident?" Jack asked.

"No, I don't think Frank has accidents. I'd say he had it planned."

"He's one coldhearted son-of-a-gun."

"Joseph said it best. Frank's an evil spirit."

Jack finished with the last stitch, and he placed Joseph's pouch over Morgan's wound. He didn't know if it would do any good, but it couldn't hurt. "Let's get you bandaged."

Ignoring Jack's objections, Morgan moved

to a sitting position once he was bandaged. "I think I'll take that coffee now."

Jack filled Morgan's cup and added some whiskey. He repeated the process for himself. "You think Frank thought he killed you?"

"Yeah, I guess he didn't make sure, or I'd be dead." Morgan didn't know if Rose had seen Frank shoot him, but Frank would be sure to tell her he was dead. He was sorry for that. He understood all too well how she would feel, since he'd experienced those same feelings less than twenty-four hours ago. He wondered if she saw Frank set fire to the farmhouse with Stevie inside. If she was another witness to Frank's crimes, there was no way she'd ever be safe until Frank was dead, or in prison for life. "Jack, he needs to be caught or Rose will never be safe. I don't even think Granny is safe around him."

"Yeah, I know. I don't think many people are safe as long as he's roaming the earth."

Morgan positioned himself on his side, and saw his saddlebag by his blanket. He reached in and pulled out Rose's Bible. He wished she had it with her because he knew it would give her strength. He closed his eyes and prayed for her to stay strong.

■ ■ ■ ■

At dusk, Corbin decided it was time to stop for the night. He figured without Frank around, they might get a good night's rest before moving on in the morning. After he helped Rose off of her horse, he told her she could soak her wrists in the nearby stream.

"Why don't you let me go? I will tell the sheriff you helped me." She knew Corbin didn't agree with Frank's actions, but she thought he was too afraid to help her.

"He might be right behind us. You see what he is capable of doing. He told me I'd have to look over my shoulder if I don't get you to Las Vegas, and I believe him." He motioned toward the creek. "Go on now and take care of your wrists. You ain't going anywhere tonight." He handed her the coffeepot from his saddlebag. "Fill this up when you're done and I'll get a fire going."

Rose walked to the stream and placed her hands in the water. The cool water was soothing on her raw wrists. She tore strips off the hem of her dress so she could wrap her wrists to keep them clean. After filling up the coffeepot, she walked back to camp. Corbin threw some beans in the pot and placed it over the fire. He shared some of his dried meat with Rose. She wasn't hungry, but she knew she had to eat something to survive.

After they ate, Rose pretended to be resting, but she was trying not to fall asleep. She thought she might try to leave after Corbin fell asleep. She saw him pull a whiskey bottle from his saddlebag and add the contents to his coffee. As she waited for him to drink himself into a stupor, she fell asleep.

The warriors knew the territory, and with the aid of the full moon, they quickly caught up with Frank. Joseph was surprised Frank was riding alone, so they kept a safe distance behind him, keeping out of sight. They followed Frank for two more hours, hoping he would lead them to Rose. They spotted a small fire off the trail, and they knew Frank saw it too, because he rode off the trail and approached the camp from a different direction.

"Wake up, Rose."

Rose jerked awake when someone kicked her on the shin. "What are you doing?"

"I wanted to tell you that your husband is dead." Frank laughed and took a long swig from the whiskey bottle he'd picked up beside Corbin.

Fear crept down Rose's spine. "What did you do?"

"I made you a widow today."

Jumping to her feet, Rose went after Frank, pummeling him with her small fists and kicking at him like a madwoman. "You are a devil!"

Frank hit her in the jaw with his fist, knocking her to the ground. "Don't worry, we'll find you another husband."

Rose remained on the ground, sobbing. If Frank was telling the truth, Morgan was lying somewhere dead and no one knew where he was. Frank could be lying just to hurt her. He took pleasure inflicting pain, just as he had to Judge. Rose cried and cried, until she could cry no more, Exhausted and alone with her fears, she remembered Morgan saying he thought it was easier to talk to God under the night sky. She looked up at the thousands of stars and started praying. A calming peace that was beyond her understanding settled over her. In that moment, she knew, without a doubt, she would see Morgan again. If there was ever a man larger than life, it was her new husband. She was determined to keep her faith in him and his strength.

Frank couldn't believe Corbin slept

through Rose's outburst. He kicked Corbin in the ribs.

Corbin rolled to his side and drew his gun.

"I could have already shot you, and you would never have known what happened," Frank said.

Corbin looked at Frank through bleary eyes. "I had some whiskey." He holstered his pistol and looked around for his whiskey bottle.

Frank held it in the air. "Looking for this? I'm glad you didn't finish the whole bottle." He pointed to Rose and asked, "How did you know she wouldn't take off while you were sleeping? You didn't even have her tied up."

Corbin saw Rose curled in a ball on the ground. "What'd you do to her?"

"I told her she was a widow." Frank laughed again.

Corbin was already regretting not letting her go. She might not have made it back to Whispering Pines, but he wasn't sure she would survive traveling with Frank. "Leave her alone, Frank. Haven't you done enough to her?"

Frank eyed Corbin as he took another drink. "Corbin, I think you're getting soft."

"I just don't see no reason to be mean to her."

Frank was tired and he hadn't decided what he was going to do about Corbin, so he sat down and drank more whiskey. He'd been thinking about taking all the men back to Denver and robbing that bank again. This time, they'd rob it during business hours and anyone who got in his way would be dead. He wanted to know if that clerk was dead, and if not, he'd be the first one to get a bullet. No one double-crossed him. After they reached Las Vegas, he'd decide who rode with him to Denver.

Joseph and the braves were watching when Frank hit Rose in the face. One of the braves started to go after Frank, but Joseph placed his hand on his arm and shook his head. Morgan had said not to kill Frank if it could be avoided, but Joseph didn't think he could avoid it if Frank hit Rose again. When Joseph saw Frank and Corbin drinking whiskey, he knew they wouldn't have long to wait for the opportunity to act.

Sooner than Joseph expected, the men were snoring. He recognized Stevie's horse, so he told one brave to release the other two horses. When the outlaws awoke, they would be spending time trying to find their horses. If they didn't find them, they would have a long walk in either direction before they found a town. Joseph planned to stay off the trail just in case more men in Frank's gang were lurking about.

While one brave was quietly moving the horses away from camp, Joseph and the other brave slipped silently toward Rose with their knives out, prepared to defend themselves.

CHAPTER THIRTY

Rose was awake, waiting for Frank and Corbin to fall asleep. She'd been worried Frankie would tie her wrists again, but when he didn't she knew she needed to make her escape. Frankie wouldn't make the same mistake twice. She turned over to see how far she was from the horses, but when she saw a brave leading them away she almost yelled out, but stopped when a dark hand covered her mouth.

"Shhh," Joseph whispered in her ear.

Rose looked at the man looming over her. She couldn't believe her eyes. *Joseph!* He'd come to help her. But where was Morgan?

Joseph removed his hand from her mouth. He helped her to her feet, and pointed to the brush. They hustled through the brush to their horses. Rose looked behind her to see if they had awakened Frank, but another brave was behind her.

■ ■ ■ ■

To Rose, it seemed as though they rode forever before Joseph stopped. Finally, she was able to ask the question she'd dreaded. "Frank told me he killed Morgan."

"He is alive," Joseph said. "But we must hurry."

From his serious tone, Rose thought Morgan must be severely injured. Tears formed in her eyes. "Is he in danger of dying?"

"No, but if we are not back by morning, he's coming for us."

"You are sure he will be okay?"

"Yes. The sheriff is with him."

"Thank you for coming for me, Joseph." Then she cried tears of relief. Morgan was safe, and they would be together again.

Joseph looked at the sky. It would be morning soon, so they needed to ride fast. "We must go."

At dawn, Morgan stood and walked to his horse. He was determined to go after Rose, and nothing Jack said persuaded him to wait longer.

Though frustrated by his obstinate friend, Jack saddled his horse so he wouldn't tear his stitches.

"If you fall off that horse, I'll leave you in the road this time," Jack threatened.

"I appreciate all you've done, Jack, but I've got to find her." How could he explain to Jack that the pain he was feeling from his wound was nothing in comparison to the pain he felt when he thought Rose had died in that fire? Nothing he could ever face would be worse than losing Rose.

Jack stopped arguing with him. If he'd learned one thing about his friend, it was his determination when he set his mind on something. Thankfully, he didn't have to help Morgan into the saddle because they heard horses riding through the trees.

Morgan and Jack pulled their pistols and waited. They spotted Joseph first, and then Morgan's eyes landed on Rose. Rose slid out of the saddle and ran into his arms.

The men took the horses some distance away to give the couple some privacy.

"He said he killed you," Rose cried. "I refused to believe you were dead. I asked God to protect you."

Morgan held on to her, understanding what she had gone through. "And He did, honey. It's okay now, sweetheart."

She looked up at him with tears streaming down her cheeks. "Joseph said you were shot. Why aren't you lying down?"

"I'm okay, honey. Are you hurt?" Morgan wanted to look at her to make sure she wasn't injured, but she wouldn't let go of him.

Rose buried her head in his chest and cried as though her heart was breaking. She was mumbling words, but Morgan couldn't understand her.

"Honey, I can't hear you." He kissed the top of her head. "Come on now, stop crying. You're safe with me."

She wiped her tears on her sleeve, but they didn't stop. "I can't stay with you. Frankie will keep trying to kill you. You will never be safe. I've seen what he is capable of doing."

Cupping her chin, Morgan urged her to look up at him. When he saw her face, he became enraged. She had blood in her hair, dark circles around her eyes, her cheek was swollen and red. He held her hands and looked at her bandaged wrists. "Who hit you? What happened to your wrists?"

"Frankie. He tied my arms to the horse."

What Morgan wanted to do was get on his horse, find Frank and beat him to death. But he wouldn't forget his promise. "Let's get you cleaned up."

"Please listen to me: Frank will never stop. He will kill you, and I can't let that happen.

I need to go far away from you."

"Rose, Frank didn't kill me. He won't kill me. And you aren't going anywhere but to our home. Jack is going to get a posse together and go after them."

"He'll never find them. Frankie is crazy." She was fully convinced that her brother was so evil that he would always evade the law.

"Honey, you're tired and scared. Things will look better when we get home."

"No, they won't. He'll come back."

He knew she was frightened and not thinking straight after what Frank had put her through. All he could do was hold her, and try to assuage some of her fears.

The men walked back to the fire, and Morgan thanked them for bringing his wife back to him.

After Joseph told them they had released Frank's horses, they decided they could stay at their camp one more day. Morgan was relieved they could stay put for several hours so Rose could rest. He thought she looked worse than he did. The two braves didn't stay in camp, but they remained close by in case they were needed. Joseph knew they would be keeping watch, and if anyone approached they would have plenty of warning.

Jack warmed some water so Rose could wash her face. When she finished, she sat beside Morgan and leaned against his chest. Even though she was secure in Morgan's strong arms, she couldn't stop crying. She'd nearly lost him, and she couldn't stop thinking about Frank's vow to kill him.

Once Rose settled down, Jack joined them at the fire to ask Rose some questions. "Do you know where Frankie was headed?"

"Yes, they were going to meet the rest of the gang in Las Vegas. They talked about going to Mexico, but they also talked about robbing a bank in Denver."

"Who was with you?"

"Corbin was the only one. I think Frankie was expecting another man to show up, but he never did." She wanted to give him as much information as she could so he could find Frankie and put him in prison before he could hurt someone else. "He knew Stevie was in the house as it was burning."

"Did you see him set the fire?"

"No, I got there after it was already burning, but I know he started it."

"Did he say that to you?"

Rose tried to think about Frank's exact words. Her memory was fuzzy. "I don't know. But he knew Stevie was inside. I tried to go in the back door to see if Stevie was there, but I think Frankie hit me. When I woke up, I was at some cabin with Frankie and Corbin. I don't know where we were."

Jack looked at Morgan. "It couldn't have been too far from the ranch since Frank left that message for you."

"He must have been hiding out at one of the abandoned homes," Morgan said.

"It was well-hidden, you would never know it was there," Rose told them.

"I never thought he rode to Purgatory Canyon each time he rustled cattle. It's too far away for him to go back and forth. It makes sense to me that he was hiding in plain sight."

"I'm real sorry about all of this, Rose," Jack said.

"I just want you to find him and put him in jail. He won't stop," Rose said. "I can't prove he started the fire, but he did, and he didn't help Stevie. Not only that, he said Joseph is the only one who can testify against him and I know he will try to kill him."

"I've already thought of that," Morgan said. He'd tried his best to keep Joseph on the ranch, but even that plan hadn't kept him safe.

"I'm sure no one saw him shoot you," she said to Morgan.

"Rose, we will get him," Jack said.

When Jack walked away, Rose looked up at Morgan. "I prayed Frankie was just trying to hurt me when he said you were dead. I didn't want to believe him."

"I guess he thought I really was dead," Morgan said. He reached in his saddlebag and pulled out her Bible. "I brought this for you."

It meant so much to her that he'd thought of the one item that would bring her comfort. Rose reached up and touched his cheek. "Thank you. I don't know what I would have done without you. I love you so much."

Morgan leaned over and kissed her. "You just said you love me."

Rose didn't want to hold back her true feelings. "I love you very much. I think I have since I was fourteen years old."

Her confession surprised him. "What? I thought you were afraid of me."

"I was afraid of you when I was young. But as I got older, I started noticing how all the women competed for your attention. They flocked to you every Sunday. That's when I started noticing how handsome you were. Of course, my older sisters had already pointed that out to me."

"Women didn't flock to me," Morgan

said, but he was smiling.

"You know they did. Every Sunday after church, it would take you forever to get to your horse. Every woman in town stopped to talk to you. Even my sisters were smitten. When I imagined my wedding at the altar, my groom was always you."

Morgan took her hand in his and brought it to his lips. "I was waiting for you to grow up."

"You didn't pay attention to me."

Morgan grinned. "That's not entirely true. I remember the pretty little gal with long blond hair who would peer over the church pew at me with those big green eyes."

Rose gave him a sad smile. "And now I've brought you nothing but problems."

"Honey, you've made me the happiest man in the world. This is nothing we can't handle." He told her how he thought she was the one who died in the fire. "I'm really sorry about Stevie, honey. I don't know why Frank would do something like that."

"He really is crazy," Rose said. "I saw it in his eyes. I never knew he was so filled with hate. You tried to tell me, but I'd never seen that side of him before. I wish you had told me about Judge long ago. Anyone who could hurt an animal would have to be insane."

"I didn't understand Frank back then, and I guess I don't understand him now."

"How did you find out it was Stevie and not me?"

"Joseph told me there was no wedding ring on the . . . body." He didn't want to tell her how badly Stevie was burned. That was one detail she didn't need to hear. "Before Joseph told me it wasn't you, I didn't know what I was going to do without you. I didn't even know how much I loved you until I thought you were gone. Granny was devastated."

Though saddened by what he'd gone through, Rose was thrilled by his admission. "It makes me happy to hear those words from you."

Morgan kissed her again. "I love you, and you'll hear those words forever." He pulled her ring from his pocket and placed it on her finger. "This belongs to you, Mrs. Le-Masters."

"Jack said Frankie left you a message. Was it my ring?"

"Yeah."

"Corbin, wake up," Frank yelled.

Corbin's eyes opened. "What's going on?"

"Rose is gone and so are our horses," Frank said.

Jumping to his feet, Corbin looked around. "How . . . when?"

"You didn't tie her up, and it looks like she played us for fools," Frank said. He walked in circles as he cursed. When he found Rose again he was going to put a bullet through her head, just like he did Morgan's. "We've got to find those horses. We can't walk all the way to Las Vegas."

"There's a small town a couple of days from here," Corbin said.

Hands on his hips, Frank glared at him. "You feel like walking for a couple of days?"

"What if she took the horses with her?"

Frank had already thought of that, but he didn't think Rose could lead two horses for long. "We've got to look."

"Rose!" Granny was sitting on the porch when she saw Morgan and Joseph riding in with Rose.

Morgan helped Rose from the saddle and she ran to her grandmother. "I'm sorry about Stevie, Granny. I'm so sorry you had to go through this alone."

"Hush, now. It's in God's hands." She turned to Morgan. "Thank you for bringing her home."

"You can thank Joseph, Granny," Morgan said.

Granny turned to Joseph. "I figured you took off after him. Next time you leave, please let me know so I won't worry so much about you."

Joseph had never considered that someone other than Morgan would worry about him. "Yes, ma'am."

Granny smiled at him. "Thank you for your help."

Rose quickly gave Granny a brief explanation of what had happened. "Granny, we need to get Morgan into bed. He's been shot, but he refuses to rest." She'd told Morgan when they got back to the ranch, Granny would make sure he stayed in bed. He wouldn't be able to argue with Granny.

Granny gave him a stern look. "You go right on up to bed. The men will carry water up for a bath, and then to bed you go." She turned her attention on Rose. "You don't look much better than your husband. Both of you take a bath and go to bed, and I will bring you something to eat. I have a lot of questions, but nothing that can't wait until you are well rested."

To Rose's amazement, Morgan didn't put up an argument. He even allowed Joseph to take Faithful to the stable.

Morgan didn't want to admit it to Rose, but he was in considerable pain. He was determined to make sure she was safe at the ranch before he relaxed. "Thanks, Granny. A bath and bed sounds good to me."

Morgan slumped in his chair while his wife bathed first. He wished he felt better so he could have a second wedding night, but he'd be content just to hold her in his arms all night.

When Morgan sat in the tub, Rose cut his bandage away and washed his back. "I could get used to this. I think I might have to get shot every month."

"I'll scrub your back every night if you promise not to get shot again." Rose tried to sound normal, but she was scared to death Frankie was going to come back once he found out Morgan was still alive.

"I like that deal better."

Rose bandaged his back again, and they climbed into bed. They were holding each other, thankful to be alive and together when Granny brought them something to eat. Granny ate dinner with them, and after she left their room, they fell asleep holding each other.

Morgan could not recall a time when he'd stayed in bed all day, but he found he'd never been as happy and content in his life as he was while recuperating. His beautiful wife was caring for him, and she was snuggled up to him at night as they discussed their dreams for the future. He had no reason to complain, and every reason to be thankful.

"Hello, Stella, Reuben." Walt had arrived at the prearranged meeting place the night before. He hadn't been back to his family farm for over a year. It was the place where he'd been born and lived until his parents died. He'd never sold the place, and he'd come here often when he wanted to be alone. He'd even slept in his old room last night, though he'd tossed and turned all night wondering if Stella would come with Reuben. He'd thought of nothing else since the day he left Denver. He didn't want to think too far ahead and make plans, in case she didn't show up, but he'd given some thought about where they would go to make a fresh start if she did. Now, here she was right in front of him.

"Hello," Stella said as Walt helped her from the buckboard.

"I'm glad you came, Stella," Walt said, not taking his eyes off of her. He was so excited she was there that he could hardly contain himself. She was the first woman he'd ever asked to take a chance on him. And she'd said yes.

Stella gave him a big smile. "So am I." She'd never thought this day would arrive. She'd prayed for years that some man would come along and take her away from the saloon. Nothing had come of her prayers, until now. She'd questioned what made Walt ask her to join him that day as he was making his getaway, but she'd never come up with an answer. It had to be fate. Nothing else made sense. It was risky going away with a man she didn't know, yet she had a good feeling about Walt. She figured she'd taken bigger gambles in her life. Working in a saloon since she was fourteen years of age was a risk every day. Men with guns, drinking alcohol, was the perfect lethal combination. She'd actually been shot once when two men had argued over a card game.

"Walt, have you seen Stevie?" Reuben asked, climbing down from the buckboard.

"A friend of mine told me he was killed in a fire on the farm," Walt said.

Reuben was shocked by the news. He liked Stevie, and he'd tried to warn him about his brother. "That had to be Frank's doing. I told Stevie not to trust him. When I met Frank I knew he wasn't a man to trust."

"I don't know if Frank had a hand in it or not, but I wouldn't be surprised."

"Does Frank know about this place?" Reuben asked, glancing around the old house that was located about twenty miles east of Denver.

"No. My family owns this land. I've never told anyone about it, so we are safe here. Come on inside the house. I just made some coffee."

The three entered the kitchen, and Walt pointed to the saddlebags he'd placed on the table. "You know how much you put in there, Reuben. I didn't spend a penny yet."

Reuben trusted Walt. Initially, he was skeptical about trusting an outlaw, but once Stella said she was riding with him to meet Walt, he was encouraged that he might actually get his share of the money. He didn't really have an option. It was either trust Walt, or get killed by Frank Langtry if he didn't help with the robbery. He walked to the table and opened the saddlebags. "Walt, thanks for keeping your word."

"Reuben, it ain't none of my business, but I'm thinking you should probably move on. Frankie knows by now that one of us double-crossed him. I don't think it's safe for you to stay around Denver. If you want, you're welcome to ride with me and Stella. I figure we'll head East and get out of this territory."

"That's why I bought the buckboard. My belongings are in the back, and I'll ride with you as far as St. Louis if you're going that way. From there, I will get passage East on a train."

"St. Louis sounds like a good place for Stella and me to make a fresh start." Walt looked at Stella as he poured her some coffee. "How does St. Louis sound to you?"

"St. Louis sounds just fine."

CHAPTER THIRTY-ONE

Six weeks later, Rose, Morgan and Granny were relaxing on the front porch after dinner when Murph reined in.

"How's things at the farm?" Morgan had sent Murph and two men to the farm to start cleaning it up to rebuild the house.

"It's going good, but I found something in the stable you need to see." Murph tossed a saddlebag to Morgan.

"What's this?"

"I reckon it belongs to Stevie, but you need to look inside," Murph said.

Morgan glanced at Granny. "Is it Stevie's?"

"Yes, that's his saddlebag."

Morgan started to hand the saddlebag to her, but Granny said, "You look inside."

He opened the flap, peered inside and his eyes widened. He looked up at Murph, and said, "What's this?"

Murph threw his hands in the air and

shrugged.

Rose looked from her husband to Murph. "What is it?"

Morgan held the saddlebag so Rose and Granny could see the contents.

"Oh, my! Where would Stevie get that kind of money?" Granny asked.

Quickly putting together the pieces of the puzzle that had long been evading Morgan, he realized he had the answer. "From that stagecoach holdup." He told them what he knew of the holdup, and how he'd happened on Stevie and Reuben on the trail. "I knew Stevie was lying to me that day. He knew the man in the buggy. Then, the day I went to Denver, I found out the man in that buggy worked at the bank there." Morgan had initially eliminated Stevie as the holdup man when he saw the man riding the palomino in Denver, tailing Reuben. Now that they had proof in their hands, he figured Stevie and Reuben planned the holdup together.

"I guess Stevie had already followed in Frankie's footsteps and we were just too blind to see," Rose said.

"We didn't want to believe he could be like Frank," Granny said.

They heard another horse riding toward

the house. Morgan looked up and said, "It's Jack."

"Hello, Jack," Morgan said when Jack reined in at the porch.

"Evening." Jack tipped his hat to Granny and Rose. "How's everyone feeling?"

"Good," Morgan said. "Would you like a cup of coffee? We have something to show you."

"If you have some made, I would be grateful," Jack said.

"Why don't you all come in the kitchen? We were going to have some pie," Granny said.

"Granny, you know the way to my heart," Jack said.

Jack dismounted, and as they walked to the kitchen, Morgan handed Jack the saddlebag and told him the story.

"So you think those two planned that robbery?" Jack said.

"I'd bet that Reuben was the brains and did the planning, while Stevie carried it out," Morgan replied.

"I'll take the money back to Denver in the morning and tell them what we know."

Rose poured the coffee while Granny served the pie. They talked about the stagecoach robbery while they ate.

Morgan figured Jack hadn't come out for

a social call. "When did you get back, Jack?"

"Last night." Jack had come to the ranch to deliver the news in person because he knew they would be worried. "Frank made it to Las Vegas. We tracked them to Mexico, but that's where the trail went cold. They aren't too helpful to the law down there."

Morgan's eyes slid to Rose, and just as expected, she looked worried.

"He'll come back here." Rose was heartbroken Jack did not have Frankie in jail.

"I agree with Rose. If Frank finds out he didn't kill Morgan, he will definitely come back," Granny said.

Morgan couldn't deny he agreed with them, but he refused to worry about something he had no control over. "We can't live our lives worried about what Frank might do."

"Morgan's right, Rose," Granny said.

Jack told them he would let them know if he heard anything about Frank's whereabouts. "Morgan, I just remembered something. That Denver bank was robbed over a month ago."

"I hadn't heard. Did they catch them?"

"No. Apparently, the robbers showed up at the clerk's home on Sunday morning and made him go to the bank and open the safe. The clerk was shot, but not killed."

"Was this before Stevie died?" Morgan asked.

"Yes, why do you ask?"

"I wonder if Stevie planned that robbery with the clerk."

"I guess it's possible," Jack replied.

"The day I was in Denver I saw a man watching the clerk. I noticed him because he'd been in Whispering Pines one day when I took Rose and Granny to town. He was riding a palomino, and that's how I recognized him in Denver. It's possible he was involved."

Rose remembered the man Morgan was talking about. "Perhaps it was a man in Frankie's gang."

"I don't know, but I doubt all of this is a coincidence," Morgan said.

"The sheriff in Denver said two men robbed the bank. The clerk couldn't identify them because they wore masks," Jack said.

Morgan had a feeling one or both of the Langtry men were involved with the robbery, though they might never know the truth of what happened.

Jack pulled a letter out of his pocket. "Granny, I almost forgot, I have a letter for you."

Granny looked at the writing on the envelope. "It's from Adelaide." She quickly read the letter and smiled when she finished. "She's coming home in a few weeks. She's bringing some children with her."

"Children?" Jack asked.

"Three orphans. She's planning on opening an orphanage here."

"Oh, I can't wait!" Rose said. "It will be so wonderful to have her home again."

"It's a shame the house burned down. It would have been a perfect place for the children," Granny said.

"Granny, that's why I have Murph and the men working over there cleaning it up. We thought you might like to have the house rebuilt. If we don't have it finished before they arrive, they can stay at the ranch," Morgan said.

Rose smiled at her husband's generosity. She wasn't surprised at his offer; he would do anything for Granny.

"I'm pretty handy with a hammer," Jack said.

"I'm sure we can get Clay out here to help us," Morgan said.

Granny was excited at the thought of having children at the farm again. "That would be wonderful. Just think, we could help so many children. Adelaide said the orphanage back East was terrible."

"Anything would be better than some of

the orphanages I've seen," Jack said.

Morgan was surprised by Jack's statement. He'd rarely heard him speak of his childhood. "Maybe they will have a better life here."

"I know Adelaide well enough to know that she will be so attached to those children she will not want to part with them if some family decides to adopt them," Rose said.

Granny agreed. "It would be difficult to let go when the time comes."

"It may take a while to find families willing to adopt, especially if the children are older. Not many people want to adopt older kids. They all want babies." Jack remembered all too well how it felt not to be selected for adoption. It was a feeling he'd never forgotten.

Jack stood to leave. "Morgan, if you are ready to start on that house tomorrow, I'll bring my hammer after work. I'll bring Clay with me."

"Murph, are we ready to start building tomorrow?"

"It's ready."

"We'll pick up supplies in the morning. Come on by here and have dinner with us, and then we'll go to the farm," Morgan replied.

They walked Jack to the porch, and when

he rode away, Granny stood on her tiptoes and kissed Morgan on the cheek. "Thank you. You are the best son a mother could have."

Morgan smiled at her. "I'm just buttering you up so you'll never stop making me pies."

"You never have to worry about that." Granny said good night and walked inside to go to bed.

Morgan and Rose followed her inside and turned down the lamps in the front room. Once all the lights were extinguished, Rose reached for Morgan's hand. "Are you ready for bed?"

"Yes, ma'am." If she thought he would say no to an offer like that, then she didn't know him. He leaned over and picked her up and carried her up the stairs.

"You shouldn't be carrying me. It might hurt your back," Rose said.

"I'm fine, and you are light as a feather." He took the stairs two at a time.

"I may not be much longer," Rose replied.

Morgan was in such a hurry to get to their bedroom, he almost missed her meaning. He walked into the bedroom, closed the door with his boot, and looked down at her. "What do you mean?"

"I've been sick a few mornings, and I've wanted some foods I've never liked."

"What have you been eating that you don't like?" Morgan asked. He hadn't seen a change in her eating habits.

"The crust on my bread," Rose said. "I've never eaten it before."

"Why haven't you told me you weren't feeling well?"

She smiled at him. "It's nothing serious, just a little nausea some mornings."

He gently placed her on her feet. "Have you told Granny?"

"No. I think I know what it is."

Morgan stared at her. "Are you saying what I think you are saying?"

"Don't get your hopes up, but I believe I am."

He pulled her in his arms. "Are you sure it's possible?"

She gave him a mischievous smile. "I don't know about you, but I think we've done everything right."

He leaned over and kissed her. "I'd say we've done everything more than right. If you are with child, it will be the second best thing that ever happened to me."

"What was the first?"

Morgan cupped her face tenderly as he looked into her beautiful green eyes. "The day you married me."

Rose started unbuttoning his shirt. "Why

don't we see if we can do it better?"

The lady didn't have to ask him twice. "I've always heard practice makes perfect."

When she finished unbuttoning his shirt, he stripped out of it, and kissed her as she ran her hands over his shoulders.

"Would you unbutton my dress?"

Morgan arched his brow at her. He thought of their wedding night. "It'd be my pleasure." When he saw the long row of buttons down her back, he said, "But I've been meaning to talk to you about the buttons on your dresses. Why are there always so many?"

Rose turned to look at him. "To torment you."

Morgan wrapped his arms around her waist and kissed her neck. "It works. I thought I'd never get you out of your wedding dress."

Rose remembered how she trembled under his touch that night, and nothing had changed. She knew she would tremble under his touch fifty years from now. "Hurry up, husband, I want to go to bed."

He liked the sound of that. "Yes, ma'am." As soon as he unfastened the last button on her dress, he started yanking off his boots and finished stripping out of his clothes. He hurried to open the window, and when he turned around, Rose was already in the center of the large bed waiting for him, watching his every move. He slowly approached the bed, lowered the flame on the bedside table lamp so it cast a soft light over the room. He wanted to see his beautiful wife. He pulled the covers back, and smiled. His eyes conveying his every thought as he crawled in beside her.

Much later, Morgan was lying on his back, with Rose's head resting on his chest. They were listening to the wind rustling through the pines, and an owl hooting in the distance.

"I've never asked what you hear when you go through the pines," Rose said.

Morgan had never told anyone other than Joseph what he heard in the pines. "To me, it always sounds like angels singing. What do you hear?"

Rose looked up and smiled at him. Over five years ago she'd told Joseph Longbow when she met a boy who heard the same sounds in the pines that she heard, she'd marry him when she grew up. She'd done exactly that. "I hear angels singing."

ABOUT THE AUTHOR

Scarlett Dunn lives in Kentucky surrounded by all manner of wildlife, and enjoys long "God walks" where most inspiration strikes. Possessing an adventurous spirit, and a love of history, particularly the pioneers of the West, she has a special place in her heart for all cowboys, past and present. Readers can visit website: www.scarlettdunn.com.